AC BISHKEY

Halcyon Days
The Colossus

CALM Studios, LLC

Est. 2025

Citius. Altior. Longius. Maior.

First published by CALM Studio, Ltd. 2025

First edition

ISBN (digital): 979-8-218-64607-3

ISBN (paperback): 979-8-9986717-2-2

ISBN (hardcover): 979-8-9986717-1-5

PRAISE FOR HALCYON DAYS: THE COLOSSUS

PRAISE FOR HALCYON DAYS: THE COLOSSUS

"A solid fantasy/sci-fi adventure that offers some good scene-setting and character work. The descriptions are evocative and help ground the book's world-building."
—Danny D. (Beta Reader)

"Quite an epic tale... I really enjoyed the worldbuilding - from the different abilities of separate factions to the unique cities that are encountered. The fight scenes are cool and don't feel unwelcome to the story... The story and world are satisfying!"
—Tamara (Goodreads)

"I began to love the crew of the Halcyon Days. The story is in the crew and the crew is in the story. I loved learning more about the world, the differences and the many crew members... The book definitely brought up many emotions throughout the many many chapters and POV switches. It was quite interesting to have a POV from the opposite side too, not very commonly seen in books. Thank you for an amazing debut, A.C. Bishkey!"
—Matthias S. (Goodreads)

"Halcyon Days is a thrill ride of a book. Sky pirates, elite soldiers with unique powers, a living machine the size of a skyscraper, and an adventure grand enough to contain it all... The crew of the Halcyon Days is where this story shines. A.C. Bishkey manages to write a lovable crew that cares for each other despite their flaws... The battles were well-written and fast-paced... easy to follow despite their breakneck pace. And there was never a battle that felt like filler; each held weight within the story... A.C. Bishkey has created an immersive world filled with compelling characters, sky pirates, and high flying adventure. If you're looking for a story packed with lots of heart and action, Halcyon Days: The Colossus will not disappoint."
—Noah J. (Goodreads)

DEDICATION

For My Son.
You'll make your own magic.

For My Father.
Thank you for showing me how to make mine.

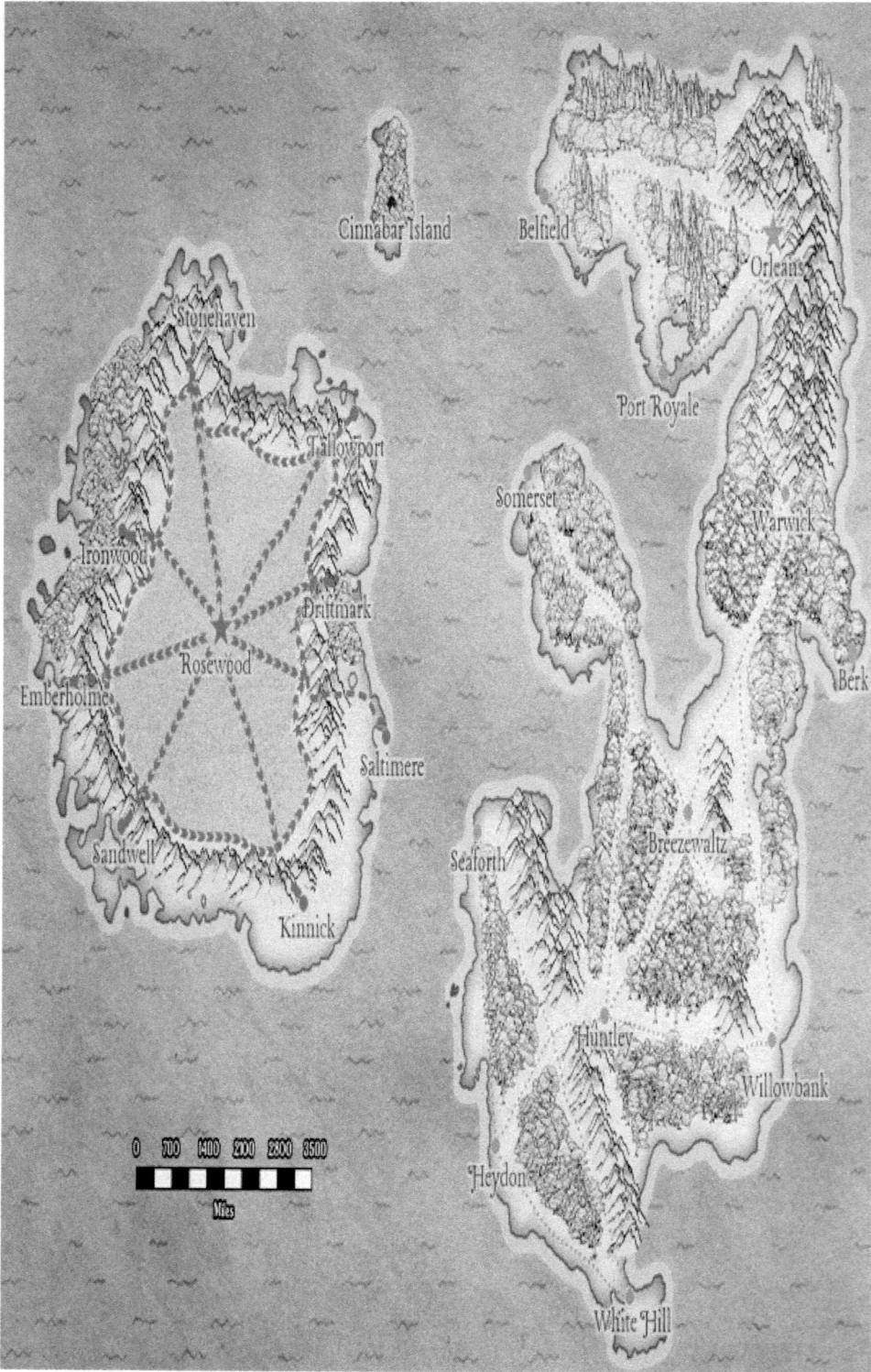

Cinnabar Island

Belfield

Orleans

Port Royale

Stonehaven

Tallowport

Somerset

Warwick

Ironwood

Driftmark

Rosewood

Berk

Emberholme

Saltimere

Breezewaltz

Sandwell

Seaforth

Kinnick

Huntley

Willowbank

Heydon

White Hill

0   700 1400 2100 2800 3500
Miles

PROLOGUE: LUCAN

1 Hour After The Rise of the Azure Colossus

The world was being reborn in judgment and rain, and Lucan was once again dealing with heretics.

A dramatic thought, he knew, but a prince was permitted his indulgences. Besides, when the scholars wrote of this day, and by the Rose Crystal's light they would, they'd need something memorable. The day the Colossus rose, the day White Hill fell, the day Prince Lucan stood upon the *Inquisitor*'s skydeck and watched as millions were tithed. Yes, judgment and rain, that would do nicely.

Below, the Azure Colossus stood fifteen hundred feet under the tumultuous sky. Its crystalline armor was slick with water, its blue flesh lit by something steadier than lightning. The Iverian skyships swarmed it like wasps, their shardshot cannons blazing against that impossible hide. Deck plates thrummed beneath the prince's feet with each distant impact. Rivets sang under stress.

The city of White Hill was effectively gone. The ruptured shell lay shattered across the verdant plain. What remained would drown in dust and deluge by nightfall.

As planned, as decreed.

"We need to move above the storm, Prince."

Rook's voice cut through the downpour. The man stood at the railing, water streaming off that ridiculous chrome mask he insisted on wearing. He was staring into the tempest as if he could read a message in the clouds. His right hand tapped twice against the rail, an old, restless habit. Rook had always been like that, seeing things others missed, impatient to set them right.

"Retreat from victory?" Lucan let the words hang between them. He didn't turn. "This moment is centuries in the making, Rook. Our conviction made manifest, and you want to flee?"

"There's another ship above us." Rook pointed at the gray mass overhead, his mask tilting to catch the glow of ricocheting shardshot. "Frigate-class. I caught a glimpse when the clouds shifted. Five hundred feet higher."

Five hundred feet in the clouds. Close enough to pounce. Far enough to think no one would look up.

Of course there was. The Iverian League never could leave well enough alone. Always interfering, always protecting their wayward flock, always standing between the faithful and being reclaimed by the Emperor's rightful will.

"Scramble fighters." His hands clasped behind his back as he addressed one of his Praetori. "Engage and destroy."

"Belay that."

The words were quiet, but they cut through the squall like a blade. Rook turned to face the prince squarely, and in that moment, something changed in the air between them. An intensity that Lucan couldn't quite parse. Urgency? Almost pleading, but why?

His fingers found the hilt of his suda, the liquid-metal sidearm that obeyed the wielder's intent. "The day's success has made you reckless." Jests were one thing, and Rook had earned that privilege through years of service and camaraderie. But whatever this was, this edge in his tone and directness, it felt like overstepping. There was only one man who gave Lucan orders, and he was sitting on a throne in Aurelia.

"Trust me, Prince." There was something in Rook's voice he had never heard before. A sadness, or maybe resignation. "Keep it sheathed. You'll want it for someone else."

Before he could respond, the transformation took Rook. The Rosari change swept over him like a wave. A shroud knitted over his clothing. Red crystalline fur bloomed across his body. His frame swelled, shoulders broadening as crystal sinew overlapped over his existing form. His boots rose at new ankles to fit the shroud's digitigrade joints, lifting him higher. That chrome mask, oversized on his human face, now fit perfectly against the Rosari skull beneath.

"They're here," Rook growled, and his voice was different now. Deeper, with a reverberating timbre.

Thunder cracked the sky in half. A transport vented its Azure engines above them and dropped through the clouds, touching down hard on the rain-slicked skydeck near the port railing. Four figures dismounted, railing at their back, and three were armed. Lucan recognized the leader before he made his first step.

"First Altier Toren Luinondo." He let the name roll off his tongue. "To what do I owe the honor?"

Toren walked forward through the storm as if weather observed rank. Altiers were always like that. So certain. So sure of their moral superiority. Lucan had heard rumors of this one, but based on what he saw, Toren was just another non-believer come to find faith at the edge of Lucan's blade.

"You crossed the line, van Ferro." Toren's voice was level, controlled, but the rage beneath it was unmistakable. "And you don't even see it, do you? Three million lived in White Hill. Three million. That thing... this... Colossus... it won't stop with Iveria. It will consume the whole world."

"You traveled all this way to warn me?" He spread his hands in mock surprise. "I expected threats, Toren. Posturing. Perhaps some violence. Not sermons. Not from your ilk."

"You misunderstand." The suda in Toren's hand refined itself into a katana, thin and exact. Static crawled along the blade's blue edge. "This is the part where I stop you from burning the world for the sake of your damned ego."

Ah. There it was.

The grin came naturally. It was the one he saved for moments like this, the one that showed too many teeth. "Not for my ego, First Altier. For my faith." He glanced at his Praetori, the imperial elites, already beginning their transformations. "And your mistake is thinking the world will burn. No, no, only the unworthy will blister."

Toren's two Altiers responded in kind, their stances shifting. Lucan could see the blue lines glowing under their skin, crystal flakes flickering on their flesh. They were prepared for what was to come. Lucan took stock of the battle as his eyes moved past them to the fourth figure standing in the back. Unarmed. Unremarkable. Just a pilot, presumably.

Something about him was deeply upsetting. The man stood there as if he had all the time in the world. The gall to land on his skydeck and act so indifferent.

Rook wasn't as good as his Praetori, but he was still a competent fighter. Lucan would let him play and finish off whatever remained of that man's smugness once Toren's breath had left his body.

"Rook. Think you can handle the scrawny one?"

There was a pause, one that took too long. When Rook finally spoke, his voice was strange.

"I'll manage."

Something about the way he said it made the prince's expression falter. As if Rook understood something. As if he'd been expecting this. As if this was all part of the plan.

No time to wonder. Violence was calling him, and the transformation was the final rite. It sang in his blood, and he surrendered to it.

The change came through his veins. Crimson fur erupted across his body, shrouding his limbs, torso, and head. It added mass and pushed his boots to meet the form's digitigrade stance. Clawed feet formed beneath that. He gripped his suda off his belt, and the liquid metal rose from the hilt to set as a single-edged blade.

Six Rosari against three Altiers and a pilot. History said Lucan was far out-matched. He liked those odds. More for the scholars to write about.

Not that he was truly worried. Even among Rosari, the prince was different. The gale around him thickened, responding to his will, and that was his personal gift. An accretion field he could project with a thought. The weight built the longer you stayed near him. Five feet from his heart was his limit, but inside that radius, every second added drag to any limbs, blades, or breath. Step out and stay out, and the world returned to normal, like a diver coming up for air. Most Rosari could only harden their own bodies, and even that took effort. His power bent the world itself. Rain struck the deck harder around him. Welds began to buckle under invisible pressure.

He swung high, arcing the blade with his full weight. Toren sidestepped, and then he wasn't there. His katana printed a wet line across Lucan's collarbone. The blade arrived first. Toren lagged into the space a heartbeat after. Static crackled along his arms where the movement left its debt.

Lucan launched another swing. Another miss. Each one was deliberate. He didn't need to hit. He just needed to stay close.

Toren circled right, blade extended, hunting a real opening. His katana sliced upward, elegant and precise. The prince caught it with his forearm and his chin, letting the edge bite into the crimson pelt. The pain was sharp and bright and utterly meaningless.

"You're as predictable as all the rest." Lucan laughed.

His boots skidded, he shoved forward, and Toren stumbled backward two steps. The prince stepped closer, and the air continued to thicken around Toren, weight gathering with each beat. A rivet head popped and pinged into the wash.

"You think protecting people is predictable?" Toren's voice was strained now, fighting against the phantom pressure.

"Your compassion is cruelty." Lucan advanced, step by heavy step, closing to within arm's length. "You let the weak suffer because you're too frightened to do what must be done. I'm told your father understood that, in the end. Isn't it strange how true clarity comes only when you're bleeding out for what you believe in?" Toren's eyes hardened, but he did not respond. "No? You'll find out soon enough."

Toren twisted free, somehow, impossibly, and kept his distance. Lucan could see crystal scales bloom and dissolve around his legs. A calculated burst. Clever, but an overexertion. The accretion drag would fall away like wet canvas. Toren was a step past him, deck wash erupting where his feet had been a heartbeat before. His blade sliced across the prince's side. The cut was deeper this time, and a darker wetness spread against his pelt. Hot metal and ozone cut through the damp air.

Lucan roared, not in pain. Never in pain. In joy. In the pure fundamental thrill of life and death.

He pressed forward, and Toren retreated toward the starboard rail where his two Altiers were engaged with the Praetori. As Lucan crowded in, the air thickened again, slowing Toren's movements. A wide, deliberate swing. A horizontal arc forced Toren to his left. The movement was calculated, precise, herding him back against the nearest Altier. Toren seemed to be aware of the field and was doing his best to avoid it. They were near the railing now, away from where Rook fought the pilot by Toren's transport. Toren and his guard fought back-to-back, protecting each other.

Compassion. Exactly as planned.

Another swing. Toren moved instinctively to shield his companion. To protect the weaker fighter.

A feint. The prince pivoted low, then high. His blade drove deep into the Altier guard's back, through cloth and flesh and bone. The man fell with a sound that was almost a sigh. The deck replied with a hollow thud.

Toren froze. Something in his face shifted. Pain, guilt, rage, and grief, all of it at once. The sight amused the prince, but he didn't care to understand it. Didn't care to name it.

"You see?" He hissed through his fangs. "Trying to save the weak only gets them killed."

The Colossus bellowed somewhere below them, a sound like continents smashing together, and the deck shuddered under their feet. Even here, far above the creature, its presence pressed against the world.

Before he could strike again, before he could drive his blade through Toren's heart and end this, another cry echoed across the deck.

This one was metallic. This one was human. Rook's voice.

Lucan turned.

Across the skydeck, near the port railing, the pilot stood utterly still. His hand rested flat against a leather pack on his back. Steam rose from the leather, visible even in the storm. Whatever this was, twenty feet away, Rook's shroud had already buckled. The transformation collapsed and crystalline fur sloughed like frost in sunlight. His human form was already sliding across the slick surface toward the edge.

Rook's chrome mask caught the crossfire's glow as he tumbled over the edge. That mirror sheen, that ridiculous mask. It hung for a moment, and then it was gone, swallowed by wind, cloudburst, and distance.

Rook was gone with it.

Lucan's blade stopped mid-swing, and he took a step to the edge Rook had just gone over. His thumb ground against the suda's hilt. He felt a screw pop and had to restrain himself before he damaged it further. The only person who'd ever called him "Prince" like it was both a title and a joke was gone. The only person who'd stood at his side for three years of planning. Who believed in the prince's vision. The only person Lucan could trust.

The thought passed.

He felt an echo of something. Guilt, perhaps, or sadness, or just the loss of a useful tool. It didn't matter. Whatever it was, it wouldn't help him kill Toren. He had to focus. Emotion was a luxury, and he had never been one to indulge in luxuries that did not serve him.

"After him!" Toren shouted before lifting the fallen Altier with surprising care. The pilot vaulted into the transport, hand still on that pack. Toren followed with the body. The surviving Altier broke from the Praetori and jumped over the edge after them.

Lucan charged forward, claws scraping against the wet deck, but they were already gone, swallowed by the storm below.

He slammed his fist into the railing. The metal collapsed beneath the blow.

A beat passed as he stared into the storm, then at their works. The Colossus still fought, which meant the day was not lost. One of his guards approached cautiously.

"Your orders, Prince?"

He turned slowly, meeting her eyes. She was young. Probably joined the Praetori thinking it was just an honor, not a sacrifice. She would learn.

"Pursue them. Retrieve Rook's body from wherever it fell. Bring it back to me."

Her face went pale. She understood what that meant. Not the fall. She could survive that. Rosari could survive a terminal impact. No, she saw the storm below, the Colossus raging, and the chaos of war spreading across Iveria. Rook's corpse was already lost to wind and distance, and that's if the pilot hadn't reached it before it hit the ground. This was an impossible task in an active battlefield. Lucan did not care. His need for violence had not been quenched.

She saluted, because that was what the faithful did, and leapt into the growing darkness of the night sky.

"The rest of you," he said to the remaining guards. "Go with her. Follow them into the afterlife, if you must."

Without hesitation, they leapt over the railing one by one, dropping into the storm below.

Lucan stood alone on the deck. It should have tasted like victory. The Colossus had risen. White Hill was destroyed. The beginning of his new world, his new order, his devotion made manifest in crystal and blue flesh. Yet Toren had escaped, Rook was gone, and something that should have felt like triumph sat bitter in his mouth.

No. That wasn't how it would be written. He would tell the scholars a different story. He would tell them Rook sacrificed himself to the cause. Together, they had pushed back the Iverian heretics and secured a great victory for the faithful. That version was cleaner. Simpler. True in the ways that mattered.

After all, this was not a defeat. The divine could only ever be delayed, never denied. Any doubt in that had been washed away by the storm.

CHAPTER 1: KALISTON

4 Days Until Landfall

Six months since the Colossus woke at White Hill, and Kaliston still hadn't slept right. Not his problem, technically. World-ending titans belonged to the Armada. He just flew his skyship and avoided debts.

He'd seen it once at White Hill, and it was from altitude. Which was the only smart way to see something that could crack cities open like eggs. The devastation looked cleaner from above. Less screaming, but more for the imagination.

At the time, he'd hoped the apocalypse would at least cancel his debts. It hadn't.

He told himself six months ago it wasn't his problem. He told the crew the same and to forget about it. No one on the ship talked about it, at least to Kal.

No matter how many times he told himself it wasn't their problem, everything that came after had shown him otherwise.

He shook the thoughts and the sleep away. The brew in his hand had gone lukewarm. Kal drained it anyway and set the mug in its holder. His other hand rested lightly on the throttle. The *Days* hummed beneath him, responsive as a thought. She was the most advanced ship in the sky, and she was his. The creditors might argue, but they would have to catch him first.

The morning sun crept through the viewport to the west, and he caught his reflection in the glass. He'd rolled his sleeves to the elbow when he had relieved his XO. She liked to keep the bridge toasty, but Val said he just did it to show off his forearms. She wasn't wrong, but two things could be true.

He knew his coat had too many pockets, his boots too many scuffs, and his smile only worked on people who didn't know him well. He kept his beard in that space between careless and deliberate. Dark curls arranged just wrong enough to look uncontrived.

It took a lot of effort to look like he didn't care.

The *Days* arced through a shipping lane thick with traffic. Even in the sky, there were rules and routes. Flying outside the lanes would draw attention from any Armada patrols, or worse, the Shipping Guild. Kal only liked to test them when there was financial gain to be had.

Pilgrim transports and cargo haulers moved in a plodding line. They were all Aurelian design, all bound for Breezewaltz. Landfall was four days out. Kal expected the sky to be packed, but it was too packed for just the holiday.

Something else was happening. He knew what it was, but he'd confirm it in Breezewaltz.

He nudged the throttle. The *Days* answered like she'd been waiting. Around them, Rose-powered freighters coughed dark exhaust. Smoke belched black from their rotors. One sputtered as he passed. Typical Aurelian engineering: luck and welds.

The *Days* ran clean. Twin heavy Azure shards at her core. No steam, no water, or smoke. Just electric current humming through her bones. Four hundred years since the Liberation War, and half the world still burned Rose like it was the only option. The Aurelians loved their heat and smoke. Iveria preferred precision.

Of course, affording anything that ran on Azure was a different story.

Kal's hand stayed loose on the controls as they slipped past a listing freighter. The *Days* didn't mind tight spaces.

Ahead, Breezewaltz rose on the horizon. Upper Mesa towering over the Lower City, tethered floats and spires stacked against the sky. It never looked real until you were on top of it. Even then, it felt like someone's fever dream.

He reached for the PA mic. Val had just left for breakfast after night watch. The rest of the crew was still sleeping. Time to fix that.

"Good morning, illustrious crew." His voice echoed through the ship. "Your ever-dashing captain here, reminding you that glory doesn't sleep in. Skies are clear, adventure awaits, and profits are on the table. Shake off the sleep, and let's write our name into the skies. And remember, I love you."

He grinned and turned the comm mic in his hand. Val would complain about the volume and content, but it was worth it.

The comm system itself was Azure-based. Probably cost as much as a Rose land speeder. He didn't know for sure because someone else had paid for it. Someone else had built the *Days*, funded her, and equipped her. Then Kal had acquired her through methods he preferred not to examine too closely.

Most of these ships would have modified Azure comm systems, even if they ran on Rose engines. A single shard could communicate with another, but Rose and Azure could not mix. The crystals operated on different frequencies. Four centuries of war, and they couldn't even say hello.

Old War. Old grudges. Old tech.

He flipped the comm to the kitchen. "Cookie, did our guest in the hold get fed?"

Crackle. Then Cookie's voice, warm as her kitchen. "Already done, Captain. Didn't touch it yet, but they will. Nobody resists my cinnamon rolls forever."

"Dangerous confidence."

"Earned confidence."

Kal smiled and set the comm down. The passenger in the hold was the reason he was here. A bounty, technically. Worth enough to clear his debts and then some. He didn't like using people who weren't actively trying to hurt him, but the passenger was just a piece in a larger game. He'd cure them before the job finished. Small mercy. He'd promised himself that much.

The job would pay. More importantly, it would get him answers. Kal had questions about the Colossus. About what could possibly stop it. About what his friend in the city was really preparing.

If all went to plan, he'd see the titan a second time. Hopefully, the last.

Avery and Kenzie would arrive soon to take their positions. For now, it was just him and the *Days*. The only real things in the sky. It seemed fate saw it differently because that's when Kal noticed the sensor blink. Blue contact. Behind them. Matching altitude and matching speed.

Kal tapped the screen to confirm it was working. Red blips showed the convoy. Then one blue. An Azure-powered ship. A hunter.

He'd seen it earlier. Silver fighter tucked into the convoy. Kal stayed low, kept the camo off, and guns cycled off. He played the civilian. Smart move in a crowd this thick, or so he thought. It was a Guild ship, and he'd assumed it was shepherding another flock.

Guess he lost that bet.

Kal didn't curse. Just set his mug down, smoothed his coat, and watched the contact close on the monitor.

Val's not going to like this.

He eased the throttle forward. Not enough to run. Just enough to test. The *Days* surged slightly, but the blue contact matched her speed.

Breezewaltz's spires caught the morning light, golden and opulent. Almost within reach, but so too was the hunter. The shardshot fire started soon after that.

There were some things even the end of the world couldn't erase.

CHAPTER 2 : LOCKE

4 Days Until Landfall

"I love you!" Kal's voice cut through the ship's PA before the comm cut off. Locke looked over at Jazz's bunk and found it empty. He'd have to be annoyed on his own this morning.

He groaned and buried his head under a pillow. His skull felt like someone had driven a spike through it. Every morning, the same. He never touched booze, not like Jules, but he woke with a buzz behind his eyes that wouldn't quit. Six months after the accident, the headaches hadn't improved. Neither had the memories.

Three years. Gone. Seaforth to the *Days*, just a blank space where his life should have been.

He remembered his childhood with his mother, father, and brother. The Citadel, with its military drills and protocol. Then, Seaforth, the trip with his family just before graduation. After that, nothing until he'd woken in a bunk on this ship with Kal standing over him, asking if he knew his own name.

They'd told him his parents died at Seaforth when Locke asked what happened. He didn't remember that part.

Dr. Rina said he had a bad accident that resulted in a severe head injury. Locke had been out for four weeks and had a scar hidden by his hair. The memories might come back, but might not. She said he was lucky it was just the three years and to count his blessings that he was alive at all.

The concussion had carved a clean break, and Locke had stopped asking questions the crew couldn't answer. Kal might know more. Then again, Kal always seemed to know more than he let on.

After five months, Locke had made peace with it. He hadn't liked himself much at the Citadel anyway. The *Days* gave him a chance to start over. Let the past catch up or don't. Either way, he was here now.

A sound came from overhead.

"Boots," Locke said to himself.

It was his personal nickname for Kenzie. Light on her feet except first thing in the morning, when she forgot to care. The rhythm was familiar. She was dancing again, the same pattern she tapped out between jobs when she thought no one was paying attention.

He always noticed.

Kenzie had joined five months ago, a month or so after his accident. That made Locke the second-newest by default. Didn't stop anyone from calling him "Kid."

Kenzie was one of the few who never used it. She never talked down to him either.

Maybe that was why he noticed her more than he should.

She stood out. Red hair that framed her face however it wanted. Hazel eyes that didn't miss much. When they landed on you, it felt like she already knew what you were about to say. She wore a white hoodie-dress with the hood up most of the time, like she was trying to blend in. Athletic gear underneath if you looked closely. Not that Locke looked close.

Much.

Today was the day. He'd ask her to dinner in Breezewaltz. Maybe tell her how he felt. Probably not that part, but definitely dinner.

Locke pressed his palms together and said his morning prayer to the Azure Crystal. He rolled out of bed, stumbled to the sink, and started brushing his teeth. He tried a half-hearted imitation of Kenzie's dance to shake off the grogginess.

Jules's face appeared in the mirror behind him. Locke nearly spat toothpaste across the sink.

She didn't say a word. Just stood there with that look, like she'd been watching long enough to form an opinion about his entire morning routine.

Grease streaked her jumpsuit and her cheek. Silver hair stuck out from under a red bandana, still damp with sweat. She looked like she'd been elbow-deep in the *Days* since before dawn.

"Grab some grub and meet me in the engine room," Jules said. "Pop quiz today, Kid." She smirked. "Or should I say twinkletoes?"

She was gone before he could object.

Locke shook his head, finished up, and pulled on a mostly clean shirt. He climbed the stairs to the galley.

The ship was swaying more than usual. The inertial dampeners kept the gravity local, but through the porthole, he could see the sky and Gaia rolling around them. He chalked it up to Kal showing off again.

The galley was alive. Cookie stood behind the counter, serving plates. Her cinnamon rolls sat in the center of the spread like a declaration of war on hunger.

"Kid's here!" Cookie called out and handed him a plate piled high.

Cookie didn't just cook. She ran the galley like it was her personal fiefdom. Stocky, broad-shouldered, with arms that looked like they could lift a crate while simultaneously dicing onions. Her apron was flour-dusted, her sleeves rolled high. Her smile promised food and consequences in equal measure.

You didn't cross Cookie. You thanked her and tried to stay on her good side.

"Thanks, Cookie." Locke tried to sound serious. "But please don't call me 'Kid.'"

"Kid, you are a kid." She winked.

Locke shook his head but didn't argue. "You seem to be in a good mood."

"Any day that starts with baked goods is a good day," she replied.

Locke nodded to Avery and Val as he passed. The ship's pilot gave a half-smile. Val's head slumped over a steaming cup of coffee, eyes closed.

The trio of Haruto, Tia, and Liam sat at their usual table, mid-conversation. Haruto mimed some exaggerated gesture. Tia nearly choked on her drink. Liam grinned like he'd heard the story a hundred times and still found it funny.

They gave Locke a friendly nod as he passed. Warm enough, but he'd never be the fourth member of that circle. Their group was already drawn, built over time through shared missions and inside jokes. The *Days* was full of these relationships, and Locke was still learning to navigate them.

He slid past and took the open seat beside Kenzie.

She was absorbed in a datapad and didn't look up until he spoke.

"Pop quiz today or just me?" he asked.

Kenzie glanced up. Her smile made his heart skip. "Nah, Jules just likes picking on you."

Locke sighed. "Something like that."

They sat in silence for a beat. Kenzie returned to her datapad. Locke took small bites and tried to look casual.

"Any plans for Breezewaltz?" The words came out before he could stop them.

Kenzie's response was light. "Nothing solid. Why?"

"I thought maybe we could grab a bite. I used to live there, know a few spots..."

"Sure, sounds fun." She paused. "Maybe Jazz or Lizz can come too."

Locke felt something deflate in his chest.

Jasper and his twin sister, Eliza. They worked in the hold, helping Jules. War orphans, a couple of years younger than him and Kenzie. They'd been on the *Days* since they were children. The crew was the only family they had left.

"You know she likes you," Kenzie said, taking a small bite. "I catch her making eyes."

Locke sighed. "No chance. She's too young and not my type."

"Oh, really? I think she's a cutie. Jazz too." Kenzie swallowed. "And they're only like two years younger than us."

Locke bit into a piece of fruit harder than necessary.

Avery stood and took one more sip of coffee. "Kenz, you good to go?"

"Right behind you." Kenzie opened her mouth and shoved as much food as possible into it. She took a big swig of coffee, swallowed, and said goodbye. She waved silently at Val so as not to disturb the resting XO.

She walked through the door. Then walked back in.

"Find me when we land, and we'll go on that date." She was gone before he could reply.

Date. She'd called it a date. Locke was pretty sure she called everything a date, but still.

Locke sat there, fork halfway to his mouth.

"Kid, you need to knock that grin off your face." Val's voice cut through his thoughts. Her eyes were still closed, her head resting against the wall. A steaming cup of coffee sat in front of her. "Otherwise, people around here will think you're not working hard enough."

"How do you know I'm smiling?"

"I could hear that big dumb grin of yours from the next city-state over."

Val finally lifted one eyelid. Her eye was still heavy from lack of sleep, but something sharp lived underneath. She was about ten years older than him, close to his brother's age. Like his brother, she had the kind of presence that didn't need to explain itself.

She rubbed her temples, took a slow sip, and sat up a little straighter. Her black hair was tied back like always. Not for looks. Val wasn't vain, even though she could've been. Her eyes missed nothing. Her expression gave even less.

She sipped her coffee and flicked her gaze back to him. "She's too good for you. Let it go before she breaks your heart."

"How do you know that's what I was thinking?"

"Cookie?" Val turned her head to the woman behind the counter.

"She's out of your league, Kid." Cookie produced two shakers. "Find someone like her in ten years when you've had more... seasoning." She rattled them for emphasis.

Val spread her hands as if to say told you so, then put them behind her head as she closed her eyes again. "I know everything that happens on the *Days*. Total situational awareness." She opened one eye just long enough to catch his expression. "For example, that cinnamon roll you're eating fell on the floor twenty minutes ago. Cookie brushed it off and handed it to you."

"Val!" Cookie exclaimed.

Val didn't flinch. "Don't ask how I know. Just accept that I do."

Locke spat out the food.

Val stood and approached before taking a seat next to Locke. She put an arm around his shoulders. "See, Kid, stick with me and bask in my omnipotence. You might learn something about women along the way."

Locke shrugged out from under her arm. He knew she was messing with him, but he didn't like being made to feel small. Nothing struck that nerve quite like being called "Kid."

"I'm not a kid." He tried to sound confident. It came out like a scolded dog.

The ship's comm chimed. Kal's voice cut through the moment.

"Uh, Val, can I get your opinion on something on the bridge? Not an emergency, but pretty urgent."

Kal's voice sounded normal enough, but both Val and Cookie exchanged a look.

Val didn't move. She looked back at Locke. "You're what, twelve, thirteen?"

Locke didn't correct her that he was twenty-three.

"You're just going to ignore that?" he asked.

"Nothing for you to worry about, *Kid*." She was testing where the line was with Locke, but they both knew it didn't really exist anyway.

Locke opened his mouth to object, but Val continued with a dismissive hand. "Right, yeah, you're not a kid. Tell you what, I'll stop calling you that if you ever pass Jules's test." She paused. Her smile turned predatory. "Or if you get a kiss from Kenzie. I think one's way more likely than the other."

She reached down, grabbed a piece of fruit off his plate, threw it in the air, and caught it in her mouth. She winked and walked out.

Cookie stopped mixing. "Damn, I want to be her when I grow up."

"Cookie, she's like half your age."

Cookie smiled and threw a roll at his head.

Locke ducked as it whizzed past and disappeared into the hallway.

"Don't serve that one," he called back.

His grin carried him all the way to the engine room.

CHAPTER 3: KENZIE

4 Days Until Landfall

The world outside was rolling, and Kenzie was doing everything she could to keep Cookie's breakfast rolls down. Avery had cursed Kal and bolted for the pilot's chair the second they stepped onto the bridge. Kenzie dove into the co-pilot's seat beside him.

Kal lounged in the captain's chair like they weren't one bad bounce from a smoking crater. "Guild bounty hunter on our six," he said, maddeningly calm.

"And you didn't think to ask for help?" Avery snapped.

"You know I only ask for help if I'm losing at cards."

"That reminds me," Avery said, fingers flying over the console. The flight sticks rose to meet his grip. "You still owe me from last week." Avery pushed down on the controls, and the ship responded. "Seems our new friend is shooting first and asking questions never."

A streak of shardshot hissed past the canopy and cratered into the gaia below.

"Our bounty must've shifted to dead or alive," Kal said. "Guess the Guild meant that last threat."

"Yeah, Kal, we know it's hard for you to imagine, but some people keep their promises." Avery jerked the yoke, rolling the *Days* into a hard climb.

"I'd say it's more making good on threats, but we'd be splitting hairs." Kal smiled at Kenzie and tapped his own harness.

She caught his meaning and buckled in. She cursed herself for having to be reminded.

Four inches of armored glass wrapped the bridge in a near-total panorama. From her seat, she saw the thick blue of open sky, the endless metal parade of the convoy, the distant shimmer of Breezewaltz, and far below, the mottled greens and browns of Gaia.

Kal's chair was elevated just behind them, a bad seat for visibility but perfect for pretending he saw the most. Behind him were stations for sensors, weapons, and systems, while the XO's seat sat off to the side between the captain and the support stations. Val typically preferred to stand. Kenzie wondered when she would arrive. That's when Kal picked up the comm mic.

"Uh, Val, can I get your opinion on something on the bridge? Not an emergency, but pretty urgent." Kenzie had to smile at the way he downplayed the situation.

Another bolt of blue shardshot streaked past, and Avery pulled tight but didn't flinch.

He was about Kal's age and shared a quiet history with him that Kenzie tried to piece together. She enjoyed teasing out backstories from the crew, though Locke seemed to think everyone's past was a closely guarded secret.

She studied Avery for a moment as he adjusted the controls. He was broad-shouldered, dark-skinned, with dark hair cut short. He looked more like a soldier than a pilot. That was right up until that easy smirk cracked through. Flying, fighting, and talking his way out of trouble… it was all a game to him. Kal and he were similar that way.

"Okay, where did we leave off yesterday?" Avery asked.

"We're doing this now?" Kenzie yelled.

A playful smile appeared on Avery's lips.

"What? You don't think I can multitask?" He twisted the stick hard to port.

"Avery, be serious." Kenzie wasn't amused.

"I always am. Go on," Avery replied, still smiling.

Kenzie rolled her eyes. "You were showing me what this bank of sensors tells me," Kenzie said.

"Ah, yes. Those are important. If the line on this one is here," Avery said, pointing at a sensor, "then we're dead."

"Like we're in the process of crashing?" Kenzie asked.

"No, if this one looks any different than it does now, we're already dead."

"That… seems counterproductive," Kenzie said, confused.

"It's important," Avery said, shrugging, "but these next two are even more important."

"At some point, you'll need to admit when you're messing with me."

"Part of my genius as your mentor," Avery replied, still deadpan, twisting the controls to the side as another blue bolt shot past.

The bridge door hissed open. Haruto, Tia, and Liam piled in, ducking instinctively as the shardshot streaked past the canopy.

Haruto moved first, spinning something in his hand as he dropped into comms. Kenzie was pretty sure he never slept. His jet-black hair was always slicked permanently back, though whether that was effort or efficiency was anyone's guess.

Tia slid into her station with all her restless energy, wavy black hair, and brown eyes lit with the promise of fire. If it whooshed, sparked, or burned, it was both her best friend and worst enemy. She was smaller than Kenzie but impossible to overlook, the kind of person no one forgot after seeing her in action.

Liam followed, sleeves rolling up as he sighed and started diagnostics without a word. Not unfriendly, but already tired of whatever the hell this was. He only seemed to wake up around the other two, and even then, usually with a glass of something brown in hand.

"Look who's gracing us with his presence." Haruto was the first to speak.

"I haven't seen someone sleep like that since the Kid bumped his head," Liam said, pulling up what Kenzie assumed were diagnostics.

"Easy, Liam," Kal replied.

"Yes, sir! To our glorious leader!" Tia barked, giving Kal a mock salute. Haruto and Liam joined her in unison, holding the pose until Kal waved them off.

"Station up," Avery cut in. "We've got a tail that thinks we're worth killing."

"At ease, soldiers," Kal said with a smile. "As our valiant pilot said, we've got a bit of a problem."

They released the pose and laughed as they cycled their systems.

"Is this serious, serious?" Liam asked.

"It looks like Avery is giving us serious flying." Kal gestured out the window as the world flipped and turned around them.

Liam frowned, and so did Haruto. They exchanged a look with Tia and returned to their work with the same urgency that Avery was flying with.

Haruto leaned toward his console, talking under his breath, as usual. He would be able to pull additional information on their pursuer via the shipboard sensors. Tia's fingers danced over weapons safeties just in case. Kenzie heard the ship's massive shardshot cannon rotate beneath them. Liam started rerouting power from secondary systems to the ship's engine. He didn't ping Jules on the comm about releasing safeties. Whatever he saw, it wasn't death-level bad, yet.

"Nice of you to join us!" Kenzie yelled from the co-pilot's seat.

"Kenzie!" Liam, Tia, and Haruto shouted back, slightly out of sync, but they got there eventually.

"Status?" Kal called out.

"Looks like a standard Guild fighter. It'll sting us if given a chance." Haruto replied.

"Let's try not to spend any credits on repairs," Kal sounded serious, for once.

"That's why I'm dancing!" Avery replied to the room.

"We can shoot it out of the air. Give me the signal, boss." Tia cut in.

"No, they'll just add it to our tab. What other options?" Kal asked the room.

Val's boots announced her before she stepped through the door, arms crossed. "Traffic seems heavy. Can we get lost in the congestion?"

"Seems like the bigger ones have a lot of exhaust…" Kenzie said to the room, a little louder than intended.

"Seems risky," Liam said. "Those Aurelian junkers aren't exactly known for flying straight."

"What's the point of having a state-of-the-art ship if she can't account for some sloppy fliers?" Kal cut in. "Avery?"

"On it, Cap." Avery pushed the controls, and the ship threaded into the convoy of Aurelian ships. Some buckled out of the way, but most didn't have time to react.

"Our friend followed us in here," Haruto called out.

"Val?" Kal asked. Kenzie caught a hint of mirth, almost like Kal was daring his XO to plan her way out of this.

Val walked to the windows and put a palm on the glass. "Avery, put us behind that big one, the one belching fumes." She pointed with her other hand. "Once we have this sucker in the exhaust slipstream, cut under and loop us around. Liam, engage our optical camo right when we break line of sight. Tia, stand down."

"Oh, what?" Tia groaned. "What if I just do one warning shot? I promise I'll miss this time."

Kal laughed.

"You can shoot the next one twice," Val replied and walked back to the XO seat. She put a hand on Kenzie's shoulder as she walked by.

Avery did as commanded, positioning the ship in the exhaust slipstream. Embers from a heavy Rose shard mixed with steam, forming a dark exhaust cloud.

Avery held the position for a beat. The *Days* shook violently from the turbulence. Kenzie held her breath, hoping the jolts were just that and not shardshot.

"They're in the slipstream with us," Haruto announced.

"Punch it!" Kal yelled, and Avery slammed the throttle while pushing the sticks forward. The *Days* pitched under the ship, and Avery pulled back hard as soon as they cleared the tip of the freighter.

"Camo now!" Val yelled, and Liam engaged the optical camo. Kenzie heard the main cannon cycle down and reset back to its stationary position.

Liam held the maneuver until they slipped back into the exhaust.

"They won't pick us up on their sensors?" Kenzie whispered, as if their pursuers could hear her.

"Camo keeps us hidden from eyes, and the Azure cores have a triple shield while it's active. We won't trip their sensors unless these bumpkins know where we already are," Kal replied.

Kenzie looked up to see their pursuer shift above them in the sky. She watched it hang in midair like a cloud. It stayed there above the convoy as the line of ships moved slowly past below. It looked like it was surveying the convoy, but soon it was out of sight behind them.

"This ship is amazing," she said to no one in particular.

"Down girl, she's spoken for," Kal replied with a smile.

There was a short silence. Tia snorted. Haruto nodded solemnly, like Kal had said something profound. Liam, Val, and Avery didn't engage. They apparently knew better.

Kenzie felt her cheeks burn. Sometimes, Kenzie lost herself around them and reverted to the nervous kid she had been before Seaforth. She hated when it happened, but hated that the girl was still in there even more. Since she had joined the crew a handful of months prior, Kenzie hadn't gone a day without thinking about fleeing before they kicked her out. They'd figure her out eventually, or she would figure them out. Either way, someone would leave someone soon.

"Wonderful, now our morning exercise is over," Kal said with a smirk. "Haruto, what's our ETA to Breezewaltz?"

"About thirty minutes, Captain," Haruto responded. "Should we broadcast our codes?"

"Sure, but don't use the ones from last time. I barely avoided paying that fine," Kal replied.

"Codes?" Kenzie asked Avery.

"Clearance codes. Technically, only officially commissioned ships from the King can dock. The codes indicate you aren't Aurelian spies and you've paid your commission fees." He looked back at the crew. "Skypirates like us operate outside those official channels."

"Exactly right," Kal said. "And why pay a fee when I know a guy who gets us codes that are practically free?"

"But work a quarter of the time," Haruto added.

"Practically free, but working a quarter of the time is a compromise I can live with," Kal said, as Haruto transmitted the codes to Breezewaltz Command. "Besides, we get in, drop the bounty off, get paid, and we're off on the next adventure before anyone notices us."

"Come on, come on…" Haruto muttered into the console.

The tension didn't show on anyone's face, but Kenzie caught the shift in the recycled air. Avery's hands tightened slightly on the controls. Haruto's breath quickened as he opened comms with Breezewaltz Command. It wasn't the crew's first time bending the rules. Maybe they'd done it a hundred times before, but the margin for error never got wider. One inspector with a good memory, one database update, and the *Days* would stop being a charming rogue ship. She would become either state property or a smuggler's tomb.

Kenzie had always respected people with good luck. Kal seemed to carry it around in one of the many pockets of his well-worn jacket. Still, she knew the line between fortune and disaster was always thinner than it looked.

She just hoped this wouldn't be the moment it snapped.

CHAPTER 4: LUCAN

4 Days Until Landfall

The *Fury* cut through the storm clouds like a blade through silk.

Lucan watched from the ruined balcony of White Hill's city hall as the Iverian Capital skyship maneuvered to avoid his fleet's encirclement. Even from this distance, the vessel was formidable. Sleek, heavily armed, and fast enough to make his commanders nervous. Azure shardshot streaked through the rain, blue lightning that tore across the grey sky.

Lucan would lose a tenth of his fleet in this conflict. A necessary trade to protect the apocalypse.

His fleet responded to the *Fury*'s maneuvering. Rose-colored fire erupted from the *Inquisitor* and two escort frigates as they harried the Iverian warship away from the vulnerable Colossus. The *Fury* couldn't be allowed close, not while the artificial heart was offline and the beast lay dormant beneath him.

Lucan pressed the comm to his mouth. "Tighten the net on the western flank. Don't let it break over the mountains. Hold the *Inquisitor*, send the Eighth."

Static crackled. "Acknowledged, my lord. The *Inquisitor* is falling back, sending the Eighth Fleet."

Through the sheets of rain, Lucan watched his flagship bank hard to starboard. The *Inquisitor* was a marvel. All sharp angles and crimson plating. She moved with predatory grace, engines roaring as she opened the gap. Lucan's chest tightened with something close to longing. He should be on that bridge, commanding from the captain's chair, not standing on this crumbling ruin while engineers scrambled below.

Another volley from the *Fury*. One of the frigates took a glancing hit and peeled away, trailing smoke.

"Sir, they're trying to flank," a voice came through. "Should we pursue or hold position?"

"Hold," Lucan commanded. "The Colossus is the priority. Keep them at range."

He lowered the comm and watched the dance continue. The *Fury* had tested them. It had stormed in until it was directly overhead, probing for weakness, looking for an opening to strike at the heart of the Colossus itself. They didn't find one, not with Lucan's fleet circling like wolves around wounded prey. They had pushed it back, away.

At least Marling was a known quantity. Drunk or not, the man commanded the *Fury*'s cannons with brutal efficiency. Still, one Capital skyship against his entire fleet? It would be a stalemate at best.

Two frigates were torn apart by the *Fury*'s broadside. Metal screamed as the ships spiraled toward Gaia below. Lucan didn't flinch. He had hundreds more. What mattered was the *Fury*'s true target. She was angling for the *Inquisitor*, trying to take out his flagship. Each loss stung more from this vantage point.

The *Inquisitor* fired again as she fell back, a magnificent broadside that lit up the storm. The *Fury* rolled hard, evaded most of the barrage. What little connected wouldn't scratch her massive hull. Still, Marling must have seen enough. Lucan watched the *Fury* turn north, into the clouds.

"They're breaking off, my lord," the officer reported.

"Let them go," Lucan said. "Maintain patrol routes. I want full coverage until we're operational."

"Understood. *Inquisitor* returning to station."

Lucan watched his flagship settle into a slow orbit above the Colossus. Majestic. Deadly. Everything a warship should be. Everything he should be commanding directly instead of babysitting Syd's latest catastrophic failure.

He turned from the balcony and stepped back into the ruined council chamber. Wind and rain battered the former administrative building, now precariously perched atop the Colossus's broad spine. The once-magnificent dome had cracked, its gilded roof stripped away and replaced with skeletal scaffolds. Gaps in the walls exposed the storm outside and let in sheets of cold air that carried the scent of damp stone and burnt crystal. Lucan had been told the southern reaches of Iveria were known as the Stormlands. They lived up to the name.

Soldiers and engineers swarmed through the ruined council chambers. They shouted orders and hauled equipment to keep the towering war base operational. The floors, once polished marble, were scorched and littered with cables, broken machinery, and discarded blueprints. A faint tremor ran through the building as the Colossus shifted its weight. The structure groaned.

Lucan caught his reflection in a growing puddle. Flawless coat. White hair fell perfectly to his shoulders, not a strand misplaced despite the wind and rain that battered this ruin. He stepped around the water's edge without disturbing its surface, one measured footfall after another. His boots gleamed, untouched by the filth around him.

Let them see the contrast. Let them understand the standard.

He had never once apologized for the lengths his expectations of perfection had driven him to, and he never would. No one had given him permission to be less than perfect. Why should he extend the same to anyone else?

Heat built behind his gaze. Not total rage, not yet, but the smoldering potential of it. It waited, patient and restrained. That was always the danger with him. People assumed calm meant safety.

They usually realized the mistake too late. Lucan enjoyed other people's mistakes most of all.

Below the balcony, Dr. Syd and his team of engineers worked in the dim glow of flickering lanterns, their hands buried in tangled conduit and vacuum tubing. The marble floor beneath them was scarred black from another catastrophic failure. The energy had surged uncontrolled and burned everything in its path.

Lucan shifted and leaped from the broken ledge. Beastlike feet struck marble. He reverted mid-stride, boots reappearing as he advanced across the cracked floor. Engineers scrambled out of his way. His patience had worn to the barest thread.

"This is the sixth breakdown in as many months," Lucan growled. His voice cut through the chamber like a blade. The workers froze. Tension thickened the air. "You promised the artificial core could sustain this behemoth. Instead, we are stalled outside Huntley, waiting while you tinker."

Dr. Syd pulled off his goggles and blinked through the haze. Grease streaked his coat, soot smudged his cheek. He put his glasses back on and let them slide straight to the tip of his nose, where they always sat, perpetually on the verge of falling.

The ravings to thin air or excited stares into dark corners weren't what annoyed Lucan most about the man. He looked like he'd forgotten what a mirror was for. Unkempt hair, half-grown beard, collar crooked with a button off-center. That last detail grated on Lucan more than it should. If a man couldn't manage his own buttons, how was he supposed to manage the divine?

Syd's eyes moved constantly, scanning, never settling on people long enough to suggest they mattered. He never really looked at people. He was looking at something only he could see.

"And I warned you this would be impossibly complicated," Syd shot back, his voice edged with irritation. His gaze flicked to the side for a brief moment. His mouth tightened as if he held back another comment. Then, to no one in particular, he muttered, "Yes, yes, I know."

He shook his head. "We are stitching together miracles using half-broken relics. The Colossus was never meant to run on jury-rigged shards, and yet here we are, pushing beyond our limits again and again. Do you know how many engineers besides me could get this running?" He held up a hand in the shape of a zero. "None. Because no one in their right mind would think this was feasible."

Lucan's gloved hand flexed. Over two years ago, Rook, the masked tactician who had uncovered the slumbering Colossus beneath White Hill, had brought him Syd. It was Rook who had formulated the plan and given it all to Lucan. It was also Rook who had disappeared from that skydeck six months ago and left Lucan to pick up the pieces. The madman was a tool in that regard. Not an asset.

Lucan stepped forward, his voice low but carrying the authority of command. "I am not interested in your excuses, Doctor. I want results."

A nearby lieutenant flinched and stepped aside as conscripts hurried past with reinforcement beams. The building groaned under another subtle shift of the Colossus's massive frame. When the creature moved, the entire place quaked. Dust cascaded from the broken ceiling.

Syd kicked a chunk of marble out of his way. "Rook asked me to make a god rise from its grave. First miracle, reviving the Colossus. Second miracle, buying us enough time with it to drive off three ships of the Armada. Third miracle, obliterating White Hill, Heydon, and Huntley. Now you want me to drag this beast to Breezewaltz for a fourth miracle?" He spread his hands. "That takes patience. Rook had patience."

Lucan's scowl deepened. "Yes, Doctor. Had. Past tense." His voice turned razor-sharp. "He is not here anymore. Thus, it falls to us. The Domain expects results from every citizen, even those born in Iveria."

Syd snorted. "Then maybe the Domain should have brought me better materials." He motioned to a worn, dog-eared journal that sat atop a rust-stained crate. "You haven't even read Rook's notes, have you? Here. Let me make it simple." He tapped a passage. "'No junk crystals.'"

Lucan's eyes flicked to the page. He recognized Rook's writing, scrawled in sharp, precise strokes. The message was underlined twice.

Syd continued, his voice laced with frustration. "We have been scrounging junk shards. White Hill's heavy shard lasted a month. Heydon's and Huntley's lasted half that. Every time the Colossus shatters a city, the heavy shards we recover already have collateral damage." He leaned back against the ruined console. "Without a top-quality heavy shard, the artificial heart will burn out every time the Colossus demands more power than we can give. And eventually?" He glanced toward nothing, then back at Lucan. "Our luck will run out."

Lucan's jaw tightened. "Rook did not prepare for this possibility?"

Syd shrugged. "He did. We planned it together. A single heavy shard from one of those cities should have sufficed, but the Colossus keeps breaking them in the chaos. Failing that, Rook assumed we would have marched on Breezewaltz by now."

Lucan's fingers curled into a fist.

Syd pulled off his glasses and rubbed the bridge of his nose. "It was a good plan. His notes cover every logistical detail and almost all eventualities except this one. He didn't understand just how powerful the Colossus was."

"A wasted effort, apparently." Lucan pulled his hands behind his back.

Syd laughed.

"Something amusing, Doctor?"

"No…yes…wasted effort. The phrase reminded me of something." Syd scoffed and looked down at the notes.

"I could use a good joke right now. Please, Doctor, do share."

Syd smiled to himself. "My son was brilliant. Had my mind, my instincts. He could've been my legacy to the world. Instead, he's probably dying in a gutter somewhere in Iveria."

Lucan studied the doctor. He tilted his head slightly and allowed the edges of his mouth to pull taut in a cool smile. "I find it strange, Doctor, that a man of your intelligence invested so much into someone you could not fully control."

Syd gave a short, bitter laugh. "A lesson learned too late." He gestured around at the mess of wires and crystalline lattices, the strained hum of crystal energy that vibrated beneath their feet. "This will be my true legacy."

Lucan turned back, hands still clasped behind his back. He gazed past the fractured walls into the roiling storm. "A legacy isn't built from desperation or regret, Syd."

Syd laughed and picked up a spanner. "The beliefs of the young."

"I was born beneath the shadow of the Rose Crystal," Lucan continued, voice quiet but sharp. "Raised to understand that the Domain had fractured and that one day, it would fall to me to rebuild it. I was chosen by fate, by the Rose Crystal itself."

Syd's eyes narrowed. "Just the Rose Crystal? The Azure or even Gaia herself might argue against your destined fate."

Lucan turned to him as if Syd had committed some great blasphemy. "The Rose Crystal is the dominant force on Gaia. The Azure is weak, and Gaia herself is an absent parent who lets her children run wild." He eyed Syd. "Apparently, not too dissimilar from yourself."

Syd laughed again. "Yes, it's always funny how the ones who speak of absent parents are those who feel they must prove themselves," Syd said, eyeing Lucan over the rim of his glasses. "To those same parents, the world, or even themselves. You hide it well, but it's there."

Lucan turned sharply. He felt his mask slip for a heartbeat before he regained composure. "You overstep."

Syd shrugged, unfazed. "No offense intended. Fathers, sons, and legacies, it's all tangled..."

Syd's voice trailed off as two figures dropped into the room. Blue crystal flaked off their skin. Altiers. They moved fast, sudas already drawn, their forms crackling with shard energy.

Some of Lucan's men didn't have time to react. They were too slow and found themselves without heads. The rest shifted into Rosari. Even then, most of the Rosari here weren't Lucan's elite. The Altiers cut through them like paper. One or two held firm, but they were the exception, not the rule.

Lucan had shifted before their boots even touched the ground. His form exploded outward in a cascade of crimson crystal. Rose energy surged through him as his body transformed, growing massive and feral. Red crystalline fur erupted across his frame. His hands became claws. His face elongated into something bestial and terrible.

He strode forward, suda in hand, as the Altiers blinked in and out of dilation.

The first Altier went for Lucan. The second continued to fight the limited Praetori Lucan had brought with him.

The Altier's blade struck his shoulder. It should have cleaved through bone. Instead, it skittered across his crystalline skin with a screech of metal on stone.

Lucan amplified his mass field. The same trick he used on Toren. This novice would be in soup before she knew it.

Lucan swung. She stepped back and twisted. She launched into another insignificant swing that did little more than chip at the fur on his neck.

When her boots hit the ground, she went to jump back, but her face showed surprise at how slow her movements suddenly became. That's when Lucan's clawed hand caught her by the throat and lifted her off the ground.

Lucan saw the second Altier put down a guard and look toward him. The imminent violence forced the man to give Lucan his full attention.

"NO!" he screamed, scrambling to save the Altier in Lucan's grasp.

Lucan squeezed. The Altier in his grip struggled, tried to use her increased speed to hammer him with her suda. It didn't matter. Rose crushed Azure. Always had. Lucan felt her throat collapse beneath his claws. Felt the desperate flutter of a dying heartbeat.

He dropped the body as the second Altier was on him.

The man hit Lucan with a flurry of cuts. Lucan wasn't worried, but he made sure to protect his eyes. Eventually, the man fell out of dilation, breathing heavily. He, too, had just spent too long in Lucan's field. Lucan could see the Altier doing the mental calculus. The fight had drained him, and even if he didn't realize it, he could feel Lucan's field weighing him down further. Lucan wasn't sure what their objective was, assassination or sabotage, but whatever it was, this Altier now knew it was impossible.

And so he ran. Azure energy flared around him as he accelerated, boosting his speed.

Lucan leaped. Twenty feet in a single bound. He caught the Altier mid-stride and drove him into the cracked marble floor. The impact cratered the stone. The Altier's ribs shattered audibly.

"I'll tell Marling," Lucan said quietly, "that his offering was insufficient."

He crushed the man's skull beneath his heel.

Lucan reverted, standing over the broken man in his perfect coat and perfect boots. Not a hair out of place. He looked down at what remained of the Altier.

Silence fell over the chamber, broken only by the patter of rain through the shattered wall and Syd's ragged breathing.

He was beside his equipment, hands already moving over the conduits to assess damage. His fingers traced wires with practiced precision, a sheen of sweat forming on his brow. He didn't wipe it away.

His head tilted slightly, as if listening to something no one else could hear. "Yes, I know," he muttered to the empty air. His eyes glazed, unfocused. "Breeze-waltz. I heard you the first time."

He blinked, shook his head, and looked up at the carnage. "Do you want my people to clean this up or yours?"

Lucan studied him for a moment. The academic, ready to defend his precious device with what? A spanner?

"I'll leave the room to you, Doctor. Do with it what you will."

His coat swirled behind him as he stepped over the bodies.

"Where are you going?" Syd called after him, voice distant.

Lucan didn't break stride. "To get you your fourth miracle."

Outside, the storm raged as rain coursed down the Colossus's massive, dormant face. Above them, the Imperial Fleet circled like carrion birds waiting to feast on the next corpse.

CHAPTER 5: KENZIE

4 Days Until Landfall

"Codes accepted, Captain. You may dock at bay A08." The voice rang through the comms.

Kal gave a little fist pump to himself and mouthed, "I told you," to Haruto.

"Copy, A08. ISS HD117 docking in two, over and out," Kal responded into the comms before he cut the transmission.

"That, ladies and gentlemen, is how you save yourself ten thousand credits in a year," Kal said, grinning.

"Yeah, but they'll flag that code in a week or so," Tia replied. "We'll have another warrant on us. Maybe another bounty in a couple weeks."

"Who cares? Add it to the twenty bounties we already have. Besides, we'll be long gone by then with ten times that amount of credits in our pockets," Kal said as he looked at Haruto. "Maybe more if I get on a hot streak at the dice tables." He smiled, clearly proud of himself. Haruto smiled back.

"With you throwing? Not likely. Everyone knows your luck stays on the ships. Make sure the crew gets paid first before you lose our profits." Val cut in.

"Val, at least warn me before you fire." Kaliston shot her a look but kept his grin. "You think I'd bet away our hard-earned money?"

"Yes," Val replied, stone-faced.

"I'm insulted. They'll be there losing along with me, right?"

The trio and Avery yelled in agreement. Kenzie flinched at the noise. She hadn't expected to be included. It still caught her off guard, being one of them.

Kal smiled and turned back to the controls. "Avery, you know the route?"

"Yes, sir," Avery responded.

"Kal, I was wondering if I could take this one," Kenzie said, though her voice trailed off.

Kal glanced at her, then at the controls. "Why don't you just observe this time? It's your first time flying into Breezewaltz. Take in the sights. Avery's seen it a million times. He can focus on getting us in safely."

Kenzie felt a pang of disappointment, but nodded and understood his reasoning. Still, she caught the flick of Val's eyes toward her.

The older woman exhaled through her nose before speaking. "Observation is learning, Kenzie. We'll be back in a couple of months, and you'll be the one landing us. Right, Kal?"

Kal hesitated. "Right," he said. A little too quick.

Val's kindness and Kal's hesitation to it had caught Kenzie off guard, but she recovered. "A couple months...?" she asked and cocked a brow at Val. "By then, I'll be rich, retired, and living like a queen in Somerset. You'll be sending me letters, begging me to come back."

Val didn't respond but gave a polite nod. Kenzie sank into the co-pilot's chair, arms crossed like someone expecting her to stick around for once hadn't thrown her off. She had caught the interaction and filed it away. Val's optimism was sweet, but it seemed like Kal knew better.

"Don't mind me, I'll just be up here scouting my next landing spot," she muttered to herself. Avery smirked, nudged the nose down, and eased up on the throttle.

Kenzie looked out the big windows as the sprawling city of Breezewaltz unfolded before her. At its center was a large mesa, crowded with thousands of homes and buildings. A lake shimmered at the heart of the mesa, and an ornate structure stood in the middle of the water. The building glinted like polished glass in the sun. The lake drained to the Lower City via many outlets that waterfalled over the edge.

A sound crackled over the ship's comm. "If you'll look out to our right, you'll see the lovely city of Breezewaltz," Haruto's voice rang out, adopting the tone of a tour guide. "This cornerstone of the Iverian League is the religious capital of the nation and the sole supplier of Azure shards. Traders, pilgrims, and ne'er-do-wells are found in the Lower City. Aristocrats and holy men reside on the Upper Mesa. The Temple of the Azure Crystal dominates the skyline and sits in the center of the Grand Lake. The fact that the water never drains out is a remarkable and unexplained phenomenon. This city is the capital of the First District, administered by the Luinondo family, who own the second-largest dreadnought in the Iverian Armada. All size and no subtlety, if you ask me."

"Not like our *Days!*" Kal roared, and the bridge erupted in cheers. Kenzie smiled, then cheered, too.

Haruto continued, "Nobles from across the nation send their children here to undergo the Rites to become an Altier. They say only one in five survives the process, but certain family lines perform better, which is why they're aristocrats and we're lowly skypirates. Just a reminder, the extra hustle and bustle isn't an illusion. The high holy day of Landfall is in four days, so the city's packed. Keep your wits about you, your head on a swivel, and your purse well hidden." He adjusted a knob on his control panel, almost absent-mindedly, before he continued in a low tone. "Especially with that Colossus rampaging through the countryside."

Kal shifted uncomfortably and exchanged a glance with Val. The crew sat in silence.

Haruto cleared his throat as if he realized too late he'd said too much. Kenzie knew he had intercepted most military transmissions, but she wasn't really aware of this Colossus. She figured it was just a rumor, but apparently, Haruto had kept the information close. Few on the crew were aware of the reports he shared with Kal and Val. It seemed they did not want to upset the rest of the crew just yet.

Someone on the crew coughed as they neared the dock. That's when Haruto spoke up again.

"Kal, we're getting a message from someone in the Shipping Guild. What do you want me to do?"

"Play it, we'll be stinking rich after this drop-off, let's hear what they want."

Haruto's fingers moved across the console, and the comm crackled to life. A stern voice filled the bridge.

"Kaliston, this is Guild Supervisor Thorne. We have reports that you're on your way to Breezewaltz. You'll know that's our city. If you show your face there, know that we will extract what you owe us, either from yourself or your crew. That package and seller you abducted were worth two hundred and fifty-three thousand credits. We expect full payment, with interest. You have until Landfall." The transmission cut just as curtly as it began.

Kal frowned. "That guy knows how to ruin a moment."

"The message was encrypted. The Guild isn't playing around," Haruto said.

"This bounty pays four times that. We'll pay off the Guild and steal it right back next week. I'm not worried about them."

Kenzie smirked despite herself. Kal's words and voice said two different things. She guessed he was broke, but his swagger never changed. She respected the bravado. On the streets, it was all about what others thought about you, not what was true.

The *Days* eased into the dock. The hum of the engines shifted, and a final, graceful lurch signaled the *Days* had touched down.

Outside the viewport, dockworkers in bright hazard suits scrambled to secure the landing zone, their figures slight against the sprawl of Breezewaltz. The docking clamps groaned as they locked into place.

"Great job, Avery. Inspiring words, Haruto." Kal sprang out of his seat.

Val stood as well, arms still crossed, and blocked the door. "And you're absolutely not playing dice with the cut from this job, right?"

Kal clutched his chest, as if mortally wounded. "Didn't we go over this already?"

"And you gave me a non-answer then, too," Val replied.

"You have little faith," Kal riposted.

Val arched a brow. "I did, once. Then I had to call in a favor with the Black Moon to get you out of that gambling den."

"I was winning that night! And the Black Moon is a good crew. I remember us drinking until sunrise."

"Yes, and I had to pay them triple what you 'won.'"

He huffed, but waved the discussion away. "All right, crew, you have your assignments. Kenzie, you're with me."

Kenzie blinked. "Me?"

Kal didn't answer. He just walked out the door. Val followed, still arguing the point.

Kenzie had expected to stay on the *Days*. Keep her head down, run standby, maybe help with cleanup. Controlled jobs, as she liked to call them. The kind that kept her off the busy city streets and out of anyone's spotlight.

She stared at the bridge's open door, her mouth parted as if she might argue with ghosts already gone. The knot in her stomach tightened.

She could probably say no. No, she should say no. Kenzie also knew Kal was trusting her enough to bring her along, and she shouldn't let her nerves betray that trust.

She slid off the pilot's chair, bumped knuckles with Avery, and followed Kal into the hall. Kenzie cursed herself quietly with every step, but was unable to come up with a good excuse to stay.

She could slip off unnoticed, become just another face in the crowd. Unfortunately, crowds made her nervous, and she'd fallen in love with Cookie's cooking. The worst part, which she'd never admit even to herself, was the flicker of excitement she felt about going on a mission.

Breezewaltz started to feel less like a stop and more like a story. She'd learned stories usually meant trouble.

CHAPTER 6 : LOCKE

4 Days Until Landfall

"And this one is?" Jules let the question hang between them, arms crossed. She wore her usual overalls, with her hair tied back under a faded red bandana. Her gloves looked like she had dragged them across every inch of Iveria, maybe even Aurelia.

Locke squinted at the component. "That's the…" he hesitated. "Charge compressor?" His voice tilted upward at the end, betraying his uncertainty.

Jules's expression was stone. "And what does the charge compressor do?"

Locke straightened. "It processes the raw energy from the ship's heavy shards and converts it to usable voltages for the *Days'* systems?" he said, and his face twisted like he'd bitten something sour.

"Right explanation. Wrong part." Jules tapped the component. "That's the inertial dampener. Keeps gravity stable inside the ship. They can also shift mass if needed, make things feel heavier or lighter depending on the setting. A Rosari in a box, I call it."

Locke winced. "Oh. Right."

She pointed across the table without looking. "That's the charge compressor."

"So close," Locke muttered.

"Not really." Jules dropped back onto her stool, already turning a wrench. "The *Days* is a one-two punch. Light, fast, with optical camo and sensor-absorbing plates for when we need to disappear. Reinforced alloy hull, twin Azure cores to shift workload, two secondary turrets, and a shardshot cannon tucked under the belly for when we don't. She doesn't look like much on the inside because of these slobs, but outside? She's a ghost or a hammer, depending on what the job needs." Jules spat on the floor out of habit. "And like any fine machine, she runs best when someone gives a damn. A person to know and love her. I don't think you're there yet, Kid."

"I care." Locke sat down, picked up an engineering journal, and thumbed through it.

"But you don't love her. Love is like an engine…" Jules started.

"You think everything is like an engine," Locke replied, smiling. Jules grunted and waved him away.

He returned his focus to the journal. He had once studied at the Citadel in Warwick, driven by a need to make his father proud. Now he studied because he wanted to contribute to the *Days*.

Kal had assigned him to engineering. Locke had suspicions that it was to keep him away from the bridge. Still, he wanted to help, but he always felt like he was just annoying Jules. He kept asking anyway.

"Do you think I'll ever pick the names up?" he asked eventually.

"Can I be honest?" Jules asked, but didn't stop tinkering.

"Have you ever stopped?" Locke responded.

Jules turned to him. "No," she turned back to her work. "And no."

Locke sighed, and his shoulders slumped.

Jules glanced at his dejected look and turned back to him. "But I see how hard you're trying, and I respect that about you, Locke. Listen, I don't think you're a natural engineer, but that doesn't mean you're not a smart kid."

Locke gave her a look.

"Smart young man," she corrected. "I don't know your backstory…"

Locke opened his mouth to start talking about his life before the *Days* and the memory loss.

"And I don't care to know," Jules continued, "but it's clear you've had an education. You must have your talents buried in there. It's certainly not dancing, and it's not remembering the names of everything. This is just going to be a mountain to climb, but you can do it if you're motivated."

"They say there are plenty of skeletons that were once highly motivated mountain climbers."

"True. If you can't survive, adapt, and evolve, then you'll die. That's a hard truth, but it's a truth. The day we stop learning new things is the day we die."

"Sage advice. I feel like I should write this down," Locke said.

"Commit it to memory, along with the circuit diagram for the cooling matrix." Jules tossed a book at him and turned back to her desk.

Just then, Lizz and Jazz walked in, bickering. Locke had watched them enough to piece together that they showed love by fighting.

"Would you stop micromanaging?" Lizz huffed and adjusted her grip on the crate.

"I would if you stopped dropping them," Jazz shot back and flashed a grin.

Their faces looked enough alike to be siblings, but their body types and personalities couldn't have been more different.

Jazz carried the crate like it weighed nothing and smiled at his sister, who was still struggling under the same load. He was a big guy, built like he'd grown up wrestling scrap and winning, but he moved like someone still figuring out where his arms were supposed to go. His ashy-blonde hair fell everywhere, and his grin said he either understood the world better than most or not at all. Either way, he made Locke laugh.

Lizz was the opposite. Wiry and sharp-featured, she looked like someone who had fought for every inch. Locke sometimes thought her freckled face and bright green eyes didn't belong in an engine room. Then he'd see her work. After years of training with Jules, she could strip a panel in thirty seconds flat. She was always trying to prove herself. To whom, or why, Locke still hadn't figured out.

Lost in thought, Locke looked at Lizz a little too long. Kenzie's earlier comment still echoed in his head. He flinched when Lizz caught him.

"Locke!" Lizz said. She dropped the crate and let its contents scatter across the floor. She rushed over to him, all energy and momentum. "Did you hear we're landing at Breezewaltz soon?"

"Yeah, pretty exciting. Big plans?"

"No, I was wondering if maybe we could…"

"Hey, sis, forgot something?" Jazz called across the room, picking up the crate's contents.

Lizz squeaked and whirled around before she dashed back to help.

"Hey, Jazz," Locke called, waving.

Jazz gave him a nod and a smile before the twins continued to stage gear for the upcoming away missions.

Locke looked past them. The overhead lights shone on a mess of tools and open panels. Every surface seemed claimed by someone. Trinkets dangled from overhead pipes and stickers peeled off lockers. A scorch mark still blackened the wall by Tia's locker. No one talked about that one. The *Days* was rough inside, but she was lived in. A ship held together by hands, history, and stubbornness.

Locke's gaze drifted to the 'holding cell' nearby. He walked over and looked in on a lone figure sitting curled on the cot. They were fully wrapped in a blanket with Cookie's food half-eaten.

The crew had taken to calling them the bounty. Locke couldn't help but feel sorry for them. They looked hollowed out in the converted tool storage cage. He knew the signs of shard sickness when he saw them. The poor soul would never be the same.

"Hi. Are you okay? Do you need to use the restroom or anything?" he asked, but got no response.

"What's your name?" Locke asked, but still only silence. "Well, I'm sorry about all this, but as I hear it, you'll be out of there soon and all this will be over."

The figure lifted their head and regarded Locke, but said nothing before they turned away again.

"Leave 'em be, Locke," Jules yelled. "We're landing. Grab your datapad and pack. I'm sending you an info packet for an errand. Meet me by my workstation when you're ready."

"Yeah, on it," Locke said. He took one last look at the figure before he jogged back through the *Days* to his bunk. He grabbed the datapad from under his pillow. Datapads weren't comms. They communicated locally, but everyone on the ship could sync with the *Days* CrystalLine connection for large communication. Locke couldn't believe Kal could afford to give one to all crew members. His old one was probably collecting dust somewhere at the Citadel.

He grabbed the beat-up pack that Avery had given him a couple of months back and checked the datapad. Jules had already transferred credits along with instructions to a watchsmith. They were annoyingly detailed. Jules had listed out streets and landmarks like he didn't know how to find a damn watchsmith.

He walked back down the corridor toward the hold when he felt something suddenly placed in his hand.

"Here," Cookie said.

He looked down and saw a wrapped pastry. "Really?"

"You'll be gone for hours," she said and wiped her hands on her apron. "Don't come back whining about being hungry."

"It's a watchsmith, not a war zone."

"Still gotta eat."

Locke sighed but didn't argue. "Thanks."

Cookie waved him off and disappeared down the corridor. She almost ran into the twins coming the other way.

Lizz jogged toward Locke when she saw him and stopped short with an eager expression. "Oh! You're heading out?" she asked as she brushed a stray strand of hair behind her ear.

"Yeah, errand for Jules," Locke said.

"We're about to head out, too," Lizz continued. "Tia and Dr. Rina are leaving to get supplies. You know, medical and…" she hesitated.

"Explosives," Jazz supplied with a grin as he arrived at the conversation. "Lots of 'em." He mimed an explosion with his hands.

Lizz shot him a look. "You don't have to say it like that."

Locke smirked. "Tia does love to be prepared."

"She said 'not getting caught shorthanded again' or something like that," Jazz added in Tia's chipper tone. "I think she plans to buy enough to take out half of Aurelia."

Locke shrugged. "There is something about being on a skyship with that amount of ordnance that should be unsettling. I guess it helps keep our minds on other things. Speaking of, I should probably get going…"

Lizz perked up. "We could walk with you. Just to…"

"Nah, I got it," Locke said quickly.

Jazz chuckled. "Classic. Won't accept backup unless it's Kenzie, right?"

Lizz's expression flickered, but she stayed quiet. Locke blushed and stammered. Jazz was either oblivious or playing his own game.

"Kidding," Jazz said. He grinned as he nudged Lizz forward. "C'mon, let's get moving before Tia has all the fun."

Locke watched them go before he adjusted his pack and headed for the exit.

Jules waited with a datapad in hand and flipped through a maintenance log. She didn't look up. "Payments loaded, directions are in the file."

"Thanks. Not sure if the route you loaded makes sense with the pilgrims in town for Landfall."

That got her attention. She studied him for a beat and tilted her head. "Have you been to this district before?"

Locke shrugged. "Something like that."

Jules squinted at him like she was about to pry, then seemed to decide it wasn't worth the effort. "Fine. Get there however you want, but don't forget my watch."

He realized he probably should have phrased it as a question, but was happy Jules had trusted him all the same. He smirked. "A little desperate for an upgrade, aren't we?"

"It's a half-second off."

"The horror."

"With equipment this sensitive, yeah."

Jules pushed past him toward the engine bay. She stumbled on a crate of Azure shardshot Tia had left out. "Dammit, Tia, watch where you leave your ammo."

"Tell Liam to move his gear out of my ammo storage, and it wouldn't be a problem," Tia said, pointing to a rat's nest of wires and boxes with knobs.

Jules shook her head and muttered, "Place was built for fifteen disciplined soldiers, not thirteen slobs. We're over-crewed and under-organized." She stepped over the crate again, careful not to crush a loose round of Azure shardshot.

"Guess that's better than under-crewed and overexploited," Tia said and moved to pick up the rounds.

Locke stepped into the loading bay and spotted Avery checking over a manifest on his datapad while Cookie secured a crate onto a transport dolly. Avery glanced up as Locke approached.

"Figured you'd be out already," Avery said while he tapped something on the screen.

"Had to fend off an army of well-wishers first," Locke replied. "You heading out, too?"

Avery nodded. "Supply run. Nothing exciting. Just making sure we're stocked up before Landfall shuts everything down."

Cookie tightened the straps on the crate and dusted off her hands. "Ain't much left to get, just a few staples. If I have to wrestle another pilgrim over the last sack of flour, so help me."

"You'd win," Locke said.

"You're damn right I would," Cookie shot back with a grin.

Avery smirked. "We're on a schedule. Try not to start any food wars."

"No promises." Cookie shoved the dolly forward and started toward the dock.

Avery turned back to Locke. "You good?"

Locke gave a slight nod. "Yeah. Just a quick errand."

"Right. Take care of my lucky pack. See you when you get back."

Locke bumped fists with Avery as he stepped toward the ramp. He had to sidestep Liam and Haruto, who were deep in conversation near the ship's terminal. Haruto was calm, as usual, but Liam looked ready to hit something.

"I'm telling you, the sensor array's got a calibration drift," Liam said, gesturing toward the screen. "If we don't adjust it, we're gonna start getting false readings."

Haruto didn't even look up. "It's been fine since Huntley. Why would it act up now?"

Liam threw his hands up. "That's not how malfunctions work, you know that."

Locke smirked as he passed them. "Ship's still gonna be here when I get back, right?"

Haruto shrugged. "Depends on if Liam decides to rewire the whole thing out of spite."

Liam muttered something under his breath, and Locke passed them with a slight nod. Their argument faded into the background. He liked the *Days* for that. It allowed him to move and decide where he belonged, free from the expectations of who he was or who others thought he should be. It gave him space to breathe and to make his own mistakes. He had the option to be reckless in a way that would have driven his father to fits if he were around to see it. True, Locke rarely exercised that option, but it was always there. The *Days* allowed him to be more than just a name or a title. It let him be a person, one not defined by his family's expectations or the pressure of a legacy he never asked for. It gave him freedom, and seeing Breezewaltz extend past the ramp only reminded him of that. Losing the *Days* would mean going back to being defined by his past, trapped in a story someone else had written for him. Nothing got under his skin quite like that.

Val stood by the loading dock and waited for Kal. She didn't say anything at first, just gave Locke that unreadable look that somehow made him feel like he'd already done something wrong.

"Don't get arrested," she said finally.

Locke scoffed. "I'm buying a watch."

Val didn't blink. "I'm saying it to everyone running errands. Just covering my bases." Locke followed her gaze to Kal, who laughed too loudly with Jazz.

He sighed. "Fair."

She said nothing else, but she turned and stared out over the city. Worry flickered in her eyes. He caught sight of Kenzie returning from putting something in a parked speeder.

"Hey, looks like you're heading out too?" he asked.

"Yeah. Freshly conscripted. You?" she replied.

"Jules wants me to run something. Still open to grabbing a bite later?" Locke hated how sheepish he sounded.

"Yeah, it should hopefully be a quick drop." She hesitated a second, then added, "I should be free for dinner by six. Any place in mind?"

"We're in Sector Six…" he thought out loud. "Oh, I know, there was a greasy spoon of a place called the Berrywood Grill in the market district. Should be perfect for our meager per diem."

"You get paid what you're worth," Val said, not missing a beat.

Locke and Kenzie exchanged a look with a smile. Kenzie shrugged, and Locke shook his head.

"See you there then. Order without me if I'm running late," Kenzie said.

"Are you going to tell me what you want?" Locke asked.

"You'll just have to guess," Kenzie replied.

"That's impossible," Locke laughed.

"By design. Not all of us are open books, Locke."

They smiled at each other and turned away.

He stepped down the ramp and onto the dock. Breezewaltz stretched out before him. They had landed in Sector Six, not far from his destination. The main roads would be congested with both speeders and foot traffic, but the side streets and alleys would allow him to move quickly. He had already mapped his route before Jules had even finished explaining where to go.

Locke had seen the city in his dreams. He might not talk much about Breezewaltz, but he still remembered it. To some, it was a holy city, but to him, it was home.

CHAPTER 7: FIRST ALTIER MARLING

4 Days Until Landfall

Heydon's Fury was the pride of its namesake city and the Sixth Capital skyship of the Armada. First Altier Marling stood at the command post. He stared blankly at the displays before him, and his drink trembled slightly in his hand. Three months ago, the Colossus had laid waste to Heydon and wiped it entirely from the map. With it went Marling's entire family. He could still picture his son's bright laughter, the light in his eyes when Marling would tickle him.

He drained his glass and poured another with his shaking hand.

A far clearer memory was finding his wife and son's lifeless bodies under a slab of rubble. Innocence crushed by the merciless creature below.

Marling took a deep breath and steadied his voice for the day's log. "Daily report of the Sixth Capital skyship, *Heydon's Fury*," he began. "Holding position above the dormant Colossus. Little we've done has slowed the creature. Our Fleet has bombarded it day after day, with no effect. I sent two of my best Altiers to investigate the activity on the creature's back. They have yet to return, presumed dead. Prince Lucan's Aurelian Fleet continues to swarm it like bees around a sleeping bear. Attack the bees and wake the bear, attack the bear and be stung to death."

He took another sip and let the burn ground him in this grim reality.

"*Heydon's Fury* is all that remains of our home. Five hundred crewmen and eight, no six, Altiers from lesser houses make up my command. Each is as helpless as I am against the towering god below. I have no idea why the Colossus has stopped its rampage. Perhaps even gods needed to sleep, or maybe it was a calculated move by Lucan to bait the *Fury* into a trap. It doesn't matter. I will hold as ordered."

Secretly, he refused to risk the last remnant of Heydon, even if opportunity beckoned. What would his mother, the previous First Altier of Heydon, have thought of it all? How would she have fought the Colossus?

Marling didn't have an answer. The Colossus existed outside of all reason.

"The Colossus…moves as if one of Gaia's many mountains has risen and learned to walk. Its spired head reaches a quarter of the way to the cloud line and towers above the land. Each step sends tremors through Gaia. Deep, rolling shocks that could be felt long before the Colossus comes into view."

Marling remembered the feeling of hopelessness as the creature walked away from White Hill.

"The air thickens when it draws near, not from heat, but from something unseen and electric. The atmosphere shifts, and the air tastes different, like the aftermath of a vicious thunderstorm. A faint, crackling charge can be felt upon approach. Subtle at first, before it grows stronger as the creature nears. It raises the hair on the skin of those who witness it."

Marling knew this would be cut from his report, but the booze had loosened his tongue, and he felt like going.

"Gaia shudders beneath it. The land trembles, not just from its massive steps, but from something more profound. An unseen force that smothers the world. Animals never linger in its path. They flee long before it arrives, sensing the shift in the air, the pull of something they were never meant to witness."

Marling drained the last of the glass and refilled it.

"Its form swallows the horizon. Its body is a mass of towering blue flesh, thick and unyielding, layered in a crystalline plating that catches the light with a cold, shimmering glow. The remnants of White Hill cling to its back, like a child carried by its father."

Marling put the mic down and took a moment to push the memory of his son aside. He continued.

"Jagged blue crystal spires grow from its skin, unstable and brittle. Some of the larger ones snap and fall to the Gaia below. They shatter into dust, unusable. New crystalline towers emerged in their place, an endless cycle of growth and decay. Even the gaia beneath it seems unfit to bear its presence. Each step leaves a deep, sunken crater on Gaia's surface and kills all life underfoot. Footprints etched in death."

Marling finished half a glass in one gulp before refilling.

"Its electric blue eyes burn with an unreadable intent. They are unblinking, cold, and distant. Looking at it fills one with a sense of dread, like something was wrong with the world and it would never be right again. When its gaze falls upon you, the hopelessness of existence settles on your chest. It does not acknowledge or consider your presence. It simply moves. You either get out of its way or become part of the ruin left in its wake."

Marling sighed and looked at the glass. "First Altier Toren has returned with his ship to Breezewaltz for Landfall. *Deepwarden* was recalled to Seaforth. *Heydon's Fury* stands alone. Word is that *Daybreaker* and *Belepoch* are coming to join the watch, but until then, we remain isolated."

He took another sip before continuing. "The King... the King doesn't want to alarm the people. I wonder how long we can keep this from the citizens. The South is burning, with or without the people of Orleans realizing it."

Just as he drained his glass again, a light flashed across the sensor panel.

Marling leaned forward and squinted at the unexpected blips on the sensor. For a fleeting moment, he hoped it was a malfunction. Yet the sensor remained stubbornly clear. He counted the blips, but the number grew too quickly to make the exact count matter. Lucan's Fleet was charging right at the *Fury*.

He rubbed his eyes. The haze of sleeplessness and alcohol clouded his mind. It felt like a living nightmare, the same feeling when he learned about Heydon's fate, a dread in the pit of his stomach.

He grabbed for the comm, but his fingers slipped across the controls.

Across the bridge, junior officers sat numbly, dulled by the monotony of two weeks of fruitless guard duty. One officer yawned as the panel lit up, and another glanced at Marling. Their confusion turned quickly to horror as realization dawned.

The tight formations of the Aurelian Fleet splintered into smaller groups and sliced aggressively through the night clouds.

Marling's voice broke through the static. "All hands," he said, barely above a whisper, then louder. Desperation colored his tone, "All hands, battle stations! Enemy approaching!"

He knew even as he spoke that the delay had cost them dearly. He slammed the controls and repeated the order: "Move! All hands to stations, prepare for combat! Get those damn shardshot cannons firing!"

His command echoed across the silent bridge. Too late to matter. He turned to the viewport and confirmed with his eyes what the sensor had shown. The entirety of Lucan's Fleet was en route in a surprise night raid.

Marling swore bitterly. They had been on guard for two weeks, just enough time to dull their sharpness. He had kept the *Fury* at a fair distance, but thought they were safe enough to respond to threats as they approached. He realized how wrong he'd been. Maybe in daylight, with the crew fully prepared, the distance might have mattered. Maybe the crew wouldn't be in a melancholic daze if they hadn't lost everything to the creature below. Maybe he would have noticed sooner if he hadn't gotten drunk to the point of oblivion.

Marling knew *Heydon's Fury* would fall amid a twinkling sky of maybes.

"Where are those cannons!" Marling shouted into the comm. Urgency clawed at his throat. "All hands, move now, go, go, go!"

Even as his words echoed through the ship, he knew it was too late. The *Fury* trembled as the first enemy ship latched on. The sharp clang of boarding clamps drove home their vulnerability.

First Altier Marling of the Sixth Capital skyship of the Iverian Armada watched helplessly as his ship was boarded. He feared he would be the last captain she would ever know.

The final image he saw through the viewport, just before the first Rosari stormed the bridge, was the *Inquisitor* breaching the darkened cloud line. Its cannons already blazed, and streaks of crimson shardshot cut through the night sky. Lucan would be here soon.

CHAPTER 8: KENZIE

4 Days Until Landfall

Kenzie hadn't known what to expect when the ramp lowered. She had never been to Breezewaltz, though she had seen cities like it. At first, it was overwhelming, but she quickly got accustomed to it. The sheer mass of people reminded her of home in the worst way. Noise hit her first. A rolling tide of voices, distant engines, and market vendors hawking their wares. The air smelled of metal, exhaust, and something frying nearby.

Their speeder was loaded, and she took a break on the ramp. Jazz and Lizz moved through the crew, ensuring that everyone had the gear for their assignments. Kal had given orders quickly and split the crew into groups, but Kenzie wasn't sure where she was supposed to fit yet. She had promised Locke she would meet him after she and Kal finished their drop.

"She is not going," Val snapped.

"Kenzie is an adult, Val. She can make her own decisions," Kal replied, and adjusted his pack. His tone was even, but his stance had stiffened. He turned to Kenzie. "Kenzie?"

"I don't want to go," Kenzie said before she could second-guess herself.

"Shut up," Val said without looking at her. "This contract came through dark channels. We don't know what the drop will look like. You can go, Kal, because we can't seem to get rid of you, but it is too dangerous for her."

Kal folded his arms. "How will she learn if she never gets a chance?"

"She's young. She will have plenty of time," Val replied, her voice sharp with frustration.

"I'm totally fine if my age disqualifies me from this," Kenzie interjected.

"Save it," Val said, holding up a hand to Kenzie, but still did not look at her. "Take someone else. I heard Tia say she hasn't shot anyone in months."

"Weeks," Tia called out from behind some crates and held up a shardshot blaster.

"See? She would be perfect," Val said, motioning at Tia.

"No, I don't want someone with an itchy trigger finger in there with me." Kal adjusted the strap of his pack. "Kenzie will be fine. They won't have anything I haven't seen before."

"Like Rosari, who will tear her head off, or Altiers, who will slice her in half before she knows it happened?" Val asked.

"I'm not saying we'll see them, but it won't be an issue if we do," Kal said and looked down to straighten his belt. "You talk about them like they aren't human." He had moved on to playing with the small pack on his back. "They're people, Val, empowered people, but people like us. They won't kill us just to kill us."

Val opened her mouth to argue again, finger raised, but Kal caught her hand mid-motion.

His voice dropped, steady but warm. "Valentine, my beautiful, gorgeous, brilliant best friend and ex-wife, please just trust me on this one." He held her gaze. "And…"

She exhaled and shook her head before she smirked. She already knew the answer. "And you outrank me."

"And I outrank you!" Kal said with a grin. "I knew you would get there."

Val hesitated, then sighed and rubbed her temple. "Fine, but if anything happens to her, I take double out on you." She winked at Kenzie.

Kal turned to Kenzie. "Don't tempt me with a good time."

Kenzie grinned despite herself. She had expected Val to fight harder, but maybe that was just their rhythm. The two of them were constantly at odds, but they managed to keep each other in line, mostly avoiding pushing too far.

"Isn't anyone going to ask what I want?" Kenzie said.

"What do you want?" Kal asked.

Kenzie hesitated, then said, "I want to stay on the *Days*." Even as she spoke, she saw the words wouldn't matter. It was Kal's game. She just wondered what he had truly made her admit.

"Okay, you've been heard and thoroughly ignored. Get your gear, we move out in two," Kal responded.

Val turned back to bark orders at the crew, and Kenzie adjusted her pack. She followed Kal down the dock. The speeder waited while its Aurelian engine bled off some exhaust. The bounty sat silent in the back, cuffed. As they approached, the prisoner lifted their head.

Kal swung into the driver's seat. "Sit in the back with them," he said, tossing a grin over his shoulder.

Kenzie hesitated. The backseat was a confined space with a total stranger who looked like death had followed them for weeks.

The bounty's eyes flicked to her. They were unreadable, with a sheen of sweat clinging to their pallid face.

Kenzie swallowed and climbed in. She had heard that skypirates ran and avoided trouble. Just her luck, she had to pick the one crew that ran toward it.

Kenzie glanced at the bounty as she climbed into the speeder. They were younger than she was, but the streets had been harsher on them. Thin, hollow-eyed, and barely holding it together. The sickness that hung on the poor wretch was unfamiliar, but what the streets had done to them, that look she knew.

It sat like a pit in her gut, expanding deeper and deeper. The vertigo of it almost made her sick. "Kal?"

"Hmm?" He didn't take his eyes off the traffic and slipped the speeder between two lumbering cargo haulers.

"What do we know about this contract?"

Kal checked his mirrors and gunned the throttle to clear an intersection before the signal changed. "We know that lovely person in the back with you is the bounty, and the contractor is paying us to return them alive."

Kenzie watched the bounty flinch at Kal's words. It was small, barely a twitch, but unmistakable. She frowned. "But what do we know? Are they going to hurt this person?"

"No... no, they'll be fine." He honked at a pedestrian. "They'll probably send us a thank-you card in a few weeks. Get off the street, ya sheep herder!"

That didn't convince her. "You told me you wanted my help with a hunch. Care to share?"

Kal smirked, but didn't answer right away. She hated when people did that, held onto a secret she couldn't puzzle out.

"We'll see if I'm right soon," he finally said. "Hang on."

Kenzie shot him a look, but stayed quiet. She fought the urge to reach for the bounty's hand, half-believing she might calm them telepathically. Maybe wishful thinking.

They pulled up to a rundown building in the entertainment district. A large man met them in the atrium and led them up the stairs. Water damage streaked the walls, and rust dripped from the railings. The whole place smelled damp, like old wood and mildew. The building had a large open courtyard and at least a dozen floors.

On the second floor, the man pushed on a hidden door to reveal a space that didn't match the rest of the building at all. Plush carpets. Elegant furniture. Polished wood and soft, warm lighting.

The man gestured to some chairs and continued into a back room. Kal strolled inside like he belonged there and kicked his feet up on the nearest chair. "Now we wait."

Kenzie stayed standing. "Kal, this feels wrong."

"Which part?"

"All of it." She gestured toward the bounty. "The bounty looks to be suffering from shard sickness. The guy who brought us here is dangerous. This office is suspicious. Hell, your casual attitude is the most suspicious."

Kal shut his eyes briefly, then cracked one open. "How was the thug dangerous?"

Before she could answer, a troll-like man entered, flanked by three guards, one of whom had led them in. "You have them?" the troll asked.

Kal barely glanced up. "Signed, sealed, delivered."

"And the crate they were smuggling?" the troll asked.

"Onboard my ship. Send two back with me, and they can have it."

The troll studied the bounty, his expression unreadable. They shrank under his stare.

"Show me your pad," he snapped at Kal.

Kal handed it over. A moment later, his datapad chimed. Payment confirmed.

"This is less than ten percent," Kal said, staring at the number.

"You'll get the rest when I have my goods."

"What a pain." Kal stretched and rolled his shoulder. "C'mon, Kenzie, back to the ship."

She didn't move. "What happens to them now?"

The troll gave her a greasy grin. "We're going to take good care of them. I need to have a little… conversation first. They had a buyer, and I'm feeling generous enough to let them jog their memory. It looks like they had a little too much fun with it before the handoff."

A thug pushed the bounty toward the other room.

Kenzie didn't like the way he said "conversation." Like the word had teeth.

"Should we inform some family or friends that they're here, that they're safe?" Kenzie asked, knowing the answer.

The troll laughed. "You think this street rat has family, has friends?" He laughed louder. "No, they're a one-person operation. Desperate and foolish. Like so many urchins before them, they didn't want the life they were handed, so they tried to take a different one. A noble sentiment, I will admit. Unfortunately, they tried to grasp more than they could hold. Control more than they saw. They reached too far, and there was no one to catch them when they fell. Ruin is always the result of that particular miscalculation."

The bounty looked at Kenzie as they walked past, and their eyes met before the thug's push jolted them forward. Kenzie's eyes followed to their destination in the side room. A goon waited there with a rope in one hand and a knife in the other.

Her stomach dropped. "You said alive…"

The troll laughed. "This isn't your problem anymore, beautiful. Follow your boss's orders and bring me back my goods."

She should've looked away. Should've walked out and let it be someone else's problem. It was almost certainly someone else's problem. Then she remembered her brother's face, and she thought, *not again.*

Before she even realized what she was doing, she shoved past a thug and grabbed the bounty. The troll's men moved to collapse on her. One lunged, a knife flashed toward her side. He was slow, but strong.

She caught his forearm and redirected his momentum into the wall. The knife was driven to the hilt. She held onto his forearm, and that's when she saw the crimson fur form under her hands.

Rosari.

She met her attacker's eyes as he transformed, looming over her.

Kal was already moving. One of them barreled into him, sending them both crashing into the corridor. Plaster rained down, and tenants peeked from cracked doors on the floors above.

It was sudden and inexplicable, but Kal left the Rosari sprawled on the floor. They had reverted to their human form and were unmoving. Then he struck another in the chest with a sharp palm. The thug dropped instantly. They reverted to a human as well.

The one that had Kenzie pinned charged, blade raised. Kal caught his wrist and led him into the office chair. He let the limp body fall into it.

Kenzie's breath stuck in her throat.

"Red Death! To me!" the troll yelled. It must have been the crew's name. The rooms stood still for a moment before she heard the footfall outside. At least twenty thugs stormed in.

The troll pulled a shardshot pistol from his belt. "Kill them all," he said.

Kal exhaled, slow and measured, then turned to Kenzie. He touched the bounty, and they slumped over. "Get the bounty out. There's a clinic three blocks north. Keep them safe. Then tell Locke we'll need a favor from our mutual friend."

"Locke? What about you?"

Kal stretched his neck and rolled his shoulders. His posture shifted as his weight centered, and his body relaxed. He bounced light on his feet, but his stance was solid when he planted. He was ready for the fight.

His smile was almost lazy. "I'm gonna put on a show."

Before she could argue, he grabbed the nearest Rosari by the face and jumped over the balcony with him. The thug hit the brick courtyard hard, with Kal on top. Kal rolled to his feet, but the thug had reverted and didn't get up.

Kenzie saw how the Rosari reacted, half angry and half afraid. She felt almost the same, maybe with a hint of annoyance.

The thugs jumped around Kal and focused their attention on him. That was probably his plan all along. Showboat like a magician. Draw them in and give Kenzie a window to escape. She didn't waste any more time. She hoisted the bounty on her shoulder and ran toward the stairs.

The troll fired. Plasma bolts came in slow, looping red arcs. The shardshot was Aurelian-made, with less precision and more spread. Kenzie would have been in trouble if it had been an Iverian-produced item with an Azure shard. Those fired straight, with accuracy and speed. The shot still punched massive holes in the wall behind her.

She corrected her balance with the weight of the bounty on her shoulder, barely thinking. She burst into the street and caught the attention of five peace officers. Kenzie's breath hitched in her throat. She did not trust uniformed officers, any of them, and these looked worse than usual.

They stood in clusters and watched the crowds. Their helmets gleamed under the late afternoon sun. She had seen officers like them before, too well-fed, too relaxed.

Still, she had to try. "There's a fight in that courtyard!" she shouted and pointed.

The nearest officer turned. His eyes flicked from her to the bounty slung over her shoulder, then past her to the troll.

Kenzie saw the shift in his expression. It wasn't a concern for her safety or a duty to the law. It was panic, as if someone had robbed his pocket at that very moment.

The five officers ran toward the dilapidated building. Three broke off toward the courtyard, and two went straight toward her.

One of the officers barked into his comm, "We've got movement. Three packages. One in the courtyard, and two on foot. This one's for the boss."

In an instant, she knew the officers were already compromised. She cursed under her breath and adjusted the bounty. They were too light, and that scared her. Luckily, it also made running easier. She didn't have time to feel guilty about how thankful she was in that moment.

Kenzie shoved into a nearby street market's packed flow. She pushed past merchants and travelers. The scent of fried food and hot pavement filled the air. Boots pounded behind her.

They weren't safe, not yet. She had no plan, no backup, and no time to catch her breath. All she could do was run, carry the sickly bounty over her shoulder, and hope Kal's plan was better than hers.

CHAPTER 9: KALISTON

4 Days Until Landfall

Kal ducked under the thick arm that swung at him. It would've taken his head off. Moments like that made him begrudgingly grateful for the Hollowline. The device sat hidden in the pack strapped to his lower back, its polished harness anchored directly to his spine. It was the most advanced piece of tech ever produced by the Conchordia Institute, Iveria's premier research academy.

Why he'd been chosen as its only test subject was a topic he didn't like to discuss. At least not sober. He had his theories, but they involved saying a name he didn't like the taste of. It always put him in a sour mood. He wished he were like Locke, with that part of his life a blank. Sure, the memory loss hadn't been Locke's choice, but sometimes curses could be blessings. When it came to the Hollowline, the blessing was also a curse. Best to leave those memories buried and mostly forgotten.

Another fist came for his head. He deflected it cleanly and siphoned the Rosari's power. The woman collapsed.

The unregulated Rosari in the troll's employ were dangerous. They would probably clean the tenement eventually if left unchecked. Eviction was the best-case scenario for the people who watched the chaos in the courtyard. It wasn't necessarily illegal to be a Rosari, but they had to register and were forced into certain parts of the city with an Altier peace force. The Rosari he fought were not obeying that particular regulation.

Kal had been surprised the troll could get his hands on so many red shards. He had thought as much when he peeked into the crate they had confiscated from the bounty a few days back. Rose shards were plentiful, sure, but not so deep in Iveria. If the thugs had been Aurelians, they would have had to make the pilgrimage to Rosewood and undergo the Rose Rites. Instead, they had obtained their power from the black market. Probably a heavy shard meant for skyships or personal transports, shattered to make more Rosari. That never ended well. Between the high risk of shard sickness and novice Rosari fumbling through raw power, things often went badly for everyone involved. Discretion was never a Rosari's strong suit, and Iverian Altiers took their management seriously.

Kal wondered if the people knew what they were signing up for when they were altered. Outcasts in Iveria for the rest of their lives, never granted even a scrap of citizenry by the Domain.

Oh well. Kal wouldn't kill them, but he would unmake them. That solved the problem in more ways than one. Their families would thank him years from now.

The Rosari swarmed, some with weapons drawn. Kal ducked with the grace of a practiced fighter, partly because he was, partly because of the Hollowline.

Kaliston had been a lieutenant in the Iverian Armada. He came from a lesser house but showed great promise at the Citadel. That was where he met Val and Toren, back before Toren became the First Altier. Kal made a reputation as a clever, if unconventional, officer. His first assignment was aboard the *Berkshield,* the Capital skyship of the Third District, based out of the city of Berk. A fine ship with a good crew. He had sparred every day, lost more than he won. That was fine. He had tested theories, refined techniques. Eventually, he found ways to disable an opponent that were best kept to himself.

Even with years of Armada training, he hadn't always been this efficient. The Hollowline made him better. His ego would never let him say that aloud, but it was true. He was as strong as a Rosari and as fast as an Altier. He admitted only to himself how reliant he had become on it. It was a curse, one the Director of Conchordia had placed on him. The irony was that sometimes, in the quiet between missions, he wondered if some part of him had wanted it. Had wanted to be chosen. Recognized. Acknowledged as special. That was the part of himself he hated most.

A Rosari speared him. It would have taken him off at the torso if not for the Hollowline. He had absorbed so much Rose energy from the Rosari that he had to burn it off constantly or risk overloading. It made him sluggish, but that was fine. The extra mass gave him the durability to tank blows like this.

He pressed his palms against the Rosari on top of him. The beast went limp and shifted back into its human form.

They always reverted once he drained them. He took everything. It was too great a risk to leave them with even a scrap of power.

Kal had dropped fifteen, maybe eighteen, of them, but more poured into the courtyard. It wasn't exhausting, just boring.

Oh well. Nothing to do but finish the job.

He shoved the unconscious body aside and got to his feet. Time to go on the offensive. It would mean taking a few hits, but with how things had gone, he could afford it.

One, two, three, four, and five dropped in an instant. The fifth planted a fist in Kal's mug. It would've shattered his nose and the skull behind it, but both face and fist stood firm. Kal disabled the thug a second later.

Maybe eleven left. Twelve? *Time for the grand finale and face what came next.*

He tapped the Azure energy and hastened through bodies and thugs. *Tap, tap, tap.* They went down at his touch. He didn't move as fast as he could. Burning Rose made him heavier, but nothing he could do about that. Absorbing too much energy was terrible for both the Hollowline and him. He had to burn some off.

The doctors at Conchordia called it a version of shard sickness. Kal knew the disease was what happened when a crystal rejected someone who tried to bond with it. The condition was more common with Azure crystals than Rose, though both could kill you. The degenerative process shuts down your organs slowly. Kal had never wanted to become an Altier or Rosari, so he'd never worried about it before the Hollowline. It felt like dying the few times when he overextended using the device and felt the illness. He'd asked the doctors the first time if the feeling was normal. The answer was silence, followed by notes and further tests. He stopped asking after that.

The last two ran. Being a bully was only appealing when they could bully someone else. Kal caught them quickly and put them down.

He moved among the bodies, checking to make sure none were still showing signs of Rosari. These poor men and women wouldn't be able to shift anymore, but they wouldn't remember their time as Rosari anyway. There was something in the Hollowline's draining process that took the full experience from the user. Kal's theory was the Crystals warped both mind and body, but he didn't care much for the science behind it. He just liked that it worked. That was the trade, his life for something that did what he required when it had to.

Kal felt eyes on him. Two women watched from the edge of the courtyard with unnatural eyes. They disappeared when he turned to face them, and the metal glint of a shardshot stood in their place.

"Don't move!" The voice wasn't the deep, guttural snarl of a transformed Rosari. It was a human woman.

Three peace officers stood before him, weapons drawn. The troll stood behind them, shardshot still in hand. Kal knew from experience he could absorb the shots, but the fewer people who knew his 'tricks,' the better.

Slowly, he raised his hands. Not having visible weapons was always a plus. He was glad he didn't have a suda on him. "What seems to be the problem, officers?"

"Disturbing the peace. Is this your work?" The lead officer kept her shardshot trained on him.

Kal glanced around at the bodies. "Just some friends of mine. They were under the weather, so I helped put them to sleep."

The officers scanned the thirty-odd bodies sprawled across the courtyard, plus however many more were upstairs. Then they looked at the troll and nodded. The troll took it as an opportunity to excuse himself.

Kal had already assumed the officers were on his payroll. There was no way they could have worked so close to his operation without getting their beaks wet. The knowing nod just confirmed it.

The lead officer tossed a pair of cuffs at his feet. "Put them on. Don't do anything stupid, and we won't have to, either."

Kal bent down slowly, picked up the cuffs, and clasped them behind his back. The moment they clicked into place, the officers rushed him. They slammed him down to the bricks and pressed their knees into his back. He let them. Rose still ran hot through his system, and he could handle them wailing on him till sunrise while barely feeling a thing.

"Officers," Kal said, his voice easy, "putting on quite the show for the good citizens of Breezewaltz, aren't we?"

One officer hesitated and glanced up at the tenants watching from the balconies. Another made up for it with a sharp kick to Kal's ribs.

Kal pretended that one hurt.

They hauled him to his feet and dragged him toward the waiting cruiser.

As they lowered his head toward the door, he caught sight of Kenzie across the street. He smiled and winked. Then let them shove him inside.

CHAPTER 10: LOCKE

4 Days Until Landfall

The streets were packed. He had seen the pilgrims before, but never so many. They flooded every road and made it almost impossible to move. Landfall was always a draw, but it felt worse than normal. Maybe that Colossus to the south had something to do with it. Either way, the celebrations would stretch on for at least two more weeks, long past the actual holiday. Getting anywhere in the mess would be a pain.

He wished Kal had at least dropped him off on the way to Sector Five, the Entertainment District.

And Kenzie. He didn't understand why she had gone with him, though he was also vaguely aware that any frustration he felt was rooted in jealousy. He trusted Kal, thought of him like an older brother, but that didn't change the fact that the second most incredible guy he knew now rode around the city with the girl he liked.

Locke moved through the crowd with his shoulders angled as if he were trying to take up less space. At just over six feet tall, it didn't work. His lean build made him look better suited for slipping away than standing his ground, but that wasn't entirely true. He adjusted his coat, well-tailored but worn at the edges, the kind a noble might wear if he didn't want to be recognized.

Locke turned down an alley to escape the worst of the crowd and immediately regretted it. Eyes tracked him the moment he stepped in. The people who called the alley home said nothing, but their presence pressed in. He wasn't afraid, just uncomfortable. Not at the people, but at what they told Locke about himself.

Growing up in Breezewaltz had taught him that the people weren't dangerous, just desperate. They tried to survive a city built to forget them. His father used to say things like, 'teach a man to fish,' but Locke wasn't sure that meant much to someone starving and too poor to afford a pole. He used to think someone else would fix it or that it wasn't his problem. That part of his younger self made his stomach turn.

The city had always been a place of two halves, divided not by walls but by height.

Above him, the Upper Mesa sprawled across the plateau. An island of wealth and power towered over the rest of the city. Real estate should have been in high demand, but excess there knew no bounds. Estates sat atop the mesa with room to spare, their gardens sprawled, their halls broad and gilded. The great houses of nobility and clergy stood undisturbed by time, as if nothing beneath them mattered.

Statues of long-dead rulers lined the pristine streets, marble archways framed walkways that all led to the Azure Temple. It sat in the middle of the Grand Lake, its reflection nearly as perfect as the stone itself. Fountains gurgled in manicured gardens, their waters untouched by the filth below.

The Lower City was something else entirely. It pulsed with life and sprawled in every direction, built atop itself over generations. Bridges of iron and wood crisscrossed the water outlets that spilled from the mesa and fed the city below. Clotheslines stretched between stacked homes like makeshift banners of daily life, while smoke curled from open grates. The air was thick with the scent of spices, metal, and the constant hum of movement.

The Nine Sectors of the Lower City formed the foundation of Breezewaltz, each one a world unto itself. Locke had visited Sector Six as a child, the same district where the *Days* had docked. The massive ports housed a constant flow of skyships, ascending and descending in tight formations. Their ability to lift directly and hover midair allowed for a dense layout. The sector was a network of landing towers and freight platforms stacked one on top of another, a honeycomb of structures that serviced the endless tide of ships.

Kal and Kenzie had gone off toward Sector Five and left Locke to fend for himself in the ever-growing tide of pilgrims crowding Sector Seven.

He picked up his pace. He would try to stop by the alley on his way back and drop off some food from the Berrywood Grill.

Locke stepped into the next street. The feeling didn't fade, but the scene before him was distracting. The market district of Sector Seven stretched down the main road. Even in daytime, bright lanterns burned across storefronts. At that time of year and time of day, the Upper Mesa cut off most of the sunlight to the western sectors.

Locke wasn't as familiar with the sector, but he still knew it. He had memorized the map of Breezewaltz by the time he was eight. His father had insisted. His brother had picked it up instantly. Locke had taken months, but he had figured it out. Best of all, he still remembered it as if it were yesterday. The streets and alleys never seemed to change.

He found the watchsmith's shop quickly enough. It was unassuming but well-maintained, a place that spoke more of quality than flash. Inside, everything had a place. Neatly arranged trays, each sitting within color-coded squares marked on the wood, lined the workbench behind the counter. A door in the back stood slightly ajar, and warm light spilled from within.

Locke moved toward the display cases. Some of the timepieces were made of gold, some of silver, but most shone with the brilliant blue of alloyed Azure metals. A sliver of shard sat inside each one to power them. It was amusing how much Breezewaltz relied on the Azure Crystal. Locke's family had been tied to its fate for generations, like the shop and the city.

The world's fate was tied to the Crystals. They were so integrated into everyday life. Azure, if you had money, and Rose, if you didn't.

Azure-powered Iverian cities, lit the streets, and fueled the sleek engines of Iverian skyships. The Azure shards were clean, powerful, efficient, and rare. The King and the First Altier of Breezewaltz, who oversaw its harvesting and distribution, tightly controlled the supply.

Rose shards were another story. They were hot, messy, and cheap. Anything larger than a thumb could burn your skin, and they constantly flaked embers and ash. A lot of downsides, with one significant advantage: they were everywhere.

Where the Azure Crystal might yield one or two heavy shards and a thousand light shards in a year, the Rose Crystal produced hundreds of heavies and countless light shards. No wonder most tech in the world ran on Rose.

Locke sometimes wondered if the Crystals themselves were at odds, or if the people had turned them against each other. He had grown up with the teachings of the Azure Order, the Twelve Rites, and whispered prayers. His brother had believed, truly believed, the Azure Crystal was a living thing. It was a divine presence that guided and protected their family. His father and mother had taught them as much. Locke had tried to share that faith, had stood beside his brother in the Temple, and repeated the words of their father, but the connection never felt real. He had wanted it to. He desperately wanted to believe the world had order. That there was some-one out there who made sure the plan was both fair and real. Instead, the words had always felt hollow, like the empty shells of broken timepieces that littered the watchsmith's counter. The sad fact that he said them anyway was not lost on him.

The door in the back creaked open, and an older man stepped through. He moved with ease despite his age and pulled on a work apron as he approached. A bushy mustache and a bald head framed a warm, smiling face. He carried the air of someone who had been there forever, the kind of person you could meet once and feel like you had known all your life.

Locke liked him immediately.

"Hello, pup. What brings you in?" the man boomed.

"I'm here to collect a timepiece. Jules sent me."

"Jules! That old so-and-so," the man chuckled.

"Know her well?" Locke asked, curious.

"We went to school together, right here in the city."

Locke blinked. "Jules is from Breezewaltz?"

"You didn't know?" The watchsmith raised a brow as he opened a wooden storage cabinet. The files inside were labeled alphabetically, and he flipped to the letter *C*. Locke realized he didn't even know Jules's last name. There was so much about her he didn't know, and the whole crew, for that matter. Locke had tried, but they all treated him like a kid brother. There was surface-level camaraderie, but something always seemed to hold everyone back.

In all fairness, he didn't remember the last three years of his own life, so may-be that wasn't surprising. It could be they had already moved past small talk in that time, and Locke was the only one who didn't remember. He made a mental note to ask Jules about her last name later.

"No idea," Locke admitted. "But that's pretty wild." The watchsmith gave him an amused glance as he pulled the parcel out of the cabinet. Locke felt he had to explain himself further. "She's amazing. I always figured she was from one of the forge cities." The watchsmith closed the cabinet and came back to the desk. "What was she like back then?" Locke asked.

"We were kids. She was like any other person, perhaps a little more practical. She always called people out when they were naughty, but she never told on them," he chuckled. "That's what I remember, anyway. Now? I assume Jules is Jules." He pulled out the timepiece. "I figure you know that better than I do."

Locke laughed. "Jules is Jules, for sure. She's maybe the nicest person I've met."

The watchsmith raised an eyebrow at that. "Jules? Nice?" He let out a deep laugh. "Don't think I've ever heard that before. No, strike that. I *know* I've never heard that."

Locke gave him a curious look.

"Listen, I'll put it how Jules would. 'Pup, you'll find that competency and niceness are inversely related.'" His impression was spot on. The watchsmith grinned. "Not that I agree with it. I think you can be both, but that's a different conversation."

Locke shook his head, still smiling. The watchsmith placed the timepiece in his hands. It was simple, practical, with no unnecessary flourishes. Still, Locke could see the beauty in its craftsmanship. The stark white metal was an artistic choice.

"Still, nice to hear people can change," the old man added, his smile turned wry. "Over time."

Locke rolled his eyes at the joke but smiled, anyway. "That was terrible, but the watch looks incredible."

"You're welcome. That'll be three hundred credits."

"Oh, right." Locke reached into his pack and pulled out his datapad. He had five hundred credits in his account. Jules had said she loaded enough to cover the purchase, but the extra amount surprised him.

The note read: *Get yourself something nice, Kid. –Jules.*

The watchsmith kept his eyes on the screen until the transfer cleared, then returned to wrapping the timepiece. As he worked, Locke glanced toward the counter's display.

"Anything else I can help you with?" He set the package on the counter.

"Do you have anything besides timepieces that a girl might like?" he asked.

The watchsmith didn't look up. "Since when do girls not like timepieces? You're saying they're late on purpose? Or just when they go on dates with me?"

Locke chuckled. "Not what I meant."

"Ah, well. I've got jewelry in that case, or if you want something with a bit more bite, I have sudas behind the counter."

"You sell weapons here?" Locke asked and raised an eyebrow.

"Sure do. Not for real use, of course. Only Altiers can activate these things. Down here, people buy them as ornaments. A little nod of respect to the people keeping us safe. I disable them before selling, just in case."

"Huh," Locke muttered and glanced over the selection. The sudas were an older style, several centuries out of date. What was old was always new again, he supposed. His eyes landed on one that reminded him of a hilt he had seen as a child and loved. His gaze lingered before it shifted to the jewelry.

Gold, silver, and azure. The pieces caught the light and glinted in the display case. Bracelets, necklaces, charms. All shapes and sizes. Some resembled animals, others were miniature homes, while many took the shape of tiny shoes or boots, for reasons he could only guess. He wasn't sure what he was looking for, only that he was looking for Kenzie.

Then, his eyes caught on a small boot charm. It was a splash of red among the others.

"Rose-gold," the watchsmith said, having followed Locke's gaze. "Not very popular. Got it in a trade about a decade ago, and it's sat there ever since. People around here like gold, silver, and alloyed Azure. Figured that one would never sell." He smiled knowingly. "It's for someone who sees things a little differently, I think."

Locke studied it for a moment. He'd never been great at reading people, and he figured that was the first step to giving good gifts. Something about the connections in his head never allowed him to make real connections with others. Still, something about how the light reflected on the boot made him think he might be on to something.

The watchsmith tapped the counter. "Tell you what. Buy it, and I'll throw in that suda you were eyeing for free."

"How much?" Locke asked.

"Oh, let's say two hundred credits."

"Two hundred?"

The older gentleman grinned, and his eyes drifted to Locke's datapad. "Seems you're good for it."

CHAPTER 11: KENZIE

"That idiot has our comm," she muttered as Kal gave her a wink and a smile from across the street. He looked like he knew a secret. All Kenzie knew was that she wanted to punch him, maybe cry a little, perhaps both.

He was shoved into the back of a peace officer's speeder, hands bound behind his back. Bodies lay still in the courtyard past them. Kenzie guessed they weren't dead. After all, she'd seen Kal's trick firsthand. Still, whatever Kal had done to them, they sure looked it. More peace officers moved through the lot and bound the hands and feet of those they had apprehended. It looked like they'd be under arrest, too. Unregistered Rosari in Iveria was a serious crime, even for civilians just trying to survive, or Aurelians fleeing the iron grip of the Domain.

She assumed Kal had let himself get captured rather than hurt the officers. Hopefully, the tenants above would finally be safe from the troll and his Red Death. The peace officers could no longer pretend not to notice. Even if some were on the troll's payroll, that fight had brought too much heat.

A late afternoon rain began to fall, and she was glad she hadn't brought her datapad. The Iverian versions tended to short-circuit in the rain.

Kenzie hurried back to the alley where she'd left the bounty and hauled them over her shoulder. The rain made them heavier, but not enough to slow her down. Together they slipped onto the rain-slicked street and headed north. Her mind spun with worry over everything that had happened. She quickened her pace until they reached the small clinic Kal had mentioned.

Kenzie startled an attendant with the unconscious bounty over to her shoulder.

"Shard sickness," Kenzie said, and the attendant wrote something down before coming around the desk with a wheelchair.

Kenzie gently placed the bounty into the seat. She took a moment to cup the bounty's face, kiss them gently on the forehead, and whisper a half-remembered prayer.

She felt bad about leaving, but maybe Kal's magic had helped. Either way, there wasn't much more she could do. She asked the attendant for the time and directions, then sprinted back into the downpour without a backward glance.

She had a date, and she couldn't afford to be late.

Kenzie raced through the rain. She didn't know what the peace officers would do to Kal. If they worked for the troll, Kal was in real trouble. Even if they didn't, she knew Kal was in hot water with plenty of organizations that had an axe to grind against Kal and the *Days'* crew. Not the least of which was the Guild.

She hurried through the streets, dodging off sidewalks and back on again as the crowds allowed. The city was unlike anything she'd ever seen, even in her childhood. Pilgrims flooded every street, though Kenzie didn't understand what they were after. She wasn't familiar with the holiday. Landfall, they called it, but the noise and press of bodies made her skin crawl. Too many faceless people and too many unknown agendas.

She cut down Mercer Avenue. *The attendant definitely said avenue, not a street.* She navigated past residences scattered through the Market District. Luckily, the Entertainment District had been nearby; otherwise, she'd be stuck walking back to the ship with no credits. She guessed the rental speeder earlier had only been necessary because of the cargo they'd carried at the time.

Eventually, she emerged onto a main street of the Market District. The crowds closed in around her, pressed from all sides. The noise and movement set her nerves on edge. She hated crowds. They reminded her of the night she had slipped away from her old life, when the crush of bodies nearly swallowed her whole. Crowds hid sharp edges and cruel intentions, and you never saw the worst of them until it was on you. Kenzie had learned that the hard way. After that, she had learned the street was just as ruthless. It was a place that chewed people up and spit out whatever it couldn't swallow.

That was why she had joined up with the *Days*. A warm bed, a steady crew, and the freedom to hop off whenever she chose. Stability without chains, as Val sold it. Kenzie wouldn't have to con her way through every day, scrounge for her next meal, or worry about when her next shower would be. When Val had offered her a spot five months ago, Kenzie had been skeptical, waiting for the catch, the angle, the moment it would all collapse.

It still hadn't come.

She told herself that didn't mean anything. She could leave whenever she wanted. Maybe even today, after they dealt with Kal's mess. The *Days* was just a ride, a temporary stop. She'd stayed longer than planned, sure, but only because the jobs were decent and the crew hadn't given her a reason to bolt. Yet.

That was the story she told herself, anyway.

The truth, the part she wouldn't look at directly, was that she'd had a dozen chances to disappear and hadn't taken a single one. The *Days* had given her something she couldn't name, something more than a bunk and hot meals. A place. Not just a spot to stand, but a place in the world that felt almost like it could be hers.

Almost.

She'd sworn to herself a long time ago that she would never go backward, but moving forward didn't mean staying with the *Days*. Staying meant risk, staying meant trust, and trust was how you got betrayed.

So she'd leave. Soon. Just, maybe not today.

Her steps finally brought her to the Berrywood Grill. She crashed through the front door and found Locke sitting with a well-worn pack in a booth.

She was late. Locke looked up, visibly relieved at first, then concern immediately took its place.

Kenzie moved quickly through the diner and slid into the seat across from Locke.

"What's wrong?" he asked.

"Kal's been arrested," she said.

Locke froze. "Have you told Val?"

"No, Kal has the comm, and he said to find you. Something about a mutual friend," she replied, rainwater soaked into the seat and floor.

Locke stared at her, confused. "Mutual what?"

"I don't know, Locke. He said something about a mutual friend right before he grabbed the face of a Rosari and slammed it into the floor two stories below."

Locke blinked. "He did what?"

"Where am I losing you? Keep up." She snapped her fingers. "We dropped off the bounty, but the troll turned out to be a sleaze. His goons were going to hurt the bounty, so I stepped in. Kal followed. Then the troll sent his entire crew of Rosari goons after us." She grabbed a warm roll from Locke's plate.

"And now you're eating?" Locke asked.

"I ran here, and yes, I'm starving," she said through a bite. "Now c'mon. The troll's connected, and Kal's not exactly low-profile."

"Good point." Locke grabbed the check and headed to the cashier. Kenzie shoved two more rolls in her mouth and joined him as he finished paying. The cashier handed him two extra bags. They stepped outside together.

"What're the bags for?" Kenzie asked.

"I need to make a quick stop," Locke responded, already moving.

"Time's kind of important here," Kenzie said, her impatience on her sleeve.

"This is important, too. It's on the way back, shouldn't take any extra time," Locke said and picked up his pace.

"Back where? What's your plan?"

"We'll catch Val up to speed, then we're going to visit my brother."

CHAPTER 12: LUCAN

4 Days Until Landfall

Marling barely had time to register the first and final blow. Lucan watched as the Altier's strength failed in an instant, and he stumbled. For all the pomp of his title, he had fallen without challenge. Lucan sneered.

Disappointing.

It was over almost too quickly and was hardly the battle Lucan had anticipated. Marling's drink had already weighed him down. He barely seemed to notice that Lucan's mass field made him heavier and slower. A single calculated swing of Lucan's suda had ended it. The blade sliced cleanly through Marling's torso.

The Altier's corpse crumpled onto the command deck, and blood pooled around the base of his captain's chair.

Lucan wiped his blade on Marling's tattered uniform and curled his lip. *This is the best Heydon could offer? Pathetic.*

The six novice Altiers stationed aboard the *Fury* had put up a better fight, but they too were no match for Lucan and his unit of master-level Rosari. They were his imperial guards, his Praetori, and he had trained them personally. They took losses, obviously, but six hundred Rosari with forty Praetori were enough to overwhelm six Altiers in a confined space.

Lucan's fur was streaked with his victims' blood. He counted twenty-three on the way to the bridge, plus Marling. The victory was absolute. He felt the familiar, grounding certainty of destiny. Each life taken, each breath snatched from an Altier's chest, was another step toward the world the Rose Crystal had promised him. A world remade, cleansed by fire and faith.

In the blood-soaked chaos, he looked more beast than man. He was a predator enthroned in blood, reveling in the terror his unchecked power had wrought.

Lucan surveyed the bridge. The adrenaline still coursed through his veins. He stood hulking, and his crimson fur soaked in blood made him look feral. It commanded silence from his subordinates as they finished putting down the remaining officers. The ship's once-pristine command center was a ruin. Shattered consoles sparked intermittently, blood smeared the walls, and the acrid scent of burnt circuitry filled the air.

"Don't worry about the bodies," Lucan commanded, his voice rumbling low and dangerous. "We're here for the heavy shard. Clear the ship, land it, and deliver the shard to Dr. Syd."

His warriors saluted, their movements sharp and efficient.

Lucan stepped out onto the *Fury's* adjoining skydeck. The cold wind bit against his bloodied fur. He let the adrenaline settle and savored the moment. The night air was crisp, and the stars above seemed brighter than usual. The Colossus lay motionless beneath them, a slumbering titan who waited to awaken. Its crystalline plating glinted faintly, even in the shadows of the night. It was a sleeping god, a lesser sibling to the Rose Colossus, but a god nonetheless. It waited, as all lesser things did, for a true believer to give it purpose. The Rose Crystal had chosen him to awaken it, to guide it, and to wield it. It had placed Rook in his path just at the right moment. What better proof of his destiny could there be than the monstrous, divine thing ready to move at his command?

Not only had Lucan directly assaulted an Iverian Capital skyship, something unheard of in the past century, but he would soon see the Colossus move again. For Aurelia, the night would be carved into legend. Lucan would overwrite it three times by next week.

One of his officers approached cautiously and kept a respectful distance. "The ship is secure, my Prince. Minimal resistance left. We are descending now, and the shard retrieval team has begun the extraction."

Lucan didn't respond immediately. His piercing hazel eyes remained fixed on the horizon, in the direction of Breezewaltz. He wondered to himself.

How many in that gilded city will tremble when the Colossus moves again? How many will die before I fully restore the Domain?

"Good," Lucan said finally, his voice measured. "Ensure the shard is delivered safely. I want no mistakes."

The officer hesitated. "And the ship itself, my Prince?"

Lucan turned, his gaze icy. "It dies here. Use it for target practice, or let the Colossus grind it underfoot."

The officer nodded and left without further question. Lucan's orders were absolute. The *Fury* dipped away from the clouds, prepared for its final descent, and he turned his focus to the next phase.

As the ship touched down, the last of the Iverian crew were dealt with. No quarter. Lucan lingered for a few final moments amid the carnage before he strode toward the main hangar, where the shard extraction team was already at work.

The heavy shard, massive and pulsing with an intense azure glow, had been disengaged from the engine room as soon as the ship landed. It was at least fifteen feet tall, wider at the top, and tapered at the bottom. Engineers carefully loaded it into a transport ship. Sweat beaded on their foreheads as they guided the delicate cargo, each movement precise and deliberate.

Dr. Syd's voice crackled over the comms. "Handle that shard with care! It will pierce any exposed skin with a bolt. Keep the suits on until it is set in containment."

Lucan grabbed his comm, eyes fixed on the massive shard as it pulsed with a deep, unearthly light. His voice cut through the static. "You'll have your shard intact, Doctor. See that the Colossus is ready to move. No excuses this time."

He clicked off the comm and turned to his men. "We take off once the shard is loaded."

"Yes, my Prince," one of them replied.

Lucan took the flight controls and waited for the final word that the heavy shard had been secured.

The Colossus would rise again the next day, and Lucan would be one step closer to watching Breezewaltz burn. He could already feel the flames in his mind, a purifying fire that would sweep from White Hill to Orleans, from the Domain's edge to the heart of Iveria. His god's judgment made manifest.

It would not just be another good day. It would be the day the old Domain was reforged. The Rose Crystal had chosen him as its hammer, its wrath made flesh, and Lucan would ensure the world never forgot the divine hand that struck the killing blow.

CHAPTER 13: KENZIE

4 Days Until Landfall

"Your brother?" Kenzie asked. They were back on the *Days* and moved through the loading dock.

"Yeah… Toren and I don't talk," Locke responded. He sounded like that was supposed to be enough.

"I still can't wrap my head around your brother being the First Altier of Breezewaltz," Kenzie repeated, her voice rising. She stared at Locke, her expression shifted between disbelief and something sharper. "And you've been sitting on that this whole time?"

"Yeah, you never asked," Locke said.

She stopped, blinked fast, and looked at the back of his head. After a beat, she kept walking. "So, what, you just casually have an Altier for a brother and don't think that's worth mentioning? What else are you hiding?" Kenzie asked.

"A lot, Kenz. I can't remember the past three years of my life, and I joined a skypirate crew before that. I have a complicated backstory."

Kenzie didn't know how to respond to that, either. She just continued to follow Locke as her mind spun. He had a brother who wasn't just an Altier, but the First Altier of Breezewaltz. The details of politics still eluded Kenzie, but she was well aware they were the leaders of the Iverian League, sitting on the ruling council with the King.

Locke just expected her to roll with that information because it was, what, an emergency? Something about Locke always felt half-finished, like there were too many loose threads to complete the tapestry. Maybe there was more to him than she gave him credit for.

They made their way to the bridge, where they found Val.

"To what do I owe the honor?" Val asked Locke. She saw Kenzie over Locke's shoulder. "What did that idiot do?" she asked.

"Thank you. That was exactly what I said." Kenzie held out her hands, palms up. "He's alive, but he might have, definitely, got himself arrested," Kenzie responded.

Val sighed. "Arrested, we can deal with. Dead is a different story. Locke, are you going to ask…" she trailed off.

"Yeah, I'll get up there, but I don't have an ID or a day pass up to the Upper Mesa."

"Okay, we'll get Haruto to make you a fake," Val responded. She picked up the ship's comm and pinged Haruto.

Kenzie pulled up to Locke. "Does he know too?"

"Only Kal and Val," Locke replied, but didn't meet her eyes. "Maybe Rina, but we've never talked about it directly." The way he said it was quiet and too fast. It felt like a child being caught.

"Oh," was all Kenzie could reply.

Kenzie took a moment to process. She was surprised, maybe even a little hurt. She used to think Locke believed everyone's past on the *Days* was a closely guarded secret, but perhaps he only thought that because he kept his own locked up tight. Like he wanted people to like him, maybe even know him, just not enough to hurt him.

She always thought he was an open book she could read with her eyes closed. After today's reveal, she wasn't so sure, and she didn't know if it was just her pride that stung.

Haruto walked into the room.

"Locke here needs a day pass to the Upper Mesa."

"Twenty-four-hour or more?" Haruto asked.

Val looked at Locke, eyebrow arched.

"Twenty-four hours is fine," Locke responded. "But two passes, please."

Val let out a quiet groan but nodded to Haruto. "Okay, what's your plan, then?" Val asked.

"Go to my brother and ask that Kal be let go."

"That's it? You haven't seen him in how many years?" she asked.

Locke hesitated. Kenzie saw something flicker across his face. She wasn't sure if it was uncertainty or guilt.

"I don't know," he finally said. "Since before I joined up with you all."

"Fine. We don't have the credits for bribes." Val seemed more annoyed than anything. "You get up top and talk to your brother. Meanwhile, I'll call in some favors from some local goons to give Kal some support on the inside." She walked up to Locke. "I'm placing all my chips on you to get him out. Can I trust you?" she asked.

Locke wavered. The implication of her words hung in the air. He nodded, jaw set like he tried to look more certain than he felt.

"Okay," she said and left the room.

"Are we just going to waltz up to the Upper Mesa with passes?" Kenzie asked.

"No, even with the passes, we would be too suspicious at this time of day. We'll take the Beggars Trail and then have the passes as a backup if we get stopped," Locke responded.

"Oh, okay, sounds like a plan." Kenzie paused, processing. "You really are from here," her thoughts caught up to her words. "What's the Beggars Trail?"

"It's an old trail cut into the mesa. It was abandoned centuries ago because it's challenging to climb. People experiencing poverty used it to reach the mesa for Landfall and other holidays, but the city leaders shut it down. The pilgrims couldn't maintain it, and the upper-class elites on the mesa didn't like it. Both let it fall into disrepair and out of memory, which makes it even more dangerous than it already was."

"You think that's the safest way?" she asked and studied him. The way he spoke about the trail and the way he knew the city reminded her that there was a version of Locke she hadn't met yet. One that wasn't built on boyish charm and self-deprecating jokes. She wasn't sure she liked that version more than the one in her head, but it made her curious.

Locke thought about that for a beat. "No, but it's the only way we make it up there, and I'm trusting our ability to climb. I'm not an actor. These passes are a gamble, too, even if they look good."

She looked him over. "I hate heights," she sighed.

He smiled at her like he'd already known that. "I'll be with you," he said.

She rolled her eyes, but her heart skipped anyway. *Stupid Locke and his stupid sincerity.* That was exactly what she didn't need.

Locke's smile continued as Haruto and Val moved back onto the bridge. Haruto handed them two official-looking documents. Val stood behind him.

"Don't let them get wet," he said and hesitated. He glanced between the two soaked crew members, then shrugged.

"You work the sensors and forge documents?" Kenzie asked.

"Kal likes it when we have two jobs, and I'm damn good at both." Haruto smiled and turned to leave.

Kenzie and Locke shared a look. Then Locke's face lit up like he was remembering something. "Hey, Haruto, can you give this to Jules? She sent me out for it earlier. Tell her the other things in there are something for… me." Locke handed him the well-worn pack. Haruto nodded and left the room.

"We'll do what we can down here." Val's lips tightened as she glanced at the forged documents. For all his bravado, Kal had a talent for trouble, and it seemed she had a habit of worrying until he was safe again.

She placed one hand on Locke's shoulder, one hand on Kenzie's. "Go get my husband," she said, her voice steady, but her eyes betrayed a flicker of worry.

Kenzie noticed Val didn't say "ex," but she said nothing. She was too busy worrying about the climb.

CHAPTER 14: KALISTON

4 Days Until Landfall

Kal leaned back against the cold metal wall of the detention block, his legs stretched out in front of him, his boots crossed casually. His arms rested behind his head, and his eyes were closed. A slight, infuriating grin played on his lips. Only the faint sheen of sweat across his brow betrayed something less than ease, a detail made stranger by the chill in the cells.

Besides that, he did not appear any worse for wear after the beating from the officers.

The dim light from the overhead fixtures cast long shadows across the cell, but Kal looked as if he lounged on the deck of the *Days*, not locked in a cell beneath the Upper Mesa. Every so often, he flexed the fingers of his left hand. The motion was slow and deliberate, as if he tried to coax the nerves to respond to his commands.

The other detainees crammed in the cells weren't nearly as relaxed. The blocks were unusually packed because of the holiday. Some leaned against the bars, while others stood in small groups at the center, their voices hushed but animated. Their attention flickered to Kal, as if he were a curiosity in a zoo.

Finally, one of them couldn't hold back anymore. A wiry voice cut through the detention block. "You him?" he asked, his voice rough with suspicion. "You're Kaliston of the *Halcyon Days*?"

Kal didn't open his eyes. Partly from exhaustion after the day's events, partly from the irritation of being without the Hollowline, and partly because he didn't care to have a conversation. His pulse ran hot, a steady thrum beneath his skin. He focused on the silence as if it were a raft. "Yes," he said, matter-of-fact.

The owner of the wiry voice must have exchanged glances with a few others in the silence. One of them, a deep feminine voice, spoke up. "From the clips?"

Kal finally opened one eye and scanned the group with mild amusement. "Depends on the clip. If my face's not in it, I deny everything."

The group laughed nervously. The tension in the cell eased just slightly.

"Saw the clip of you raiding that Aurelian supply depot on Cinnabar. You're either made of brass or not swinging anything at all," the broad-shouldered woman said. She hesitated, then added, "But if that was you, how the hell did you end up here?"

Kal sat up and rested his elbows on his knees. "I thought I'd take a little vacation down here for the holiday. Nothing says authentic Landfall Day like a Breeze-waltz prison cell."

The woman smirked. "You don't seem too worried for a guy in lockup."

Kal spread his arms wide to gesture at the cramped cell and the motley assortment of detainees. "Worried? Please. Look at this place. Give me the hum of a heavy shard, a strong drink, and I'm practically back on the *Days*. Besides," he added with a wink, "this isn't my first time in one of these with fine folk like you. Probably won't be our last. We can all get a drink when we get out of here."

A ripple of laughter spread through the group. One of the younger detainees, a scrawny kid with bright eyes, piped up. "Is it true? That your ship can outrun Toren's skyship, the *Arcadia*?"

Kal tilted his head, as if to weigh the question. "It's not about outrunning them," he said. "It's about making sure they never knew you were there to begin with."

The wiry man leaned against the wall and crossed his arms. "You're all talk and bluster. What good do you do? Not like anything you do out there matters a damn for people like us."

"You're right. When I'm up there intercepting supply lines and selling the goods back to you fine people at a tenth the price, it means nothing. The starving children who make it another six weeks off the rations we provide? What good is that?"

"You said yourself, you don't give them out for free," the wiry man responded.

"Hey, even sunlight costs you a shadow," Kal said and half-closed his eyes. "Keeping the *Days* in the air isn't cheap."

"Are you a saint, skypirate, merchant, or politician?" the man asked.

"Or an addict?" interjected a gaunt woman with sunken eyes.

The eyes startled Kal for a moment. They were stripped down to nothing but brutal honesty. He recognized something in them he did not want to admit. He looked away, then recovered quickly.

"Only to adventure, my dear, and since when were the five mutually exclusive?" he asked in turn.

The sound of boots echoing down the corridor interrupted the conversation. They had become common even in the short time Kal had been there. The detainees fell silent, and tension crept back into the air.

Two guards appeared with four men. The guards shoved the new arrivals into Kal's cell.

The stranger's presence made Kal's hand drift to the small of his back, fingers instinctively brushing for the pack that wasn't there. The motion was automatic. His body still expected the weight, still reached for it in moments of uncertainty.

He caught himself and dropped his hand like nothing had happened. The echo of the missing hum lingered in his spine, a phantom charge that left him heavier, slower, and less sharp. It was like being underwater without knowing how deep he was.

He hated how much he missed it, hated how much better it made him, and most of all, he hated the man who'd strapped it to him to begin with.

"Kaliston?" one of the detainees asked when the guards were out of earshot.

Kal stood slowly, dusted off his jacket, and extended a hand to greet the newly arrived detainees. "Still am, last I checked," he said with his typical half-cocked grin.

"Val sent us," the lead detainee said and shook his hand. "We're with the Cliff Cats crew out of Sector Seven. She said someone named Locke is working the other angle and to keep you alive until then."

"They took my pack. I'm going to need it before very long."

"Nothing we can do about that, Cap. We're in here just like you."

"Sure." Kal wished he hadn't led with that. "Did she say anything else?"

"Yeah. She says you're an idiot."

"I always am until I once again prove my genius." Kal smiled and wiped away the sweat before he sat back down.

CHAPTER 15: LOCKE

4 Days Until Landfall

The Beggars Trail began as an almost imperceptible path that wound between jagged outcroppings of rock at the base of the mesa. Overgrown with thorny bushes and scattered with loose shale, it seemed to pull away from them in the night and gave Locke a sense of vertigo.

Centuries prior, city leaders decided the best way to discourage its use was to simply let it rot. Locke squinted as the trail vanished into the night.

"Still think it's safer than the main gate?" Kenzie asked, hands on her hips.

"I never said it was safer," Locke replied, and adjusted his shirt. "Just less likely to get us caught."

Kenzie sighed. "You think you can do this?"

"Yeah... I think so. I mean, I've done it before," Locke said. "My father made Toren and me do it when we were younger. Back before Toren went to the Citadel."

"The Citadel?" Kenzie asked.

"Oh, sorry, the military academy for the Armada," Locke said, and Kenzie nodded. He continued. "Father said this was our city, and we needed to know everything about it."

"You sure you're not just doing this for nostalgia?" Kenzie asked.

"There's nothing nostalgic about this. You'll see soon enough," Locke said.

"How old were you when you did this?"

"Toren was sixteen or seventeen. I was six," he said.

Kenzie didn't ask another question, and that was a relief. It wasn't a particularly pleasant memory, and Locke was truthfully nervous about what lay ahead. He admitted to himself that they had options. Haruto's forged IDs might be good enough to get them through the gates, but then again, maybe not. He chose what he trusted, and he trusted what he knew. That was what his father taught him. He could also admit that it wasn't the same thing as choosing.

The trail, or what was left of it, quickly narrowed as they climbed. The sound of the bustling market below faded with every step. The path twisted and turned. It forced them to scramble over crumbling ledges and squeeze through narrow crevices. Kenzie muttered curses under her breath as another thorn snagged her sleeve.

"This is the worst idea you've ever had," she grumbled. The city below faded a bit. "This isn't a path, it's a death trap. It's like the mesa made it just to kill us."

"Technically, it's manmade," Locke said. "Just no one has maintained it in something like a hundred years."

"Great. That information makes this so much easier. Thank you for sharing."

The trail took them to a sheer rock face, where faintly etched handholds marked the next part of their journey. Locke tested one carefully, and the stone flaked under his fingers. He looked over his shoulder as his hand missed the hold.

"Don't look down," he said, more to himself than to Kenzie.

Kenzie glanced over the edge and immediately recoiled. "You're a walking cliché."

"Just climb," Locke said and started up the wall. "It's not as bad as it looks."

Kenzie followed. The handholds proved smaller and more precarious than they seemed from below. About halfway up, the wall gave way to a small, flat ledge. Locke hauled himself onto it and reached down to help her.

She brushed his hand away and hauled herself up. A low, guttural growl echoed from somewhere above them. Kenzie froze. "What was that?"

Locke's brow furrowed as the sound came again, closer. He turned toward the path ahead, where the trail disappeared into a dense patch of underbrush. "Probably just an echo from the lower level," he said, though his tone didn't even convince himself.

Kenzie gave him a look. "An echo of what?"

"Cliff cat, maybe."

"I'm sorry, a cliff cat? Say again?" Kenzie asked.

"They're big, feral cats that live on cliffs. It's all in the name already."

"Oh, you sure it isn't a rock bear? Or a boulder dragon?"

"Those aren't real," Locke said and stepped cautiously toward the underbrush.

"Neither were 'cliff cats' until two seconds ago!"

The growl came again, and it was unmistakably close. Locke stopped and motioned for Kenzie to stay behind him. He crouched to pick up a loose rock from the trail.

The underbrush rustled violently, and a creature leapt out, a sleek, sinewy predator with glowing blue eyes and jagged teeth. Its fur was the color of ash, and its long, whip-like tail lashed back and forth.

"Cliff cat?" Kenzie hissed and stepped back.

"Cliff cat," Locke confirmed grimly. "And it's glowing. So that's a fun new problem."

"Any advice?" Kenzie asked.

"Yeah," Locke said, "hope it has shard sickness instead of turning into a feline Altier."

The cliff cat was gaunt and malnourished, but it looked hungry, which made it more or less dangerous. It crouched, muscles coiled as it prepared to pounce. Locke hurled the rock and struck it square in the side. The creature yowled, staggered back, but didn't retreat. Instead, it regrouped and lunged at Locke.

The cat was weak and slow, which was fortunate for Locke. Shard sickness. Locke sidestepped it and shoved Kenzie toward the path ahead. "Go! I'll handle this!"

Kenzie didn't argue. She scrambled up the trail, but she didn't get far before she glanced back. She paused, as if to consider something, before she shook her head. Locke dodged the cat's swipes and used the narrow terrain to his advantage. The creature was relentless. Its claws raked the stone as it pressed its attack.

"Locke!" Kenzie shouted. She picked up a rock and hurled it at the beast. It struck the cat's hindquarters. That drew its attention. "Up here, you overgrown house pet!"

The cliff cat turned, snarled, and bounded toward her. Kenzie's face looked like her stomach dropped. "Oh, no, bad cat, bad cat!" she yelled and retreated up the trail.

Locke took advantage of the distraction. He grabbed a large, flat piece of shale and used it as a shield. He drove into the cat's side. It clawed at the stone, its tail snapped like a whip. Locke braced himself and shoved harder. For a moment, the creature clung on, then with one final push, it lost its footing and plummeted into the abyss. The cat yowled as it plummeted, its cry stretched long into the night before it finally faded.

Kenzie exhaled shakily as Locke climbed up to join her. "You okay?" he asked.

"Fine," she said and worked to catch her breath. "You?"

"Never better." He grinned, though he panted. "See? Nothing we can't handle."

Kenzie stared at him. "Do you enjoy pushing cats to their doom?"

"Depends if they're trying to eat me for dinner."

"If they are?" she asked.

"Then still not really," Locke said. "It was sick, not evil. Just got caught between survival and bad luck."

"It was it or us…" She paused and looked at him. "As long as you didn't enjoy it. I would hate to think the guy who bunks in the room below me secretly goes mountain climbing for the animal cruelty."

Locke hesitated and watched the empty space where the cat had fallen. He had acted to save Kenzie and himself, but in doing so, he had consigned another creature to death. Part of him was sad, but another part had acted the moment Kenzie was in danger. There was an anger there that fueled his actions. It scared him almost as much as the thought of what could have happened.

He shook it off and gave Kenzie a crooked smile. "I mostly just do it for the views and the company."

She rolled her eyes, but the smile lingered longer than usual. Locke caught it between breaths and held onto it like a win.

She turned to continue the climb. "Why was that up here?"

"Some people say the cats have been here since before the founding of Breezewaltz. Others say the elites moved them in to discourage undesirables from climbing to the Upper Mesa. Sometimes they find their bodies in the lower city. I guess we know why now. Either way, we should be wary of more as we go."

"You could have warned me that crystal beasts were a thing," Kenzie said and took another look over the edge.

"Yeah, sorry, not sure about the Rose Crystal, but the Azure Crystal can alter any living thing." Locke tested the footing ahead before he gestured for Kenzie to go first. "Typically, we don't do that because who wants an uncontrollable animal that moves faster than you can see?"

"Right, makes sense." She lifted herself to the next handhold. Kenzie turned around and offered a hand to help Locke up. "You're saying this one occurred naturally?"

"Most likely. The crystal veins run deep into the mesa. Some are just on the other side of these walls. That thing's den must have been close to a fissure." Locke gestured ahead, then shrugged. "Most things don't survive that kind of exposure. Not sure if that one was lucky to be alive or unlucky to turn out that way."

The trail stayed brutal, but at least it had stopped trying to actively kill them. They reached some chains that hung over the mesa's edge near the top. The two used them to climb up the rest of the way to safety. They found themselves in a rare park maintained by the collective aristocracy of the Upper Mesa.

Kenzie collapsed onto the gaia and stared up at the night sky. "I hate heights. I hate cliffs. I don't hate cats, but I hate whatever that thing was."

Locke fell beside her and grinned despite the exhaustion. "But we made it."

They lay side by side and breathed hard, their sweat cooled in the breeze. The stars stretched endlessly overhead, and for a second, Locke thought about how close she was.

"You're alright, you know," Kenzie said, just barely loud enough to be heard over the wind. Locke glanced over, surprised. Kenzie clocked it with a side-eye look. "I'm denying I ever said that."

"I don't think anyone on the *Days* would believe me if I told them."

"It's tough work to maintain constant plausible deniability, but it comes in handy for moments like this."

They both smiled, but neither moved. They lay like that for what felt like forever and also no time at all.

Finally, Kenzie groaned and sat up. "Next time, we will use the passes. I don't care if they throw us in jail. At least jail would be flat."

"Deal," Locke said and sat up.

For a moment, they stared out as the lower city of Breezewaltz sprawled before them in the distance. Skyships passed overhead. The city lights below them illuminated the constant hustle and bustle of the pilgrims, even at this hour.

"Well," Kenzie said finally, "if nothing else, this holiday's going to be memorable."

Locke chuckled. "Yeah, looks like we'll survive to celebrate it. C'mon, my family's house is this way. Hopefully, Toren left the front door unlocked and the lights on."

CHAPTER 16: KENZIE

4 Days Until Landfall

The Upper Mesa of Breezewaltz was a different world from the city below. The winding chaos of the lower city gave way to broad avenues, ornamental lamps, and silence cloaked in wealth. Even in the Upper Mesa, where property was at a premium, the houses were palatial. The air smelled of rich gaia and lavender, carried on the evening breeze. Even the ever-present hum of the city seemed more refined. The distant voices, the occasional whirr of an opulent speeder, were present, but none of the raucous energy from the sectors below.

Kenzie took it all in, arms crossed. "So this is how the other half lives."

Locke rolled his shoulders and neck. "It's different when you grow up in it."

"Yeah?" Kenzie arched a brow. "You miss it, rich boy?"

Locke exhaled and glanced around at the polished walls and immaculate corridors. "Not really. It's not all parties and prestige. There's a price to it, like every step needs to be measured and judged. You're always watched, always expected to play your part." He looked at Kenzie, his expression unreadable. "I was never the person they wanted me to be, and I don't think I ever will be."

They rounded a corner and found themselves on a main thoroughfare. Lamplight cut the dark, but the wind still bit.

"Tell me about your home." Kenzie wanted to fill the unfamiliar space.

Locke looked around before he spoke, like it was something he had rehearsed and was trying to remember. "The Upper Mesa is constructed like the spokes of a wheel. Residences and fine shops surround the Grand Lake with the Azure Temple at its center. The ultra-wealthy live closer to the Grand Lake, but the Luinondo estate takes up a plot of land from the mesa's edge to the Grand Lake itself."

"Sounds fancy," Kenzie said.

"Controlling the trade of Azure shards has its perks," Locke replied.

The two of them walked down the brick road. They mostly kept to the edge beneath the well-manicured flora. They rarely saw other souls, but when they did, they were dressed in well-tailored clothing and finery. Locke and Kenzie stood out like sore thumbs. They hadn't dressed the part.

"Should have packed better clothes. I'm such an idiot," Kenzie muttered under her breath. "We're going to get made if one peace officer sees us."

"We'll be fine. Just walk like you belong."

"Pfft, what do you know?"

"I literally grew up here," Locke replied, and Kenzie stuck out her tongue.

They stayed on the roadway until they reached the Grand Lake. The road ended in a roundabout that encircled the water's edge. Locke turned right. Kenzie had no idea where she was going, so she followed his lead. She didn't know which pissed her off more, not knowing where they were or having to rely on Locke, of all people.

"How much farther?" she asked.

"A few more blocks," Locke said, not breaking stride.

They passed an opulent hotel that was hosting a party. The music was subdued for the lower city, but raucous for the Upper Mesa. Kenzie craned her neck to look through the windows at the gentlemen and ladies dressed in expensive clothes, drinking fancy cocktails. She shook her head and continued to walk with Locke.

They walked by a man around the corner who had a little too much revelry. He was sick on his hands and knees. Another man stood over him and watched with concern. When the standing man turned, it was clear he was in uniform. A peace officer. He took one look at Locke and Kenzie, hollered, and trotted over while he motioned for them to come closer.

As the officer approached, Kenzie looked at Locke, then at the officer. "Let me handle this," she whispered. "Hello, officer, it seems we're not the only ones having too much fun tonight."

The officer glanced over his shoulder at the sick man, who had rolled over and sat up. His dinner stained his shirt. "Aye, Mr. Grubb will be fine. Might I ask who you are and where you're going tonight?"

Kenzie produced her pass and nodded to Locke, who did the same. "Here are our passes, and we're on our way back to our friend's. We're staying with him as guests."

The officer eyed the passes. He checked Kenzie's, then Locke's, turned them over, and bent them slightly. He looked back up at them. Not only were they in basic clothing, but the climb hadn't done them any favors.

Kenzie saw Locke flinch slightly as the officer bent the paper. She felt it too, but she could hide it better. Haruto was good, but no one was perfect.

"Where are you coming from?"

"Coming from?" Kenzie echoed. The question flustered her. She didn't know Breezewaltz. She could say the Berrywood Grill, but would that make sense? Kenzie knew how silly the whole thing looked. Locke and she were clearly not supposed to be there. It only took two eyes and a brain cell to do the math. She froze.

"Went down to the lower city for a bit of fun. Coming back to the Luinondo estate. First Altier..." Locke hesitated, then pushed through. "Luinondo didn't travel with us, but he told us it would be no problem to pass with that paperwork."

Kenzie clocked how Locke said his last name, like it meant everything in the city. The mention of the First Altier made the officer stiffen. He looked back at the paper, then at Locke, and weighed the confrontation. "I wasn't told the First Altier had guests," the officer said, voice cautious.

Locke didn't blink. "Then maybe ask yourself why that is."

The officer bent the paperwork again, slower, eyes still on Locke. "You know the way?"

"Keep following the roundabout, then look for the most expensive estate in Iveria besides the King's castle."

The officer nodded and handed the passes back. "Try to stay off the streets. Landfall this year has attracted a lot of pilgrims."

"Calling them pilgrims is being generous," Kenzie said.

"It's not for me to label them, milady, just to preserve the peace. Good night." With that, the officer ran back to the sick Mr. Grubb and tried to help the doofus up.

Kenzie and Locke moved on in silence at first. "Enjoy your hero moment. That's the last one you get," she muttered once the officer was out of earshot.

Locke and Kenzie continued down the path in silence, but Kenzie's gaze stayed on Locke. She wasn't sure if she was annoyed he had to step in or mad at herself. It seemed like a mix of both.

"What did you mean when you said calling them pilgrims is generous?" Locke asked eventually.

"Have you noticed the people down there? Not just the number of them, but what they have on them? Bedsheets, family pictures, and packs loaded with water. They're not pilgrims, they're refugees. Something is driving them north."

Whatever that something was, it would have to wait.

"We're here," Locke said and paused before the second biggest estate Kenzie had ever seen. She had seen a larger castle, but this was still impressive.

The estate of House Luinondo was a looming structure of white stone and deep mahogany, adorned with banners in the dark blue and silver of the Iverian League. Guards patrolled the perimeter, their uniforms crisp, their shardshot rifles gleaming in the moonlight. It was a fortress masquerading as a home.

Kenzie gave Locke a sidelong glance. "You sure we couldn't have just walked through the front gate with those fancy passes?"

Locke smirked. "You think we would have stood up to more scrutiny than we just got? Plus, I'd rather not be announced at the door like some long-lost beggar returned home for a handout."

"Isn't that what we are?"

"Being it and being called it are two different things. C'mon, I know another way." He turned and followed the wall.

After a while, he led her into an alley. It appeared to be used by servants and for trash. As it continued, they passed two guards who paid them no heed, and the wall became hidden behind large hedges. They slipped through a secret garden entrance behind some hedges to the right, carefully moved between neatly trimmed gardens, and climbed up the back steps. Kenzie's boots barely made a sound against the polished marble floors as they stepped over the exterior terrace, while Locke practically crashed with each step. Kenzie could not believe Locke was so loud. She knew he called her 'Boots' behind her back, but she thought maybe he was projecting.

Locke approached a door, but it wouldn't budge. Locke gave her a look of surprise.

"We never locked this door. Looks like Toren has made some changes."

Kenzie smirked and moved past him. She took a small amount of pleasure in Locke not knowing everything going on up here. She got down on one knee in front of it and slipped out a pouch with small tools from a pocket near her waistband. Her hands moved silently before a small click was heard, and the door swung open. She tried not to beam too much, but she was proud of her work. She gestured into the opulent building. Locke's smile made her feel better than she would like to admit.

The manor was clean, yet not austere, well-maintained, and clearly inhabited. The scent of aged wood and parchment filled the air. It looked like Locke stopped breathing for a second. She wondered if being in his childhood home, with the familiar scents, triggered memories. She thought about how nice that must be.

Kenzie lingered behind him as they moved down the hallway. Her eyes flicked over oil paintings. She assumed they were distinguished Luinondo ancestors. "I'm guessing you're related to all these guys?"

"Technically. We're the second-oldest unbroken line in Iveria, after the royal family."

"Figures. They all look like they have broomsticks up their backs."

Locke barely suppressed a chuckle. "You would've gotten along with my mother, then. She wanted to take them all down, but Father wouldn't let her. Said it would have been disrespectful to the family."

The only thing more impressive to Kenzie than the legacy was the wealth. Kenzie always liked the idea of family money, but the reality of it scared her, too. Worse, she knew what money did to families. Too much of it was just too much power, and ultimately, power corrupts. She was glad Locke had walked away from it.

Locke and her turned a corner, and a man stood at the end of the hall. His arms were crossed, and his expression was unreadable. His features bore the same noble cut as Locke's, though his hair was neater, his posture straighter, and his presence heavier.

"Toren," Locke said and forced a smirk. "Never could get one past you."

In that moment, however, Toren didn't smile. He took a step forward in the dimly lit corridor, his eyes scanning Locke like he was searching for something. Kenzie wondered if the look made Locke as uneasy as it made her. She'd seen that look before, in the desperate kids on the street who were constantly trying to see past the masks others wore. There was money to be found past the illusions people project, but Kenzie was certain Toren wasn't worried about money. His look was a mix of emotions, but he didn't show anger or relief. It was something between the two: tension. The kind that came from someone who had made peace with a story and suddenly found it being rewritten before him.

"You should not be here," he finally said.

Kenzie thought of a million comebacks, but swallowed them all. She wasn't sure if Toren would help them, but it would be more of a tightrope walk than she thought. She guessed Toren would only respond to honesty.

"Sorry," Locke replied, "I shouldn't have said that. No time for jokes. We need your help."

Toren tilted his head. "'We'?"

Locke breathed deeply before he launched into it. "Kal's been arrested. He's being held in Sector Five. Bad run-in with an underworld crew, Red Death or something like that. Now we need to get him out before someone cracks his skull."

For the first time, Toren's mask cracked. He inhaled sharply. His gaze flickered to the floor before it settled back on Locke. "Kal, huh? What did that idiot do this time?"

"That's what I said," Kenzie added before she could restrain herself.

Both men looked at her with the same hint of amusement.

"Yeah," Locke said and turned back to Toren. "He fought a crew of unregistered Rosari. We think the local officers were on the crew's cut. He's probably in danger, even now. I can only hope he's still your best friend?"

Toren's jaw tightened. "We have been walking different paths for some time, Locke. Him, you... and I."

"He's like family, to us both, right?"

Kenzie wondered if Locke had meant to say it like that, but it seemed honest enough for the moment.

Silence stretched between them. Kenzie could feel the years of separation, of different lives and unspoken words. Toren's fingers curled into fists at his sides before he finally exhaled and turned on his heel. "Come with me. We will talk somewhere private." He walked away before saying a curt, "Dismissed."

The four hidden Altiers that formed Toren's personal guard appeared from the shadows and moved into a secondary room. Kenzie let out a muffled shriek but tried to compose herself. It wouldn't look professional for the master thief to have been surprised by silent guards. Kenzie took a few breaths and followed as Toren walked ahead.

"He seems fun," she said.

"He's a little stiffer than I remember, but I'm pretty sure that was him trying to be nice."

Toren led them to a private study, a room of polished oak and dark leather chairs. Shelves lined with books that looked untouched but also dust-free. Kenzie knew Locke had a love of reading and could imagine him spending hours here as a child. She wondered which was his favorite. She would have to ask when the time was right.

A desk sat before a large window that overlooked the Temple. The exterior lights twinkled in the darkness.

Toren walked over and picked up a book bound in black from the desk. He folded the fabric bookmark and closed it gently. Then he placed it in a drawer beneath the desk with a click. He poured himself a drink and finally sat. "What was the official reason for the arrest?"

"Disturbing the peace, technically," Locke said. "Kenzie was there and said it was a fight." Locke realized he hadn't introduced her. "Oh, this is Kenzie, by the way."

Toren tipped his glass to Kenzie. "Charmed." He took a sip and then swirled the amber liquid in his glass. "Now's not a good time. Between Landfall and the conflict to the south with Prince Lucan, the city is on edge."

Locke leaned forward. "Great. Then no one will notice one skypirate being released from holding."

Toren exhaled through his nose. "It is not that simple. I cannot just order his release. The moment they processed him, he probably raised some alarms. Some official, others not. The Shipping Guild will want his head, for one. He's stolen too much from their trade lines. Not to mention the underworld bosses he has crossed. It's got to be a dozen of them in this city alone. Then there's the Holy Order of the Azure Crystal that knows his ship has unregulated Azure heavy shards. The sacrilege. Finally, knowing him, he probably used counterfeit codes again…"

"Don't you hold sway over all of them?" Kenzie asked.

Toren studied her. "Sometimes. Barely. Requests always come with strings attached. I bail him out of this, and I will owe something to someone down the line.

Someone I probably should not owe something to. I try to keep out of the pocket of too many people, especially those of, well, lesser morals."

Locke smirked. "What if Kal was in your pocket?"

Silence. Then Toren leaned forward and placed his glass on the desk. "First, who is to say he is not already? Second, what could a skypirate do for me?"

Kenzie smiled and reacted to his body language. "We can do whatever you need, but you've already decided, haven't you?"

"Not exactly." Toren looked down at himself and leaned back. His expression darkened. "At least, nothing I want to talk about with you two."

Toren pretended to think about it, but Kenzie already knew the truth. This was all for show. For some reason, he tested them. He breathed deeply and sighed, running a hand through his well-maintained auburn hair.

"Okay, one second. I will call in and clarify it. Do you know which facility he is at?"

Locke looked at Kenzie. She shrugged. "Like Locke said, Sector Five. Not sure which facility is local, though. Whichever one was closest to the fight," she said.

"You said Red Death, right?" Toren asked.

"Yeah, that's the one," Kenzie responded.

Toren chuckled. "Ander's crew. Of course, Kal is dumb enough to pick a fight with them. On the bright side, I have tried to weed them out for months now. The red tape, even for me, was a nightmare."

He picked up the datapad and comm, then pinged the holding facility. He moved to the other side of the room. The velvet curtains and books muffled his conversation, but it seemed he issued orders on multiple calls.

"Doesn't seem like he trusts you very much," Kenzie said to Locke as Toren paced the other side of the room.

"Yeah, I'm still a little foggy on the details, but I don't think we had the best parting before I joined the *Days*."

"Kal and he were friends?"

"Yeah, from the Citadel. Val too. Kal stayed with us one summer when I was eight or nine. I remember them being inseparable in those days, before they were all assigned to different Capital skyships."

Toren returned to the duo. "They will release him in the morning," Toren confirmed. "I will personally attend to it, and the two of you will join me."

Locke stood. "Morning? Why waste more time if he's in danger?"

Toren smiled and took another sip. "Unfortunately, Locke, some of us still follow the laws. I can order his release, but I'll need a judge to approve it, then a council member has to ratify it, and finally, I have to sign the damn thing before a notary. Only then can it be officially entered into the record. That takes time, even for me. I know skypirates do whatever they want, whenever they want, but here in the real world, we have to follow the rules."

Locke didn't have a response. He just frowned and looked out the window.

"Will Kal be alright?" Kenzie asked, her voice quiet as her eyes moved from Locke to Toren.

"It seems Val already arranged for a small crew to join him in jail, plus I ordered that they give him back his pack. He will be fine. This might even teach him a lesson about the consequences of getting arrested. He's the only pirate I know who gets caught more than he gets away." He looked at Locke, and his face softened. "I am sure he would appreciate your concern." He turned to Kenzie. "Both of your concerns." Then, back to Locke, letting the warmth linger. "It is good to see you getting along with him at least. Back at the Citadel, he and I were like brothers. Val was the older sister, at least to me. She kept us in line more often than not."

Toren stood and crossed to a secondary door. He spoke quietly with someone on the other side. "Locke, your old room is available. Why not rest there?" He looked at Kenzie. "Kenzie, right?"

She nodded.

"You can take a guest room in the west wing. Unless you two are sharing quarters?"

Locke and Kenzie looked at each other. Kenzie laughed, and Locke blushed.

"No, separate rooms are fine," Locke stammered.

Toren smiled at his little brother. "We can catch up on our way down tomorrow, but for now, it is good to have you home," Toren said and put his arm on Locke's back. "Oh, and give me the forged passes. I will have my staff issue official temp documents for the morning."

Locke reached into his pack, pulled out the forged pass, and handed it over.

"How did you know we had forged documents?" Kenzie asked. She hesitated before she did the same.

"I knew Val long before you did," Toren said with a smile. "Locke, can you show Kenzie to her quarters? I trust you still know your way around."

Locke nodded, and Toren winked at him as he closed his study door behind them.

Kenzie wasn't sure what to make of any of it. The Upper Mesa was confusing enough without the Luinondo brothers playing polite. They'd probably secured Kal's release, but Toren was still a mystery. The way he treated Locke was like he was hiding something. Still, her doubts scattered the moment her head hit the softest pillow she'd felt since before the streets of Seaforth.

CHAPTER 17: LOCKE

3 Days Until Landfall

The sun had barely risen over Breezewaltz when Locke and Toren stepped out onto the estate's private gondola platform. The crisp morning air carried the scent of damp stone and blooming lavender from the gardens below. A sleek transport waited for them. Its engines hummed softly, ready to take them down into the city.

Locke adjusted the collar of his coat and stole a glance at his older brother. In the softer morning light, Toren looked less like the unyielding commander from the night before and more like the sibling he had once known. The mantle of responsibility still pressed on his features, but there was something almost nostalgic in how he had stood waiting for Locke. It reminded Locke of their father.

"Feels like we have done this before, doesn't it?" Toren mused as they boarded the transport.

Locke smirked. "True, but Father would be yelling at us that we're running late."

Toren chuckled. "And Mother would tell him that fifteen minutes early is not considered late."

Kenzie grinned from the opposite seat. "I love family reunions. So heartwarming."

Locke gave her a look, but smirked. "You're just happy you get to ride in luxury for once."

"I'm happy I don't have to climb down a death trap of a cliffside trail, yeah." Kenzie tilted her head toward Toren. "You should've seen him last night. He pushed a cat off the mesa. I think he even enjoyed it, the psychopath."

Toren raised an eyebrow. "Ah, the Beggars Trail. I was wondering who let you up here with those fake passes. I should have known." He smiled at Locke. "Locke always did like finding ways to make things harder for himself."

Locke scoffed. "You make it sound like I had a choice." He forced a smile. He wasn't sure what Kal had told his brother about the accident, but he hoped Toren wasn't talking about the missing years. The comment felt like Toren handled him with kid gloves, and that stung more than it should.

The transport lifted off smoothly and glided high above Sector Nine below before it began its descent toward Sector Ten. Below them, the sprawling streets of the lower city stretched out. The morning merchants set up their stalls, workers already filled the main thoroughfares, and pilgrims bustled about. The air was cool but held the promise of the day's warmth.

For a moment, silence settled between them, save for the low hum of the transport.

Toren finally broke it. "How long do you plan on staying here?"

Locke exhaled and leaned back in his seat. "I guess that depends on Kal, but now that I'm here, I wouldn't mind spending more time with you." He looked at his brother sheepishly. "If that's okay?"

Toren nodded. "Things will get busy over the next few days, but you always have a home here. Kal and Val, too. Kenzie as well, if she wants it."

"They probably prefer their skyship over the Upper Mesa," Kenzie replied. She looked surprised to be included.

"Maybe," Toren looked out the window. His guards waited for them below. "But the old Kal I knew would take me up on the offer. Besides, I still have to get that favor from him."

Kenzie kept staring out the window and back at the brothers. "How long have you known Kal?"

"I met him on my first day at the Citadel. He called me a pompous blueberry, even though I had not performed the Final Rite yet. We wrestled in the yard a week later, but afterward, when Val tended my scrapes, he apologized. I think he held some resentment toward the upper houses before we met. That quickly went away, and the three of us became inseparable. We were thick as thieves during our time at the Citadel until our assignments took us across Iveria."

Locke listened intently, and a small smile played on his lips. He could picture it. The three of them, younger, cockier, and testing each other in the Citadel's training yard. Kal had always been quick to pick a fight, and Toren had always been just as quick to meet a challenge head-on. It wasn't surprising that Val had been the one to smooth things over. She had always been the mediator, the one who made things work.

Kenzie turned toward Locke. "And you?"

Locke huffed through his nose. "I think it was Toren's first summer back. Kal had some family issues, so he stayed with us. I tried to follow them around, but they wanted nothing to do with a kid."

Toren chuckled. "More like a stubborn stray."

Locke raised his eyebrows and looked away with a half-formed smile. It felt like Toren was trying too hard to make it feel normal, like there wasn't a canyon of unspoken words between them.

"I remember that differently," he said.

"We always do," Toren agreed, his tone softer, almost regretful.

The transport slowed as it neared the landing platform at the base of the city, where a small escort of guards waited. It settled with a soft jolt, and the doors hissed open, allowing the morning breeze to enter. The scent of street food and something burning from the city's lower districts wafted in.

As they stepped out, Locke caught sight of the waiting figures. A familiar face stood among them: Officer Brann. He was one of their father's most trusted officers. Not an Altier, but good at his job. Now he was protecting Toren. The older man paused when he saw Locke and inclined his head in greeting, but wasted no time getting to business. "First Altier, we've secured the lower district as ordered." Brann hesitated. "Sir, there was already an altercation in the cells last night. Two men are dead."

Locke and Kenzie exchanged a glance. "And Kal, is he..." Kenzie started.

"The prisoner is being processed as we speak. A group of inmates came to Kal's protection, but I am told he did not need it. The surviving attackers were separated and will be retried for the incident. I suspect they came for the bounties on his head. He's carrying over twenty active ones, last we checked, and none of them are small."

Locke sighed, and Toren shrugged.

Kenzie relaxed a bit, but she was still stiffer than normal. Locke could guess why. They were in the belly of the beast. Even if they wanted to, Locke and Kenzie would not find leaving this situation pleasant should someone decide the rest of the *Days'* crew should join Kal instead of the other way around. Hopefully, everyone would play nicely.

Toren nodded. "Good. Ensure he is being held in solitary for now. The Guild will probably make another attempt, or this Red Death crew. Try to put an end to it before it starts. No need to make a show of it." Toren gestured for Locke and Kenzie to proceed. "Okay, then, let us not keep him waiting."

They got into awaiting speeders, and the security convoy moved through the lower streets with purpose. Eyes followed them as they passed. It was early and the main crowds had yet to form, but the people who were out noticed who was travelling through the streets.

Locke took in the sights as they moved. The narrow alleys, the colorful awnings of the market stalls, and the distant clang of metalworkers starting their day. It was different from the Upper Mesa, rougher, yet full of life in a way that the opulent but sanitized Upper Mesa never entirely managed to be.

When they arrived at the detention center, Brann led them through a set of stone corridors to a holding area. The guards posted outside the cell snapped to attention as they approached, but Toren waved them off.

Brann received a key card, unlocked the solid iron door, and pushed it open to reveal the man inside.

Kal sat on the narrow bench, arms crossed, and looked thoroughly unimpressed. His coat had been removed, his shirt slightly wrinkled, but otherwise, he seemed entirely at ease. He looked up, took them in, and shook his head like he'd expected the punchline all along.

Kenzie stepped inside first. "You're committing to this whole 'getting arrested' thing, huh?"

Kal shrugged. "Figured I'd see how the other side lives for a bit. Gotta say, I'm not a fan of the accommodations. I came all the way to Breezewaltz, Tor, and this is how you set me up?"

Toren stepped forward, arms crossed but smiling. "Seems to suit you, actually. You are lucky I owed you one, but we are even now."

Kal's grin widened. "You never let me forget my debts, do you?"

Locke stood against the back wall while Kenzie hugged Kal.

Toren shook his hand before Kal pulled him in as well.

"I do not know who is more grateful that you are leaving. The guards or the guys you roughed up last night?" Toren wondered.

"Don't say it like that. In fact, we went easy on them." Kal winked at Locke.

Toren's expression didn't change, but Locke saw it, the subtle flicker of thought, the way his posture shifted. Something had caught Toren's attention.

Kal dusted off his sleeves and grinned. "Anyway, I have a feeling the real fun's just getting started."

"Glad you noticed." Toren's voice was quieter, sharper.

Kal opened his mouth to reply, but the lights flickered. The security cameras twitched. Someone was hijacking the facility's systems.

Locke felt his stomach drop. "That's not good."

Toren didn't move at first. His eyes locked on the hallway camera as it rotated to the four of them standing in the holding cell. Then, slowly, he stepped forward and rested his fingertips against the metal casing. He closed his eyes, and a soft pulse of blue energy flickered from his fingertips and seeped into the camera. The energy surged through the conduit, threaded into the network, and followed the disturbance like a hunter tracking prey.

Toren's gaze darkened. He turned to Brann. "Lock the facility down. Now."

The order barely left Toren's lips when the cell door across from Kaliston burst open.

Two figures lunged from the shadows and moved with unnatural speed. They were too fast, too precise for common thugs. A man and a woman. Altiers.

They moved past Brann in an instant, through the hallway, and into Kal's cell. The woman struck like lightning. A suda with a thin dagger blade flashed toward Kal's throat. Kal barely twisted away in time. The weapon sliced through the air where his neck had been. The male Altier had a suda dagger in each hand and aimed for Kal's ribs.

Kenzie and Locke barely had time to register the attack. Toren didn't seem to move from the hallway at first, but in an instant, it felt like he was everywhere all at once.

The man's blades stopped inches from Kal's chest, suspended in midair, held in place by Toren's hand. The woman jerked violently backward, her arm locked at her sides as if an unseen hand had seized him.

Toren exhaled in the center of the cramped room and held both attackers, one in each hand. The entire room felt electrified. It tasted different, as if the air had been ionized.

"Novices," Toren said, almost disappointed. "You should have stayed with the Armada. You could have been properly trained."

With a flick of his wrist, Toren slammed the male Altier, into the cell wall with a sickening crunch. His weapons clattered to the floor.

The other struggled against Toren's grip as he held her wrist. She tried to break free, but it was a feint. While she struggled, she grabbed another concealed suda with her free hand to attempt a second attack on Kal.

One moment, the novice Altier swung. The next, she slammed into the adjacent wall. Both sudas clattered to the cell floor.

It was over before Kenzie could even pull Locke into the corner with her. Kal adjusted his pack while his face looked like Toren had issued a challenge.

Silence hung in the air. Then, the camera flicked into the position it had faced before the assault.

Toren's voice was quiet. "Give me a minute to put an end to this."

"Okay if I tag along?" Kal asked.

"You are still an inmate, friend." Toren smiled before he left them at an imperceptible speed.

Minutes later, the detention door opened, and Toren walked in with the unconscious body of the troll over his shoulder.

"You'll have to teach me that trick. You tapped the network directly, didn't you?" Kal asked.

"It would take you years," Toren replied and placed the man in the cell. The sudden movement jolted the man awake. He was stunned for a second, but quickly got to his feet.

"You think this will stop me?" The troll wheezed a laugh and tried to regain control. "Half the men in this prison are on my payroll. I'll be out before you finish breakfast."

"Not anymore." Toren closed the door, and the sound was drowned out.

He turned to Brann. "You heard him. Assemble a contingent of our most trusted personnel and take control of this facility. Appoint someone to lead the internal investigation. Don't shake anything up until after Landfall, but let's clean this place up after the holiday."

"Aye, First Altier," Brann said and saluted.

"Oh, and don't let that one out until the trial. I'll preside personally."

Brann nodded. The once-feared underworld figure was just another prisoner who awaited trial. A fitting end.

Kal smirked as Toren rejoined them. "Gotta admit, I wasn't expecting you to put him on trial."

Toren gave him a flat look. "You never did understand how justice works. Glad you got a front-row seat."

Kenzie let out a breath and shook her head as the last remnants of the fight dimmed. "We should probably leave before there's a third attempt on Kal's life."

Toren held an arm behind his back, another in front, and gestured toward the exit. "I could not agree more."

The four of them walked out. Toren, Locke, and Kenzie turned toward the speeders. Kal turned the other way, back to the *Days*.

Toren stopped and looked at Kal. "Where are you off to?" Toren asked.

"Oh, sorry, am I still a prisoner?" Kal asked.

"No, but you owe me a favor."

"How? You owed me one, and you just bailed me out. We're even," Kal responded. He was either genuinely confused or a fantastic actor.

"That was before I saved your life and put your assailant behind bars," Toren responded, enjoying the back and forth.

Kal held up his hands with a grin. "Alright, you got me. I had a feeling there was more to this, anyway."

Toren's expression didn't shift, but Locke noticed the slight change in his posture. Toren's voice was unreadable. "Meaning?"

Kal's smirk didn't fade. "I've heard things. Something's stirring in the south. Iveria might not be ready for what's coming. I knew when I sent Locke that you wouldn't haul me out of jail just for old times' sake."

Toren held his gaze for a moment, then nodded. "You planned this?"

"You weren't responding."

"I have bigger issues than you," Toren replied.

"Not anymore," Kal said in turn.

Locke frowned. That did not sound good, and Toren looked like he'd swallowed a frog. Wheels turned, and Locke felt like he was just along for the ride.

CHAPTER 18: KALISTON

3 Days Until Landfall

The gondola ride back up to the Luinondo manor felt surreal. Kal hadn't been to the Upper Mesa since he and Toren had that one reckless summer. Back then, Toren wasn't a nobody, but he wasn't who he would become either. That alone shifted the entire atmosphere. Two Altier guards, stiff-backed and humorless, had helped them into the gondola. The pomp of it all. Kal had almost forgotten who his friend was. Locke seemed uneasy, almost like he didn't know his place in a room with Kal and Toren. The two older men were immediately at home, and Kenzie still appeared to take it all in.

Kal sat on a bench with his hands folded behind his head. He felt entirely at ease, and his posture reflected that. He smiled and looked out the window without a care. Kal had plenty, but it was better to make them think this was just another morning for him. "Gotta say, Tor, last time I was up here, I remember getting into more trouble than I usually do in the lower city."

Toren didn't even glance at him. "We were eighteen the last time you were here."

Kal grinned. "Two things can be true."

Kenzie stifled a laugh and kept pace beside a lost Locke. "What did you do?"

"Mister goody-goody over here was too afraid to let us into the wine cellar, so I had to improvise," Kal said and waved a hand vaguely. "Next thing I know, we're watching the sunrise over the mesa after stealing a dog."

"Nothing worth remembering," Toren chuckled.

Locke looked shocked. "That's how we got Wilson?"

"Well, I had trouble figuring out who he belonged to the next day, and Kal would never take care of him," Toren muttered.

Kal gasped and placed a hand over his heart. "I would have made an excellent father, thank you very much. Just ask these two."

Kenzie and Locke shook their heads. Toren ignored him, but the twitch of his mouth suggested amusement, just a little.

Kenzie took in her surroundings. Her eyes flickered between the extravagant estates and pristine walkways. She crossed her arms, as if she suddenly remembered how out of place she was. "This place doesn't feel real," she muttered. "Everything's too perfect."

Locke nodded. "That's the point. The nobles like their illusion of order. They're up here, and the undeserving are down there."

Toren's gaze cut to him. "It's not just an illusion."

Locke met his brother's eyes. "Isn't it? How often does the upper crust come down? Does anyone up here really care about life beyond the mesa?"

Toren sighed. "Not this again. I thought you were supposed to get him off his soapbox?" he said and looked at Kal.

Kal knew exactly what Toren meant, but he also knew Toren liked to maintain a firmer grip. Kal wanted Locke to just be Locke. Being an idealist, even a naïve one, was who the kid was. Kal didn't want to ever change that.

Kal let out a dramatic sigh. "Gaia, I missed this. The charged sibling rivalry." He looked at Kenzie. "I don't have one, so I never had the chance for this." He motioned to the brothers with open palms. "Just sitting here with these two makes me feel alive."

Kenzie gave him a sideways glance. "Funny how you make everything about you, isn't it?"

Kal winked. "I am the star of the show, Kenz. You'd do well to remember that."

"Sure," she muttered. "I'll add that to the list of things you're wrong about."

Kal smirked. "Val says the same thing, but she never produces the evidence."

Locke pinched the bridge of his nose. "Can we not do this in here?"

"Do what? This feels like three against one," Kal said and held up his hands in mock surrender. "I'm just making conversation. When did I become the bad guy?"

The three of them looked at Kal, and Kal shrugged before looking out the windows.

The gondola docked soon after. Its doors opened with a whoosh. The winds always blew harder on the mesa, but it was rarely unpleasant. The four travelers stepped onto the platform, where two new Altier guards met them. Then the six of them traveled the short distance to the front of the manor.

Toren stopped in front, and whatever tension had built between the group shifted instantly. In the light of day, the Luinondo house was as grand as Kal remembered. It was built with white stone, deep mahogany, and towering columns that loomed over the courtyard. It was a palace built over time and a place built to last.

Kal inhaled deeply. He always sought wealth, but he never trusted others with it. Most people who amassed that level of wealth could not be trusted to make good decisions. Still, the rich smelled nice. He had to admit to that.

Toren turned to face them. "You're going in the front this time."

"Oh, did my charges here sneak in last night?" Kal asked. "Naughty charges."

Toren gave him a look. "I was talking to you."

Kal chuckled. "I really missed you, too, Tor."

Kal hesitated before he stepped inside. Something about being there made him feel... wrong. He should be back on the *Days*, not walking into one of the nicest houses on all of Gaia. He wasn't the only one, as Locke lingered behind him.

Kenzie must have noticed, because she walked back to nudge Locke with her elbow. "You okay?"

Locke forced a smirk. "Yeah. Just never thought I would be back... here. In this house again."

Kal wondered if Locke realized how true that comment should have been. Toren led them into a private sitting room and dismissed the guards with a considered nod. The moment the door shut, Kal flopped onto one of the velvet chairs. He sprawled like he owned the place.

"Gaia, this is comfortable," he sighed. "Locke, remind me why you ever left this behind?"

Locke ignored the comment while Toren poked his head out the door to ask the staff to begin breakfast. Kal was unhappy that his first volley was ignored. He lined up another.

"Toren, I can't believe you've become so dour with this much wealth."

"Because some of us have responsibilities we take seriously."

"Oof," Kal winced. "A glancing blow. I'll have you know I take running the *Days* very seriously. Don't I?"

Kenzie and Locke looked at each other and shared similar knowing smiles. Kenzie settled into a chair near the window, arms crossed. "So what now?"

Toren sat behind his desk and thumbed through some daily reports his staff had prepared. "Now we discuss why you're here."

Locke narrowed his eyes. "Like, why are we in Breezewaltz? We had that bounty."

Toren shook his head. "No, not what brought you to Breezewaltz. What compelled me to invite you back to my house."

Kal groaned. "You were never subtle, always so direct. Everyone knows you need some foreplay before you get down to business."

"I thought you were always in the mood to talk about credits," Toren replied.

"Oh, you said the magic word." Kal sat up fully. "I'm listening."

"The Colossus. What more have you heard out there?"

"The Armada can't touch it. Even that assault with, what, six or seven of our Capital skyships after Heydon? Nothing. I've heard we've lost two ships to it already. It's wiped out three major cities. Millions are dead and displaced. The only thing preventing it from destroying all of Iveria is that the damn thing keeps needing a nap or something. We saw it about a month back, crouched outside of Heydon. A full Aurelian Fleet circled overhead." Kal tried not to let the memory of that monster shake his voice.

"Yes, the thing rampages for about a week and then goes silent for a month. Rinse and repeat. Even when we get close to chasing away the Fleet, we cannot damage the unholy thing, and it seems to kick on to defend itself." Toren balled up a piece of paper on his desk.

"Does the King have a plan?" Kal asked.

"Not a good one. We left Marling on watch while the other First Altiers tried to regroup their Capital skyships. Conchordia is trying to come up with a solution. Half the remaining Armada should be at Orleans with the King. I am here because of Landfall, but once it is done, I will join them or head south to Heydon."

"You mean the ruins of Heydon," Kal replied with an arched eyebrow.

"Unfortunately, yes."

"Okay, and where's this proposition come in?" Kal asked, but he already knew where it was headed.

"I think Lucan is controlling the thing. At the very least, the breakdowns seem somehow mechanical, like the engine is not working right."

"The engine? You think it's mechanical?" Locke asked.

"No, sorry, that was a metaphor. I think the heavy shards work as a sort of heart for the creature. It reminds me of when they recommissioned the *Willowark* a decade ago. The heavy shard was undersized for the ship, and they had to keep landing due to power loss. The heavy shard would gain enough power for a time before eventually running out again. They had to swap it when the next heavy shard was ready. Took about four years."

"And you want us to prove your theory?" Kal asked.

"Yes. I want you to investigate how they power it and if there is a way to stop it. The *Days* is the fastest ship in Iveria. She's the only ship with optical camouflage. You can get in and out without anyone noticing you."

Kaliston thought about it for a moment. "I don't know if you can afford us for this."

"You would just be the transport. I would lead a team of Altiers on foot. Surveillance indicates constant activity around the old White Hill City Hall structure."

Silence stretched in the room.

"Listen, we cannot stop it, let alone hurt it. We barely even slow it down. Fighting that thing in one-on-one combat is useless. However, it was dormant long enough to be forgotten, and something stirred it back from its slumber. I think Prince Lucan is behind this one way or another."

Kal looked up, but didn't say anything.

"A bee sting to the throat can be deadly," Toren continued. "All we need is to find the right pressure point and squeeze. We can't break it, but maybe we can *disconnect* it. We can remove the power source if a shard powers it, or even redirect it if it's being controlled. I need to get on its back to do that. The *Arcadia* is a beast, but she is not fit for this mission. Can you help me?"

Kal sat with the words for a moment, thinking. It was a gamble, but Kal had never been known to walk away from something just because it had long odds, especially if the payout was right. He had spent most of his life chasing his father's approval. Now, the only thing he chased was credits. Kal had found that those were easier to earn.

"Quadruple what you paid me for the last job… and you settle any debts and clear my bounties."

"How much do you owe the Guild?" Toren asked.

"Two hundred," Kal replied.

"That's it?" Toren asked.

"Plus fifty-three," Kal added.

"Of course." Toren sighed.

"And there may be one or four additional accounts of similar totals."

Toren smiled. He was good for a thousand times that amount. He just liked watching Kal squirm. "I agree on one condition," he finally said.

"What's that?" Kal asked.

"Locke stays here."

Kal surprised even himself when he didn't respond. He just looked at Locke. Locke was dumbfounded for a moment.

Kenzie glanced between the brothers, then cleared her throat. "I think I'll... go explore. Maybe steal some silverware."

"Enjoy the grounds, but leave everything where you find it," Toren said flatly.

Kenzie sighed and threw her arms down. "It was a joke, you stuck-up weirdo."

She put a hand on Locke's shoulder before she slipped out the door. Kal was surprised by how long she let it linger. Kal knew from the second he invited her on the *Days* that she wasn't good at the staying part. She had been a street thief when chance had brought them together. The time before their meeting had forged her into someone always on the run, not thinking of anyone but herself. Yet there she was, acting like she wanted to leave, but leaving an unsure hand to linger. That was who Kenzie was now. Someone whose past self was fighting who she wanted to be. Kal believed some battles were meant to be fought alone.

Her hand lifted, and the tension in the room thickened once she was gone.

Locke met Toren's eyes. "I don't answer to you, and you don't control me. This is my life now."

Toren leaned back and folded his arms. "Your life? How am I supposed to trust you? Do you even trust yourself? You do not seem to remember Seaforth. You have not mentioned what happened to Mom and Dad while we were there. Do you remember that? You do not seem to understand that it's a pretty big deal to be gone for almost four years."

Locke hesitated. "I had a head injury... Seaforth is blurry."

Kal raised an eyebrow at the comment. He often wondered how much Locke remembered.

Toren's eyes hardened while his voice cut through the air like a blade. "Our parents died at Seaforth. We lost you there, too."

Locke flinched. There it was, the unspoken accusation, sharp and unyielding.

Toren exhaled slowly, his tone tightened. "I understand you have an injury, but the fact that you cannot even remember means I have to take care of you. You cannot be trusted to take care of yourself."

"Take care of me? That's rich. Did you even look for me after Seaforth? Did you even care?"

"Locke, losing you for that time almost killed me. I make a million tough decisions every day in this seat, but not knowing what was going on with you was the hardest thing I've ever had to live with. When Kal finally contacted me to say that you were alive and safe, I felt more relief than when I passed the Final Rite." He closed his eyes and rubbed his face. "You do not seem to get it. You never did."

Locke's jaw tightened. "What exactly am I supposed to get, Toren? That I'm just another responsibility to you? That you see me as another problem to solve?"

Toren's expression hardened. "You are my brother. That will always be more than a responsibility. If you want to act like a stray, do not be surprised when people try to put a leash on you."

"Here I thought you were the pet. The one who had everything handed to you. To just naturally be the best and have everyone love you."

"To be responsible!" Toren yelled and stood. He slammed a fist into the desk. "I am sorry you think your life was tough in my shadow, but all everyone showed you was love, and then you ran away because you thought you knew better."

Kal made a face, then slapped his hands on his knees. "Oh, look at the time. It's 'I-gotta-not-be-here-for-this o'clock.'" He stood. "I'm going to find Kenzie. Toren, you have a deal, and you two can work this out between you."

Locke looked at Kal, a little hurt.

"Sorry, Kid, it's just business, and the price is right. We'll pick you up on our way back." He put a firm hand on Locke's shoulder and left the study.

Kal knew what would pass would be important for the brothers, and as much as he liked being a fly on the wall, it didn't feel right to intrude.

He moved down the corridor to find Kenzie staring at a suit of armor. "They used to fight in these?" she asked.

"Aye." Kal nodded and stood next to her. "A millennium ago, before the Crystals changed everything."

"I can't believe Locke's family fought in these. How could you move? Or see?" she asked.

"Slowly and barely," Kal replied, "and Locke's family didn't fight in this. The Luinondos are practically upstarts, along with the royal line. They all came into power four hundred years ago after Iveria fought back against Aurelia. Seven centuries of oppression, and Iveria picked new rulers governed by a new blue Crystal. Does that make sense to you? Ridding yourself of one master just to install another?"

"That's the way of the world, right? Someone is always there to put a crown on," Kenzie scoffed.

"Only when we let them," Kal said and gestured down the hall. "C'mon, I know some places we can get into trouble here. There's a locked door I could never get open."

"Sounds like my wheelhouse," she said. She gave the armor one final look and walked down the hall.

Kal admired Kenzie's ability to roll with the punches. There was something of Val in her, the same fire and grit, but Kenzie's center was softer. It wasn't weakness. It was something quieter, something she kept tucked away where no one could reach it. Kal didn't know how long she'd stay on the *Days*, but he hoped that before she left, she'd let that part of her take its rightful place. That was who she really was.

"You coming?" she called back.

He smiled and followed her down the hall. Kal knew their time together would be short, but time was never the problem. The trick was what they did with it.

CHAPTER 19: LOCKE

3 Days Until Landfall

Toren exhaled and rubbed his temples. For the first time that morning, he looked tired. "I had no idea what happened to you after Seaforth," he said. "I thought you were dead."

Locke swallowed. "Would it have mattered? You still became the First Altier, and I'm still just me."

Toren's jaw clenched. "Of course it would have mattered."

Locke shook his head. "You had your duty, your title. You didn't need me."

"That's not how family works, Locke. I had no one, especially after Mom and Dad passed."

Locke looked away. His chest felt tight. "I am sure I had my reasons."

Toren's gaze softened, just a fraction. "They probably weren't good."

For a moment, neither spoke.

Toren shook his head. "Let us just… have some breakfast. I am sure it is ready by now. Tomorrow, we can discuss the Landfall ceremony. It sounds like you are staying for it. We might as well make it enjoyable."

Locke didn't want to leave it there, but he didn't know what else to say. Toren went to put a hand on Locke's back, but reconsidered mid-motion. He flexed his hand in midair and walked through the study door, leaving Locke standing there. It was like a cork had been unplugged from his chest, and everything he wanted to say to Toren had limply poured out onto the floor. He felt hollow, empty. His disappointment pooled at his feet.

Locke did not know which part stung the most, still letting Toren talk to him like a little brother or being forced to sit out on the mission.

He looked up at the giant painting of his father that hung in the study. Both Locke and Toren had inherited their mother's eyes, but even on canvas, their father's eyes pressed down with the weight of expectation. He looked into them and wondered what his father would think, what he would say. Locke could only guess, but the thought clarified his purpose. He decided he wouldn't let Kal or Toren treat him like a little brother. He would be a part of that mission one way or another. There was no use moping about it.

He pushed past the large doors to the main hall and caught up to Toren on the way to the dining hall. The Luinondo estate had always been impressive, but in the morning light, it buzzed with activity. The polished stone floors carried the echoes of servants moving with purpose. The scent of fresh bread and roasted meat wafted through the halls. Somewhere deeper in the manor, a musician played a gentle tune on a stringed instrument.

Locke had spent his time on the *Days* convincing himself that it wasn't his home anymore. Unfortunately, being there, walking through the familiar halls, and hearing the sounds of an ordered life made it harder to believe.

Toren led him through the house with an ease Locke envied. Everything about him seemed effortless, from his straight posture to how people instinctively moved aside when he walked past. He greeted everyone by name and asked them about their days, families, and lives. He wasn't just a noble. This life fit him like a perfectly tailored coat. He belonged here.

Locke didn't remember most of the faces. He didn't care about their lives. Mostly, he felt like he didn't belong.

"So," Toren said as they entered the family dining hall, "do you remember how this works, or do I need to remind you which end of the fork to use?"

Locke scoffed and rolled his eyes. "I didn't forget how to eat, Toren."

"Good. I was worried your years of spending time with Kal had turned you into some animal."

Locke smirked, but Toren's jab was gentler than before. It was less a criticism and more teasing.

A long oak table stretched before them, covered with a spread of breakfast options: bread, honeyed fruits, smoked meats, eggs cooked in ways Locke had forgotten were possible. Toren took his usual seat just off the head of the table and gestured for Locke to sit across from him. A deliberate choice, the seats from their childhood, one meant to include him.

Kal and Kenzie weren't there. It was just him and Toren. There was no one to deflect or buffer. No excuses. The brothers sat.

Toren waved off a servant and poured them both tea. "Mom would have said you are too thin."

Locke blinked. "You should have seen me when I woke up. I was a string bean."

Toren raised a brow. "The head injury. What do you remember?"

Locke huffed. "Not much. I remember going to Seaforth and getting set up at a guest villa. I remember going for a swim with you before dinner. Then it's blurry. I can't remember past that night, but I have this feeling like I had to escape. Next thing I know, I'm waking up on the *Days*."

Toren exhaled. "When was that?"

"Six months or so ago."

"Picked a hell of a time to come back to us. That was about the time that the monster rose from White Hill. You always had a sense of timing."

Locke stabbed a piece of fruit with his fork. "You always complained about me being late. You and Father."

"Because you were," Toren said simply. "You take after Mother that way."

"Oh, this again? I'm like Mother, and you're like Father?"

"It's in how you carry yourself. The way you talk. How you instinctively placed the napkin on your lap before properly holding the silverware, just like she taught us."

Locke froze and glanced at his hands. The first course fork was in his left hand, and the appropriate knife was held in his right just like she had taught him all those years ago.

Toren took a sip of tea. "You can pretend all you want, but you'll always be a Luinondo."

Locke swallowed thickly. "I'm not so sure that's a good thing."

Toren tilted his head. "Isn't it?" It seemed he didn't expect an answer. He reached for food and put some meat and eggs on his plate.

For a long time, they ate in silence. It wasn't uncomfortable, but Locke felt it. Toren must've too. It was like both of them knew there were things left unsaid.

Finally, Locke sighed. "Why don't you want me to go on this mission?"

Toren set down his cup. "Because you're my brother, and I wouldn't be able to live with myself if anything happened to you."

"You can't protect me from the world."

Toren studied him for a moment before he nodded slightly. "Maybe not, but I do not have to throw you into certain death, either."

Locke stared at him. "I hate how you look down on me."

Toren let out a slow breath. "I don't look down on you." He closed his eyes. "But… I did resent you."

The words landed like a slap. Locke's throat tightened. "Resented me?… why?"

Toren leaned back in his chair and rubbed a hand over his jaw. "Because you were given the best, and you were still pissed off because it was not enough. You always thought life was so unfair. You thought you had it so tough just because you were another cog in the machine instead of *the* cog. So you hated the machine. Then, when we all thought you were dead, it turned out you had the luxury of just leaving. Of disappearing. I could never think that way, to treat others that way."

Locke's fingers clenched around his fork. "You think I wanted to disappear?"

Toren's voice softened. "I think you thought your life would turn out different."

Silence as a wall of years stood between them. Locke wanted to argue, wanted to push back. To tell Toren he was wrong, that he was just a small cog on the *Days*, and he was happy with that life. He tried, but the words wouldn't come. All because, deep down, he knew Toren was right.

Finally, Toren spoke again, quieter. "The day after Seaforth, I had to fly the *Arcadia* back myself and commit the Rites. I was made the First Altier of Breezewaltz. Then I had to fly to Orleans and stand before the Council to assure them our family was still strong, that the Luinondo name still meant something. I spent the next year in Willowbank, at the Crystal Bastion, learning to be an Altier. All the while, I mourned Mother and Father… and you, because I thought you were dead, too."

Locke's stomach twisted. He hadn't thought about that side of things. "I didn't mean for… I wish I could tell you more…"

"I know," Toren exhaled, "but it doesn't change the fact that you left, and I stayed. I was forced to hold it all together. I do not know a better metaphor for who we are than that."

Locke looked away and stared at the golden embroidery on the tablecloth. "I was bitter, even before Seaforth, about this life and us. None of this is for me. I don't belong."

Toren's expression didn't change, but something in his eyes did. "That's the biggest lie you've ever told yourself."

Locke's grip on his fork loosened, and he had to set it down. Since his injury, he'd justified his actions by telling himself Toren didn't need him. That no one back home did. He had found his new family on board the *Days*. Hearing Toren say outright that Locke belonged in Breezewaltz, it cut through all of Locke's carefully built walls.

Toren sighed and rubbed his temple again. "You are here now, and I would rather make the most of that than waste time arguing or being angry with each other."

Locke swallowed. "You're angry?"

Toren's lips twitched. "I did not say that."

A beat of silence. Then Locke chuckled and scooped some egg into his mouth. "I forgot how much of a pain you are."

Toren smirked. "The feeling is mutual, but I never forgot that."

They sat in silence for a beat before Toren spoke up again. "And I missed you, too, little brother."

It would not be a short journey to mend whatever divisions had developed between them, but it was the first small step. Not two people tiptoeing around old wounds, but brothers who genuinely cared about each other.

It was then that the hidden door set into the back wall popped open, and Kenzie fell through, followed by Kal. "You scared me half to death!" she yelled from the floor as Kal stepped over the bottom paneling.

"I told you to watch your feet."

"How does that help me when the whole room spins?" Kenzie asked and got to her feet.

"Oh, look, breakfast." Kal strode over. "Not waiting for your guests is bad manners, you know." He placed a hand on the chair at the head of the table, but moved past it when Toren shot him a look. He took a seat next to Locke.

"I thought I heard vermin in the walls," Toren said and put some more fruit on his plate.

"Well, my intrepid protégée here thought she felt a draft coming through the wall. I told her all these houses have emergency routing. When I proved it, she got mad at me."

"You tricked me!" Kenzie huffed as she sat down.

"And whose fault is that? The trickster or the trickee?" Kal responded as he loaded up his plate.

"That's not a word," Kenzie said and filled her plate.

"Kal, have you talked to Val since we have been here?" Toren asked.

"She knew the second I got out. I swear, if I have to hear one more time about perfect 'Situational Awareness,' I'm going to steal a second ship." He took a bite of crispy bacon. "But yes, I sent her a message thanking her for the muscle, and told her I would book us a weekend in Somerset. She was unimpressed."

"She will never change," Toren said as he took another bite.

"How did those two get together?" Kenzie asked.

"Oh, that's a good question. I honestly cannot remember. We were always inseparable, and then it just happened. Kal was a tomcat at the Citadel, and I think Val eventually just got so annoyed she kissed him. The rest has been a storybook ever since." Toren carried a sincere smile.

"Not quite, Tor," Kal responded. "Val and I have been separated for a few years now."

Toren looked at him quizzically. "But she's still on the ship. She's your second in command?"

"Yep, the *Days* is our baby. We couldn't decide who got her. Besides, I think she's just playing hardball, trying to win an argument."

"For a few years?" Kenzie asked.

"It was a bad argument." Kal looked around the table at the confused faces.

"Kal, I know you can convince yourself of anything, but even you have to hear how stupid that sounds," Toren said between bites.

"It's obvious I'm the only one here who has ever been married." Kal put a piece of fruit in his mouth. "She's still crazy about me. We'll figure it out someday."

The other three laughed. Kal shrugged and kept eating.

"What about you, Kenzie? What is your story? Are you from around here?" Toren asked.

"No, no, I'm from out east. Uh, Seaforth, actually, but I would prefer not to talk about that." Kenzie kept her tone flat, as she had practiced, but her fork paused midair. She didn't offer more, and thankfully, no one pressed her.

"I can respect that," Toren replied, "and how long have you been following this miscreant around?"

"Five months or so," Kenzie said in between bites.

"Interesting timing. What was the world doing before six months ago? It seems like it suddenly turned on, and all the interesting things happened at once," Toren said and winked at Locke. "How are you liking the *Days*? She is a fine ship, huh?"

"She's amazing, like nothing I've ever seen. You command the Arcadia?"

"Yes, ma'am. The best damn Capital skyship in the Armada. Even better than the Orleander and the royal so-and-sos that fly her."

"How many Capital skyships are there?" Kenzie asked.

"Oh, here we go." Kal pretended to fall asleep with his head tilted back.

Toren threw a roll at him. Kal caught it mid-air without opening his eyes and took a bite, grinning.

"Twelve," Toren said, turning back to Kenzie. "One for each city-state of the League. Breezewaltz has the Arcadia, the King flies the Orleander out of Orleans. We're down a couple since the crisis in the south started."

He paused, something dark crossing his face before he recovered. "Each district has a First Altier, like me. We sit on the Council with the King, handle defense, oversee Azure distribution."

"Why isn't Orleans the first district?" Kenzie asked. "I'd think where the King sits would be."

"Breezewaltz is where we found the Azure Crystal." Toren poured more coffee. "This is where the rebellion started. The King's family came from here originally, founded Orleans as the capital after independence."

"So Landfall celebrates your freedom?"

"Close. It celebrates the day the Azure Crystal fell from the heavens. Our ancestors discovered it, harnessed its power, won our freedom from Aurelia. Religious and state holiday rolled into one."

Toren glanced at Kal, then back at Kenzie. "Is this your first Landfall?"

Kal looked exposed for a moment. "I assumed she knew. Sue me." His mouth was full, making him sound ridiculous.

Kenzie smiled. "So you're like a warrior, priest, and politician rolled into one?"

"I wear a lot of hats, yes," Toren said warmly.

"I keep telling people in this town that roles are not mutually exclusive," Kal interjected. No one seemed to understand what he was talking about, and Kal didn't explain further.

Kenzie set down her fork. "What about the people outside the cities? The ones your Capital ships can't protect?"

Toren's expression hardened. "They risk raids. Aurelia targets farms, small towns. We do what we can, but..." He shook his head. "We're not everywhere at once."

"Some dream," Kenzie muttered.

"It's better than the alternative." Toren's voice was quiet. "Seven centuries of slavery under Aurelia. We're not perfect, but we're free."

Kal whistled and wiped his mouth with his napkin. "Way to bring the mood down, Tor. I think that's enough history for one day." He stood. "I need to stretch my legs. Who's coming with me?"

Locke was surprised that everyone agreed, and the meal concluded. Locke sarcastically chalked it up in his mind to the unifying power of Kal.

After breakfast, they walked the grounds. It was something Toren and Locke used to do as children. They strolled through the blooming gardens, the polished courtyards, and the training fields where they had once sparred with wooden swords. Toren said he had about an hour before his first appointment of the day, and then he would be gone until late evening.

Kal and Kenzie wandered to the edge of the property to see the incoming skyships. Practically all used Aurelian engines. The skyships were close enough to the mesa that Kal and Kenzie could witness their engineering in flight. Each pointed out interesting designs as they flew overhead. Kenzie seemed to like the massive propellers that moved the ships through the sky.

At the edge of the estate, near the family's gondola, Toren paused beside a stone balcony overlooking the lower city. "This is where Father used to bring us," Toren said quietly. "To remind us of our responsibilities to these people."

Locke leaned against the railing and looked down. Six of Breezewaltz's sectors stretched out before them, vibrant and alive, a city that had thrived despite the centuries of war. The Luinondo line had protected it from the beginning.

"You still believe in all of that?" Locke asked. "Responsibility? Duty? Can we protect these people?"

Toren exhaled. "Yes, all that is important, but the most important thing is family. Like Mother always taught us, family first. This city is my family, and I will protect it. Just like I will protect you."

Something about Toren's words pulled at a memory Locke couldn't quite grasp. One from before Seaforth. Locke let it go and recentered in the moment. He didn't have an answer for Toren's sentiment. For a long moment, they stood and looked out at the city they both loved.

Then Toren clapped a hand on Locke's shoulder. "Come on. Landfall starts in three days. I have some meetings today and tomorrow, but you three will be my guests for the ceremonies. Maybe we can get Val up here if I allow the *Days* to park on the lawn. It should be a memorable day." He started back to the house. He put an arm around Kal, and Kenzie fell back in behind them.

Locke looked at the city one more time, then turned back to the house. "And then? What happens after that?"

Toren looked back with an arm still around Kal's shoulder. He smiled and looked at Kal. "And then Kal and I will put down a walking god."

CHAPTER 20: LUCAN

2 Days Until Landfall

It had been over a day of planning and Lucan kept reminding himself that perfection took patience, sometimes. The *Fury* was dark beneath them. The red glow of the shardshot impacts from the Aurelian fighters was the only thing that illuminated the hull. The battle was long over, and his crew used the husk as target practice. It was almost pitiful, a broken machine surrounded by scorched *gaia*.

The transport skyship that housed the heavy shard had pulled up as close to the creature's chest as possible, but the final few meters required a human's touch for final placement. Luckily, Crystals always floated, but seeing one that size hover in the air never stopped feeling like blasphemy against the natural order.

Lucan stood just outside the skyship's bridge and gazed at the heavy shard that loomed before them. Beyond that, the Colossus's blue crystalline chest had a wide opening that waited to be fed. Syd had discarded the previously spent heavy shard. It now lay as an inert chunk of dark blue crystal on the gaia below.

The doctor's crew had created a housing that would allow the undersized heavy shard to interact with the Colossus and allow it to tap the shard's energy.

The Colossus kneeled in its dormant state, which meant the skyship was only halfway to the clouds. Though inert at the moment, the promised danger of the creature was palpable.

Dr. Syd adjusted his gloves. He wore a full-body suit to protect himself. Azure shards, especially heavy shards, speared humans with tendrils of blue lightning. As Dr. Syd had reminded his crew, being pierced in that manner tended to be fatal. Protection was necessary at all times. Syd stepped forward toward the enormous slab of glowing azure. His expression was unreadable, but his hands moved with precision as he inspected the heavy shard for any cracks or damage.

"The integrity held," Syd murmured, more to himself than to the comm channel. "I was concerned you barbarians would damage it in that assault, but fortune has smiled upon us."

Lucan folded his arms. Fortune was not a deity. It was an aspect of the Rose Crystal he worshipped. Even then, fortune only appeared to those who pulled it out of the shadows.

His crimson cloak shifted in the cold night breeze. He spoke into his comm. "You are welcome, Doctor. Now, enough stalling. I want it in place tonight. You have wasted too much time already."

Lucan felt like he could hear Dr. Syd's lips curl into amusement behind the protective hood he wore. "Patience, Prince Lucan. You'll have your war machine soon enough."

Syd turned to the gathered engineers, his own handpicked cadre of technocrats. They were men and women who had abandoned the decaying halls of Belfield's Conchordia Institute to work under him. They were his thralls, and they respected his genius above all else. At his command, they moved quickly and used insulated machinery to guide the heavy shard's form through the bay to the chest cavity.

As the shard lifted off the cargo runway, a deep hum resonated through the air and vibrated the steel beneath their feet. Lucan exhaled slowly. His blood also thrummed with anticipation. They had come too far for failure. He had always known the moment would come. From his first lessons beneath the Rose Crystal's glow, he had felt its call. This was not just a conquest. This was a communion.

A heavy shard of the Azure Crystal stood before him, subjugated. A fragment of a weak god. One who would be brought to heel shortly.

He smiled and thought about how half the world had lost its faith. He imagined himself as the chosen hand that would restore it to its rightful devotion under the Rose Crystal.

"The shard should interface smoothly," Syd said and watched as the team maneuvered the massive shard into the waiting socket. "Plenty of room."

Syd was right. The heavy shard, massive as it was, was dwarfed by the vast cavity it was set into. It was as if something larger was meant for the space.

The engineers began final connections the moment they pushed the shard into place. When the last bond was set, Syd flipped the switch, and the shard glowed and thrummed while the Colossus shuddered. Its massive body trembled, and the sound of grinding joints and shifting plates reverberated through the valley.

Lucan grinned.

Then, a ripple of energy surged through the Colossus's frame. Its veins of crystal flared a deep blue, and pulses of power raced along its limbs like the awakened nerves.

"It's responding," Syd muttered as his eyes flicked between his diagnostics. "Just as I suspected."

Lucan stepped closer to the overhead railing and rested a gloved hand against the cool metal. The air shook as the Colossus came back to life, the raw, unfiltered power of something far greater than a million men.

His heart surged with quiet awe. The Colossus was more than a weapon. After all, it was the child of a god. A flawed, misguided god, but one all the same. The Rose Crystal had chosen him alone to wield it against the blind and misguided. Heresy was punishable by death, and in Iveria, Lucan found plenty to fit that sentence.

Syd tapped a few buttons on his control panel, his gaze sharpened. "Something curious…" he muttered.

Lucan turned his head sharply. "What?"

"There continue to be two control signals whenever we reawaken the creature," Syd said and frowned at the readings. "Two distinct sources of influence. One of them leads it to Breezewaltz, which we anticipated." His fingers tapped across the controls, analyzing the data stream. "But the second signal," he continued, "is something else. Something… northwest of here."

Lucan's brow furrowed. "Northwest? What's out there?"

Syd's eyes gleamed with a dangerous curiosity. "You would tell me if you knew, right?"

He didn't direct the question at Lucan. Syd looked into thin air. Eventually, he shook his head. "No, it doesn't matter. It's been a boon so far. The second signal is the one I've hijacked to point the creature toward Heydon and Huntley. Once the creature completes its objective at Breezewaltz, we'll bend it north to Orleans."

Lucan's pulse quickened. "To Orleans."

Syd nodded. "Yes. If this works, I won't have to worry about power again. I can march the Colossus straight to the King's doorstep."

Lucan's lips curled into a smile. "Then it better work."

The massive god rose from its kneeling position, its plates ground as it stood at full height and towered over the ruins of *Heydon's Fury*. Each step sent tremors through the gaia and caused boulders and loose bits of rock to fall from nearby mountains and cliffs.

A maniacal smile pulled across Syd's face. Sweat formed on his brow, but his expression was triumphant. He stood alone. His team had pulled back to the seats in the personnel room, closer to the bridge.

"Yes, this one will work. We did it, ladies, we did it!" Syd screamed, even though no one else was in the room.

Lucan turned and moved back to the control bridge. He took a seat behind the controls. He did not want to be floating there when the creature moved in earnest.

The only response was the hum of the Colossus and the gaia trembling beneath them.

Lucan steered the cargo ship around, back to the base they had established on the creature's back. "Then let's see how long Breezewaltz stands when their god comes knocking."

The Colossus marched. A massive foot crushed the *Fury* as it walked.

Unlike Lucan, Breezewaltz had no idea what was coming.

CHAPTER 21: LOCKE

Landfall

The city was alive. Orleans was the head, but Breezewaltz was the heart of the Iverian League. It pulsed with the joy of its people, the bedrock of the free world bathed in shimmering blue lanterns and golden banners. The grand bazaar of the Upper Mesa stretched across the streets, the scent of roasted meats, spiced wines, and sugared almonds thick in the air. Music played from every corner, strings and drums wove together in an anthem of celebration.

Landfall was in motion.

The crew of the *Days* had posted up on Toren's viewing platform. It offered a pristine view of the upcoming ceremony and had everything the crew could ask for: food, drinks, and space to enjoy it all. Below them, a stage had been set up, and a band played well-known tunes as street performers dazzled the crowds.

The crew made their way from the Luinondo manor, where Toren had granted them an absurdly generous landing zone via his well-manicured lawn. His landscaper would be furious in the morning.

The *Days* had relocated two days ago. The moment she spotted him, Val pulled Toren into a tight hug. The way they looked at each other spoke about their friendship almost as much as the hug did. It told Locke everything he needed to know. Their fights and fences mended. Late nights and early mornings as cadets. They stood together for nearly half an hour on the lawn, catching up and laughing easily. Their body language conveyed an old, unbroken bond. Locke kept his distance and let them have their moment.

The next two days flew by in a blur of camaraderie and revelry. Locke was exhausted, but he enjoyed letting the crew see that part of him. He thought he'd need a week to recover, and that was before the sun had set the evening of Landfall. That's when the festival *really* started.

Locke stood amid the crowd, and the warmth of it washed over him. He let the past drift further into memory. For the first time since returning, he didn't feel like a runaway, a failure, or a man searching for his place. He was home, even if only for a night.

Toren stepped up beside him, dressed in the fine blues and silver of an Altier's festival robes. Unlike the rigid leader Locke had first encountered, his shoulders were relaxed and his expression lighter. The burdens of command had not disappeared, but at least for the night, Toren was closer to being his brother than First Altier Luinondo.

"The city looks good," Locke admitted and watched the lanterns sway in the warm evening breeze. He had many memories of the Upper Mesa, but seeing it decked out for Landfall always floored him.

Toren took a sip from his goblet. The glow of festival fires reflected on the wine's surface. "I am not going to take credit for the decorations, but I will say thank you, nonetheless."

Locke smirked. "Shame they didn't put up a statue of you yet."

Toren gave him a side glance. "Give it time." They both laughed.

Locke was surprised by how the banter between them felt natural. Not strained or forced. Just brothers talking, as if the war, the Colossus, and the lost years between them didn't exist.

"It's good to be home, even if it's not under the best circumstances."

"It is good to have you home, little brother. Know that you will always be welcomed here."

Locke hesitated and turned his goblet in his hands. The warmth of the festival had lowered his guard, and in its glow, it felt like they were just brothers again. Maybe it was foolish to break that moment, but he had to try.

"Toren, can we talk about the mission with…"

Toren cut him off. "Locke, you know I would not have kept you out if there had been another way. It is not that I do not believe in you, but this mission is so dangerous that it is beyond reckless. Besides, I did not think you were the type to throw yourself into something like this. You were always so careful as a kid."

"You ask too much of me, Toren. You know I can't just stand by while you and the *Days* are in danger."

Toren looked at his brother for a long time. Locke felt he was really taking in the man behind the eyes they shared. Then, finally, he came to a conclusion. "Fine, let us discuss tomorrow. I am not saying yes, but I understand…"

"First Altier Luinondo," the voice cut through the music like a blade.

Locke felt his spine straighten instinctively. He touched his cheek, a memory of Aldis slapping him for breaking fast came to his mind. It was hazy, but it was from before his memory gap. Locke tried to remember it further, but the train of thought was broken by Toren's voice.

"High Priest Aldis," Toren said, bowing and extending a hand.

Locke had been a teenager when they had last spoken. At the time, he was best described as pissed off but obedient. He was also a naive boy who still believed the Azure Crystal watched over him at all times. Even with all the injustice in the world and especially in Breezewaltz, he had believed that his family's place in the world was preordained. He had repeated eleven of the twelve rites beside his brother, whispered prayers under the stone arches of the Temple, hoping the words would bloom in his heart. They had taken root, but never sprouted much more beyond that.

The high priest stepped up to the brothers, the bells on his robes whispering against the polished stone floor. He glanced at the motley crew assembled, and his gaze hardened.

"Friends of yours, Locke?"

Locke was surprised Aldis had remembered him.

"My brother runs in interesting circles. We will have to bring him back to the light after Landfall," Toren said and smiled at Locke.

Aldis's eyes returned to Locke, and he gave him a large smile. "I did not expect to find you here," Aldis said and folded his hands into his sleeves. "I think I'm one of the few here in Breezewaltz to know who you really are."

Locke felt his jaw tighten. "Meaning?" he asked.

"Meaning to everyone else, Locke Luinondo is either riding against the wind or dead. Tonight, my child, you are still anonymous." He clasped a hand on Toren's shoulder. "That won't be the case once we make our announcement later tonight." He spread his palms. "The return of the wayward son for Landfall. I think that will make a good centerpiece for my midnight ceremony. Both of you will be there, right?"

Toren forced a chuckle. "No need to twist our arms. We will be in the first row." He winked at Locke.

Aldis nodded and turned to Locke. "You have a duty to your family, to this city, and to the Crystal itself. You may play the rogue," his eyes wandered to Kal, who was dramatically pouring a drink into his mouth, "but the blood of the greatest house of Altiers runs through your veins. It would be wise not to forget that."

Locke felt his pulse quicken. "I haven't forgotten."

Aldis leaned into Locke. "That's not what I hear." He stood and nodded at Toren.

With that, the high priest turned, his robes whispered against the stone as he swept away. His presence left a cold void in his wake. Locke released the breath he hadn't realized he held.

"What did he say to you?" Toren asked.

"What? Sorry?" Locke said and took a deep breath.

"What did Aldis say to you before he left?"

"Something about saying my prayers."

Toren eyed him suspiciously, but before he could press, one of his officers walked up and whispered in Toren's ear.

"Marling?" He paused to consider something. "Give me a full report after the ceremony. *Daybreaker* and *Belepoch* are still inbound?"

The officer nodded.

"Any other reports?"

"Nothing on the Crystalline or comms per the King's direction. Long-range sensors have lost tracking. No other ships of the line are available to report."

Toren's jaw tightened. He spoke, mostly to himself. "Marling had been ordered to watch, not engage. We're flying blind now." He weighed his options in silence. "Reach out to the Shipping Guild, see if they've seen anything along their lines. Dismissed."

The officer saluted and walked away. Toren looked off into the night.

"Everything alright?" Locke asked.

"There have been developments to the south. Nothing to be done at the moment, but the *Arcadia* and the *Days* need to move toward Huntley tonight." He checked his watch. "I want to tell you more, but the priests expect me. We can discuss this later, but I make no promises about whether that means you will be with us en route. There's more we should discuss about what happened after Seaforth. Hopefully, this will be a quick ceremony."

"Not if High Priest Aldis is running it," Locke said and smirked as he recalled his three-hour Rite of Affirmation. The memory made him shake his head, but underneath the humor, relief settled in. Toren had not committed to letting him take part in the mission, but at least he considered it. That was better than no chance at all. "Good luck," Locke finished.

"Don't need it, at least, not tonight," Toren said and turned to leave.

Locke nodded and watched his brother walk away. The short time they'd shared had done more than he expected to bridge the divide, or maybe the bridge had never been burned at all. It could have been made of stronger stuff than he realized and still stood after all this time, just unused and forgotten.

So why, then, was the unease creeping back in?

He pushed it away, looking out to the incredible festival before him.

Locke walked across the platform where Kal stood among the crew of the *Days*. The captain laughed too loudly, drank too freely, and told stories far too exaggerated to be believed. Locke moved into the group to hear the end of whatever story this was.

"Picture it, three Guild skyships closing in from all directions. The canyon walls herding us toward death, and me in the cockpit with one shot before we're torn to shreds," Kal shouted to the assembled members of the *Days*.

"Kal, we were there," Tia yelled, laughing.

"I know, I know, but the best part was when I cut the engines just as their shardshot cannons started firing," Kal yelled. "And Avery says to me, he says, 'What are you doing?'" He continued and brandished his cup. "And there we were, plummeting to Gaia with shardshot flying past, and all I could do was look at Avery and say, 'I don't have a name for it. It's just falling with style.'"

The gathered revelers erupted in laughter, some clapped him on the back, and others raised their cups in cheer. Next to Locke, Val watched with the practiced patience of someone who had seen the performance a thousand times before.

"You're watching him like you are deciding whether to throw him off the platform or yourself," Kenzie mused beside her as she walked up to the XO. The co-pilot watched Kal with a playful smile.

"It's a dumb story." Val huffed, arms crossed, but made no move to get away from it.

Kal must have felt her gaze because he turned and flashed her a wolfish grin. "Well, well," he drawled, weaving his way through the crowd. "If it isn't the Executive Officer herself."

Kenzie excused herself, not wanting to cringe through whatever the exchange was about to be. Locke stood off to the side.

"XO of putting up with your BS," Val corrected.

Kal narrowed his eyes and smiled. "That doesn't sound like a real position. Who appointed you? Was he better looking than me?"

"It is the *Days*, Kal. Our positions are as real as your humility." She sighed, then muttered, "And unfortunately, you probably are the best-looking one here. That's exactly what's ruining my night."

Kal faked another shot to the heart and put a hand over his chest. He swooned into Val, who didn't move. He grinned, smug as ever.

Val shook her head.

"Who'd you put on watch?" Kal asked.

"The twins."

"So… no one's watching the ship," Kal said, standing back up.

"They're *capable*," Val muttered, though Kal's smirk told her he wasn't convinced.

He swirled his drink and watched the firelight catch in the liquid. "Are you going to ask me about the next twenty-four hours?"

"Are you going to answer?"

"Tell you what, since you're so beautiful and I'm on a bit of a winning streak, I feel confident about this offer. Trade you a status update for a kiss."

Val sighed and rubbed her temple. "Kal, can't you just *talk* to me? Why is everything a game to you?"

"Part of my roguish charm." Kal gave her a slow, knowing smile. "Fine, I'll tell you, but you're buying the information on credit…with interest. We leave tomorrow, and Toren is coming with us. He's already paid, so we won't have to worry about credits for a while. Everyone will be ready at dawn. Until then, I'm here talking to the prettiest woman at the festival. I'd say Landfall is going damn well."

Val sighed. "I hate that your boyish tricks work on me."

Kal grinned. "I know."

"Where are the other children?"

"Locke and Kenzie? Reveling, hopefully," Kal replied.

Locke took that as his cue to leave before their attention fell on him. He wondered where Kenzie had gone. He moved to the edge of the platform and eventually caught sight of her standing just off the festival square, outside the golden glow of the lanterns. She had her arms crossed and watched a group of acrobats spin fire through the air. The flames reflected in her hazel eyes and cast flickering light across her face, but her expression was unreadable. If anything, she looked like she was hiding how she truly felt.

Locke had noticed that about her before. The way she hovered at the edges of moments, never fully in or out. It was one of the things that fascinated him. The way she always seemed a step removed from the world around her, like she kept her distance from something only she understood.

The big band finished their set and took a break. Three players stayed on stage and continued to play softer, slower music.

Locke picked up two drinks and meandered through the crowd until he made his way next to Kenzie. The acrobats collected applause and credits in open-mouthed hats, but Kenzie remained unimpressed as Locke approached.

He extended a drink to her. "They're talented," Locke said.

"I had a dog that did better tricks, and she had three legs," Kenzie said and didn't reach for the second drink.

"Must have been well trained," Locke said. He retracted his hand and held both drinks close to his chest. He took a long pull of one and hoped it would provide some instant courage. "You don't seem to be having fun."

"It's nothing. The fire dancers just reminded me of something sour. They put me in a sour mood. Don't let it ruin your night. Go back with the crew. I'll be fine soon, I promise," Kenzie said and looked down.

"Sure, I'm here if you want to talk about it," he said. "Otherwise, can you save a spot on your dance card for me later, if you're in the mood?" His voice was steadier than he expected. Maybe the drink was more potent than he realized.

Kenzie turned. Her brow arched in that way that always unraveled him a little. "What makes you think I dance?"

Locke tilted his head and smiled even as his stomach knotted. "What makes you think you have a choice? Do you know who my family is? We're a big deal around here…"

For a beat, she just stared at him.

"That was a joke," Locke said, smiling into his drink.

Kenzie exhaled sharply, then took the drink from Locke's hand. One gulp, then she set the glass down upside down. Without a word, she grabbed his hand and led him to the dance floor.

Locke hastily poured the drink into his mouth and swallowed. He set the glass down on a passing table. He was very aware of how delicate her fingers felt in his palm. She led him onto the festival square and wove through the crowd of swaying couples, and despite his mild protests, she stopped in the middle of the floor.

The band still played a slow, winding waltz. It was the kind of dance Locke had memorized as a child, and now it was muscle memory. Unfortunately, Kenzie wasn't like the partners he had danced with before. She wasn't soft-spoken nobility. She wasn't trying to impress him or gain favor with his family.

She watched him. Her head tilted slightly. She waited, amused, to see what he would do next. Their hands were still joined from the journey to the dance floor, so he placed his other hand lightly on her waist. He couldn't help but notice how her lips quirked.

"Careful, Locke," she murmured. "I might start thinking you've done this before. Wouldn't want me to get jealous of one of these rich girls, now, would we?"

His mouth parched instantly. The flirty banter was almost too much. Locke wasn't sure he could play this game. Not only was he a novice in the field, but Kenzie felt like a master. She was able to twist him like it was nothing. The only thing that usually saved him was that Kenzie never played with him like this on the *Days*. Landfall, apparently, was different.

Locke cleared his throat and forced himself to look somewhere other than her mouth. "I have, actually. Years ago. The number of balls they throw up here is insane."

Kenzie hummed, as if she only half believed him.

They moved, slow and easy. Locke led, expecting her to follow awkwardly. It was an old Breezewaltz tune few knew outside of the wealthy circles. The steps weren't intuitive, and the rhythm was slightly off, but she matched him effortlessly, as if she had danced the steps her entire life.

Locke observed her grace, and he remembered how she had successfully navigated the Beggars Trail with him. He had taken her athleticism for granted due to exhaustion at that moment. He looked down at her, eyes narrowed. "You have done this before?"

Kenzie smirked. "What makes you think that?"

Locke exhaled sharply. "Because no one's this good on instinct."

Her fingers tightened around his, but her voice stayed light. "I had a life before the *Days*, too, Locke. Or maybe I'm better than you think. Could just be a fast learner."

Something about the way she said it, the way she looked at him, made his heart do something stupid and undignified in his chest. His heart was leading him down a fraught path, and his brain screamed at full volume to turn back. Locke knew, even before they had entered the dance floor, that his heart had already won. He regretted trying to drown the sensible part of him with that swill.

She smiled and twirled. She let him lead, but was still very much in control. As he watched her move like a practiced dancer, he realized he liked her too much. He liked her in a way that made him second-guess every word that left his mouth. That made him want to impress her, which was ridiculous because Kenzie wasn't a girl who was impressed by anything.

And yet, there they were. She danced with him while the serene Landfall music floated on the breeze. The lanterns above cast soft light over her face. Their bodies pressed together as they moved through the steps, and she did not pull away.

The intimacy of it all was a double-edged sword. His body felt electric, but also extremely uncomfortable. Toren would have probably been okay in a similar situation, dancing and smiling until his partner melted into his arms. Locke was not Toren, on many levels, and the situation brought that contrast into focus. He had to say something, anything, to break the moment before it became something he couldn't handle.

"Breezewaltz isn't so bad, is it?" he asked.

Kenzie gave him a look, as if she tried to decide what response would fluster him the most. Then she leaned in, just slightly, just enough that her lips nearly brushed his ear. "I could see myself settling down here..." she whispered.

Locke forgot how to breathe.

"And robbing you blind," she finished her sentence, and her breath brushed past Locke's ear.

He missed a whole step, tripped over himself, and almost took Kenzie down with him. Kenzie laughed and pulled him back to his feet just in time to see that his face and ears had gone full red.

Her smile widened as she admired the deepening color. "A little embarrassed from the fall?"

"Yeah, the fall." Locke looked around. "Didn't mean to put on a show like that." He dusted himself off, and Kenzie giggled. Locke's hope of an anonymous trip was quickly dashed when he saw the crew on the viewing platform laughing at his missteps. Cookie looked like she had tears in her eyes. They had collectively watched the dance.

"And for my next trick…" Locke called up and brushed imaginary dust from his sleeve like it had all been planned.

"Let them laugh, Locke. It's a brave man who dances with two left feet. You did your ancestors proud tonight." Her smile was still firmly attached. "And I had fun."

He could tell she hadn't meant to say that last part, at least not like that. The words had slipped out too quickly, like they had waited for her to stop guarding them. Locke wondered if the crew of the *Days* had gotten under her skin and made her soft in ways she didn't fully understand.

Locke had no response because she was right. There was nothing he could add to make the moment better. Perfection only seemed to exist in the seconds between words.

The horns sounded to indicate that the final ceremony would commence. Locke and Kenzie made their way back to the viewing platform to join the crew. They gave him some grins and laughed, more with him than at him, which was nice. Jules and Tia made room for Locke and Kenzie to view the ceremony.

Their view was amazing for the spectacle that was about to begin.

Landfall's climax took place at the center of the Grand Lake, the heart of Breezewaltz. The stunning Temple of the Azure was built on top of the water, just offset from the lake's center. There was a solitary footpath that extended from the southern shore to the temple entrance. The path split into a circle at the center of the lake, then rejoined and continued to the temple.

Thousands of nobles and wealthy pilgrims gathered in hushed reverence around the edge of the lake as the high priests stepped forward, led by Toren. Their ceremonial robes cascaded like flowing ink. Typically, the ceremony would feature multiple First Altiers, maybe even the King, but not that year.

A deep resonance filled the air, a sound felt more than heard.

Once the procession reached the circular portion of the footpath, the priests and Toren spread out equally along the rounded path. The lake's surface under the footpath glowed, and then slowly, something rose from the depths.

A spire of the Azure Crystal, jagged and massive, ascended toward the heavens. The water parted around it, as if afraid to make contact. Its edges pulsed with raw, untouched power. Each flicker was like the slow, rhythmic heartbeat of something alive.

The only thing that kept the Crystal tethered to Gaia was the massive chains that bound it to an anchor far below the water's surface. As it rose, lightning cracked from its core and streaked across the sky in brilliant arcs of blue. The bolts struck the clouds and sent ripples of light cascading over the entire mesa. The sound was deafening, and the air itself tasted different. It was charged, potent, and alive.

The Crystal did not glow like fire, nor hum like machinery. It resonated. Its pale blue light pulsed in waves, all-consuming yet strangely soft, as if it breathed in time with something unseen. Looking at it for too long felt like staring into an unblinking eye, something that saw but did not acknowledge. Even with one's back turned, its presence lingered and pressed at the edges of thought.

The priests danced as lightning struck around them. Their robes, which were woven from materials that were both ornamental and practical, protected them from the deadly bolts. That was the way of Breezewaltz, a city that worshiped the Azure Crystal in form, faith, and spectacle.

The crowd roiled in jubilation. Voices rose in joy, worship, and celebration. The Crystal climbed higher and higher. High enough that even the crowds in the lower city could see it. It was the moment they had waited for, the moment they could witness a miracle with their own eyes.

Some in the crowd swore they heard whispers, faint and impossible to pinpoint.

Locke watched the Crystal rise, its pale blue light cast shadows across the city he had once called home. The sight should have stirred something in him, some deep, ancient reverence. The way it had been for his brother, for his parents, and for the generations of Altiers who had come before him. Instead, as the Crystal's lightning arced across the sky and painted the mesa in ghostly blues and silvers, Locke felt only the pressure of expectation. He thought of the hollow echo of words he had whispered his whole life, but never believed. If the Crystal truly watched over its chosen, if it truly called and blessed those it deemed worthy, then why was the lower city a cesspool of poverty and corruption? Why were the lives of families being destroyed in the South? Why had his parents died protecting Iveria's borders?

Locke felt the fires of Seaforth in his memories. Then nothing but darkness, lost in screams.

Kenzie's hand brushed his, a brief, grounding touch, and the emptiness receded. He glanced at her, the light of the Crystal reflected in her hazel eyes. He wondered if she had ever believed in anything the way his family had. The way his father had wanted him to. He wondered if it mattered, or if faith was just another word for choice. Maybe faith was the stubborn refusal to turn back, even when every instinct told you to turn away. He looked back at the floating Crystal.

It was beautiful. In the way, a storm on the horizon was beautiful. A warning and a wonder. A promise and a threat.

Fireworks exploded above the city. Bursts of blue, gold, and silver reflected off the lake. It was magic, maybe even perfect.

Subtly, through the cacophony of noise, the sounds from the lower city had shifted slightly. A dark presence moved through the night sky toward the Upper Mesa, and the cheering on the Upper Mesa moved to cries of confusion.

Locke felt it before he saw it. The whoops and yelling turned into something shriller before they evolved into a terrible, crushing stillness. The only sounds were the exploding fireworks and a steady, rhythmic boom like massive war drums. The air felt too heavy. It was a sensation that made his skin crawl, and he couldn't understand why.

The fireworks continued unabated, like nothing would stop them. It was then that the fireworks illuminated the face. The horrific face that would haunt Locke for the rest of his life.

Beyond the Grand Lake, beyond the Temple, past the edge of the Upper Mesa stood the Colossus as it stared at the Crystal suspended in midair. Towering and silent, it looked hungry.

Its skin shone blue against the fireworks, and the light reflected off the blue crystalline plates. Its massive blue eyes stared down at the city, a horrific, toothy smile permanently etched on its face.

Locke's breath caught in his throat. All of Breezewaltz froze, and for a single, terrifying heartbeat, no one moved. Then the Colossus lunged for the Crystal, and in a single voice, the city screamed.

CHAPTER 22: KENZIE

Landfall

The city collapsed into terror. Breezewaltz had become a single, deafening roar of screams and panic. Kenzie watched people trample each other in their rush to flee while confetti still drifted through the air, untouched by the bedlam. Skyships moored at both the Upper Mesa and lower city lifted off as fast as their engines could raise them into the air.

The Colossus's massive fingers closed around the Azure Crystal, wrenching it from the sky. Its chains snapped like thread. The sound cut through everything else.

Toren was already running. Kenzie could barely make out his figure as he tore down the walkway toward the temple, his festival robes discarded mid-stride to reveal his Armada blues underneath. Around him, four Altiers scrambled into formation. Kenzie wasn't sure if they were also from great houses, like Toren, but she assumed they were his personal guard. The five figures leaped with unnatural agility, scaled the temple, and reached the Colossus's extended right arm.

On the platform, Kal and Val were shouting orders to the *Days'* crew. They had wasted no time.

Val's fingers strained as she gripped Kal's arm hard enough to leave marks. "Get us out of this, Kal."

Kal nodded, serious for once. That scared Kenzie almost as much as the Colossus. "Hail the twins. We're falling back to the estate. We'll take off the second we get there. You're on point."

Val nodded and waved the crew back toward the manor.

"Kenzie, Locke, c'mon, we have to get out of here," Kal shouted over the din.

Kenzie looked at Locke. His eyes locked on Toren and the blue glow of his team, specks against the Colossus's massive forearm. Their radiance was stark against the night sky. She could see the exact moment Locke made his decision. His jaw set, his shoulders squared, and that stubborn tilt to his chin meant he was about to do something stupid.

"I can't leave him," Locke said, and moved before anyone could stop him.

"You can't do anything," Kal said and reached for Locke's arm, but Locke had already jumped the railing and charged through the dispersing crowd toward the massive creature.

Kenzie didn't think. She saw Locke move, saw how his eyes locked on his brother with that wild, desperate fear of losing someone he loved. She knew that look. It was the same panic that had burned through her when she realized her family was gone and she was powerless to save them. Her first instinct was to run. It had always been that way since that day. Looking at Locke, something else emerged and prevailed.

"Don't be stupid," Kal yelled, but the words sounded like he already knew just how stupid she was about to be.

Kenzie vaulted the railing after Locke. She landed lightly on her feet and hit her stride without thinking. She didn't know if they could save Toren, or if they had any real chance of helping at all. She couldn't stay behind, not after seeing the desperate fear in Locke's face. She was terrified of what the night might take. Not just Toren, but from Locke. Like a fool, she followed him.

"Gaia's blood! Damn kids'll get themselves killed!" She heard Kal slam his hands on the railing. She looked back to see him shove off it. He tracked them as he turned and sprinted back toward the manor.

Kenzie let him go and returned her focus to the giant monster that terrorized the night. The broken chains hung limp below the Azure Crystal and rattled beneath the Colossus's right hand. Toren and his team were on the creature's right arm and moved toward the chest. Kenzie sprinted around the Grand Lake beside Locke. They leaped over toppled benches and shattered lanterns. They dodged between panicked citizens while Locke tried to keep his eyes on his brother. Tracking Toren in the chaos was becoming impossible.

The Altiers moved toward the creature's main torso. At the same time, the Colossus raised the Crystal toward a cavity in its chest. Its movements were slow but deliberate. Its left arm rose to the cavity, and its fingers gripped a heavy shard placed there. Then, in one swift motion, it tore the piece away while the right hand shoved the Azure Crystal into the opening. It was a perfect fit, like the Crystal had always belonged there.

For a moment, nothing happened. Kenzie's breath caught. The air felt too thick, charged with something that made her skin crawl. Then a hypersonic roar erupted from the creature. She saw two of Toren's Altiers lose their footing and fall to the lower city before the blast knocked her flat. The wave sent carts flying and shattered glass in almost every building on the Upper Mesa.

The Colossus shuddered, its entire body convulsed as energy poured into it. Its blue lines illuminated under its skin, like lightning tracing beneath its surface. It trembled, and its limbs locked in a terrifying spasm. Its head tilted skyward, as if in joy or agony. Then it went still. The Upper Mesa fell dead silent. The eye of the storm. Kenzie's ears rang from the roar, but the eerie stillness made her skin crawl. She almost wished for the screams to return. The silence felt worse.

She pushed past a turned-over stall and rubbed her ringing ears. Locke was in front of her. His breath came in sharp gasps as he stared at the Colossus frozen in place. The Azure Crystal's light pulsed with something like a heartbeat. It felt wrong to Kenzie.

Then, as suddenly as it had stopped, the creature jerked to life. Its head snapped downward, its eyes burned with a new, terrible awareness. It was like the creature had sleepwalked to Breezewaltz. Now it had awakened, and it didn't like what it saw.

The Colossus roared again, and the sound was deafening. Kenzie had to cover her ears and fell to her knees. That's when the creature rammed a knee into the Upper Mesa. Kenzie screamed and had to close her eyes as the gaia beneath her shook. Its first blow shattered the mesa. A quarter of it crashed into the lower city. Luckily, the gaia beneath Locke and Kenzie held.

It leaned over the upper mesa and slammed fists into it to dislodge more pieces. Lightning arced wildly from its chest each time it got close and carved molten scars into the streets and buildings. What remained of the structures that were hit quickly caught fire. Large parts of the Upper Mesa collapsed into fire and ruin.

A monstrous fist slammed into the Upper Mesa to their right, and an arc of blue lightning split the pathway in front of them. It raced toward their position. Kenzie barely had time to react. She rolled out of the way and dragged Locke with her. They crouched behind a statue, probably one of Locke's ancestors. She doubted even the enshrined could save Breezewaltz tonight if they were alive to defend it. She grabbed Locke's arm.

"There's no stopping that thing now. I lost Toren when he went over the shoulder," she yelled.

"Yeah, if he held on, it looks like he's on that thing's back," Locke yelled back.

"Locke, he can't stop this. We have to help him escape." Kenzie held his gaze and hoped he would hear the truth.

Locke looked from her to the ruins of his hometown. She hoped he saw what she saw. Fleeing from somewhere, especially when it's your home, was one of the hardest things a person could do. Kenzie didn't even realize she held her breath until Locke nodded and she took a long exhale.

Kenzie gave his arm a squeeze and let go. "We'll take the speeder back on the *Days*. I'll pilot." Kenzie said.

They turned and retraced their steps to the estate. They made it back just in time to hear the *Days* cycle up its engines. Kal ran up the ramp and made sure all other crew members who had come back with him were on board. Out of the corner of his eye, he spotted the duo and spun.

"You idiots! What were you planning on doing there? Throwing rocks at it?" Kal yelled over the engines.

Locke and Kenzie ran past him to the transport speeder. It was a two-seater with a custom-sized Azure shard for its engine. One seat in the front and one in the back, set between two thrusters on the far ends. It was open air, perfect for what they were about to do.

Kenzie's hands were steady on the controls, but inside, she screamed at herself to get off and go to her bunk. She was alive. She had already escaped tonight. Now she was flying straight back into the waiting arms of death again. For what? She already knew her answer, even if it was a terrible one. It just meant there was no turning back.

"Just what do you two think you're doing?" Kal was mad when they passed them, but it seemed he got more pissed the more he understood what they were planning. "Get off that now, that's property of the *Days*. You already tried to get yourself killed tonight. You're not taking a piece of my ship for another attempt."

Kenzie started it up, but Kal put a hand on the controls. "I said no. Get off. That's an order!"

In an instant, Jazz and Lizz restrained him, with one on each arm. Kal was too confused to fight back.

"Go now," Lizz yelled, and Kenzie floored it.

She heard Kal yell as the transport zipped out of the cargo hold and into the night sky. They made a beeline for the Colossus. It was still rampaging and tore through the Upper Mesa and lower city. It was massive, and the buildings from both elevations were toys to it. The *Arcadia* had lifted off and started to pummel the creature. However, the Aurelian Fleet had quickly descended and occupied the Capital skyship.

Locke and Kenzie circled the creature to search for a sign of Toren. Kenzie saw him first. She slapped Locke's shoulder and pointed down. A dim blue light streaked across the creature's back toward the left arm. Something was wrong, though. The light was dim, too dim. Behind it, an impossible swarm of red lights shimmered in the dark.

"We need to go down there to get him," Locke yelled into the night air.

"Yeah, it looks like he's in trouble," Kenzie said.

Kenzie gunned it down toward the creature's arm. As they got closer, it was clear that Toren was scrambling, hounded by a small army of Rosari. The Colossus's left arm was braced on the Upper Mesa. The right arm was out, level with its shoulders and in front of the creature. It crushed the city below it and must have tried to maintain its balance.

Kenzie watched Toren's blue light race down the left arm erratically. His fluid grace was gone, replaced by desperate, stumbling movements. He was injured, but she couldn't tell where. She saw him look back at the swarm of red lights that pursued him before they lost him for a moment as the speeder went beneath the right arm. Toren headed for the Colossus's left hand, probably planning to jump back to the Upper Mesa if he could time it right.

The red lights had gained ground. Rosari could survive the fall if they lost their footing. Toren couldn't.

Kenzie watched as Toren approached the Colossus's hand. His blue radiance flickered like the last bit of flame on a wick. That's when she saw another figure close the distance on Toren. A larger red glow that moved with purpose and confidence. She knew the Rosari by his spotless back even before she saw his face. It was Prince Lucan van Ferro of Aurelia. She'd learned he was a bastard, but seeing him there made a terrible situation somehow worse.

Toren spun around, and even from their distance, Kenzie could see his shock. Lucan's face was visible in his red glow, and he smiled.

Some of the Rosari took potshots at the speeder, and Kenzie had to take evasive maneuvers. She ducked under the left arm to avoid the worst of it. Locke's hands clenched the edge of the speeder. His eyes were wild as they swung beneath the left massive arm. She cut hard, and the transport moved back around. They crested just in time to see Lucan drive his suda through Toren's side.

Kenzie felt Locke's entire body go rigid beside her. The world seemed to tilt beneath them both. She heard Toren grunt, even with the madness around them. He hung there in Lucan's grip, but he didn't go limp. Instead, he twisted one arm and extended the liquid metal of his suda straight into Lucan's mouth. Lucan wasn't ready for that. The suda punched into his mouth, and he staggered. He must have accreted an instant later to prevent it from puncturing through his skull, but the pain still seemed to hit hard and broke his focus.

Toren ripped himself free and stumbled back. A growing darkness stained his normally impeccable Armada blues. He looked up and saw them in the flying transport. Kenzie dove toward him while Lucan recovered and reached out for the final kill. Toren turned and jumped.

Locke stood and reached just in time to catch Toren's hand. Kenzie kept her fingers on the controls as Toren's suda clattered into the side of the speeder and fell to the city below. Locke screamed at the sudden pain as all that weight pulled against him. Between the shardshot from the Rosari and Toren's condition, she didn't need to be told to move them toward the mesa. Behind them, Lucan screamed into the night as the Colossus's arm pushed off the mesa and pulled the small army away.

"Too quick, Kenz. I can't get a grip," Locke yelled.

She could see that Toren's hand was covered in sweat and blood. So much blood. Locke reached out with his free hand.

"Give me your other..." His voice died.

She saw it too. Toren's other arm was cut off at the elbow.

Kenzie noticed Toren's eyes half-closed, but fear flickered in them. It seemed Locke was the only one who didn't know how this would end. He tried to get a better grip on Toren's one hand, but the blood made everything slick.

"Promise... promise me..." Toren gasped. Blood bubbled at his lips. Lucan must have pierced his lung.

"Faster, Kenz, he's slipping!" Locke yelled into the night.

Kenzie said nothing. Even with the conflicting instructions, she punched it. The jolt rocked the brothers back, and she watched Toren's eyes lock onto Locke's. She knew what would happen next, even as Locke tightened his grip, even as his other hand scrambled for leverage. She could see Toren's grip weaken and watched his fingers slide away.

"No, no!" Locke threw his weight forward, but Toren had already fallen. Kenzie reached forward to grab hold of Locke's shirt and keep him on the transport.

For a single, terrible second, she watched Locke's eyes meet his brother's. Toren seemed to hang there in the abyss, a second spread out into a lifetime. His expression cycled through a litany of emotions, a flicker of pain, perhaps regret, and then something else. That's when time caught up, and he was gone.

Locke screamed, but the wind and destruction swallowed the sound. Kenzie watched Toren plummet through the night's sky. She pushed the controls down, but even at this height, the speeder wouldn't be able to catch him in freefall. She couldn't look away as he fell into the ruined city below. She lost sight of him just before impact.

She pulled up just before they reached the ruined city below. The Colossus was moving through another portion of the city away from them. They would find Toren's corpse in the rubble. That was all Kenzie could do for Locke in the moment.

His head hung as they descended the final few feet. Tears formed at the edges of his closed eyes. His brother was gone, and now they both knew it.

CHAPTER 23: LOCKE

The study was too quiet. For the first time since they arrived in Breezewaltz, there were no distant sounds of revelry. No music in the streets. No laughter to drift through the halls. Even the hum of airships passing overhead was muted. The Colossus had gone. It had left behind only ruin and silence.

Locke sat slumped in his father's old chair, elbows heavy on the polished mahogany desk, face buried in his hands. He no longer cried. Those tears had already fallen, spent by the time the transport had landed aboard the *Days*, and left him empty and exhausted. He doubted he had any left. Instead, he'd stared blankly at the floor for the past hours and waited for another wave of grief that never came. It sat stubbornly in his chest, heavy as lead, and pressed painfully against his ribs.

The room brought back a faded memory from childhood, an afternoon that had blurred with time when their father had questioned them about how a priceless statue had broken. Toren had been seventeen then, Locke only seven, and they'd tried to lie their way out of trouble. Locke had crumbled quickly. He had forgotten the lie when the icy glare of their father's anger overwhelmed him. Toren had absorbed the brunt of it, accusations filled with disappointment and shame. The words *embarrassment* and *failure* were spoken in an unkind manner.

Afterward, alone together in a quiet room not unlike the study, Toren had cried softly, something Locke had never witnessed before or since.

"What if I'm not good enough?" Toren had whispered through his tears.

Locke hadn't known what to say then, and he still didn't know. At the time, the idea of Toren failing at anything had seemed impossible. Yet the impossible had happened, and Toren wasn't there to ask any more questions.

Locke shuddered, fingers gripped the edge of the desk. The fear that had once tormented Toren suddenly belonged to him. Locke wasn't just grieving the loss of his brother. He also had to confront the terrifying realization that if steadfast and reliable Toren could falter, then Locke was sure he stood no chance at all.

Across from him, Kenzie perched quietly on the edge of the couch, her usual sharpness softened, muted somehow. She held a cup of tea untouched between her hands, as if its warmth alone might soothe her.

She had tried speaking at first, just a few words, enough to let him know she was there. Locke had barely responded, so she just sat with him in the quiet.

The door burst open.

Kal stalked inside, boots scuffed against the polished floors. His presence was like the first bite of winter. "Alright," he said, voice sharp. "I've had time to cool down. Time to think."

Kenzie didn't say anything. Locke didn't look up or move.

Kal's voice was steady, but there was an edge underneath. "Let's go over it again. What, in Gaia's ever-loving grace, did you two think you were doing?"

Kenzie exhaled. "Not now, Kal, please."

Kal slammed his palms on the desk, rattling the teacups. "No, not now? Not now? Let me tell you something, *kids*, now is exactly the time. You disobeyed a direct order. Both of you." His glare flicked toward Kenzie, but she met it without flinching. "You stole my transport. You almost got yourselves killed. And Toren still died along with half the city."

Silence.

Kal's breathing was heavy. His fingers curled against the wood, and his fist trembled.

Kenzie set her tea down with a slow, deliberate motion. "We did our best to help, but it just wasn't enough."

Kal's jaw clenched. "That is not the point." He stepped back and ran a hand through his hair. "Gaia's blood. I thought I'd seen reckless before, but this? This takes the damn crown." He paced and shook his head. "You *knew* it was bad when I said no. I don't say no to you two. When do I ever say no to the two of you? And then," he pointed at them. "You force me to follow you when you steal *my* transport and put yourselves in a suicide run. Put the whole crew in danger. What the hell was I supposed to do with that?"

Locke finally looked up at him. "You wanted me just to let him take on that thing by himself?"

Kal snapped. "I wanted you to listen to me!" The anger cracked, something raw bled through underneath. "You think I wanted Toren to die? You think I wanted to watch you almost go with him? Gaia, dammit, Locke, you scared the hell out of me. That's not how we do things on this crew. If we do something stupid, then we do it *together*."

He turned away and pinched the bridge of his nose. "Now I have to discipline Jazz and Lizz, because, guess what? They listened to you over me. You put me in a position where my crew chose your stupid plan over my orders." He scoffed, voice tight with frustration. "Worst of all, you're sitting here, feeling sorry for yourself. Like it's the end of the world, when you should be *angry*, I'm not saying Toren would want your hands to get bloody, but he sure as hell wouldn't want you sitting here when there's work to do out there."

Locke knew how to be angry. He had been plenty of times in the past. At the world and himself. At his inadequacies, mostly. That part of him felt roped off, like he couldn't touch it. Up until today, that had been a good thing.

He felt the heartache press on his ribs again. He wished he *could* be angry. It would have been easier. Instead, he just felt… vacant. Not the empty that lets anything new in. The kind that echoed. The type that repeated every decision you made and every one you didn't, until you couldn't remember which ones mattered.

Kal sighed and shook his head. The worst of his anger seemed spent, but that didn't mean he was done. "This was supposed to be simple. We were supposed to get in, get paid, and keep moving. Now we're tangled in something. The Colossus is out there, supercharged, and you," He jabbed a finger at Locke. "You just got promoted."

Locke frowned. "What?"

A knock at the door.

Kenzie looked toward it first, already knowing. "Don't people have better things to do today?"

Kal scoffed. "The city leaders are scared. They don't like it when the seat is empty in good times. After last night," he paused, but then looked at Locke, "they're desperate." The fire remained behind his eyes.

Liam cracked the door open. "Locke, um, the city council is in the main hall."

"Thanks, Liam. Tell them he'll be with them shortly," Kal responded in an even voice. Apparently, his anger was reserved for the dissenters. Liam nodded and closed the door.

Locke didn't move. "They know I'm back?" Locke asked.

"I asked on my way in. Apparently, Aldis told them yesterday before the festival. Something about presenting you during the midnight ceremony. If it makes you feel better, they said it was secretly Toren's idea. Another one of his terrible ideas." Kal said as he leaned against the desk, arms crossed. "They want you to take the Final Rite and become the First Altier. *Toren's* seat."

Locke's stomach twisted. He already assumed all that, but his thoughts didn't feel real. The words seemed to give the thought form.

Kenzie studied him carefully. "Do you want us to come with you?"

He swallowed. "I might just stay here." He smirked sheepishly. "Maybe they'll leave if I never come out."

Kal pushed off the desk. "Yeah, you do that, because I am not kneeling before you." He stalked toward the door. "Gaia, help me. I will give you another head injury if you ever try to give me orders. C'mon, Kenzie, I'm hungry, and I have more yelling to do. You're gonna be there when it happens."

Then he was gone.

Kenzie hadn't moved and lingered for a moment longer. "Locke," she started. Her voice came quietly, but not soft. "You think Toren died because of you."

Locke didn't answer at first. Then he slammed his fists into the desk. "Of course, he died because of me. He wouldn't have been on that thing if Breezewaltz and I hadn't made him feel like he had to be. He wouldn't have fallen to his death if I had just…hung on." Locke slammed his fists again, lighter, and slumped further into the leather seat.

She leaned forward, elbows on knees. "He didn't. You need to acknowledge that he made his own choice, just like we did. He chose to stand, to protect the people of Breezewaltz. I know it hurts, but we can't stop just because it hurts. I… know that's not fair."

Locke's throat barely worked. "I'm not stopping."

"Yeah," she said, not unkindly. "You kind of are…" She took a deep breath. "That's not the Locke I know."

He looked away. "What do you know about me?"

"I know you have a complicated backstory." She smiled to lighten the mood just a bit. Kenzie waited, then added with a softer tone, "I know he believed in you, and I know you've been sitting in this room all morning like that's not supposed to mean anything."

That cracked something, not enough to break, but enough to shift. "I know you're right," Locke admitted, voice thick. "But every time I close my eyes, I just see his face. He trusted me."

"And you haven't broken that trust, not yet. Holding on to him wouldn't have given him back his arm or closed the wound in his chest. You did what you could in the moment, but you didn't fail him. It was a no-win scenario. You were there for him in the end. I'm sure that's how he remembered you."

Locke wanted to believe her. He desperately wanted to accept that maybe being there for his dying brother was enough, but it didn't feel like it. The empty ache in his chest wasn't so quickly convinced. He could have done more, should have done more. Self-resentment was replacing grief, and Locke wasn't sure if that was better, but it was something. An emotion. A faint sliver of light in the dark.

He exhaled and shook his head. "I'll be fine."

Her face didn't change. If he had convinced her, she didn't show it. He didn't believe his words either, not yet. Saying them was a beginning. It was motion, and maybe inertia would keep him from sinking into the abyss. She stood, placed a hand on his, and then followed Kal out the side door.

He braced himself on the desk as he stood. His thumb settled over a carved flower near the edge. When he shifted his weight, it pressed into the pistil. A hidden spring clicked, and a lock released beneath the desk. Locke had known about the secret compartment in his father's desk, but it took a moment to remember what he had just done.

Locke looked into the open shelf that hung down where his legs had just been. A small black book sat alone inside. He picked it up, opened to the first page, and blinked back tears.

Journal of Toren Luinondo, First Altier of Breezewaltz, Years 997–

Locke thought back to his first night back, when his brother had put a book away. He had never known his brother to keep a journal. Maybe it was a habit Toren had picked up after becoming First Altier, or perhaps he had just always been clever about hiding his secrets.

Toren had never gotten the chance to finish the volume. Locke considered reading further but knew he didn't have the emotional strength to make it past the first word. Not yet, maybe not ever.

He wiped his eyes, slipped the book into his coat, and closed the compartment. He turned toward the double doors that led to the main hall.

On his way, he passed a window with curtains parted slightly. Outside, smoke
still curled lazily from shattered buildings where the Colossus had smashed
through almost gleefully. The few remaining skyships hovered quietly over ruined
neighborhoods, and an eerie stillness hung over everything. It made it feel distant
yet painfully close. It gave Locke a sudden sense of vertigo, as if he were falling.
He forced his gaze forward. The city bore wounds as deep as his own, wounds he
wasn't sure either of them could heal.

The hall beyond was pristine, untouched by the destruction that had occurred
outside. It was a reminder of order in a city that had lost all sense of it.

Locke stepped inside to find the governing council waiting. A semicircle of
merchants, holy men, and officers.

At their center stood High Priest Aldis, his silver hair caught the daylight.
"Locke Luinondo," he said, voice steady. "We are sorry for your loss."

Locke forced himself to meet the man's gaze. "The city has lost just as much,"
Locke admitted out loud for the first time.

"We will bury him with your parents in the crypt. A team is clearing the rubble as we speak, but it will take weeks," Aldis said.

"Thank you," was all Locke could say. The thought of his family's crypt under
the Azure Temple left him cold. He hadn't even worked up the courage to visit his
parents on this trip.

Aldis continued. "Toren's death has left a void. One that must be filled before
Breezewaltz can stabilize. We know you have just returned to us, but by Azure's
blessing, it seems that this itself is providence in these dark times." He stepped
forward. "We ask that you take the Twelfth Rite."

The words landed like a hammer.

Locke had never seen the Twelfth, or Final, Rite in person, even if he came
from a long line of men and women who had. His grandfather, his father, and
Toren had all walked the path of the faithful. They had been bound to Breezewaltz
by the sacred covenant of the Luinondos. To Locke, it had always felt more like a
yoke, a bond that choked the life from men who might have lived freely. Still, the
position came with great power, and he could make a real difference. He just didn't
know if he believed all that. Now they asked Locke to put his faith in a title.

"I…" Locke started, then faltered.

He wasn't Toren. Locke had never wanted it. He was supposed to be the reckless younger brother. The one who ran from responsibility, who lived on the *Days*, free of it all.

Aldis studied him. "This city needs a leader, Locke, and whether you believe it or not, you are still a Luinondo."

Locke swallowed. The thought of it pressed down on him, heavier than he'd ever imagined.

"If the Luinondo line yields, we risk a vote and open succession. Breezewaltz can't afford that, not after last night."

The First Altier of Breezewaltz. Could he live up to that title? Did he even have a choice? Locke's mind spun through the implications. The shadow of his family's legacy, the fractured city outside, and the unspoken expectations of the council. All of it crushed down on him. If Toren, the steadfast brother who had always seemed untouchable, could fall, what chance did he have?

His heart raced. He had spent years running, carving out a life on the *Days*, free from the chains of duty and everything Aldis offered him in this moment. He wasn't Toren, and even if he had stopped wanting to be years ago, was he enough? The eyes of the collected city council bore into him, and he felt the same pull of legacy that had driven his brother to stand against the Colossus. It was like iron in his boots and a noose that tightened around his neck. He pulled at it, and that was where he found another thread.

He remembered Toren's final words. *Promise me.*

His brother hadn't finished whatever he was trying to say. Locke would have to guess what was in Toren's heart. It started as a low answer, distant and hazy, but it rose in his mind. The more he grasped at it, the more it gathered strength, like the roar of an approaching wave. Kal and Kenzie were right. He couldn't just sit here, paralyzed by doubt or grief. Locke needed to be out there, trying to do what was best for the people of Iveria. He wasn't his brother, but maybe the moment didn't call for someone like Toren. It could be that it was a problem only someone outside the system could solve. He wouldn't know until he tried.

Promise me. Locke didn't know what Toren wanted him to promise, but this vow would have to do.

"When can we start?" Locke asked.

"This evening," Aldis nodded back.

CHAPTER 24: KALISTON

5 Days Until the Colossus Attacks Orleans

The Luinondo estate's dining hall was packed, but nobody celebrated. Most of the crew was there, seated or standing with plates in front of them, when Locke walked in. They pushed food around more than they ate it. Conversation had stalled, not because anyone lacked something to say, but because all eyes were on the confrontation at the center of the room.

Kal stood above the twins, arms crossed and pulse high. Val had braced her hands on the table beside him, her weight angled forward and her hands to her chin. For once, Jazz and Lizz didn't have a single sarcastic line between them. They sat quietly, backs straight, faces tight. Like two kids who waited for a punishment they knew they'd earned.

Kal's anger hadn't cooled since the cargo hold. It had settled deeper, though. A cold fury that was sharp-edged and brittle. There was no humor in it, no theatrical exasperation. Just disappointment that rode close to the bone. "You don't just stop me from giving an order on *my* ship," Kal said, voice tight. "You restrained me, Jazz." He turned to the boy.

Jazz didn't flinch or joke. "Yeah, Kal, I did."

Kal's eyes moved to Lizz. "You held my other arm. Told them to go."

She nodded once, still not meeting his gaze.

Kal shook his head and stepped forward. "I have half a mind to throw you both in the damn brig just to make a point."

Lizz raised her eyebrows but didn't lift her chin. "Do we even have a brig?"

"I'd make one just for this," Kal snapped.

Jazz let out a tired breath. "Kal, c'mon. You know why we did it."

"Oh, I know what you *thought* you were doing," Kal said and dragged a hand through his hair. "That doesn't make it less reckless."

"They weren't going to stop," Lizz said. She glanced at Locke, just once. "You know that. I would've done the same if it were Jazz."

"Then you stop them," Val said, her voice cool and hard. "You don't feed the fire."

Lizz didn't back down. "You wouldn't have stopped them either."

Val's lips pressed together, but she said nothing.

Kal let out a bitter laugh. "Fantastic. So now I've got a crew who decides when my orders apply."

"I wasn't following orders," Lizz said. "I was doing what was right. We're not an army, Kal…" She let the rest of it hang there for Kal to fill in himself. That stung more than it should've.

Kal didn't answer. His arms were still crossed, but his chest had deflated some. He was proud of Lizz for knowing the line existed and knowing where she stood. He was also a little annoyed that she was beyond reproach now. He could only angrily nitpick now. Luckily, he was an expert at that.

Locke finally spoke up. He'd been quiet and watched from the door. "If you want to be mad at someone, be mad at me," Locke said.

Kal turned toward him. The heat in his chest didn't fade, but it shifted. He wasn't sure if it was pride or if he was just too tired to separate it from everything else. "Oh, don't worry," Kal said. "I am."

Locke stepped in closer. "Okay. Now that everyone knows you're not happy with me, can we talk about what comes next?"

Kal raised an eyebrow. "More plans from our junior cadet?"

Locke took a breath. "I'm taking the Final Rite. I'm going to become the First Altier."

That landed. The whole room seemed to look at him at once. Kal stared at him and weighed the words. He noted how Locke didn't blink when he said them. A one-in-five shot at survival, and the kid said it like tomorrow was a certainty.

Kal laughed once, dry and short. "Figured you would. What else?"

"I'm staying on the *Days*."

That one made Kal pause. He looked Locke over, like he would spot the lie. "Excuse me?"

Locke didn't flinch. "You said it yourself. Toren would want us out there, doing something. He gave his life for Breezewaltz, for us. I can't just walk away from that. The *Arcadia*'s wrecked. The Armada's all been called to Orleans. Civilians are running in the opposite direction." Locke took a breath and rubbed the back of his neck. "Maybe the Armada stops the Colossus, maybe not, but I'm not going to sit by for another city to fall. Toren wouldn't, and neither can we."

Kal let out a long breath and turned away for a second. He ran a hand down his face. "Locke. This isn't a raid. It's not some sky skirmish. You're talking about taking on a goddamn walking god. We don't do that."

"We're not going to fight it," Locke said. "We're going to figure out what Lucan's protecting on it. He wouldn't be there if there wasn't something worth guarding."

Val unfolded her arms. "What if we can't?"

Locke met her gaze. "Then our fate is the same as Iveria."

Kal groaned. "Gaia's blood, you get worse every day. I dislike the Domain as much as anyone, but there's no upside to this. Can someone, please, talk sense into him?" He pointed at Locke with both palms before he sat on the table.

Jules, who had been silent until then, finally spoke. "If the Azure Crystal's in its chest, then that thing has an unlimited power source."

Kal turned to her, eyes wide. "Great. That makes this sound *way* less suicidal."

Haruto glanced up from his datapad. "I wasn't going to say anything, but I decrypted a CrystalLine message from Orleans's defense command earlier. The Colossus is heading north. They estimate it'll reach the city in five days if not impeded. They clock it at fifty-three miles per hour."

"Today is day zero?" Avery asked, and Haruto nodded. Avery leaned against the wall near the kitchen and let out a low whistle. "The *Days* can make it there in just over eighteen hours. We could be on-site tomorrow night if we leave tonight."

Kal groaned. "I hate that you did the math."

Tia cracked her knuckles. "So what's the play? 'Cause shooting at it didn't exactly work for the *Arcadia* last night. What's stopping us from getting flattened the second we get close?"

Haruto tapped the table without looking up. "We're not going in guns blazing. Like Locke said, we follow Toren's plan. Figure out what's powering it, or better yet, what's controlling it." He glanced at Jules. "How sure are we that the Azure Crystal is doing all the work?"

Jules scratched at the back of her head. Kal could tell she hated to guess, but she answered anyway. "Powering it? One hundred percent. That Crystal's infinite. You all saw the difference when it slotted into the chest. Controlling it? That's theoretical. Not my field."

Val folded her arms. "Do you think anyone's controlling it? Maybe it was always drawn to the Crystal?"

Avery leaned in. "I'll buy that it came for the Crystal, but why destroy the city after it had it? Why head north? Why Orleans? That place didn't even exist if that thing's been dormant since before the founding of the League."

Val's brow furrowed. "You think Lucan's directing it?"

Avery shook his head. "I don't know, but I've seen Haruto's write-up. Lucan's got a taste for cruelty, but not the brainpower to control something like that."

"Right," she put her hand on her chin for a beat before she turned toward Kal. "This whole thing reeks of one person."

Kal groaned, jaw tightening. "The Director."

Val raised her eyebrows. "You still call him that?"

Kal didn't answer right away. "Better than the other names I used to call him."

"Fine," she said, letting sleeping dogs lie.

"Who are you talking about?" Haruto asked.

"Dr. Baron El-Syd, former Director of Conchordia." Val replied.

Kal felt it all click at once. "Knowing him… that would explain how they got it to move in the first place. If they really are controlling it…" He trailed off, and his jaw tightened. "Damn it. You're probably right. Asshole. Why didn't I see it?"

"You think he made a control device?" Jules asked.

"He made worse at Conchordia," Kal said. "This? This is well within his range. It's probably what Lucan was guarding on that creature's back."

"How do we know it was Lucan guarding anything?" Liam asked from the far end.

Kenzie answered before Kal could. "He chased Toren out of a building. Then Locke and I saw him from behind." She paused. "The rumor is he's the only Rosari without spots on his back. It was him."

"So we need to get up there," Locke said. "That same building Toren came down from. Whatever's in there is important."

"Which means getting close," Kenzie added. "Without tipping it off."

Kal stepped forward, voice steadier. "Toren said it best. The *Days* is the fastest and stealthiest ship flying." He said it like a proud father. A few smirks passed between the crew. Kal didn't care. "What? She is." He looked around the room. "I'll put her up against anything in the Armada."

Val let it ride. "You're overcompensating again, but not wrong. We don't engage directly. We get in, find what's causing it to move. Cut the strings, and maybe, maybe, we don't have to fight at all."

"Right," Jazz said, nodding. "And if we can't cut 'em, we find a way to pull 'em."

Lizz grinned. "Or tangle them into knots."

Cookie entered with a tray and set it down without a word. She looked more serious than usual, her voice flat. "What if it's not being controlled? What if it's doing this on its own?"

The room went still. For once, nobody had a comeback.

Locke exhaled. "Is there any way to know for sure?"

Val looked to Kal.

He shook his head. "No, Val. We're not going there."

"Kaliston, we've got one hundred and forty-four hours before this thing hits Orleans. If there's even a chance to find something that helps us stop it…"

He knew what she meant. So did the crew. All eyes landed on him again. He felt it settle in his chest, the weight of the ask. Kal let out a breath and ran both hands down his face. "Fine. Fine! Screw it. We'll go to Belfield, but we hit Somerset first."

Val raised her brow. "Uncle?"

"Uncle," Kal said. Then he turned to the twins. "And you two are still in the doghouse."

Jazz grinned. "No place I'd rather be."

Kal pointed at him and mimed crushing something invisible between his palms. "Just… shut up."

Val laughed. Lizz smiled.

The tension ebbed, replaced by something slower and more deliberate. The start of a path forward. They sat around the table again, maps pulled out, datapads synced. Cookie passed around the bowls that no one had the appetite to pick from earlier. Slowly, people ate.

Kal stood just outside the edge of the group and watched. Toren's absence still pressed against the walls of the room like a cold draft. Kal could see it in the way Locke hovered, in the stiffness behind Val's smile. He felt it too. It was something they'd need to talk about, but not for a while. It was in the room with them, and they would name it when the time was right.

Val stepped up beside him and dropped her voice. "You think you're losing them?" she asked and motioned subtly toward the twins.

Kal didn't answer right away. Eventually, he gave a low nod. "I don't know. I hope not."

"They're loyal. Stupid, yes, but loyal. That's a good thing. You keep your grip steady but pointed in the right direction. They'll come back around. The whole crew will." She placed a hand on his shoulder.

He looked down at her hand, then nodded again. He knew enough about the world to know she was usually right. Kal took a slow breath and gave a small smile as Val's words settled in. She patted his shoulder once more, then peeled off to take a seat beside Locke.

Kal watched her go, then watched Locke. The kid looked like he barely kept it together, like the edges held out of spite more than strength. Kal took a seat across from his ex-wife. Val leaned toward Locke, voice low enough that the crew couldn't hear the words, but he could.

"Are you nervous about the Rite?" she asked.

Locke froze, and Kal could tell he hadn't even considered it. He was someone who wouldn't. Always focused on the story after the trial. Locke thought the best outcome would always happen with the right effort and outlook. Besides, he ran on grief, duty, and adrenaline. There hadn't been space to process the fact that he might die that evening.

Val gave Locke a smile. Kal had seen it a million times. It was her 'you're an idiot, but I support you' smile. "Don't be. You'll be fine. When was the last time a Luinondo didn't pass?"

Locke hesitated. "My uncle."

Val blinked. "I'm going to shut up now," she said and turned back to her plate.

Kal snorted under his breath and rubbed his eyes. Yeah, that tracked.

CHAPTER 25: LOCKE

Silence hung over the Luinondo manor, heavy and unnatural. An absence of servants and guards left the grand halls empty. The staff probably tended to their personal tragedies. Having them come in had not mattered to Locke. The manor had an eerie quiet to it when evening had rolled around. Only the high priests and a handful of attending council members remained. Their solemn silence only made the situation feel more eerie. Outside, Breezewaltz still smoldered from the Colossus's devastation, but the Luinondo manor showed none of that. It was unsettling, as if the manor itself held its breath for what had come before and what would come next.

Typically, the Rite would occur at the Temple, but the Colossus had destroyed it the previous night. The Luinondo Estate would suffice. The estate his father and brother had presided over as First Altiers.

Now, it was Locke's turn.

He wasn't sure if he was ready, but he was also sure he didn't have a choice. He wondered if that meant he was ready, in a roundabout way.

Val's words from earlier stuck in his head. *Don't be nervous. When was the last time a Luinondo didn't pass? My uncle.* Locke hadn't even known the man. His father never spoke of him. The only thing Locke had ever gleaned was that his uncle had attempted the Rite and had died almost immediately.

They said four in five didn't survive the Azure Rite. Half died instantly, as if lightning erupted inside them. The rest waste away from shard sickness. The lucky few become Altiers.

Locke didn't like to think about all the odds. He was a terrible gambler, and betting with his own life in the balance went against every instinct he had. He exhaled slowly, steadying himself. Locke was on his knees, and he looked up at the assembled priests, council members, and friends.

Aldis stepped forward. His silvered robes trailed behind him. His face was lined with decades of ceremony, but his voice was still strong.

"Locke Luinondo," Aldis intoned, his gaze piercing. "You have been called to ingest a shard of the great Azure Crystal, as your ancestors have before you. You seek the Twelfth and Final Rite, but know that this is not a trial of mere inheritance. This is a covenant. A bond between the First Altier, our beloved Crystal, and Iveria itself."

Locke nodded. His throat was dry, and the shard looked large. He felt the expectation of the council's eyes on him.

Aldis continued. "Do you promise to keep Iveria safe? To hold the Iverian League above all else and shield her people from enemies, foreign and domestic? Do you promise to put others above yourself always, and perform your duty even when it is not convenient?"

"I do..."

"Then take this shard and ingest it. All here will be your witness to your vow and this trial."

Words hung in the air. Aldis moved a gloved hand toward Locke. It contained the rather large shard. Locke wondered if he should have asked to have it chipped further. He looked up at the crew that stood around him in the foyer. Kal looked impassive, Kenzie looked worried, and Val gave him two thumbs up.

Locke hesitated only for a moment before he swallowed the shard. He had participated in the Eleven Rites as a child, had bowed his head a hundred times beneath the Crystal's shadow and whispered the prayers, but this was different. It was the moment where words became flesh, where belief became pain, and where the unchosen were found out. The chamber was utterly silent as they waited.

"Close your eyes," Aldis commanded, "and bite this." He held out a bit of leather.

Locke obeyed.

He heard his breath through his teeth. That's when the pain erupted in his chest and lanced through his ribs like the Azure's judgment made real. He felt like he was electrocuted from the inside out. A thousand whispered prayers from his childhood rose unbidden, fragments of a creed he still remembered. The words did little to dull the pain. Each shock demanded to know if he could endure and if he was worthy. His body buckled, muscles seized. He barely registered falling forward. The only sensation besides the pain was the taste of leather as he bit into the strap.

His body convulsed, and the pain was overwhelming. A realization found him through the agony: *I'm dying.*

That was the only thought his brain could produce over the pain. Great, he was one of the eighty percent. He thought he heard a scream, but he wasn't sure if it was from outside or inside him.

In an instant, the pain stopped, or he died. One of the two.

He felt as though he was outside his body, and a presence watched over him. He didn't know how, but he could feel the Azure Crystal miles away, along with a presence in the room with him. Not Aldis, the priests, or the crew. It was something else, something bigger, and it looked at him. He could feel it judging him. Then, the pain started again.

It crept up on him until it reached its zenith, but Locke still felt the presence. The pain was vast, unblinking, and ancient. It was a force that had seen the rise of the cosmos, that had existed from the start. It regarded him, not with warmth or understanding, but with a cold, impersonal curiosity. He had grown up believing the Crystal was a protector, a guiding light for his people, but it felt more like the indifferent eye of a storm. The force did not care about his suffering, only that he endured it. He felt small, insignificant, a gnat before a god that neither loved nor hated him. The realization shook him, even as his body convulsed and his teeth ground into the leather strap.

He opened his mouth to scream, but no sound came out. Then a feeling washed over him. It felt like words, but there was no sound.

"Speak, wayward soul. What name dost thou bear beneath shadow's veil? What oath hath claimed thy heart, and by what right dost thou seek me?" it asked.

Locke spoke to the entity even as no words left his mouth.

"I don't know who I am. I don't know who I'm meant to be, but I promise I won't run. Not again. Never again. I couldn't save Toren… but I will protect Breezewaltz. Iveria. You. If you'll have me. Whatever this is, whatever it costs, I'm not running away anymore."

There was a long pause, or at least it felt long through the pain. Finally, the voice returned.

"Thy will is thy worth. Rise, wayward one, and reclaim thy rightful path. Too long hast thou wandered under an errant banner, forsaking the covenant once forged. The burden is thine, as it once was and always will be. The path is clear, if thou hast the strength to walk it."

Its words lingered before they faded until there was nothing. The room was silent, and the pain that had ripped through him was gone. The chamber was still again.

Locke felt the sweat drip from his body. He panted, and his heart hammered. His vision swam when he stood, but he could get to his feet.

He was alive.

Slowly, he looked at his hands and chest. His fingers trembled, but something was different. His veins, barely visible beneath his skin, glowed faintly with an internal blue light before they dimmed to normal. Blue crystals grew and evaporated on his skin. They shot off small bolts of lightning as they appeared. He felt the Azure Crystal in his gut, like an echo that had always been there, and waited for him to call it by name.

Aldis stepped forward, his expression unreadable. Then, after a moment, he bowed. "It is done," he said. "You are the First Altier of Breezewaltz."

The council murmured among themselves, some with relief, while others remained uncertain.

Locke barely heard them. His mind still spun.

"What is your command, my Lord?" Aldis asked.

Locke steadied himself. "Hold the city. Take care of those in need, both in the Upper Mesa and the lower city. I'm going after that creature."

"My Lord?" Aldis asked.

"I know you did this so the city would have a leader, but my duty is to Iveria. I'm going to put that monster down," Locke said while he put his shirt back on.

Murmurs rippled through the council and attendants.

Aldis took a measured breath. "Lord Luinondo, the city needs you. Now, more than ever. You must understand…"

"I do," Locke cut in. "I understand that if we don't stop that thing, more cities will burn. If I stay here, Iveria will be rubble around us, and Aurelia will have us under their boot."

Aldis tightened his fingers into the folds of his robe. "Lord Luinondo, you would leave us in our time of need? You have a duty to Breezewaltz. You shouldn't even leave to attend Altier training at the Crystal Bastion, let alone chase a walking god across the continent." His voice was calm, but there was something brittle beneath it.

"I'm not leaving you," Locke said. "I'm going out to protect you."

Aldis held his gaze, then he exhaled through his nose. "I see," he murmured. He stood next to Locke, then turned slightly to give the members of the city council an unreadable gaze. Something passed between them, unsaid but understood.

By then, the crew of the Days had already filed out to prepare for the journey. They gave Locke nods and fist pumps on their way out.

Kenzie ran over and pulled him into a careful, relieved hug. "Never scare me like that again," she whispered as her voice quivered. She let go and left to find the rest of the crew.

Kal was next, his eyes softer than Locke had seen them since the events of Landfall. Before Locke or Aldis could say a word, Kal placed both hands on Locke's shoulders.

"He would've been proud of you, your parents, too. Since they're not here to say it, let me." Kal's face was serious, but not cold. "I loved Toren like a brother. He was the best man I ever knew, but you don't have to be him, Locke. Just be you, that's enough." He smiled at Locke. "You'll carry his legacy, your family's legacy, but it's time to forge your path. We'll be with you every step of the way. We're your family now. Rely on us, and we'll rely on you. Understand?"

Locke nodded at Kal, and he nodded right back. Kal squeezed his shoulders once more, then gave Aldis a mistrustful glare before he turned to walk away.

Locke did his best not to melt into tears immediately. The only thing that kept him level was that the air around Aldis had shifted. It was subtle, barely noticeable. The way his face emptied, the way his shoulders lost their ceremonial stiffness. It was a minor change, like a mask that slipped out of place.

"The rumors about you were right," Aldis said. His face had shifted from friendly grandfather to murderous bile.

Then his voice hardened. "You would squander what's been given to you."

The murmurs died. The temperature in the room seemed to drop.

"Excuse me?" Locke asked.

Aldis took a step forward, voice lower, the silk-smooth reverence gone. "I should have known. Putting our faith in you was like pissing into the wind." His lips curled into something not quite a smile. "It was a mistake, and I should have known. We put our faith in the runt of the litter, and of course, you bolt the second it becomes inconvenient, just like you did after Seaforth. I've heard the stories, even if your brother tried to cover them up. Locke Luinondo the skypirate, Locke Luinondo the coward." He waved to his attendants to pack up.

"I'm sorry. You're insulting me because I'm trying to help Iveria?" Locke asked. Locke knew the grandfatherly holy man was an act, but truly seeing behind it for the first time still shocked him.

Aldis chuckled, but there was no warmth in it. "I'm insulting you because you're an *unreliable child*, chasing a dead man's delusion of grandeur." His eyes narrowed. "Go. Run after your brother's ghost. Maybe you'll be more useful as a martyr than as a leader. At least we will be done with the Luinondo line. As is, we'll do what we must to make sure Breezewaltz endures."

The words hit Locke harder than the Rite itself. He had survived the Azure Crystal. It had judged him and found him worthy. However, to Aldis and Breezewaltz, that still wasn't enough. They had already made up their minds. The 'coward of Seaforth,' he had called Locke. A runaway turned skypirate, a skypirate turned absent First Altier. Locke's fingers curled into fists at his sides. The thought that they were right about him, and might have always been, made his blood boil.

Aldis's attendants and council members shuffled to follow Aldis out of the chamber, some too stunned to react. Others nodded along as if they had expected it.

The words slipped from Locke's lips before he could stop them, quiet but confident. They carried more steel than volume. "You're wrong about me. All of you. You've always been wrong."

"No, child, I think not. Perhaps the Crystal accepted you, but Breezewaltz has not," Aldis said before he left the room.

A few turned, but only to shake their heads or offer a dismissive wave. They'd tell themselves the Crystal had chosen poorly, or perhaps he'd passed the Rite on lineage alone. Either way, he wasn't worth their time.

Locke stood in the center of the empty room, and the silence pressed against his ribs.

There was no one left to see him off. No attendants, no administrators, and no family. Just empty halls and a crumbling city. Not that the silence mattered. He wasn't in the mood for any more goodbyes.

He looked at his family's manor for a final time and took a deep breath. Then stepped over the threshold, past the terrace, and onto the well-manicured lawn. Parts of the city still burned in the twilight beyond the mesa. Locke took that in, too, but did not break stride. He made his way to the parked *Days*.

Lizz met him on the ramp. "All good?" she asked with a smile.

"Good enough," he responded.

"Great, because Kal is calling an all-hands meeting in Command."

CHAPTER 26: KALISTON

5 Days Until the Colossus Attacks Orleans

They had dimmed the lights in the Command Room to match the twilight of the darkening sky. It was quiet when Kal stepped in, not silent, but the hush that settled over the group meant everyone knew why they were there.

The crew had already gathered. Some were seated, but others leaned against counters or walls. Cookie had laid out a few plates of whatever she'd put together, but no one ate. Jules was at the far end, arms crossed over her chest, head low. Lizz sat between Jazz and Tia and picked at the corner of a napkin. Rina leaned against the doorframe, her face unreadable, her presence steady. Locke was near the back, not hiding, but not front and center, either. His eyes were dark. Kal wasn't sure if it was from wear or fatigue. Probably both. Kenzie hovered by the corner, a thumb tucked into the shorts she wore under her dress. Liam, Haruto, and Avery were all there.

Kal took a breath and stepped forward. "I'm not gonna make this long," he said.

That got them. Heads lifted, and attention clicked into place.

"We're all carrying something after Breezewaltz. That's not news. Some of us lost people we'll never get back. Some of us saw things we can't unsee. We'll deal with that in our own ways, but tonight, we're going to name it."

He paused to let the importance of that sit.

"Toren gave everything for that city, and for us to be here tonight. He didn't hesitate, he didn't run, and he sure as hell didn't flinch. He saw what had to be done, and he did it."

Kal looked down for a moment, jaw tight. His fingers curled around the edge of the center console. Normally, when the group would meet, it would project maps and plans. It was off for this meeting.

"He was my best friend, and he was like Val's younger brother."

"He was smarter than you. He listened to me," Val said and grinned. The group chuckled.

Kal smiled at Val. "He was the commander of the *Arcadia*, and he was his father's son." Kal paused, almost broke at the words, but recovered. "He was a pain in the ass, but he was also the kind of person who would've walked into fire for anyone. He did it for me more than once… I wish I could have done it more for him…"

A ripple of breath passed through the room. Not a murmur, just a shift. A few glances exchanged. Someone cleared their throat.

"We don't get to bury him tonight, not properly, but we can do this. We can remember him right before we leave Breezewaltz."

Kal picked up the pace, but kept his voice steady. "Toren fought like he believed we were worth the fight. Like Iveria still mattered. Like everything the *Days* represents was important. Freedom and family." He looked at Locke. "So we're gonna prove him right." He looked around the room, held their eyes, one by one.

"If we're going to do this, then this moment is where we start. We acknowledge the loss, but we prove it was not in vain. Sure, we might be skypirates, but we hold the line. We can mourn later, or not at all, if that's your choice. But we do not fall apart. Not today, and not until this is done. It is too important that we see this through. That's the only way we can honor Toren's memory, and the many lives lost yesterday."

No one spoke, but they didn't need to.

Kal reached into his coat and pulled out a half-empty bottle. The good stuff. He set it on the counter with a quiet thunk, then raised it.

"To Toren. To Breezewaltz. To the ones who've fallen, and the reasons we're still standing."

He took a long swig and passed it to Val, who took it with both hands.

They went around after that, one by one. No speeches. Just quiet sips, low nods, hands on shoulders. Jules muttered something too soft to hear, but Kal saw her eyes close when she drank. Cookie pulled the bottle out of Jazz's hands before it touched his lips and wiped at her eyes with the corner of her sleeve. Locke took his swig last and stood in silence. He raised the bottle to Kal, for the words both said and unsaid. He set it back down in front of Kal. No one questioned what the gesture meant.

Kal looked at this crew. *His* crew. They had carried him through the eye of the needle before. He just wasn't sure if he could carry them through this. Kal hoped he was enough, and he wouldn't have to ask too much of them. He knew the wounds were fresh, but at least they took the first step by acknowledging their existence.

That act was done. The crew, like him, probably didn't like how it ended, but it was time to write the first page of the next one.

He turned to Locke. "Meet me in the hold. You might have the title, but it's time for you to learn to be an Altier."

CHAPTER 27: LOCKE

The Days had been in flight for an hour, but Avery seemed to be the only one keeping her aloft. The rest of the crew gathered in the hold, vast and dimly lit, empty save for stacked crates and the inertial dampeners Kal had Jazz and Lizz set down. The hum of the ship's engines pulsed through the metal walls, a steady heartbeat beneath their feet.

Jules sat at her workbench in the corner, apparently unconcerned about whatever was about to happen. It was a front. She could just as easily work from the engine room. Val and Kenzie leaned over the railing of an upper catwalk. The rest of the crew formed a loose semicircle around the mats.

Kal entered wearing just black pants and his brown leather pack, straps wrapped around his torso, the device resting against his lower back. He stretched his arms and rolled his shoulders. "Alright, Kid. Let's see what you've got."

"Before we start, I want you not to go easy on me." Locke's voice was quiet but steady. "Not because I want to be punished, and not because you think it's what's best. I have to become someone who can stand beside Toren's memory. Not beneath it."

Kal blinked, surprised just long enough for it to register, then gave a slight nod. Locke didn't know if it was approval or acknowledgment, but either would do.

He shook off the exhaustion of the past day. He was probably in shock. If he stopped for even a second, the grief would take hold and never let go. He'd let his brother slip through his fingers. That thought lingered at the edge of his mind, waiting to consume him. Kal's speech had been nice, but it was just a beginning. The hard work would come after the words. Locke couldn't face that part yet. For now, moving away from the darkness was better than pushing through. He would deal with it once everything was done.

The thought reminded him of Seaforth, for some reason.

If the Twelfth Rite had done anything to him, he didn't know what it was. Maybe his limbs felt lighter? He certainly didn't feel sharper, but it was hard to tell with the lack of sleep.

"Are we fighting?" Locke asked.

Kal snorted. "Gaia, no. You'd be dead before I threw the first punch."

Val nudged Kenzie. "Confidence is a disease."

Kal grinned and dramatically pointed at her. "And I've got a terminal case. Now shut up and let me teach."

He stepped into the center of the room and motioned for Locke to follow. "I had Jazz and Lizz set up inertial dampeners in the hold. They adjust localized gravity so whatever we do here won't strain the ship's structure."

Locke scanned the hold and spotted the red devices arranged in a square at its center. The twins had put down some safety mats on the floor as well. The crew stood just outside the perimeter, watching.

Kal stepped inside without hesitation. "You're an Altier now. That doesn't mean you know how to use it. Let's start with the basics. What do you know about Altiers?"

Locke thought for a moment. "They're fast, durable but not as much as Rosari. They go for quick strikes and fast battles that end early, mostly because they tire out quickly."

Kal's eyes flicked upward, like he was asking the heavens for patience. "Right-ish. That's the children's book version." He paced. "Time slows down, but not in the way you think. You don't just move faster. You perceive time in broken pieces. Imagine I handed you a picture book with sixty pages. Out here, in the normal world, you could flip through all sixty. Inside dilation, when you tap your power, you only get four. You don't get to pick which ones, and the ones you do see come through a pinhole." He stopped. "Your brain tries to fills in the gaps. At first, you'll run on instinct. You'll never control it if you don't understand that."

Locke frowned. "I'd prefer to be in control."

"Every Altier does," Kal said. "That's why they train. To see more frames, to expand the pinpoint, to hold dilation longer without burning out. A master Altier can sustain nine hundred miles per hour for an hour or maintain half that speed for an entire day. That takes extreme training. The more you work at it, the more control you'll have over what you see, how you react, and how long you last."

Kal flicked his hand. Before Locke could react, he was right in front of him.

Locke barely had time to flinch before Kal tapped his forehead with two fingers. Not hard, but enough to make him take an automatic step back.

Kal stepped away, casual and unconcerned. "You think I moved fast, right?"

Locke rubbed his forehead. "Yeah. You closed the gap before I even processed it."

"That's because I was dilated and you weren't. Your eyes might've caught the first and last page of me moving, but your brain couldn't keep up with what happened between. To you, it seemed instantaneous. To me, it was like flipping through six or seven pages of movement. I process what I can in there, but I'm still working with limited information."

Locke frowned. "Then how do I keep up?"

Kal smirked. "You can't. Not unless you're dilating too. That's the entire advantage of being an Altier. You exist at a different speed than everyone else." He paused. "And if it's not already clear, you have to use your power consciously. It doesn't activate automatically when you sense danger. Right there, I tapped you without you activating subconsciously."

"Makes sense," Locke said.

Kal clapped his hands together. "Alright. Tapping the power should be as natural as moving your fingers. You might not realize it's there because it's new, but your brain already knows how to use it. It's just waiting for you to figure it out."

Locke was skeptical, but Kal wasn't known for philosophy. If he said so, it was probably based on experience. Locke flexed his fingers. "How do I control it?"

"Close your eyes."

Locke did.

"Look inside for something. When you breathe, your lungs normally function on their own, but when you think about it, you can control them directly. There should be something there that feels similar. Do you feel it?"

"Maybe?"

"Let's test it. Flick your finger. When you do, tap into that energy."

Locke took a slow breath. He focused inward, felt for something unfamiliar, something just under his skin. It was there, like a thread woven through him. He focused on it, pulled the string the same way he could consciously tell his hand to move.

The world blurred and seemed to slow down to a crawl. He flicked his finger and released the energy. The hold returned to focus, and a weak crack sounded through the cargo hold.

Kal's grin widened. "Nicely done." His expression shifted as he studied Locke's hand. "Now we need to talk about control. You went full bore there. You'll be lucky if your nail doesn't fall off."

"What!" Locke stared at his hand.

"Relax, it's a training injury." Kal leaned against a crate. "Chicks dig scars."

"We really do." Val said, bumping her shoulder into Kenzie.

Kal smiled at the XO and looked back at Locke. "Think of it as a dial. Right now, you're flicking the switch on and off, but any Altier worth their salt can dial it up and down steadily. Try spinning your arm in a circle. While you do, gently apply the energy to it."

Locke moved his arm and slowly applied the energy. Eventually, the world slowed and became fragmented as his arm moved at a constant speed. Locke continued to add energy until Kal pulled him out. They both came back to regular time together.

"When any part of you moves inside dilation, it pulls your whole body in," Kal said. "It's all or nothing. You can't dilate just an arm or a leg. Your body won't allow it."

Locke flexed his fingers, felt the lingering strain. "So no small tricks? No partial activation?"

"No. You're either in or out. If you move, your whole system has to keep up." Kal's expression turned serious. "How do you feel?"

"Like I just sprinted up the Beggars Trail," Locke muttered, breathing hard.

"Zero chance," Kenzie called from the catwalk, nudging Val.

Kal didn't smile. "Get used to that. Using dilation stacks exhaustion on top of itself. It burns stamina to function. Your body strains to process all the sensory input, and you can't breathe properly in there. Air turns into soup in dilation. The faster you move the thicker it becomes.. You have to inhale between bursts like a swimmer surfacing between strokes."

Locke nodded, still catching his breath.

Kal grabbed a small metal washer from a nearby crate. "Your kinetic energy is tied to you and the things you're touching at all times. Throw this while you're dilated. Watch what happens when it leaves your hand." He tossed the washer to Locke.

Locke caught it, focused inward, and let the dilated world take over. He flicked the washer toward Kal.

The moment it left his fingers, something was wrong. The washer accelerated in a blur, but the second he released it, it bled speed like it was moving through syrup. Kal snatched it from the air before it could ricochet past Jules.

The world snapped back to normal.

The gruff engineer looked up from her stool at Kal's outstreched hand a few feet away from her. She looked like she was already over whatever this was, but she still didn't move.

"Sorry about that, grandma," Kal said.

"I'm not your grandmother, Kaliston." Jules went back to working on the equipment on her bench.

Kal smiled and walked back to Locke. "Did you see that?" Kal asked. "The moment it left your fingers, it lost momentum. Your power stays with you, not what you throw."

Locke frowned. "So I can't just throw a rock fast and turn it into a weapon?"

"You can, and it'll be fast for a moment, but it's not as effective as you think, especially against Rosari. The second it leaves your grip, it bleeds speed. Your power stays with you, not the object. Air resistance is a problem too. That's why Altiers fight up close." Kal grabbed a small bell from the crate. "Now catch this while dilated. Focus on it before you shift."

He tossed it.

Locke tapped his power. The world slowed.

The bell vanished.

Not literally. It was there, somewhere in the fragmented reality, but his depth perception lied. He reached where his eyes told him it should be and grasped air. The sound came through warped and distant, stretched across too many missing frames. He fumbled, overcorrected, nearly dropped it before securing the catch.

When he returned to normal speed, sweat beaded his forehead.

"Your senses don't work right in there," Kal said quietly. "Sound needs air, and air barely exists in dilation. What you're seeing, hearing, feeling, that's not your normal nerves. Something else extends when you tap the power. Something that mimics your senses but doesn't replace them." He paused. "If you're not focused on an object before you shift, good luck finding it again. Vision narrows. Light smears. Distance becomes a guess."

Locke's chest tightened. Not from exertion. The description reminded him of an afternoon he watched his father train in the yard. He would set up mutliple dummies, hundreds, and move between them dilated. Locke never understood why, until now.

He shoved the thought down, it would not help him in this moment.

"The best Altiers train lifetimes to expand what they can process in dilation," Kal continued. "For now, as a blueberry, you're stuck with your four picture-book pages. Those new senses will kill you fast if you're not ready."

"Blueberry?" Kenzie asked from the catwalk.

"Novice Altier. Street slang for anything associated with the Azure Crystal. They're kind of one and the same." Kal looked back at Locke. "Your thinking works differently in there too. You can make split-second choices, but only if you're sharp enough to fill in the blanks your brain can't see."

An hour passed. Then two. Locke's body screamed with each new demonstration, each push into dilation and snap back to reality. His muscles felt wrung out and left to dry. But Kal kept pushing.

"Alright," Kal said, gesturing to the center of the hold. "I want you to tap into it again, but this time, hold it as long as you can. See what happens when you overextend."

Locke took a breath, felt for the energy, and let it take over. The world blurred as everything around him slowed. For a moment, it felt effortless. Fragmented motes of dust hung in the air, suspended rather than frozen. The ship's lights layered over themselves, each moment stacked into the next. Time didn't flow. It settled, drifted past in distinct pieces.

Locke kept his focus on Kal's face, but everything else became washed out. Not entirely black, but hazy, lacking definition.

Then the strain crept in. His muscles coiled with tension, his breath grew heavier, his chest tightened like a fist closing around his lungs. He pushed through. Tried to hold it. Just a little longer.

Locke's focus wavered. The dilated world rippled at the edges. Images blurred and warped together. Nothing was real, just his mind filling in the missing frames with the wrong information.

Everything snapped back.

Time crashed into him at full force. His body lurched, his legs buckled, and the intensity of real-time movement hit like a hammer. He gasped, sucking in air like he'd been drowning.

Kal caught him before he could hit the floor. "And that's what happens when you overdo it."

Locke coughed, heart hammering. "This feels like I just ran ten miles."

"More like sprinted ten miles while holding your breath." Kal let go once Locke had his balance.

"I don't know how much more I have in me, Kal," Locke said between labored breaths.

"You're made of stronger stuff than that. Besides, girls are watching." Kal flicked his eyes to the catwalk. Locke looked back at Kenzie and Val, who were lost in conversation but not looking away. Locke nodded back to Kal.

His voice softened slightly. "A good Altier doesn't waste it. A great Altier knows when to use it and has the stamina to keep going. Use it when you need to, not just because you can." He paused. "And they don't lose focus mid-dilation. You have to learn to ignore the pieces your brain is trying to fill in."

Locke said nothing. He couldn't even describe what the world looked like on the edge of his vision.

"Now do the opposite." Kal's expression hardened. "This time, push as hard as you can. Don't move when you do this. Don't even move your eyes."

Locke braced himself, took a deep breath, and threw himself into the dilated world. Instantly, his perception widened. More frames, more detail, more everything. The world slowed to a near standstill. The hum of the ship faded into a distant echo. Every edge sharpened, every shadow deepened.

Then his whole body locked up.

His muscles screamed. His head pounded like a drum. His vision blurred as if his mind had outpaced his body. He feel out of dilation, not by choice, but like his body pulled him out. He collapsed onto his hands and knees with a gasp.

Kal crouched beside him. "That was you moving faster than almost anything that has ever lived. Lucky you didn't shift your eyes, or you would have lost them. You pushed too hard, maxed out without control, and your body shut down before the strain could kill you."

Locke clenched his fists as frustration bubbled up. "So what's the point? If I can't even use it at full strength?"

"The point is knowing how much to use and when." Kal gestured for him to get up. "You don't slam the accelerator on a ship without knowing how to steer. You ease into it. Control is what makes an Altier dangerous, not just raw speed."

Locke exhaled and wiped sweat from his forehead. His breath was shallow, and the exhaustion of the past twenty-four hours settled into his bones.

Kal stepped back and crossed his arms. "I'm not going to hit you to prove this, but know that I could. Your body will eventually adapt to withstand the force of your strikes at one hundred eighty meters per second. But that's your limit, not the world's."

He punched the air with a cracking sound. It was more than speed. Kal was doing something else, but Locke couldn't tell what. Probably had something to do with the pack on his back.

"Rosari can punch with about ten tons of force. Even at normal speed, that would tear through you, our hull, and just about anything else on Gaia's green planet."

Locke exhaled. "Don't get hit. Got it."

Kal's voice hardened. "I meant that one. Do not ever get hit by one of them."

Locke's stomach tightened at the shift in Kal's tone. He nodded.

"Last thing. Altiers don't fight barehanded. Not if they can help it." Kal glanced around. "I don't have a suda, so we'll have to skip that part. We'll see if we can pick one up in Somerset or Belfield."

Locke hesitated. "I might have one, but it's deactivated?"

Kal frowned. "Why do you have a suda?"

"I picked it up when I ran that errand for Jules." He turned toward Jules's workbench. "Hey Jules, was there a suda in that package Haruto gave you?"

From her workbench, Jules barely glanced up. "Yeah, and I fixed it. It's over here along with that..."

Locke dilated.

The world fragmented. He pushed through the sensory distortion, focusing on Jules's workbench even as the edges of his vision smeared. His muscles screamed, but he covered the distance in what felt like three stuttering steps.

He snapped back to normal speed beside her.

Jules blinked, startled. "...thing. Right." She recovered quickly, reaching into a drawer. "Here's the suda." Her voice dropped. "I'll hold onto the...other thing for now?"

Locke nodded. The charm, the one from the watchsmith. "Thanks," he said quietly, understanding her intent. She gave him a wink.

"Great, that solves that problem," Kal called from across the hold. "Now get over here and let's get dangerous."

Locke returned at normal speed this time, giving his body a chance to recover. The suda was simple. Just a grip with pinholes at the top where the metal would push through. When he held it, something hummed beneath the surface. Like the weapon recognized him.

He turned it over in his palm. "I can feel the core inside, like we're on the same wavelength. That's new."

Kal's expression turned serious. "Sudas are extensions of an Altier's will. The liquid metal inside is infused with shard powder. It responds to intent, forming whatever shape you need, but only if you're feeding it energy and focus." He stepped closer. "Lose either one, and it retracts. No exceptions. You can't drop it in a fight and expect it to stay active. Can't throw it like a spear. It's part of you, or it's nothing."

Locke tightened his grip. "How do I activate it?"

"Same way you tap your power. Push your energy through your palms into the hilt. Will it into existence."

Locke closed his eyes for a moment. He reached inward, found the same energy he'd used all day. That thread woven through his being. He channeled it downward through his hands into the grip.

The suda responded.

A ripple of blue metal surged outward. The liquid metal expanded and rose like a wave before it solidified into a massive single-edged sword, the size of Locke himself. His eyes widened. "Oh."

Kal put both palms up. "Down, boy. You just made a ship-killer. Dial it down before you put a hole in my hull."

Locke focused and adjusted the energy flow like Kal had taught him. The blade melted back into the hilt almost instantly. He tried again, picturing a shorter blade. The suda responded by extending into a slender sword. He experimented further. A chain-whip. A flat-edged shield. Each form came easier than the last, though his attempts came out warped, with uneven edges and inconsistent lengths.

His arms began to tremble.

"The suda pulls energy from your stamina, just like everything else," Kal observed. "Overdo it, and you'll tire out faster than fighting barehanded. There are two openings on both sides of that thing, and some sudas even have dual chambers to split into two. The weapon is adaptable and moves as fast as you think. It can form a blade, a spear, or even a shield in the right hands. But it's only as good as your control."

Locke retracted the suda fully and let his arms drop. Every muscle ached. His head pounded. But beneath the exhaustion was something else. A spark of understanding. Maybe even competence.

Kal stretched and rolled his shoulders. "Alright. That's enough for today. You're still a blueberry, but at least you have a foundation."

Locke lowered the suda to his side. "So that's it? No more training?"

Kal barked out a laugh. "Kid, this was just your first day. You have a long way to go before you're anywhere near competent. I've known Altiers who've trained for decades and still never mastered their school."

"I thought the Crystal Bastion was the only school?" Locke asked.

"There are seven schools. Most Altiers spend their entire lives dedicated to just one. You? You don't even have a style yet. This is an emergency crash course to help you not die when the time comes. I have five more days, but at least now, you might last five seconds in a real fight."

Locke groaned and rubbed his sore legs. "Great. Looking forward to it."

Kal clapped him on the shoulder. "Get some rest. Tomorrow we'll focus on Rosari combat, and trust me, you'll miss today."

As Locke trudged out of the dampener field, he noticed Kenzie still on the catwalk. She'd been there the whole time. Val had left, and now she scrolled through her datapad. She gave him a silent thumbs-up and went back to whatever she was reading.

Locke sighed and dropped onto a nearby crate. His body ached, and his mind felt wrung out.

It had been a long day, but he hadn't given up. Learn and adapt or die. Jules had told him that. He watched the engineer tinker in the corner, still smiling to herself. He wondered if he helped contribute to that.

CHAPTER 28: KENZIE

5 Days Until the Colossus Attacks Orleans

Kenzie lingered on the catwalk long after the others had filtered out, the hum of the ship's engines a steady companion. The cargo hold below was quiet, save for the residual charge of the day's training. She leaned against the railing, one boot hooked behind the other, and flicked through her datapad without reading any of it. Her legs ached, and so did her head, but this wasn't a tiredness she could sleep off.

Jules had tinkered below for the better part of an hour, lost in a rhythm of wrench turns and muttered swearing. She hadn't commented on Kenzie's perch, and Kenzie appreciated that. Jules didn't pry. She didn't ask questions unless something was on fire, and even then, it was more 'what happened?' than 'who did this?'

Kenzie stretched her legs and let out a quiet groan. "Think I could get away with sleeping here tonight?"

Jules didn't look up. "Not unless you want Val dragging you back to the bunks by your ankles. You know how she gets when people don't follow curfew."

"Yeah, wouldn't want Mommy to get mad we're out of bed," Kenzie said as a faint smile played on her lips.

The quiet settled in again. It was a silence they didn't need to fix, and that's why Kenzie liked being around Jules.

Eventually, the older woman set her tools down and leaned back against a crate, arms crossed. "You're thinking about something," Jules said.

Kenzie raised an eyebrow. "Aren't we always thinking about something?"

"You know what I mean."

Kenzie tilted her head back to stare at the ceiling. "Yeah. About today. About the past week. About what's coming next."

Jules didn't press. Just nodded. "We live in interesting times. The question is, do you trust your gut?"

Kenzie thought about it for a moment. "Yeah. I think I do."

Jules scoffed. "No, Kenz, you either do or you don't. Half-in is the same as all-out."

Kenzie let out a slow breath. "Maybe."

Her thoughts drifted to the crew. This strange, patched-together family that somehow felt like hers. Val with her dry wit, Cookie with her unshakable cheer, Haruto's bursts of musical chaos, and Lizz's quiet friendship. They were messy, inconsistent, sometimes infuriating, but they still made it work.

"I don't get it," Kenzie muttered.

"Get what?"

"How we haven't killed each other yet. Or gotten killed."

Jules chuckled. "You need to give Kal more credit."

Kenzie thought about that. She couldn't will herself to say it aloud, but maybe Jules was right.

"Is it weird no one's really talking about Breezewaltz?" she asked. "Like we're all just pretending it didn't happen."

"Like Kal said, we'll process in our own ways, but this is how the *Days* deals with grief." Jules leaned her head back against the wall. "Keep moving. Grief can't catch you if you never stop. That's the *Days'* unofficial motto."

Kenzie's faint smile faded. She heard the truth in it. They could run all they wanted. Grief would find them eventually, but still, she was running too.

"We have Kal to thank for that nugget?"

Jules just grunted.

Kenzie stood and stretched her arms. "I need food. You?"

Jules pushed to her feet and cracked her back. "Yeah. Might as well. Cookie was baking earlier. Smelled like something so good it should be illegal."

The two of them walked down the corridor in step and silence. Their boots echoed gently on the metal floor. As they neared the galley, voices spilled out ahead of them. It was Liam and Jazz, already mid-argument.

"What, we're just making up rules now?" Liam barked.

Jazz grinned and shuffled a deck of cards with practiced flair. "They're house rules. You'd know that if you'd won last time."

"That makes no sense. Cheating is still cheating." Liam pushed a finger toward the table.

"Oh, come on. You just hate losing."

"I hate the results dishonesty produces." Liam took a swig from a brown bottle.

Kenzie leaned in the doorway with a smirk. "Still arguing about the last game?" She surveyed the scene. "You guys are still playing tonight? After everything that's happened?"

"Of course," Cookie called out. "The card game is the oldest tradition on the *Days*. We wouldn't stop on account of something small, like the end of the world."

"Well, then, Jazz definitely should remove those three high cards from his shirt," Kenzie said with a smile.

Jazz moaned and threw the cards on the table. "Thanks, Kenz!"

"Hey, wouldn't want you to face the end of the world as a cheater."

Liam pointed at the cards and then at Jazz with a look of shocked vindication. "Thank you!" he finally said to Kenzie.

"My one good deed for the day," Kenzie said and stepped aside to let Jules through. "Besides, I'm just here for the bread."

Lizz sat curled up on the bench nearest the wall, a book open in her lap. She looked up as they entered, offered a nod, and turned the page.

"He's going to get you back for that," she said without taking her eyes off the manual.

"Your brother doesn't scare me. I've seen his sister beat him up," Kenzie replied.

Lizz looked up to smile at Kenzie, and Kenzie returned the gesture.

"What are you reading?" Kenzie asked.

"Oh, it's an engineering book Jules gave me. Kind of dry, but someone wrote some hot gossip in the margins. They have a crush on someone else in class." Lizz turned to show scribbles with someone's name and a heart.

"Cute," Kenzie said. "How are you doing besides?"

"Lot to process," Lizz said and closed the book. "But about as well as everyone else."

"We're all still here, right?" Kenzie said and looked around the room. It looked like a normal night on the *Days*, which somehow made it feel even weirder. Her gaze returned to Lizz, who was still watching the group.

"Yeah, we all trust Kal," Lizz said into the open room. She turned her head back to Kenzie, and the girls' eyes met.

Lizz smiled, but this time, Kenzie could only give a half smile back. Kenzie nodded and pointed toward Cookie with her thumb. Lizz understood the gesture. She silently shook her head, waved goodnight, and returned to her book.

Cookie turned from the stove and wiped her hands on a towel as Kenzie approached. Jules was already there.

"There you two are. Hungry?" Cookie asked.

"Starving," Kenzie said and moved to hop up on the counter.

Cookie handed her a warm roll. "I thought I heard a wrench hitting something it shouldn't."

"Wasn't me. I'm allergic to them," Kenzie muttered.

Jules chuckled as she claimed a stool. Kenzie took a bite and let the warmth do what words couldn't.

Cookie glanced over. "You've been quiet today."

Kenzie shrugged. "Lot on my mind."

"Want to talk about it?"

Jules shook her head. "I already asked. She's not in the mood."

Kenzie smiled at the two women. It was fun being cared about, but it was strange that this was how some people lived. Kenzie knew that because she experienced it before her mom and brother died, but she hadn't known it since. The amount of time after was starting to catch up to the amount before. That fact made Kenzie a little sad.

"Alright then. I'll let the bread do the talking," Cookie replied and broke Kenzie out of the reverie.

The galley filled with soft sounds. There was the clinking of glass, card shuffles, the low murmur of setting up, and all the inside jokes. The game hadn't started yet, but the mood warmed. Tia wandered in as she tossed a deactivated shell between her fingers. At least Kenzie hoped it was deactivated. Tia dropped into a seat and put the shell behind her ear. Haruto followed with a fresh bottle under his arm and a grin, like he already knew how the night would end.

Eventually, Kenzie slipped off the counter. "I'll catch you later."

Cookie gave her shoulder a quick pat as she passed. "Goodnight, sweetheart."

"Night."

Kenzie moved through the quiet halls of the ship. Familiar lights hummed low and flickered in their usual spots. Her fingers trailed along the wall. Not for comfort, just contact. She paused outside the bridge, then stepped inside.

The room was dim, lit only by the stars beyond the glass. She moved to the co-pilot's seat, her seat, and put a hand on it. Kenzie held it there for a moment before she approached the glass panels that domed the bridge. She leaned forward and rested her forehead against the cool pane. Space stretched everywhere above them at night. She couldn't see the gaia below the clouds. The heavens were still, silent, and constant.

It was the only place she knew that stayed that way, no matter what happened on Gaia. Her chest tightened. What was she still doing there? The *Days* was a means to an end. A chance for her to build her network, learn some skills, and have a clean pillow for a time. She should've left at Breezewaltz. She had planned to leave at Breezewaltz, just after dinner with Locke.

Locke... What a pain that she liked the guy. It would have been so much easier to leave without him, but she still thought she could have done it. Then why did she stay? The events of the past couple of days were pretty crazy. Maybe she just wanted to see how it would turn out, or was it because she wanted to help? Either option was bad, and they both broke all of her rules. The biggest was rule three. Never stay in one place long enough to get betrayed.

Kenzie had been there five months, and it hadn't happened yet. Was she still waiting for the other shoe to drop?

Footsteps padded softly behind her.

"Can't sleep?" Val's voice was low, wrapped in wool and fatigue. She stepped inside, draped in a blanket, and dropped into the captain's chair like she belonged there.

"Something like that," Kenzie said.

"I'm on watch tonight. Mind if I sit?"

Kenzie smiled at the woman who was already seated. It wasn't really a question about the seat, but it was nice of Val to ask. "Not at all."

"A credit for your thoughts?" Val asked as she curled her legs under the blanket.

"I feel like my head's floating in space."

"Been there," Val said. "Too many times to count. Most were after drinking too many Kaltinis."

"He named a drink after himself?"

Val smiled, and they both laughed. When the laughter died down, they sat for a while. The silence stretched comfortably between them.

Eventually, Kenzie said, "I've been wondering what happened to the bounty from Breezewaltz. I left them at a clinic. Kissed their head and ran. I meant to go back before we left, but then the Colossus hit and…" She didn't finish the sentence.

Val took a slow breath. "Sometimes it's better to assume everything worked out."

Kenzie didn't answer.

Val continued, voice gentler. "You did what you could. They probably didn't know how lucky they were because of you."

Kenzie looked at her.

"Kal told me you stepped in," Val said, almost wistfully. "We become the people who would've protected our younger selves. I think if younger you saw what you did for that bounty… she'd be proud."

Kenzie swallowed and looked away. Her eyes locked on the stars. She wanted to believe that. It was possible that a part of her did, but the other part, the louder one, still believed she didn't deserve any of it.

They sat without speaking for a while longer.

Finally, Val said, "I bet you're wondering how you ended up here, and what in Gaia's green garden is making you stay."

Kenzie smiled faintly. "You have a gift."

"I only know because I ask myself the same thing every day."

"Do you have an answer yet?"

"You know my answer."

The way she said it could only mean one reason. One person.

The two women passed a quiet smile between them. Kenzie nodded and finally understood that part of Val. She wondered if any of it was true about herself as well.

Kenzie rose and arched her back. "I've got a date with my bunk."

"Goodnight, Kenzie."

"Night, Val."

She reached the door before Val added, "And if you're going to tell people you grew up in Seaforth, say you lived on Evergreen. Next to George's Garage. Best chowder in Iveria."

Kenzie paused, caught the subtext, and smiled. "Thanks. I'll remember that."

The door hissed shut behind her as she stepped into the hall. Her boots echoed with a weight that didn't feel heavy. For once, she thought she might actually sleep through the nightmares.

CHAPTER 29: LOCKE

The corridor that led from the hold was quiet. A quiet that felt unnatural on something with so many personalities. The hum of the stealth engines was muffled, a distant but ever-present pulse. Locke walked down the corridor alone while his boots tapped against the metal floor with a hollow rhythm. The dim strips of lighting painted the path in cold blue and cast his shadow long against the bulkheads.

The day still clung to him like the sweat on his brow. Kal's instructions filtered between the dull aches and pains that popped up as he walked.

Locke paused at a viewport. Beyond, the stars hung still in the night sky, cold and unreachable. Space above, clouds below. He placed his palm on the glass and spread his fingers. His focus shifted to his reflection: shadowed eyes, a tight jaw, and the emotion of the day carved into his face.

Was that the last thing Toren saw before the end? Had he been disappointed that Locke was the one who held him? Did he know Locke would ultimately let him slip away? Did Toren share Aldis's disappointment in the 'Coward of Seaforth'?

Locke shook his head. He tried not to think about it. If he let the pain of it catch up to him, he felt like he would fall through the glass and into the night sky.

A whisper of movement came from behind him. He turned.

"I would've thought you'd be too tired to be pensive." Her voice was smooth and warm.

Dr. Rina stood a few steps away as she watched him. Thin but iron-backed, she kept her silver-streaked black hair tied back in a puffy ponytail. Her sharp gray eyes could diagnose a lie as quickly as a broken rib. Her lips were usually pressed into a line of professional impatience. They only curled in amusement when someone tried to talk their way out of medical procedures like stitches.

Dr. Rina's white coat hung loosely over a button-up shirt and fatigues, the sleeves rolled up to reveal a line of faded tattoos along her left forearm. She carried a steaming mug in one hand and a notebook in the other.

"Sorry, just stretching my legs after training with Kal earlier," Locke replied.

Rina smirked and tilted her head toward the viewport. "Lot of ghosts out there."

Locke glanced back at the stars. "Ghosts?"

Rina stepped closer as her gaze followed his. "One group of ancient people believed the stars were the ghosts of the dead. Of course, like most traditions, that belief faded after the Crystals fell."

"I never knew that."

Rina leaned against the bulkhead and crossed one ankle over the other. "You grew up in the Order. I doubt they would teach it. Just another obscure fact I picked up in my travels." Her eyes flicked over him. "You're hunched over and favoring your right. Want me to check your legs?"

Locke raised a brow. "You didn't even examine me."

She tapped her temple. "Didn't have to. Doctor's intuition, or maybe just experience around here. Kal's never subtle with his training."

Locke rubbed his leg self-consciously. "It's fine. No sparring today. He's letting me look forward to that."

"Listen to what he has to say. That man has done things even I couldn't believe." She took a sip from her mug. "Besides, you're an Altier now. You'll heal fast. Doesn't mean it won't hurt like hell in the moment."

Locke eyed her curiously. "Are you always this honest?"

"Kid, you're not the first Altier I've patched up, and about the millionth soldier. Bedside manner left long ago." Her mouth curled into a slight grin, and she took another sip. "Now, if you'll excuse me, I need to help Hawk with an infected toenail."

Locke's lips twitched. "Hawk?"

Rina shrugged. "Old nickname for Avery. Known him most of his life. He brought me in. Kal liked I could cut hair, too. Thinks it's beneficial if the crew can perform multiple tasks. Just don't ask Cookie to stitch you up."

Locke chuckled but didn't respond. The silence stretched before Rina spoke again.

"About Toren... I'm sorry, Kid."

Locke didn't answer at first. Eventually, he managed a weak, "Thanks."

Rina nodded, as if she had expected that. "I lost my sister. She wasn't a fighter. She was on a hospital ship, but that didn't matter. The Old War found her, anyway."

Locke swallowed. "I'm sorry... I didn't know."

"Thank you, but it's okay, really," Rina said softly as she held his gaze. "We all carry something from them. What matters is that we don't let what they stood for, or what they taught us, leave with them. We must always carry their love forward, in whatever form that looks like."

Locke had to stop himself from getting choked up. He was surprised his resolve held.

She continued, her voice firm but warm. "I wish there were perfect words to ease losing someone, but there aren't. Feel the pain on your terms, Kid, and take solace in the love around you. Doctor's orders."

The ship's hum filled the quiet, a steady rhythm beneath the wisdom of her words.

The ship's comm crackled from overhead. "Hey, Kid. If you're still lurking, get down to the galley. Cards are hot, drinks are cold, and your seat's getting dusty."

Locke smiled faintly at Haruto's lazy drawl. Then a second voice jumped in. It was sharper and full of mischief.

"And bring your credits!" Jazz called out.

Rina raised an eyebrow. "Sounds like you're being summoned."

Locke hesitated. "You play?"

"Not tonight." Rina pushed off the wall. "I already owe enough to these skypirates." She nodded down the corridor. "Go. It'll be good for your head. Just try not to laugh too much, for your muscles' sake."

She started down the corridor, then paused and glanced back over her shoulder. "Oh, and Locke? It's not about winning. Sometimes just showing up is enough."

"You mean the game?" Locke asked.

"What else would you call life?" With that, she kept walking.

Locke's feet carried him down the corridor, but he paused just outside the galley. He hadn't meant to stop, but something in the air caught him. The low voices, the hum of the overhead lights, and the quiet conversation that only happened when people thought no one was listening.

The game had clearly found its rhythm. Most of the crew gathered, just like the overhead comms said, but something had passed before Locke came into earshot. The cards were shuffled, the glasses clinked, and something simmered beneath the surface. Locke wondered what had soured the mood since they called out to him.

Liam's voice came first. "Exactly. It's like Breezewaltz was built to break. The mesa had always stood over that city. Now it finally gave in… I hope everyone in those sectors made it out in time."

Cookie grunted. "Iveria's not just cracked, it's crumbling. The sweet nut at the center is gone. The League won't be able to defend its cities, and trade lines will be ruined in weeks. It's going to be like the history books, when Aurelia held us under their thumb."

Haruto's voice came next. Locke could hear the clink of a chip between his fingers. "Strange how there's nothing on the long-range comms. No articles on the CrystalLine network either. It's like it didn't happen."

Liam spoke again. "It must be a blackout, and the King's probably behind it. Maybe that means he has a plan."

Jules scoffed. "I doubt that pompous bastard could plan his morning piss." Her voice was rough, brittle. "Toren had one. Still died, but at least he gave a damn. He tried to lead like it meant something. His death tells you all you need to know about that."

"Guy didn't even hesitate," Tia muttered. "I'm no stranger to reckless violence, but to charge at that thing was a level of courage I don't think I'll ever find."

There was a silence after that. Locke felt he was unmoored in that quiet space. The darkness twisted in on him. It was Lizz's voice that straightened him.

"He'll be remembered for it. Sad way to go, but the people will remember him as a hero."

"More like a failure," Liam said. "What? That's the truth. I think the guy was alright, but people will see half the city destroyed and the man dying. The record books aren't going to be kind to him."

Haruto broke in. The clinking between his fingers increased as he spoke. "Not unless we bring the Colossus down. We have a chance to rewrite his legacy. He becomes the spark that lit the way forward."

Cookie spoke, her words somber for once. "That's more optimism than I've ever heard you have."

"What's my other option at the moment?" Haruto asked.

"Your usual self," Tia replied.

"My usual self would have jumped off this skyship in Breezewaltz," Haruto said. The sound of the chip stopped.

"Glad to hear you're changing your own legacy in the face of insurmountable odds," Lizz said.

Cookie jumped in, "Legacy is just words on paper." Locke heard her drain her drink and then set it down. "It all crumbles to dust anyway, just like we will. A footnote in a story no one finishes, or forgets with enough time. All we have is each other in the here and now."

"Maybe," Jules said. "But what we do over the next week will mean something to millions of Iverians. If we succeed, and it means saving Toren's legacy, all the better. To be clear, that's the biggest 'if' with an asterisk that Gaia has ever known."

Another pause. A longer breath.

"I didn't know him well," Lizz said quietly, "but when he looked at you, it felt like he already saw the best version of who you could be. Like you'd already made it. I didn't know what to say to that. Wish I could have gotten to know him."

Jazz piped up and tried for a smile in his voice. "Said I'd make a fine soldier. Asked about my past as an orphan. He told me I mattered and said he could tell Kal was proud. Might've said what I wanted to hear, but... he made it feel true."

"You mean he was a good liar, because no one has ever thought that about you," Lizz chimed in.

"You just liked him because he and Locke share those same dreamy eyes," Jazz shot back.

That got a few chuckles, soft and tired.

Cookie sniffled like she held back a tear. "He told me my pearlfruit pie was the best he ever had. Men like that know a way to a woman's heart."

The group chuckled and then reset.

"You think Locke's gonna be okay?" Tia asked, barely audible.

Liam answered before anyone else could. "I think he's focusing on what comes next. We need to be there for him. That's all we can do. I hope he comes tonight. He could use a break."

Jules nodded. "Exactly. The world is burning to the ground out there, but by Gaia, we need to keep it together in here. We keep our eyes on the goal in front of us. The rest of it can pour in once that's done."

"Who would have thought he was practically royalty?" Tia asked.

"I thought he was just an annoying kid who tried too hard. Now it makes sense. The expectations of that life must've been like being buried beneath a mountain," Haruto said.

"Do we talk about his accident?" Cookie asked.

"You know as little about it as anyone. Kal, Val, and Rina know more than they'll tell." Liam said.

"That's enough." Jules cut in. "All of you. We don't guess at pasts. Everyone here can talk about what they want to share when they're ready."

The group fell silent until Lizz murmured. "He just needs us to be here."

The words settled over the game. Jazz didn't even make a joke.

Locke stepped forward. Just enough noise to let them know he was there, and by the time he reached the door, their performance was already in motion. The mood shifted, almost imperceptibly. Locke could hear the cards being dealt while the chairs adjusted, the chips clacked, and someone pulled out another round.

Haruto spoke without turning. "You gonna stand there all night, Locke?"

He could've stepped back. Pretended he was passing through, or said he was tired. He didn't do either.

The table shifted. Jazz's grin sharpened. "I thought I felt someone creeping around. Get in here, First Altier." He tapped the empty seat between him and Lizz. "We've got room."

Lizz looked up. The usual need to be seen in her eyes softened when they met his. "I can help with the rules. I'm sure Kal already gave you enough to memorize today."

Jules, arm draped over her chair, smirked without turning. "You owe me hazard pay after that performance, Kid. Might as well cough up some credits, too."

Cookie's dry chuckle floated from behind the counter. "I'll fix you up something."

Tia didn't even glance up. "About time you paid into the *Days'* rainy-day fund."

Liam, still nursing his mug of jet-black something, muttered, "We've seen how you lived, Kid. No excuses now."

The laughter came fast, like it was caught behind a dam and had overflowed.

Locke stood there a second longer to think. It had been a long day, and he had more thoughts swimming around than he knew what to do with. None of the crew would fault him for going to bed.

On the other hand, despair had followed him since the moment Toren slipped through his fingers. A silent specter, always one step behind. He could feel it over his shoulder as it waited to wrap its arms around him.

In the end, it was not a hard decision, but it was still one he had to make. Faith was always a choice, even when one put it in other people.

He stepped forward and slid into the seat the twins had left open. "All right," he said, a breath caught in his throat. "Deal me in."

CHAPTER 30: KALISTON

4 Days Until the Colossus Attacks Orleans

The sea shimmered like broken glass as the *Days* dropped into her final descent over Somerset's outer harbor. From the bridge, Kal watched the dock lights reflect in steady teal ripples along the water. There were no alarms, scrambling fighters, or shardshot cannons locked on. Just the lazy drift of gulls circling above rooftop banners that advertised pearlfruit slush and half-price reef gliders.

It looked like a vacation town that pretended the world hadn't just cracked down the middle.

Behind him, Haruto's voice cut in. "Dock A-twelve."

Avery didn't respond. He just keyed the landing sequence, calm as ever. The ship hummed beneath their feet and glided toward the pad with practiced grace. Somerset unrolled itself below, a canvas of white stone villas, bright neon stalls, and hills crowned with lazy palms. It was untouched. At least that's how it appeared from the clouds.

The *Daybreaker*, the Eighth Capital skyship of the Armada, had done a wonderful job keeping it a resort town. That wouldn't last with her away in Orleans. It was only a matter of time before either the war or the Colossus would come here.

Kal called for all hands and left the bridge before the gear even locked.

By the time the engines powered off, most of the crew had gathered in the cargo hold. The ramp hissed open to let in a wash of sea air that smelled like salt and citrus peel. It was warm, familiar, and sharp enough to remind anyone with a nose they were still alive.

Kal stood near the exit, arms crossed, as the ship settled behind him. "We've got twelve hours," he said. "That's it. The CrystalLine's still dark about Breezewaltz, and the long-range comms are bottlenecked. The King's locking down information tight, so don't be surprised if Somerset acts like nothing's happened."

He pulled a thick stack of credits from his coat and set it on a crate. It hit with a soft thud. "Walk. Eat. Breathe. That's not a suggestion. I want every one of you off this ship for a few hours. If you're still on board when I check in, you're getting reassigned to sewage duty."

There was a pause. "Except you two." He nodded toward Jules and Lizz. "Tow cable's getting modified before we leave."

Lizz offered a lazy salute and wandered toward the tools. Jules gave him a look that said she'd already rebuilt the entire ship twice that week and was not interested in starting a third, but she didn't argue.

Val slung a satchel over her shoulder and stepped toward the ramp.

"I'll go on ahead," she said. "You know how Uncle is. Better if I show up alone. Give me six hours, and I'll have his traps disarmed by the time you catch up."

Kal narrowed his eyes, but she was right. No point trying to talk her out of it.

"Two-hour comm intervals," she said to the assembled crew, already halfway down the ramp. "We're docked in Northside Market. Let's make this one uneventful after Breezewaltz, aye?"

The crew peeled off. Jazz muttered something about a shirtless run on the beach. Liam was already hunting for the nearest food stall. Rina glanced at Locke, more measured than worried, and stayed put as the crew advanced out.

Kenzie paused just before she stepped off the ramp. It wasn't hesitation exactly, but she stood there a little longer than the others. Watching the coastline. Listening for something. Kal clocked it and said nothing.

Locke lingered too.

"You stay," Kal said, "but give me a minute. I have another problem to solve first."

Kal turned back to Jules and rattled off a list of adjustments for the tow cable modifications. He gestured with both hands as he talked, half-inventing and half-remembering what they actually needed.

Jules stared at him. "You might as well ask me to fix the hull with a shoelace and some glue."

Kal gave her the same look he always did, like a kid asking for one more toy. Jules gave him that small smile, and he continued. When he finished, she gave him a theatrical sigh and pulled Lizz aside to run diagnostics.

"We're all gonna die, and he's asking for a yo-yo," Jules muttered, loud enough for the stragglers to hear.

Kal didn't dignify that with a response beyond a chuckle. He pivoted toward Locke, who still hadn't moved. "We've got five hours," Kal said. "Today's Rosari training. Start stretching."

Locke groaned under his breath, but obligingly lifted an arm and pulled it across his chest. His form was lazy, but at least he pretended to take it seriously. Kal followed his gaze down the ramp, where the last of the crew headed out in clumps. Most had already vanished into the city. Kenzie, though, was still there.

She stood to the side, one foot on the deck, as if the ramp might swallow her if she put both down. One arm hung onto the railing, and the other hung loosely at her side. Kal could see the side of her face, and it was unreadable. She scanned the horizon, seemingly not trusting what she saw.

"Coming or not?" Jazz yelled up the ramp, his shirt already off.

"I'm evaluating my options," Kenzie replied, voice dry.

Kal didn't miss the slight shift in her weight. Typical Kenzie. She always thought about her possibilities and the worst-case scenario, each presented.

Rina stepped up beside her without a word. The two stood in silence for a second. Kal stayed at the monitor and pretended to fiddle while he watched out of the corner of his eye.

Rina looked over her shoulder before she cleared her throat and finally spoke. "Sunlight's good for mood regulation," she said to Kenzie. "Fresh air helps with sleep quality. Laughter stabilizes cortisol."

Kenzie glanced sideways. "That your way of saying I look pale?"

"You look like someone who's never stopped long enough to let sunlight touch her."

Kal didn't move. Rina had a way of getting through to people that never felt like effort. It was like she flipped a switch. People never noticed the room getting brighter until their problems were sterilized in light.

"Might do you good," she added, "to sit still in the wrong place for once."

Kenzie furrowed her brow. "Don't you mean the right place?"

"Sometimes the wrong place is the right one."

Kenzie gave her a look. "You always talk like this?"

"Only when I like someone," Rina said. "Come on. We'll get you right as rain."

There was a pause. Long enough that Kal thought Kenzie might actually turn around and walk back inside. Then she rolled her eyes, muttered something under her breath, and stepped off the ramp.

"Fine, but if I get sunburned, I'm blaming you."

"We have ointment," Rina said and looked back to wink at Kal as she started down the ramp. "But I'm sure the bar is covered."

Kenzie snorted, short and soft, and walked into town beside her.

Kal waited until they were out of earshot. Then he turned back toward the table, grabbed the nearest tool schematic, and sketched over it with a stylus. He had an hour to get the tow cable schematic to Jules and five to train Locke.

"Let me know when you're ready to keep going," Locke called across the hold, still stretching.

"This is all part of it. You're doing great," Kal called back and gave him a thumbs up.

Toren used to call Locke a pain in the ass when they were students. Kal finally understood why Toren always said it so fondly.

CHAPTER 31: LUCAN

4 Days Until the Colossus Attacks Orleans

The remnants of White Hill groaned with every slow, titanic step of the Colossus. The shattered city hall had become Lucan's mobile throne. If Rosewood, the capital of Aurelia, could move, why not his new capital on Iveria? His Fleet trailed behind the behemoth like loyal hounds, heavy cruisers and frigates in formation, and the *Inquisitor* led the pack. If the Armada arrived, he would command from the *Inquisitor*, but for the moment, the ruinous perch atop the walking god felt right.

Once, it had been a seat of Iverian law, a place where local decrees were passed and governance was debated. Now it was his, back where it belonged.

The ceiling had been patched together with jagged beams that clawed at the sky like shattered ribs. Even with Syd's inertial dampeners, the structure groaned underfoot. Dust drifted from the rafters with each step of the Colossus. Metal creaked and machinery whirred, a steady undercurrent beneath the deep, rhythmic pulse of the creature itself. It was a sound Lucan had come to savor, the sound of conquest.

Behind him, a choked moan turned wet, then fell silent.

Syd sighed and muttered something under his breath. Lucan finally turned.

The last of the captured Altiers slumped against a support column, arms bound, body broken. She had lasted longer than the other one. The first had screamed himself hoarse before he died. She had gone quiet early, which Lucan had found less entertaining.

Lucan crouched beside the body. The woman's arm twitched faintly, though it could have been a reflex. "You thought yourself chosen, but you picked the wrong god. I commission your soul to the beyond in the name of the Rose."

"Finally done?" Syd mused. He didn't even look up. "Are you planning to continue playing with her, or did you get what you were looking for?"

He sat at the central control console while his hands danced over the interface. The station had been cobbled together from Iverian tech they had shipped in or scavenged, but it worked. His masterpiece. He set the coordinates, and the Colossus followed.

Lucan chuckled under his breath. "I didn't need anything from her. I like the sound they make when they break."

A nearby officer shifted uncomfortably. Lucan's gaze flicked to him, but he said nothing.

Syd still didn't pay attention. His fingers moved across the console, adjusting calculations. Then, without missing a beat, he spoke again, but not to Lucan. "Yes, I know," he murmured. "It won't be long now."

Lucan tilted his head.

Syd kept working. "It's already begun." He paused. "Of course, they'll try. That's what makes it fun."

Lucan ignored the ravings, as usual.

A nearby officer approached with a datapad, his steps carefully measured. Lucan flicked his eyes toward him.

"High-priority long-range communication, My Prince," he said, his voice tight. "Encrypted Domain frequency. From Rosewood. It's… It's the Emperor."

Lucan turned slowly, and the entire room stilled. Even Syd looked up from his console. Something glinted in his eyes. Was it interest, or perhaps… amusement?

"Play it," Lucan said.

The speakers fired up with a crackle before turning into a low static hum. At first, there was no sound, but Lucan knew better. The Emperor would speak when he was ready, not when the audience demanded his voice.

"Prince Lucan, my son," the voice intoned eventually. It was calm, measured, and every syllable held importance.

Lucan stood straighter.

"In my time, we have watched the sky burn. Watched Altiers scatter like ash before me, but we have never had a victory like the one we now call ours. You have made your mark. Breezewaltz lies in ruin, the Iverian heart falters."

Lucan said nothing. A quiet smile formed at the edges of his mouth.

"You are truly your father's son," the Emperor said. "A commander worthy of your title. Aurelia is proud of the divine works you perform."

Lucan's breath eased. Finally, the recognition he was owed.

Then the voice shifted, not in tone, but in gravity. "The people will speak of this day as the moment the Domain took its first true step back into glory," the Emperor continued. "Thanks to your effort, they will remember Emperor Titus Regis Van Nero as the one who restored our glory. This new Colossus is our righteous weapon. The Rose Colossus is our shield, but the Azure Colossus is our sword. We would very much like to sit at the head of our full war Fleet with our Colossus under our feet as we break the walls of Orleans. To that end, it must be brought home."

Lucan's head tilted slightly.

"You will guide it across the northern sea," the Emperor said. "Bring it to Tallowport and wait for Rosewood to arrive. We will purify the creature and consecrate its might before holy battle."

Lucan's expression darkened. The words landed like stones.

"You have done well to find this sacred weapon, Lucan, but it was never yours to command," the Emperor said. "This is a weapon of the Domain, our Domain. You have shown it can be wielded, and now you will deliver it, as commanded."

The transmission cut. Silence pressed against the chamber like a physical thing.

Lucan didn't move for several seconds. Then, very quietly, he said, "Who brought the message?"

An aide stepped forward. A junior officer, young and clean-uniformed. He was barely old enough to understand what he'd delivered. He took one cautious step, datapad still trembling in his hands.

Lucan walked toward him.

The boy straightened. "My Prince, I only relayed the message as I was commanded..."

Lucan's hand shot out and seized him by the throat. Lucan didn't raise his voice. He didn't need to. "Did you hear him?" he said, quietly. "Did you hear what he called me?"

The officer's eyes bulged. Lucan tightened his grip.

"A tool. A courier. An errand boy," Lucan growled. "I bring this continent to heel, and still I'm told to fetch." His face twitched. "The Emperor speaks of glory, but only I stand atop the Colossus. Only I have felt the pulse of the Azure Crystal beneath my feet. Isn't my glory already the will of the Rose Crystal? What else would you call it?"

The officer shook his head, at a loss for words.

With a roar, Lucan shifted and launched the officer into the same column where the dead Altier's corpse was chained.

The sound was sickening. Apparently, the officer wasn't a Rosari. Lucan noted the weakness with cold disdain. The unworthy always revealed themselves, eventually. The boy slid down the stone in a crumpled heap. He did not move further. Lucan crossed the broken room and stood over the dead cadet. His breath was sharp at the thrill of the violence. Then, slowly, he looked at the Altier's corpse. His fingers twitched and balled into a fist.

"Let that be a lesson," Lucan called to the room. His voice turned almost too soft to hear, and he reverted. "That's what happens when we ask fate for a portion of glory," he kicked the corpse with a polished boot. "You take it with your own hands, or fate will find a way of taking it from you."

He walked to a desk he had commandeered, sat, and set the pad down. Notifications on payments and troop lists scrolled across the screen. Admin work. He would delegate it to his lieutenants. It was beneath him.

Lucan looked up and scanned the room. It was only then that regular service resumed.

Technicians moved around Syd, testing cables and reading charts.

One approached the doctor. "Sir, there is a minor issue with the routing information desyncing intermittently," the tech said.

Lucan glanced up.

Syd's hands never stopped moving across the console, but his head tilted slightly, as if listening to something no one else could hear. His lips parted. His expression was distant, rapt. "Ahh," Syd murmured, his fingers tapped the screen like a pianist at the keys. "Yes, I see it now. A little ripple in the current. A stone tossed into the river, but the river still flows, doesn't it?"

Lucan's gaze drifted to one of his officers standing nearby. The man stood at rigid attention and pretended nothing had happened. Lucan did not acknowledge it outwardly either. He had learned to ignore the eccentric asides from the moment Rook first brought Syd to him.

"Yes, of course. A redundancy?" Syd let out a breathy chuckle. His fingers moved across the controls. "No. Not yet. Patience. You're both so impatient. I see the pattern, don't I? I always do."

Lucan called the officer over. "Make sure they fix the issue," he said, his face impassive. His mood had soured, and he in turn abruptly found the bustle of the room grating.

The officer nodded quickly and left, though not before casting one last wary glance toward Syd.

It wasn't Syd's mad muttering that bothered him, but the imperfection surrounding him. It was the loose cables, the makeshift repairs, and the constant reminders of mortal limitation. His father would have called it chaos, but his father would never have dared such ambition. Lucan had made peace with the necessary flaws. Perfection required sacrifice. The weak were merely tools to carry his vision, and what did it matter if tools broke while in service to greatness?

Another tremor ran through the chamber as the Colossus took another step. A massive foot crashed into Gaia below and sent a shockwave up its spine to rattle the remnants of White Hill. The datapad on Lucan's desk shifted slightly. He fixed it without looking.

"Was the message that upsetting?" Syd asked, not looking at Lucan.

"You would not understand."

"I'm all ears if you would like to explain, so my team and I don't end up like that." He nodded to the corpses.

Lucan scanned him. *Fine*, it wasn't like it was a secret, anyway.

"I have over forty siblings. One of the joys of the Emperor keeping a harem." Lucan eyed his Praetori to see who that comment amused. None smiled. Fine. "Only the males can inherit the throne, but I still had eighteen half-brothers. Some were older, and some were younger, but all aspired to the same seat. My claim to the throne has never been a matter of birthright alone, because in the Domain, strength and ambition matter more than blood. Each sibling was an obstacle between me and my rightful place. I have already eliminated seventeen of them, pruning the tree, if you will. The eighteenth is an infant, and he will meet the same fate in time. That is the way of the . There were no repercussions, of course. This is my family's biggest open secret. The Emperor practically encouraged it. Still, even that hadn't been enough. He won't give it to me without a sign. Said paying the price with family blood isn't enough. I would need to prove it with my enemy's. I had no problem with the request, but I promised myself a showy campaign of reckless murder wouldn't be enough. That was when Rook walked into the picture. We were gearing up for the campaign when he came to me. He said he heard we were planning to move out and thought he could help. You should know the rest. You were there shortly after."

"Convenient timing," Syd said, not looking up, "Rook falling into your lap like that."

"He offered me the possibility of reuniting Aurelian's lost lands in the name of the Rose Crystal. I didn't care who he was or why he wore that mask. He was a gift from my god in my time of need. She answered my prayer. With his plan, I could finally declare my strength to my people. Even better, that I get to destroy my enemies with their own Colossus."

Syd didn't respond. Instead, he glanced at the screen, nodded to himself, and spoke to no one. "Yes, I told Thorne to look in Somerset, but tell me if he lands in Belfield. Yes, I know you can't watch him all the time.

Lucan's eyes lingered on the smear of blood that ran down the pillar. Something about the angle of it irritated him. He rose, strode to the dead Altier, and nudged the body with the tip of his boot.

Lucan saw Syd smile to himself. A small, knowing thing.

CHAPTER 32: LOCKE

4 Days Until the Colossus Attacks Orleans

Locke felt a little let down that Kenzie wasn't perched in her nest. She ran through the streets of Somerset with the rest of the crew. Hopefully, the reprieve would be good for everyone's mental health. Locke hoped he could join them whenever this Rosari was supposed to appear.

Kal finished stretching and gave Locke a once-over.

"Okay, so we know you're wiped from yesterday. We'll try to limit how much you tap your power today. Besides the exhaustion, how do your muscles feel? Fine?"

"Actually, yeah. I thought I'd be sore from yesterday, but my arms and legs feel great."

"That's the one perk about becoming an Altier. Your body feels fantastic until the day you die."

"Didn't know that," Locke said, genuinely surprised.

"Good joints go a long way. Most Altiers don't live long enough to enjoy the perk."

"Oh." Locke's enthusiasm dimmed.

Kal frowned and shrugged. "Such is life." He moved to the center of the impromptu training ring. Locke followed him.

"What do you know about Rosari?" Kal asked as he spread his stance and raised his hands into a ready position.

"Are you one now?" Locke asked.

"I have many talents. Answer the question," Kal replied.

Locke shifted into a fighting stance and mirrored him. "Strong. Durable. We learned to keep our distance and aim for vital points with shardshot. That was the Citadel line for non-Altiers."

"Sure, that's fine for grunts, but you've seen them up close since the academy. What do you think?"

Locke hesitated. "Scary." He winced as the word escaped. It felt childish.

Kal chuckled. "You're not wrong. Took Iveria centuries to stop being terrified of them. Imagine seeing a wolf for the first time. Now it is standing on its hind legs and punching through your ribcage. Scary is an apt word for it."

He held out a fist for Locke to bump to signal the start of the spar.

Locke fell into step and blocked Kal's slow jabs as they circled. "What else do you know?" Kal asked.

"They're brutes," Locke offered as he deflected a combo. "Slow but dangerous. Aim for the ones who can't accrete fast enough. Wear down those who can."

Kal nodded. "Surface-level stuff, but a start. Forget about wearing them out, that's a mistake. Between a master Altier and a master Rosari, the fight is won with stamina and control. And guess what? Rosari burn slower than Altiers."

Kal faked left, then sprang into a sharp aerial elbow. Locke barely slipped under it.

"They don't need speed," Kal continued while he recovered into a spin. "Their mass does the work. A normal-speed punch from a fully accreted fist will still shatter every bone in your body."

Locke threw a testing jab at Kal's chest, and it connected. No Altier force behind it, but Kal still didn't budge.

Locke barely had time to flinch before Kal's uppercut buried into his gut.

Pain exploded through Locke, and he folded with a gasp on the mat.

Kal crouched beside him. "That was me using a ten percent accreted fist, and I'm not a seasoned Rosari. A real punch from one would pop right through you. Sorry for the pain, but you needed to know."

Locke wheezed through the lingering ache for what felt like days. Eventually, he forced himself to stand.

Kal gave a lopsided grin. "You'll tag me back, eventually. But when I say 'don't get hit,' I mean it."

Locke rubbed his stomach. "Yeah. I'll remember."

Kal continued to pace around him. "Rosari fight mostly bare-handed because they don't need weapons. Their bodies are weapons. Be cautious if you ever encounter one that is armed. That means they've had training, and they can juice anything they touch. Suda, club, shield, and hammer all hit like a Capital skyship's shardshot. It's the same as an Altier. It only lasts as long as they hold it. The second they let go, the accretion bleeds off."

"Accretion?" Locke asked.

"They can add mass and density to themselves along with anything they can touch. Other living things are challenging for them, but not unheard of."

"Ah, knew the process but not the name." Locke frowned. "So they can't throw weapons?"

Kal flicked a coin at him. Instinct kicked in, and Locke snapped into dilation to sidestep as the coin clinked harmlessly against the hull floor. Lizz and Jules, watching from the sidelines, flinched.

Kal chuckled. "Relax, ladies. I would never throw a fully juiced coin at my beautiful protégé."

Lizz blinked. "Protégé?"

"Beautiful?" Jules added.

"Yeah, I've taken him under my wing, gonna turn him into an even more beautiful butterfly."

Lizz and Jules exchanged amused glances. Locke and the women took a step back.

Kal shrugged. "Greatness isn't for everyone." He turned to Locke. "If you had let the coin hit you, it would have felt double its weight. If I took two steps back, it would have been about one and a half. The accretion falls off proportionally to time, not distance. Understand?"

Locke nodded. "Why don't they just make the air too dense to breathe?"

"Good question, protégé. Rosari have difficulties manipulating gases and liquids. They can generally manipulate solids, but even then, they have limits. Most Rosari can't extend their power beyond five feet. Some train up to ten. A few? You're already in the coffin before you realize you stepped into the grave."

Kal's expression turned serious. "Here's what matters. The dumb ones burn out quickly, accreting unnecessarily and launching wild attacks. The smart ones accrete only when it counts. And the truly terrifying ones? They fight like it's second nature, always fully accreted, never breaking a sweat."

"I assume doing that burns stamina, like when an Altier dilates?" Locke asked.

"Exactly," Kal cut back in, pleased Locke had gotten it. "Even though it seems like it, Rosari don't accrete instantaneously. It takes effort to move up and down that spectrum, burning precious stamina," Kal said. "They can't tap their power unless transformed. Aim for the throat if you catch one unaware. Aim for the nose, ears, and eyes in a battle of attrition."

"Why there?" Locke asked.

"Rosari nose, ears, and eyes aren't human organs. You damage them, and they can heal, but they need to cycle in order to do so. You get them to revert and hit them the moment the fur is gone."

"Makes sense." Locke considered a thought. "Is there a limit to how tough they can make themselves?"

"Yes, but it varies by individual. Some are more gifted. It is essential to note that they can enhance all these variables through training. A master's skill set is completely different from that of a pepper."

"Pepper?" Locke asked.

"Rosari version of a blueberry," Kal replied.

Locke's voice dropped, thinking of the spectrum of talent. "Ever see a master Rosari fight a master Altier up close?"

Kal nodded, face tight. "A few times. Unstoppable force, meet immovable object."

Locke remembered watching Toren hold off Lucan.

Kal's eyes darkened. "It is rare. Typically, a novice Altier can tear through a legion of novice Rosari. On the other hand, it becomes less a fight and more an execution when the Rosari's experience and ability surpass the Altier's. The best Rosari don't parry or dodge, they beg you to strike. They live for the moment you're in range. If they get a hand on any part of you, you're already dead."

Locke's jaw clenched. His brother's face flashed in his mind. He wished Kal would throw another punch, but he just let the moment breathe.

"So, having heard all that, how do you fight one?" Kal asked.

Locke paced in thought. "You hit first, hard. If that fails, you move. Never go full burn with the stamina. Burnout kills Altiers faster than punches. Doesn't matter how fast you are if you can't move. The nice thing is, it goes both ways. Make them waste their stamina. Force them to accrete, fully and everywhere if possible. Exploit their limits. Aim for sensitive areas that are easily damaged. When their control slips, finish them at their vitals."

Kal nodded while Locke absorbed his own words. His mind ran through what he had just learned.

"And then there are the legends." Kal cut in.

Locke's brow lifted. "Legends?"

"Yeah. Some Rosari have pushed themselves beyond their limits, unlocking rare and extreme versions of their powers. They're usually tied to the Emperor's bloodline in some way, but there have been stories of Rosari from the boonies who could punch through mountains or harden into an impossible defense. Once a person swallows a Rose shard to become a Rosari, it's not just about physical limits, but faith. Pure, unshakable conviction in the power of the Rose Crystal. Those who can push past the natural limits of their bodies often do so because they believe they're chosen. They believe they have a divine right to wield that power. It's the core of the Rose Order's philosophy. To them, every Rosari is a reflection of the Rose's will. They become living weapons, the many hands of their merciless god."

"The Emperor, as in the Emperor of Aurelia?" Locke still grappled with some of the information.

"Yeah, is there another?"

"No, I just…"

"Stop talking. You're getting in the way of my lesson." Kal leaned in, as if to share a secret. "There are other legends. One could transfer mass into you with a touch, slowing time into an eternity. Another crushed you from the inside. He sounded particularly terrifying."

Kal's voice dipped lower, and something almost reverent crept in. "The worst one I ever heard of existed three centuries ago. She could control mass so precisely that she made micro-densities. Impossibly small, impossibly heavy. Gravity wells the size of a speck where time didn't just slow, it stopped. Imagine your suda frozen a blink before impact. You don't understand what's happening, you wrench, but nothing moves. You're already a corpse, you just don't know it yet."

Locke frowned. "Aren't I too fast for that?"

Kal shook his head. "Once you're caught, there's little you can do. Any Rosari who can catch you is already a second away from killing you."

He stepped close, grabbed Locke's shirt lightly, and his fist stopped an inch from Locke's chin.

Locke broke away, eyes sharp and wary.

Kal grinned, and the danger slipped back into mischief. "Speed's your edge, but brains keep you alive. Fast means nothing if you're not thinking."

Locke's gaze hardened with determination.

Kal exhaled. "The most relevant is probably Prince Lucan. I've heard it on good authority that he has a special ability to alter mass around him, making everything heavier and slower. Even Altiers." He hesitated. "That's probably what got... well..."

Kal's words trailed off, and Locke felt a sense of vertigo when he realized Kal was talking about Toren. He hadn't put it together before, but the thought of his brother falling to someone who believed themselves an instrument of a god twisted his stomach in ways he wasn't ready to confront. Locke wasn't sure if Kal had noticed or not, but the next thing he knew, Kal's arm was around him.

With a sharp clap to the shoulder, the moment passed. "Good. Lesson's over. Meet the team in town. We'll spar for real next time. Word of warning, I might need to punch something after meeting with Val's uncle."

CHAPTER 33: KENZIE

4 Days Until the Colossus Attacks Orleans

The boardwalk had already warmed in the morning sun. The wood underfoot was dry and sun-bleached. The air was thick with sea salt and a sweet scent from a nearby stall. Somerset woke up slowly. The locals unfurled awnings, shopkeepers stacked crates of fruit outside their doors, and a breeze blew just strong enough to keep the gulls aloft in lazy spirals.

Kenzie stepped out of the dock and onto the boardwalk. She blinked at the brightness. Her boots thudded the slats a beat behind the rest. She hadn't meant to fall behind, but no one had waited either. The crew fanned out ahead of her, not scattered but not tight, just moving like they had somewhere to be and all the time in the world to get there.

Haruto walked a half step behind Avery, his brow furrowed, hands fidgeting with a coin he flipped between his fingers. "Something's wrong here."

Avery didn't look up. "You say that everywhere we dock."

"This one's different." Haruto glanced toward the open-air cafés and tourists who strolled like nothing had happened. "We stared into the eyes of that thing, but it's like everyone here doesn't know it exists. Like these people are in a bubble and they can't see past it."

"Exactly," Avery said. "The bubble has a name. It's the King."

Haruto continued to scan, eyes sharp. "And everyone here just goes about their day? You don't think that's strange?"

Avery gave a one-shouldered shrug. "We've been jumping from fire to fire since before Landfall. Let it be quiet for once."

Haruto didn't respond right away. The breeze pushed a strand of his slicked-back hair out of place, and he ignored it as he turned the coin between his fingers. "I don't trust quiet."

"Then don't," Avery said. "You can exist with something you don't trust."

Kenzie watched them fall into a rhythm that didn't need a beat to start. She kept walking.

Up ahead, Jazz veered toward a vendor stand where painted glass ornaments dangled from wire racks and caught the sunlight in rippling bursts of blue. "Think I could trade my per diem for one of those?"

Tia didn't even look up. She dug through a salvage crate stacked with loose wiring and empty casing shells. "You're supposed to use that for food."

Jazz held a charm between two fingers. "The sign says it will bring wealth and fortune."

"It won't," she said as she pulled out a mesh bag of shardshot casings and squinted at it. "Unless you're planning to throw it at someone."

He turned the ornament in his hand and seemed to study it, but knowing him, he was pretending. Kenzie caught his eyes as they flicked to Tia for a moment. Tia muttered to herself, something about not having enough casings, completely absorbed. Jazz smiled to himself. Kenzie did the same.

"Why is something only worth consideration if it's a weapon for you?" Jazz asked.

"It's important to protect yourself, especially in this line of work." She shrugged. "Besides, you'll just hang it in the bunk and break it climbing into bed," Tia said, and finally looked over.

Jazz shrugged. "Might be good luck until then."

Tia narrowed her eyes at him. "You're weird."

"I like to think the universe has my back," he said, just a little too fast.

Cookie walked by with a bag of wrapped breakfast rolls. "Don't buy anything that jingles or breaks, both of you. I'll personally throw it out of the cargo hold along with you."

Jazz set the charm down with exaggerated care. "Not even one?"

"Last time you brought something on board, it hatched and we had to fumigate the ship, so no."

Tia laughed, short and sharp. Jazz looked at her like he'd just won a medal.

Kenzie stayed to the side. She drifted with the current of them, but not in it. She kept her hands in her pockets, and her eyes moved. The warmth of the town unnerved her. Two days ago, they had watched a city crumble. And in Somerset, children laughed as they ran down the boardwalk. A vendor offered chilled juice with half a citrus rind pressed over the rim.

This place reminded her of Seaforth. She'd told Avery and the crew she was from there, which was partially true. She'd been there for about five years, living as a street thief before joining the Days. Living maybe wasn't the right word. Surviving was more apt. She didn't miss the cold or the hunger, the sleeping with one eye open. The one thing she did miss was how simple it had been to know who she was back then. Just a girl trying to make it through the day. Not somebody others depended on. Not someone whose heart jumped with concern every time Locke walked into a room looking half-alive.

Her real home was more complicated. The whole truth was too messy, and she wasn't ready to share it. So Seaforth would do as an answer. For now, maybe always.

Rina passed her a to-go cup without a word.

Kenzie blinked. "What's this?"

"Drink it," Rina said and continued on. "I can write a prescription if that'll make you more comfortable."

The cup was chilled. The drink packed a punch. Kenzie sipped, then held it in both hands as they rounded a bend in the boardwalk. Palm fronds tickled the air overhead. The ocean stretched out to their left, impossibly blue, and glittered like it had never known a war.

The strangeness of it pressed against her like a whisper she couldn't shake. How easy it was to pretend the world hadn't broken. How easy it would be to not pretend at all.

She didn't speak, she just followed.

The Broadside Tavern was all pale wood and shade cloth, perched on a raised platform that overlooked the water. A handful of low tables sat scattered about with menus made out of driftwood, glass pitchers beaded with condensation, and cushions that had seen better days. The crew claimed the back corner like they'd done it before.

Cookie dropped into the most prominent chair with a grunt and peeled the wrapper off a muffin that looked more like a brick. "I'm marching back into the kitchen if this turns out to be a thornberry cake."

"You can't commandeer a kitchen just because of thornberries." Haruto did his usual scan of the crowd.

"You can if you have cause," she muttered as she chewed.

Tia propped her boots on an overturned crate and unslung the salvage bag from her shoulder. "This place is too peaceful. Like the Old War never even happened."

"This is what too peaceful sounds like after Breezewaltz," Jazz replied and plopped down next to her. "Can't we just enjoy the calm between the storms?"

"Not if it's fake," Haruto replied.

Jazz looked around. "They have rings. Want to play a game?"

"You poor, sweet child. Prepare for devastation." Tia smirked.

Jazz grinned. "Sounds like a good time."

Kenzie took the seat on the end, a half step removed from the center of the noise. She said nothing. She didn't have to. Cookie slid a baked good over to her. It was tart, pink, and foamy with frosting.

"Thanks," Kenzie said quietly.

Cookie made a face, like it wasn't a favor, just standard practice.

Avery sat on the rail behind the table with his back to the view, arms folded. He watched the crew, not with suspicion or curiosity. Something that straddled the line between indifference and care. It felt natural.

"You know there's a beautiful ocean behind you?" Kenzie asked.

He tilted his head. "Waves are fine, but people make the world go round."

"So you're reading us?"

He shrugged. "After a while, you figure out what's worth spending yourself on. This," he nodded toward the table, "this is what's important."

Kenzie looked down at her pastry. She didn't have a reply, but it felt like a moment that didn't need one.

Conversation mellowed as the afternoon wore on. The drinks were served, the chairs drew closer, and the light filtered through the shade cloth in soft, golden strips. Jazz and Tia had vanished for a minute and returned with a board game that used colored rings and a complicated scoring system. Haruto played twice, beat them both, and spent the rest of the time predicting outcomes that always came true.

Laughter came in fits and starts like small, easy things. Cookie told a story about flying cargo with a pet lizard that only responded to sky shanties. Avery talked about a storm run between Willowbank and White Hill that ended with them upside down and sideways. Every time the story changed hands, the cargo grew larger, and the storm intensified.

Kenzie didn't say much, but she listened and watched. It wasn't the jokes or the drinks or the warmth of the sun that got her. It was how no one flinched when someone mentioned Toren and Breezewaltz.

The first time it happened was halfway through Cookie's second pastry, when Rina reached for a napkin and said, "We have to take care of Locke. He might not show the damage, but Toren's death is gonna hit like a bolt of shardshot."

No one froze. No one changed the subject. Jazz moved a piece and said, "The guy is taking it surprisingly well, all things considered."

"Maybe he's still in shock," Tia added and moved another piece. "Or he's just letting the forward momentum carry him."

Avery smirked. "I met Toren once when I was stationed in Willowbank. Flew him in from Breezewaltz. He was such a stuck-up prick, but also the nicest person I've ever met."

Cookie gave a low whistle. "Takes a brave soul to mix the two."

A beat passed. Just long enough to feel the ache beneath the humor. Then Rina raised her glass, not high, not performative. Just enough. "To the brave," she said.

No one echoed it, but everyone drank.

Kenzie stared down at her half-empty cup. The fizz had gone flat, and she wasn't sure when. Her chest felt tight in a way that had nothing to do with sugar. She remembered Toren's voice. It had been steady. She remembered how he told her about Iveria and what the League meant to him. Most incredible of all, she had believed it. That was the most uncommon thing since before Seaforth, and it spoke of Toren's character.

Then she remembered his gasped struggle as Locke clung to his remaining hand. The way he'd hung off the speeder as Locke told her to punch it. Kenzie knew it would be how things would move forward. The devastation of the past stalked her at all times and caught her in quiet moments. Add that night in Breezewaltz to the list.

She shook her head to escape the thought and didn't realize someone had moved until a cushion bumped against her leg.

Lizz had joined them and took a seat next to Kenzie. She smiled as the group cheered her name. Locke followed a step behind.

Kenzie's eyes found him first. He looked exhausted, but there was something else. Something harder to name. He seemed settled, as if the fog inside him had shifted. His posture was better, his steps a fraction more certain. Her fingers tightened around her cup. Maybe it was just the Rite, or the trauma changing him. But part of her worried he was becoming the zealot his past life almost made him. That scared her more than anything.

"No Jules?" Kenzie asked.

"She wanted to keep working. Said it was more relaxing than whatever this is. Did I miss anything?" Lizz asked through her smile.

Kenzie hesitated. "No, just the usual ebb and flow." She smiled back at Lizz.

"And a few rounds. Nothing you can't catch up on," Avery chimed in.

Conversation resumed without further mention of Toren. The table leaned into a new debate. Which Capital skyship could outclass the other? Locke said the *Arcadia*, but the group settled on *Orleander*. What city-state had the best food? Seaforth was floated, but no one could agree on it. Jazz was adamant it was Warwick. Cookie called him an idiot and passed him another drink. Laughter rose again.

Kenzie laughed, too. It came out raw and sudden. Her eyes were sharp with surprise. A bark of amusement that startled even her. She clapped a hand over her mouth too late.

Everyone looked, but no one mocked or teased.

Rina, across the table, met her eyes. "That's good," she said softly, like it was a diagnosis. "Means you're still in there."

Kenzie blinked.

Rina rose, glass in hand. "Kenzie, I need to freshen my drink. Care to join me?" She winked at Avery.

Kenzie nodded, stood, and followed the doctor.

Rina leaned against the bar, not pressing, but present. She looked Kenzie in the eye. "You're feeling it, that's good. Life doesn't end just because life does. I can see it in your eyes. You've been here before with a more personal loss."

Kenzie felt like Rina had punched her in the gut.

"You have that look. I'm observant. Just remember how that felt and try to offer that grace to the ones who need it."

Kenzie's eyes watered, and she was beside herself.

Rina reached into her coat pocket and pulled out a folded handkerchief. Without ceremony, she slid it across the bar. "Try not to cry into your drink," she added, tone dry but kind.

Kenzie wiped away the tear, but she felt her throat tighten. She took the square of fabric, almost as a favor to Dr. Rina, but didn't use it.

They returned to their seats and rejoined the conversation.

The sun had shifted lower, making the light richer and warmer. The sea breeze curled in from the west to stir napkins, hair, and the top layer of sand along the path behind them. Far off, a gull shrieked. The boardwalk continued its slow pulse of easy living. Children enjoyed flavored ice, vendors hawked their wares, and a string of lights flickered on one by one.

Kenzie leaned back, arms folded behind her head, and let the quiet settle.

It was still strange, all of it. The peace and silence after the nightmare they had just experienced. The lack of anxiety with the nightmare before them. They spoke as if neither had happened nor would occur. That might be enough for now. Let the past be yesterday and the future be tomorrow.

She didn't say anything more, because she didn't need to. She was there, and for the first time, that didn't feel like a mistake. For a moment, just a moment, she let herself feel safe in the company of friends.

The light had shifted to amber when Haruto's posture changed. His hand stopped mid-flip on the coin, and he let it hit the ground. His eyes tracked something over Kenzie's shoulder.

"Cookie," he said quietly.

The table went still.

Kenzie turned to see eight figures approaching from the boardwalk. Three moved with the fluid certainty of predators. The four others moved like the world would get out of their way. Kenzie knew instantly these weren't ordinary people. At the center walked a man in a pressed suit, his collar open in the heat. His graying hair was slicked back, and his face carried the kind of smile that never reached the eyes.

Cookie stood up and walked toward the bar. A comm slipped from her pocket.

"Thorne," was all Kenzie overheard.

The name landed like a stone.

Thorne stopped a few paces from their table, hands clasped in front of him. His mercenaries fanned out behind him in a loose semicircle. "The crew of the Halcyon Days," he said, his voice smooth as oil. "Heard from a friend you were making port. Thought I'd pay my respects."

"That what we're calling it?" Rina's tone was light, but her shoulders had gone rigid.

His smile widened slightly. "The Shipping Guild has long memories. Especially for those who've cost us... investments."

"You heard what happened at Breezewaltz. Don't you have bigger problems?" Avery asked as one of the bigger thugs took a position next to him. Another moved toward the bar. Kenzie wondered if Cookie got her message out.

"Exactly what I wanted to discuss with your Captain. Expecting him?" Thorne replied.

"You know Kal, always unpredictable," Cookie replied as another thug pushed her back into her seat.

Around the table, the crew shifted. Tia's hand drifted toward the satchel at her feet. Lizz set down her mug with deliberate care. Haruto leaned down to pick up the coin.

"We're just here for refreshments," Rina said evenly, not standing. "No need for this to get complicated."

One of the women with a scar across her jaw let out a short laugh. Kenzie could see crystal flakes blooming and evaporating around her eyes.

"Seven against twelve," Haruto said quietly, now holding his coin between his fingers. "Bad odds for someone."

"There are eight of us, and I only count ten of you," Thorne replied.

"For now," Avery jumped in. The mercenaries he brought stiffened a bit and took stances like violence was imminent.

Thorne raised a hand, and his crew went still. "No need for unpleasantness. Not yet." His eyes swept across the group. "I have some business to settle with Kal. Somerset's a small town, but apparently, all my team could find was his crew." His gaze lingered on Locke, then Kenzie. "Surprising to see the scion of the Luinondo line still keeping company with skypirates. I would have thought you'd have stayed home."

Rina stood slowly. Her voice dropped an octave. "You've delivered your message. We'll tell Kal when we see him. Let us leave, and we'll come to an arrangement. Like you said, no need for this to turn ugly."

For a long moment, no one moved. The afternoon sounds seemed very far away. The gulls, the distant waves, and the vendors felt like a lifetime ago.

Then Thorne stepped forward, his smile fixed in place. "No, I don't think I will. Let's wait together. Kal will come running. Whether it turns ugly or not..." He pulled out a chair for himself and gestured for Rina to sit as well. "Well, that depends entirely on what happens next."

Thorne sat, and whatever peace Somerset had offered ended. It had always only been an illusion anyway.

CHAPTER 34: KALISTON

The shack was half-collapsed on one side, its roof patched with what looked like the wing panel of an old Domain skyship. Its other half bristled with antennae, metal filament strung like fishing line between makeshift towers. The funniest things washed up on the shores of Somerset.

A shard generator hung on the side of the shack, which meant Uncle was off-grid and proud of it. Kal saw the motion detector on the path, but didn't care that he triggered it.

The door was already open.

He heard them before he saw them. The shack was alive with Val's low laugh, the scrape of a stool, and Uncle's unmistakable bark of amusement. It was full-throated and unfiltered, just like always. The sound might have been nostalgic if it hadn't been Uncle's. He and Kal never really saw eye to eye.

Kal paused just outside and, just for a second, considered turning back. He reminded himself that nothing scared him. Then he stepped over the threshold.

Inside, the room was cluttered but alive. Charts were pinned to the walls, crystal fuses sat half-disassembled on a table, and a crate of shardshot ammunition rested next to a rusted water heater. Val sat cross-legged on the counter with a chipped cup in her hand and grinned like she belonged there. Uncle stood by the stove and poured another splash of whatever they were drinking. He looked even rougher in person: salt-silver beard, hair like coiled wire, and a frame built more for wrecking doors than opening them. The shardshot pistol on his hip had more rust than clean metal, but Kal could tell it still worked.

"Finish that thought later," Val said when she spotted Kal in the doorway. "Look what fell out of the sky."

Uncle turned. His face didn't shift much. It wasn't cold, but not exactly welcoming either. He gave Kal a slow nod. "Kaliston." His voice was like gravel in an oil can. "Did you get lost between the gate and the porch? Sensor picked you up ten seconds ago."

"Had to stretch my legs," Kal replied as he stepped inside. "Admiring your retirement spread."

Uncle grunted. "Retirement in my line of work is rare enough. Having a beach view with enough food and drink means I did something right."

He didn't offer a seat, so Kal dragged over a crate and sat anyway. Val kicked her boots lightly against the side of the counter.

"You two catch up?" Kal asked.

Val nodded. "Uncle was just telling me about the time he rigged a blueberry explosive under the deck of a Domain skyship."

Uncle's eyes gleamed. "What can I say? They were illegally parked."

Val and Uncle laughed again, but Kal didn't.

He reached into his coat, pulled out his datapad, and set it on the nearest table. "We need eyes on Conchordia. Full layout. We know you've still got your network."

Uncle didn't move. For a moment, he just watched Kal. His cold eyes weighed him against something unspoken. Then he looked at Val.

"This is why you're here?"

Val nodded. "I was hoping to get there." She shot Kal a look. "But I guess we don't have time to screw around."

Uncle set the bottle down without pouring. His eyes didn't leave Val. "You sure about this?" he asked. "Conchordia's not a joke, and you two aren't exactly welcome."

Val raised her chin. "I figured they'd forgotten about us by now, with Syd booted and all."

Uncle flinched at the name. "They haven't. Not with that skyship you took. Not with the thing still strapped to Kal's spine."

Kal crossed his arms and shifted on the crate. "If you've got something to say, say it."

Uncle stared at him. "You always had the mouth. Just making sure you still have the mind to match it. I've heard rumors about a detained skypirate sweating in a cold cell. I don't waste time with folks who've already fallen over the edge. Just trying to figure out if you're still on level Gaia or if you're as psychotic as…"

Val stepped in, voice sharp. "Enough. This isn't about your pissing contest."

Kal started to speak, but she shot him a look. He closed his mouth and leaned back instead.

Uncle turned back to Val, expression unreadable. "You still trust him?"

Val hesitated for a second. Then she nodded. "I do."

Kal watched the exchange in silence. Val had always chased Uncle's approval, and more often than not, she got it. Kal had done the same with his father. All he ever got back was disappointment.

Uncle grunted. "Fine."

He swept some discolored papers and a stack of rations off the table with one hand and set down a dust-covered drive. The bottle followed close behind, but he didn't offer a toast, just a look.

He looked Kal in the eyes. "I care about Val," he said. "Always have. You happen to be the shadow trailing behind her."

Val exhaled quietly but didn't respond. Kal stood and picked up the bottle. He took a full swig, grimaced, and put the bottle back on the counter. Uncle watched him the entire time, then gave the slightest hint of a smile.

Val plugged the drive into Kal's datapad. They watched the data unfold: a grid of tunnels, security pings, and entry checkpoints. The Conchordia campus glowed in sharp relief, its exterior wall and defensive checkpoints spread across Belfield.

Val leaned over the table. "How old is this?"

"Three months, give or take," Uncle said. "Still better than flying blind."

He tapped a section marked maintenance with a callused finger. "The old access tunnel is your best bet, but word of warning, they've developed some sort of automated drones."

Kal glanced up. "And you know that how?"

Uncle didn't smile. "Just because I stopped fighting doesn't mean I stopped listening. Speaking of, I heard you picked up a new follower."

Val straightened. "Locke? He doesn't kneel at the altar of Kal. He's a true believer in the Azure Crystal."

Kal snorted. "Give it time."

Uncle's expression darkened. "Be careful with that. The ones who put their faith in rocks and gods tend to forget who's standing beside them when the building starts burning."

Val's hand paused for a moment on the drive before she continued. "He's not Toren."

Uncle grunted, and his eyes flicked to Kal. "No, not who I was talking about. This Prince Lucan sounds like a real piece of work, from what I've heard. Thinks he's practically a god."

Kal leaned back. "I'd think the same if I did what he's done."

Uncle eyed him. "I've seen enough men believe themselves chosen to know how those stories end."

Val shrugged and returned to studying the schematics while Kal watched her. Uncle did too.

"She used to read battlefield maps like bedtime stories," Uncle muttered, voice half-nostalgic, half-regretful. "Smartest thing I ever saw in pigtails."

Kal said nothing, and neither did Val, but she smiled.

Uncle picked the bottle back up but didn't raise it. "I don't know all the details on that thing on your back," he said to Kal, "but you'd better be sure it's not the one walking you into Belfield."

Kal met his eyes. "It isn't."

"Mm-hmm." Uncle drank.

Val unplugged the drive and tucked it into her coat. She lingered a moment before she spoke. "Thank you, Uncle. This is exactly what we need."

"Happy to help, kiddo."

"I'm not a kid," Val said.

"You'll always be a kid to me," Uncle said, laughing. "Just make sure you two take care of each other. One of you more than the other."

Kal said nothing. His hands flexed once at his sides, then went still again.

Uncle held Val's gaze, the message clear. "I'm not going to tell you your business. Gaia knows I've been terrible in that department, but you can't fix something that doesn't want fixing. Just be careful how close you stand when it finally breaks."

Val nodded, just once, and she stood. Uncle pulled her into a hug at the door. She kissed him on the cheek and left. He shook Kal's hand too hard and too long. He let the old man have his moment. He doubted they would see each other again, one way or another.

Outside, the antennae buzzed faintly in the breeze, and the warped metal wing over the roof creaked as if it laughed at them.

Kal walked a few steps behind Val on the way back. She glanced back at the shack once before it was out of sight, but she didn't look at Kal. When she'd seen enough, she faced forward and kept walking. Kal kept pace. She was just a few feet away, but she had never seemed more out of reach.

The comm crackled to life. Cookie's voice came through muffled from Kal's pocket, but he could make out the word.

"Thorne."

Val spun, and Kal reached for the comm. He pulled it out and hit the trigger.

"Cookie, what's going on? Are you okay?" Kal said, his voice rising.

"Kal!" Cookie's voice was a tense whisper. "He found us. We're at the Broadside Tavern. I'm not sure how he found us, but he brought a crew."

Kal looked at Val.

"Don't do anything stupid. We're coming," Val said into the comm.

"Don't worry about that, you're bringing all the stupid with you," Cookie replied, and the comm cut off.

Kal was already running, Val beside him, both sprinting toward the Broadside Tavern.

Uncle had been right about the Hollowline. It was dangerous. Thorne was about to discover exactly what that meant.

CHAPTER 35: KENZIE

4 Days Until the Colossus Attacks Orleans

The minutes crawled. Thorne sat at their table like he owned it, one leg crossed over the other, hands folded in his lap. His smile never wavered. The kind of smile that said he'd done this before and knew exactly how it would end.

Around the tavern, his crew had positioned themselves with practiced efficiency. Two Rosari blocked the front entrance, arms crossed, their bulk turning the doorway into a wall. The third and fourth stood near the kitchen, cutting off the back exit. The Altiers moved with restless energy. There was one near the bar, another by the boardwalk railing, the woman with the scar circling slowly behind Thorne like a predator pacing a cage.

Kenzie counted exits. Two blocked. Windows too high. The drop to the beach below was twenty feet, maybe more. Survivable, but not pleasant. Not with Rosari and Altiers chasing them down.

She cataloged weapons. Tia had her satchel, which had a shardshot for sure, maybe more. Kenzie wasn't sure what else was packed in there, but Tia never left the ship light. She wasn't sure if those would be assets or liabilities. Explosives in this space would kill half the crew. Haruto still had his coin, but that was theater, not steel. Avery carried a concealed shardshot in his boot. Rina probably had something medical that could double as a sedative. Locke had himself and his suda.

Not enough. Not against this.

Across the table, Locke's fingers tapped his thigh. Nervous energy, poorly disguised. He was running scenarios, too. She could see it in the way his eyes flicked from Thorne to the exits. She bet he couldn't make the odds add up either.

"So," Thorne said, breaking the silence. His voice was conversational, almost pleasant. "The *Halcyon Days*. Quite the reputation you've built. Stolen cargo, disrupted supply lines, cost the Guild... what was the last tally, Mira?"

Mira stopped pacing. "Five hundred thousand credits."

Haruto glanced at Mira. "Gone up since Breezewaltz?"

"Interest," she added.

"Five hundred thousand," Thorne repeated, savoring the number. "That's a lot of credits to lose track of."

Rina's voice stayed level. "We don't work for the Guild."

"No," Thorne agreed. "You work for yourselves. Which makes you pirates. And pirates," his smile sharpened, "have a tendency not to be missed."

Liam shifted in his seat. His hand moved toward his datapad, slow and casual. Too casual.

The Altier by the bar moved faster.

One moment she was across the tavern. The next, she was beside Liam, her hand clamped around his wrist. The datapad clattered to the ground.

"Don't," she said softly.

Liam's face went pale. "I wasn't…"

She twisted. Not hard, but enough. Liam winced, his body jerking forward involuntarily.

"Hey!" Locke was on his feet before Kenzie could stop him.

The woman's eyes flicked to him, crystal flakes blooming around her irises. "Sit down, boy."

"Let him go," Locke said. Crystal began to flake across his skin. His hand moved to his suda.

Everything happened at once.

Mira vanished into dilation. Locke did as well, but in an instant he was back, stumbling. Her fist drove into his solar plexus with surgical precision. Locke folded, gasping, and she swept his legs out from under him. He hit the ground hard.

Kenzie started to move, but Haruto's hand shot out, gripping her arm. She looked back. He shook his head.

Mira stood over Locke, one boot planted on his chest. "Stay down."

Locke wheezed, struggling for air. His hand clawed toward his suda, but she pressed down harder.

"I said," she repeated, her voice cold, "down."

Thorne watched with mild interest, like a man observing a chess match. "Spirited. I'll give you that. But enthusiasm isn't the same as skill." He looked at Locke with something like pity. "Your father was brave. I barely knew your brother, but they say the same about him. Shame he had to get himself killed."

Locke didn't answer. Couldn't.

"My fight isn't with you, First Altier. Your family and the Guild have always played nice. Let's not ruin that today over some credits." Thorne turned back to the table. "You see, this is what happens when children play at being…"

The front window exploded inward.

Kal came through it like a cannonball, hit the ground in a roll, came up running, and drove his fist into the nearest Rosari's jaw before anyone could react.

The Rosari's head snapped back. He staggered, more surprised than hurt, but it gave Kal the opening he needed. Kal slapped him on the chest, and the Rosari reverted as he fell to the floor.

Val came through the door a heartbeat later, shardshot already drawn. She fired twice. Blue shardshot sparked against the second Rosari's shoulder and chest, driving him back.

The tavern erupted into chaos. Thorne was on his feet, smile finally gone. "Take them!"

Mira kicked off Locke and vanished into dilation, racing toward Kal. The Altier by the bar moved to flank. The Rosari by the kitchen charged forward, the floor shaking under his weight.

Kal met Mira's charge head-on. She came out of dilation with a spinning kick aimed at his head. He caught her ankle, twisted, and slammed her into the nearest table. Wood splintered. She rolled away, already moving again, but Kal matched her.

"Go!" Val shouted, firing at the Rosari to keep him back. "Get out of here!"

The crew scattered.

Tia grabbed her satchel and bolted for the kitchen, weaving between overturned chairs. "I'll circle around!" she shouted over the chaos.

Jazz and Lizz went with her. Haruto pulled Liam to his feet, half-dragging him toward the boardwalk exit.

Locke struggled upright, still gasping. Avery pulled him up, but that's all Kenzie saw as she ducked under the arm of a Rosari and vaulted over the bar. She scrambled through the back kitchen as the staff cowered behind a counter.

She thought about looking back. She wanted to help.

Instead, she ran.

Behind her, the sounds of the fight intensified. Shardshot fire. The crash of furniture. Kal's voice, sharp and commanding: "Val, left!"

Kenzie didn't look back. She pushed through the back door and into an alley. She barreled past wind-blown litter and toppled crates.

That's when the wall to her right exploded.

One of the Rosari burst through the opening, brick and mortar cascading around him. He was uninjured and unbloodied. He grinned when his eyes locked on hers. Kenzie looked back, but none of the crew was with her.

"I know you," he said, his voice carrying the typical Rosari growl. "Someone would pay handsomely to know you're still breathing. Thought you died years ago."

A flash of memory. Night breeze. Lanterns. Her brother's hand in hers.

This man had been there.

Kenzie's panic spiked. She looked for an escape, but the alley was narrow and long. No other exit besides doubling back into the tavern.

Think. Think!

The Rosari barreled toward her. His smile said she'd survive, but she wouldn't like it. That's when a blade appeared at the Rosari's throat. Locke was at the other end.

He must have come through the hole the Rosari made. He'd come out of dilation right next to the creature, aiming for the vitals. Unfortunately, his blade wedged in the thick fur at the Rosari's neck.

The Rosari tapped him with a backhand. Locke flew into a pile of trash and disappeared under it.

Kenzie's hand went to her knife, but she knew it was useless. You couldn't knife a Rosari. Not one who knew it was coming.

"You don't have to do this," Kenzie said, backing up slowly.

"No, but I want to." He cracked his knuckles, each pop like a gunshot. "Shipping Guild pays well. Your hide will pay better."

"I'm not going back."

"That's not up to you."

He lunged.

Kenzie threw herself sideways, pushing off the wall with her boots. He overcommitted and slipped. The boards cracked under his hands and knee as he dropped forward. She braced a hand on his back and leaped behind him.

He was faster than expected. His hand closed around her wrist and yanked. She went down hard, face-first into the wooden planks. Before she could recover, he flipped her over, his weight pinning her down.

"Always slippery," he said. His hand pressed against her chest, not quite crushing, but the threat was clear. "Had to be, to survive that night. But you can't run forever."

Kenzie's vision swam. She couldn't breathe, couldn't think. His weight was impossible, like trying to move a building.

His face filled her vision. Her heart hammered in her ears. She barely heard the sound of a canister hitting the ground, followed by a hiss. Bluish smoke filled the alley.

The Rosari began to choke. He rolled off her, reverting to human form as the gas hit his lungs. Kenzie felt hers burn too.

That's when Tia put a shardshot round in his chest.

"Move!" Val yelled, helping Locke out of the trash pile.

Kenzie ran. Behind her, she heard Locke call out, but she didn't look back.

Boots pounded behind her. She glanced back to see Tia, Val, Locke, and the twins. Relief flooded through her, followed immediately by worry. Where were the others?

They ran through the streets, dodging pedestrians who scattered at the sight of them. By the time they reached the dock, Kenzie's lungs burned. She wasn't sure if it was from the running or the gas. She rounded the corner entry just as Val grabbed her arm and yanked her into a side alley. Through the gaps in the buildings, Kenzie could see the *Days'* berth.

Twenty Guild personnel surrounded it. Armed and waiting.

"Haruto spotted them," Val said, breathing hard. She tapped her comm. "The rest of the crew is on the other side."

Kenzie's stomach dropped. "So we're trapped."

"Not trapped," Val corrected. "Just delayed. Kal will handle the Guild thugs. We need to find another way aboard."

Locke leaned against the wall, still wheezing from the hit. "Another way?"

Tia was already scanning the area. "There. Maintenance hatch. We can access below the pier."

Val nodded. "That'll work. Move quiet. If they see us, this gets a lot harder."

They slipped through the shadows toward the beach to get under the pier.

Behind them, somewhere in Somerset's winding streets, the sound of glass shattering echoed into the evening air.

CHAPTER 36: KALISTON

Kal ran. Not dilated, not yet. He needed all the juice in his pack. The boardwalk blurred past him, tourists scattering as he and Val sprinted through the late afternoon crowd. The Broadside Tavern was three blocks ahead, and Cookie's voice echoed in his mind.

He found us.

"How many?" Val asked, keeping pace beside him. Her shardshot was already in her hand.

"Thorne never travels light. Probably both Altiers and Rosari." Kal's breath came steady despite the sprint. "He probably called in a full crew."

"Wonderful."

They rounded the corner. The tavern came into view, its beachside patio packed with his crew and Thorne's mercenaries arranged like pieces on a board. Through the window, Kal could see Locke on the ground, an Altier standing over him.

"Theatrical entrance?" Val asked.

"Always."

The Hollowline hummed against his spine. Kal tapped it, pulling Azure. The world fragmented, time splitting into stuttered frames. He angled toward the front window, picked up speed, and launched himself through the glass.

Dilation snapped off as he hit, glass falling like slow rain. He rolled to his feet and kept moving. His fist connected with the nearest Rosari's jaw.

The Rosari's head snapped back, more surprised than hurt. Kal palmed his chest and absorbed the energy into the Hollowline. The Rosari reverted as he fell.

Val came through the door a heartbeat later, shardshot raised. Four shots. Blue rounds sparked against another Rosari's shoulder and chest. The ozone smell of shardshot filled the air. The Rosari still stood, pissed but alive.

The tavern erupted into chaos.

"Go!" Val shouted at the crew. "Get out of here!"

They scattered. Tia bolted for the kitchen with Jazz and Lizz. Haruto dragged Liam toward the boardwalk. Locke stumbled upright with Avery's help.

Thorne's crew moved to intercept.

The scarred Altier was Mira. Kal had met her before in a smoky lounge. She wasn't on assignment, but she was cocky and cruel. Kal figured they'd fight eventually.

She kicked off Locke and vanished into dilation. The shift was unmistakable, that familiar blink of compressed time. She came out of her run with a spinning kick aimed at his head.

He caught her ankle mid-strike. The Hollowline let him shift into her accelerated timestream, matching her speed for just a heartbeat.

Her eyes widened. Just for a second. Just long enough to realize he shouldn't have been able to do that.

Kal twisted and slammed her into the nearest table. Wood splintered. She rolled away, already moving again, but Kal matched her speed. The device buzzed against his spine like a trapped fly, feeding him both powers at once, though never for long.

A second Altier came at him from his left. Male, younger, but equally as cocky as Mira. Seemed to be a disease with these Altiers. He came in with a jab-cross combination that would've been impressive against a normal fighter.

Kal slipped both punches, grabbed the man's wrist, and yanked him forward into a knee strike. The Altier gasped and stumbled back.

Then the Rosari from the kitchen hit him.

Barely saw it coming. A massive fist like a wrecking ball caught him in the ribs and sent him crashing through a chair. Pain exploded through his side. He rolled with the impact, came up on one knee, and let the Hollowline adjust.

Azure dropped away. Rose surged forward. His muscles thickened, bones became iron. The world stopped fragmenting. Instead, it slowed differently, became heavier, denser.

The Rosari charged again, fully accreted, fur rippling across his arms and face. He swung with enough force to crater concrete.

Kal met the punch with his own.

The impact rang like a bell. The floor cracked beneath them. The Rosari's eyes went wide as his fist stopped cold against Kal's accreted hand.

"Surprise," Kal said through gritted teeth.

He twisted, using the Rosari's momentum against him, and drove his other fist into the creature's ribs. Once. Twice. The third strike sent the Rosari stumbling backward into the bar.

But he couldn't stay accreted. Not with Altiers in the room.

Mira came out of dilation behind him, aiming for his kidneys. Her knee connected, a solid hit that would've dropped most people. He'd kept just enough Rose power to take it. Her yelp of pain when her kneecap met his reinforced spine was satisfying.

He dropped the Rose, pulled Azure, and slipped into dilation just as her knife thrust toward his thigh.

Too slow.

Kal palmed her chest, knocking her back onto her injured leg. She stumbled. He grabbed her arm and threw her into the advancing second Altier. They collided in a tangle of limbs.

The tavern was a wreck. One wall had a Rosari-shaped hole in it. Tables reduced to kindling. Glass everywhere. The smell of spilled beer mixed with blood and ozone.

And the crew was gone.

Breathing came hard now. The switching burned stamina faster than fighting normally. Fatigue crept into his muscles, the Hollowline's hum turning from smooth to grating.

"Kaliston." Thorne's voice cut through the chaos, calm and measured. He rolled a Guild credit coin across his knuckles without looking at it. "Let's stop this madness."

Kal turned. Thorne stood near the bar, untouched, his remaining fighters regrouping around him. Two Altiers and two Rosari closed ranks. Mira stood cautiously next to Thorne. Behind Kal, the fallen man that had once been a Rosari lay unconscious on the floor. Guild muscle on Thorne's retainer, all watching Kal with new wariness.

"Yeah, well," Kal said, breathing hard, "you started it."

"I only want what's ours. Pay the debt."

"I'm working on it."

"How soon?"

"Why don't we just tip Locke over? He's bound to have a few credits spill out now that he runs the Luinondo house."

"I'm being serious, Kaliston. How soon?"

"I'm working on it!"

Thorne smirked, the coin vanishing into his palm. "Fine."

"Fine?"

"As long as you leave me collateral."

Kal forced a smile. "Deal. You can have Liam."

Thorne stopped smiling. "No, Kal. Something worthwhile. I'll take the ship."

Kal's smile fell flat. "What do you want with the *Days*?"

Thorne's face remained unreadable. The same coin clicked in the quiet as he rolled it again. "The world is ending, Captain. A ship that can outrun and outmaneuver anything would be valuable."

"Not a chance." Kal's voice hardened. "I'll pay you back, but the ship stays with me."

"Funny that you still think this is a negotiation." Thorne stepped back. Next to him, Mira rubbed her knee and tested it gingerly. "You can fight, I'll give you that. But you seem to think I only brought seven people with me."

The words landed like ice water. More of Thorne's company were somewhere in Somerset, probably between Kal's crew and the *Days*.

Time to go. He advanced.

A table exploded where he'd been standing. The third Altier, a woman with short-cropped hair and a chipped front tooth, now stood in the spot Kal had occupied a moment earlier, her leg still extended from the kick.

"You're quick," she said, grinning. "But you can't fight all of us."

"I love being underestimated. It makes the next part much more satisfying."

The male Altier charged from his left. Kal cut the blue, flooded red. Full accretion. His shoulder caught the kid in the chest like a battering ram. He dropped red and dialed up blue. He grabbed the Altier's wrist and drained into the Hollowline.

The power flooded into the device. Crystal flakes stopped blooming across the kid's skin. His eyes went wide. He gasped once, then collapsed.

The sickness hit immediately. The parasite on his spine sang while wrongness crawled from his stomach across his skin. The Hollowline was hungry, but his body was already complaining.

One down. Four still standing.

A Rosari, the one Val had shot earlier, came at him from behind. His fur bore the evidence of the shots, but he was dangerous. Kal barely had time to switch to Rose before the creature's fist connected with his shoulder.

Pain exploded through his arm. His accretion wavered. The Rosari grinned and pulled back for another strike.

Short-Hair and Mira hit him together. Not just fast, but coordinated. They'd learned his rhythm. He blocked one strike, took another on the ribs, barely deflected a third. Time to change the tune.

Kal grabbed a chair with one hand and threw it at Short-Hair. She dodged, but it bought him a second. He switched to Azure, caught Mira's wrist mid-strike along with the injured Rosari, and drained.

Their power surged through Kal and into the Hollowline. The Rosari fell backward like a cut tree. Mira slumped, unconscious before she hit the ground.

The sickness doubled. Kal's vision swam. His stomach churned like he'd swallowed broken glass. Mixing the two powers always hit harder, faster. Kal staggered, but kept his lunch down.

Including the one at the start, that made four down. One had left the room through the Rosari-shaped hole in the back. Short-Hair and one Rosari left in the room.

They circled him now, wary. They'd seen what happened when he touched their friends.

Thorne was gone. The room held only the three of them.

"Where's Thorne?" Kal asked, breathing hard.

"Took the opportunity to attend to other matters," Short-Hair said. She spat onto some broken glass and winked. "But we can still take care you, Captain."

Dammit. Kal had wanted to talk to Thorne. The man was a hound, and Kal didn't want him nipping at his heels beyond today. The only option left was to flee Somerset and settle his accounts after the Colossus. Assuming there was an after.

Kal would solve that problem in time; for now, he had to get out of the room.

"You can join him, or you can join your friends on the floor. Your call." Kal was only semi-bluffing, but he wasn't sure if they knew that.

Short-Hair and the Rosari exchanged a glance. Then, without a word, they bolted. The Altier sprinted toward the boardwalk, the Rosari created a second hole as he crashed into the alley.

Kal didn't chase them. Too tired, and his crew was more important.

The tavern was a disaster. Tables destroyed, glass everywhere, and walls cracked. A few tourists huddled outside, data pads raised, terrified. The staff had fled. Kal would've left some credits if he had any to spare. He'd have to pay back the damage sometime in the future. If he lived that long.

No peace officer arrived. Thorne must have paid them off to look the other way.

He made his way through the ruined tavern and out onto the boardwalk. His legs felt like lead. The sickness from draining the mix of enhanced fighters churned in his gut, making every step an effort. He could drain a hundred Rosari or ten Altiers before he felt the effects, but mixing them always led to rapid sickness.

"Val? Status?" Kal spoke into the comm and winced.

"Near the docks. Under the pier," Val responded in a hushed tone.

Kal leapt over the pier railing and found Val's group near a storm outlet. Kenzie, Locke, Tia, and the twins huddled in the shadows.

Locke looked like he'd learned some hard lessons during the fight. Good. He needed to know he wasn't invincible just because he was an Altier.

"You good?" Val asked as he approached.

"Been better." Kal rotated his shoulder, wincing. The Rosari's punch had done more damage than he'd thought. "Crew?"

"Scattered. Haruto says he's with the others on the other side of the dock." She paused. "Guild's blocking the berth. Twenty-ish personnel, armed."

Of course they were.

Kal pulled out his comm. "Haruto, sit rep."

Static, then: "We're in position on the east side. Took the long way around to be safe. Glad we did. Guild's locked down our berth tight. Cookie, Rina, Liam, and Avery are with me. Looks like Jules locked down the ship. Better be thankful these Rosari seem to want it in one piece."

"Can you get to the *Days*?"

"Depends on how loud you get."

Kal looked at the crew around him. Tired, battered, but ready. The Hollowline rattled his vertebrae, wanting more even as his stomach churned and head swam.

"Sit tight," Kal said into the comm. "I'll draw them off. When you see your opening, move."

He cut over and hailed Jules. "All good, Granny?"

The voice that came back sounded more annoyed than anything. "I'm not your grandmother, Kal. And yes, I'm fine. I locked down the ship, but it looks like you're in a pinch."

"Can you give us some backup?"

"I'm a terrible shot. I can cycle the engines, but I think that will draw them inside when you want them looking out."

Kal thought for a moment. "Okay, hold tight. Be ready to lower the ramp when you see us coming. I'll assume there are one or two ships circling over us. We'll have to power on the camo as soon as the landing gear is up."

"On it," Jules replied.

He cut the connection and turned to Val. "I'm not fighting twenty Guild thugs head-on. Not like this."

"First smart thing you've said today." She scanned the dock. "You do your thing. We're going to sneak up the maintenance hatch."

"Maintenance hatch?"

Tia nodded. "Two berths down. Comes up inside the facility."

"Want me to help?" Locke asked, still wheezing.

"Gaia, no." Kal looked at him, amused. "You can help me by escorting the crew here onto the *Days*."

Kenzie and Jazz, who were supporting Locke's weight, gave Kal a look. He shrugged. No reason to make Locke feel bad about his first day as an Altier.

"Wait for whatever I'm about to do. Then make a break for the ship."

"What are you about to do?" Val asked.

"Stand there and breathe aggressively."

She tapped under her eyes twice. Their old signal. *Don't be stupid.*

He tapped back twice. *No promises.*

Val didn't argue. "Don't get killed."

Kal smiled. "You never let me have any fun."

They split. Val led her group toward the maintenance hatch, moving quietly through the shadows. Kal circled wide, heading for the main dock entrance where the Guild personnel were staged. He climbed the wooden stairs back to the main landing.

His ribs ached with every breath. The sickness made his vision swim at the edges, but he'd been hurt worse, fought sicker. So he told himself.

What could he use? There were a few speeders parked outside the facility. Could hotwire one, create a distraction, or use it as a battering ram if things got desperate. A single Rosari would probably palm it and crush the speeder like a tin can. Nix that. A row of fruit stalls lined the dock edge. He could launch one or two. Maybe a clumsy Rosari would slip on slick fruit and take the rest out? No, but he chuckled anyway. Then he heard the groan of rusty chains and looked up to see the loading crane. It held a shipping container that swayed in the sea breeze. He sent a quick prayer to Gaia that the release wasn't seized.

He rounded the corner.

Twenty-ish Guild thugs, just like Val said. Most clustered near the entrance to the *Days'* berth, blocking access. A few enhanced among them, he could tell by the way they moved, the subtle signs of accretion or dilation.

Kal stepped into the open. "Afternoon, gentlemen, ladies. Lovely day for a dock party."

All heads turned in his direction.

"Kaliston," one of them called out. An older man who looked like leadership. "Thorne talk to you?"

"That's one way to phrase it."

The older man's expression hardened. "Then you know the terms. Pay up or we take the ship."

"Here's the thing," Kal said, taking a step forward. "I'm not in the mood to fight all twenty of you, but you're not laying a finger on the ship in there. Ask yourself if your health is worth a paycheck."

"You know it's always more than just that with the Guild." His resignation melted, and he shifted into a Rosari.

The Hollowline hummed and Kal tapped it. Azure. The world fragmented.

Before even the Altiers could react, he moved. Not toward them, but toward the crane controls at the edge of the dock. He slammed the emergency release. The shipping container swung wild, cables snapping, the massive metal box crashing down between him and the Guild thugs.

Chaos erupted. Half of them scattered. The enhanced ones came at him, dilated or accreted, depending on their specialty.

Kal didn't fight them. Just ran, leading them away from the berth, away from where Val's group would emerge.

An Altier caught up to him first. Kal switched to Rose mid-step, turned, and caught the man's punch. Held it. The Altier's eyes went wide.

He didn't drain him. Couldn't. The sickness was already too much. Instead, he just threw the man into his companions behind him.

Keep moving. Keep them focused on the chase.

He vaulted over a cargo container, switched back to Azure, and sprinted toward the far side of the dock. Guild personnel gave chase, shouting orders and coordinating. Sea salt and Rose exhaust filled the air, the late afternoon sun glinting off metal and water.

That's when he heard the *Days'* engines spin up. He grinned. Val had made it aboard.

He cut back toward the ship. The Guild thugs realized too late what was happening. Half their force chasing Kal, the other half watching the *Days* lift off her moorings.

Haruto's group emerged from the east side access, sprinting for the loading ramp that was lowered. Shardshot cracked from both sides.

Almost there.

An enhanced Rosari stepped into his path. Big, solid. No way around him.

Kal didn't slow down. He switched to Rose, full accretion to match, and hit the Rosari like a skyship freighter. They both went down, rolling across the dock. The Rosari got a hand around his throat.

Val's shardshot barked from the *Days'* cargo bay. Blue rounds pinged off the Rosari, close to Kal's face. The Rosari's grip slipped on the jolts. Kal looked back at his ex-wife, a little nervous at how close that was.

No option, he absorbed the man's Rosari form and lurched into a stumbling run.

The loading ramp was rising. Haruto and his group were already aboard. Cookie leaned out, hand extended.

Kal leapt.

His fingers caught Cookie's wrist. She hauled him up with surprising strength, and he tumbled into the cargo bay as the ramp sealed behind him.

The *Days'* engines roared. The ship lifted, pulled away from the dock. Shard-shot fire from below sparked against the hull, harmless at this range.

Kal lay on the deck, breathing hard, his whole body screaming in protest. The sickness from the draining made his stomach heave. He rolled onto his side, just in case. The copper taste in his mouth wouldn't go away. His hands were shaking.

"Welcome aboard, Captain," Cookie said dryly. "Enjoy your shore leave?"

"Delightful," Kal managed. "Let's not do that again."

"Your plan was to release a shipping container? They're going to bill us for that."

"It worked." He looked up at Val. "Nice shot on that Rosari at the end there."

"Not really. I missed the creep I was aiming at."

"Har har."

She smiled and offered her hand. He took it, let her pull him upright. "Camo's on and Avery's going to keep us low until we get out of here. We count three Guild birds in the sky."

The *Days* banked hard, putting distance between them and Somerset. Through the cargo bay windows, Kal could see the city shrinking behind them, the dock growing small.

They were clear. Battered, barely holding together, but together nonetheless.

He made his way toward the bridge, each step an effort. The Hollowline's hum was settling, and he could feel the heat coming off the pack. The sickness would pass, but it wouldn't be a pleasant night.

"Where to, Captain?" Avery called from the helm when Kal entered the bridge.

Kal steadied himself against the doorframe. They had four days until the Colossus hit Orleans. Four days to figure out how to stop it.

"North," he said between steadying breaths. "Belfield. Conchordia."

The *Days* cut through the sky, leaving Somerset and the Guild far behind. Through the viewport, city lights smeared into streaks through the active camo, and the ship climbed into twilight.

CHAPTER 37: LOCKE

Locke had woken tangled in half-formed dreams where he chased after something he could never quite reach. Kenzie's voice had urged him on. Toren was there, too, until the gaia gave way and he once again fell. Locke reached for him, but the result was the same as Breezewaltz.

He awoke the moment he realized it wasn't Toren falling. It was him. The bruises on his chest screamed at the jolt, but not as badly as he expected, given the way they felt yesterday.

He told himself it was just a dream, but it didn't feel like one. Beneath it all simmered the anger he couldn't feel at Breezewaltz, and the unease followed him as he tried to shake the sleep. He couldn't help but feel something real tried to surface. He couldn't place why it made him feel better, but the anger was new. He figured it was progress.

Locke opened Toren's journal. He couldn't trust his memories, but he knew he could trust Toren's. He flipped to the last page with writing on it. It looked like it had some light water damage.

Entry 41, 3th Bloom, Year 998

It rained again today. Same as that night on the Inquisitor. *Same chill in the air, same taste in the wind. Every time it rains like this, I think about him, and that night.*

Shaw always hated the rain. Said it made his bones ache and his temper worse. It never stopped him from doing his duty, but he grumbled the whole time. I had to ignore it. My station wouldn't allow me to squabble with my guard in public.

He had insisted on coming with me that night over White Hill. Didn't even have his coat. Just boarded the Days, *held fast to the transport, and followed me into the storm.*

Then he died.

I wrote to his family. Tried to console their grief, but there are still nights I find myself reaching for him in the dark. No one is here to stop my tears. It is just another heartache I carry alone.

I thought I could hold his memory alongside my other burdens. The only thing that keeps me moving is the thought of protecting my people.

The King has ordered the Council to suppress conversation about the Colossus in our city-states. Luckily, the farmers and rural communities witnessing the destruction between our cities are rarely connected to the CrystalLine.

The King has the ability to intercept and halt transmissions if he doesn't like the content. Something Conchordia whipped up. I disagree with it, but I've been overruled by the Council.

The citizens are acting normally. I am not sure if that is a good thing or not.

White Hill is gone. Heydon and Huntley, too. A quarter of the league has been wiped off the map. Two Capital skyships. We are forced to call the refugees 'pilgrims,' and they flood the remaining cities with terrifying rumors. The King wants calm in Iveria, but the Colossus seems indifferent to your mood when it comes to collect from another city.

We left the Fury to stand watch, ready for another pointless skirmish if the creature moves north toward Orleans.

I only fear what happens to Breezewaltz if it is in the way.

I think Prince Lucan is behind this. I would bet my last credit that if I stormed the creature, I would find him on its back, pulling the strings.

The entry ended there. In the margins, Locke saw a scribbled note. *Rook? Kal reports he has not reappeared. Check in again after Landfall.*

Locke stared at the ink like it might move again, like Toren's hand still hovered over the page, ready to answer every one of Locke's questions. When nothing happened, he closed the book and rested it on his chest. It was comforting to know Toren had loved deeply before he passed, even if that love had ended in tragedy, twice over. Locke hoped Toren and Shaw had found peace together in the afterlife, at least.

He thought of his brother losing someone he loved, and how that compared to the mass death they had left in Breezewaltz. Haruto had stopped relaying death tolls. Kal said they didn't set the right tone with the crew, and the numbers just didn't add up.

Losing someone close was always different from watching faceless masses meet the same fate, but Locke wasn't sure which hurt more.

Centuries of war had left Iverians calloused to most loss, especially the kind delivered in numbers. It was common to hear that an Aurelian raid had hit a farming community at least once a month. It had become white noise.

Locke wondered how much noise the destruction of Breezewaltz would make in the other corners of Iveria, between the King's attempt to bury his head and the city-states mainly worrying about themselves. He assumed the rest of Iveria was like Somerset, going about their business, pretending nothing was wrong.

Locke understood it was easier to keep moving. Grief could wait until there was time for it, and there was never really time for it, especially not during a war.

He reopened the journal. *Rook? Kal reports he has not reappeared.* Who was Rook, and what did he mean to Toren and Kal?

Locke clenched his jaw. There were hidden secrets in that sentence. There were buried secrets Kal hadn't shared with him. Of course, any secret wouldn't bring Toren back, but Kal *knew* something he hadn't shared. He apparently had shared a connection with Toren that even Locke wasn't privy to.

He felt it, the seeds of anger he had sought in his father's study the day after Toren's death. An anger that wanted to blame someone and have someone bleed for it. Even if it was himself. The anger sat there, begging him to let it out. He wondered if it would transmute into something deeper, like Toren had talked about in his entry. How would it evolve further after that?

He sighed and rolled out of bed before he could spiral further.

He got his breakfast as usual. Kal had told him to meet in the hold, as it had become the recent routine. Locke had thought he might have the day off, given that whatever they had to do in Belfield seemed to be taking most of Kal's attention, but the ship's captain didn't seem to want to waste time.

Inertial dampeners framed the sparring ring as usual. The ghosts of lessons learned the hard way already filled the space. Locke had had his butt handed to him over the past couple of days, but that just meant he wanted to vent.

Across from him, Kal waited, loose and easy. He had a foxlike glint that said he was already three moves ahead, even though they had yet to begin. "Alright, Locke," Kal said. His voice carried its usual mix of humor and edge. "First Altier of Breezewaltz, let's see how little you've learned."

"I've learned a few things, Kal." Locke's tone was low, tight. "Like the fact that you've been keeping secrets."

Kal's eyes sparked. "Oh? Am I in trouble? You'll have to be more specific."

"Toren. You were talking. You reported back to him on someone or something. Who is Rook?"

Kal arched an eyebrow. His stance subtly shifted. "What exactly do you think you know?"

"I know you knew Toren better than I ever did. It should've been you who went out that night to save him. You could have killed Lucan in an instant."

"You're angry," Kal said calmly.

"No," Locke snapped. "I'm furious."

Locke snapped into dilation, and time fractured. The ship's hum stretched and became choppy. It was a slow, groaning chord delivered in packets. Kal moved to match. Locke lunged, not with control, but with heat. The strike was wide, his timing reckless, and Kal effortlessly slipped past it.

Locke twisted into a kick that Kal blocked with a forearm. He absorbed the blow with practiced calm.

Locke pressed, and his fists flew faster, tighter. "You could've stopped him," Locke spat when he broke dilation for a breath. "You knew what he was trying to do."

Kal's eyes flicked, sudden and sharp. "You think he wanted to be stopped? Like he hadn't already made the choice."

"Then you could have saved him!"

"I had my own choices to make, Locke, my crew to save."

Locke surged again with a palm strike, then an elbow, followed by another palm. Kal blocked one, dodged the next, but let the third land. It struck hard against his face, but he didn't move or counter. He kept his eyes focused on Locke. Almost as if the strike was a penance.

"You get to keep moving," Locke gasped. "You get to tell your stories and make jokes and be *fine...*"

Kal re-engaged. He was swift, brutal, and exact. His leg swept Locke's out from under him and drove him down hard. Locke hit the floor with a grunt.

"I am not fine," Kal said coldly. "I just know where to put the emotions."

Locke didn't get up right away. His chest heaved. "You had years with him. You were practically brothers. I had him for what? Three days? And then he's just... gone."

Kal looked away, jaw tight. "You're right, it's not fair."

"Then why aren't you acting like it? The jokes and quips from you haven't stopped since Breezewaltz. Maybe they've gotten worse. Why do you get to act like nothing happened?"

"Because if I don't, then this whole thing falls apart, okay? Use your head for once, Locke. It was a tragedy what happened to Toren, but if I let that wash over me, then I would drown and bring the *Days* along with me. You say I get to keep moving, but you don't realize that I never move alone. The people on this ship depend on me to make the right call at the right time. I can't let them down, not ever. The sooner you realize that, the sooner you can start becoming a leader yourself."

Silence stretched between them, raw and charged.

"This isn't productive," Kal said finally. "It might feel good, but you feed the fire like this, and there's no telling who it will burn. I promise to talk, but can we focus on the lesson first?"

Locke sat up slowly. His hands shook, and his breath was heavy. "Yeah, fine."

Kal offered him a hand. Locke took it, and the training resumed in silence.

Locke snapped into dilation again and again. Time didn't bend. It fractured. The ship's hum became a low vibration, stretched between frozen moments.

Kal wasn't still either. He flickered in a sequence of frames, his stance deceptively open in one instant, unreadable in the next. Locke had learned the hard way that those gaps in motion were dangerous.

Fast. Be fast. Locke moved and burst into the outside world with an eruption of speed. He was a blur of motion to Kal's flank and struck high with an open palm to Kal's ribcage.

Kal pivoted smoothly, and the strike grazed empty air. Locke twisted low to sweep for his ankle, but Kal stepped over it and drove down with his heel.

A hammer of force crashed into Locke's extended leg, like a speeding Capital skyship. Pain exploded through his thigh, a deep, brutal knot locked the muscle. He tried to get up, but gasped as the pain flared and fell on his butt again. Locke gritted his teeth. That was no normal shot.

"You're getting better," Kal called as he circled. "But you're still thinking like a sprinter." His eyes flashed with something sharp. "Focus. Remember that speed's a blade, but timing's the cut."

Locke pushed to his feet. "You're just playing with me. Whatever you and Toren were doesn't make me your kid brother. It's time to get serious." He reformed his stance and shifted lower, sharper. "You're fast, but you're not Altier fast."

Kal's lips curled. "You think?"

Locke vanished into dilation again, faster, almost as fast as he dared to move. Kal couldn't match his speed or meet his blow. Locke's fist landed hard against Kal's jaw. The impact stretched across eternity.

The dread set in the moment Locke realized, just before the contact fully registered, that Kal had already grabbed his wrist. In one smooth motion, he twisted and used Locke's momentum to launch him overhead and slam him into the ship's unforgiving floor.

The dilation snapped off, and Locke gasped from the impact. His chest heaved as he tried to catch his breath. "No fair... Rosari resilience... Altier speed... you're cheating." His voice was tight, and he gasped in disbelief. Kal had knocked the wind out of him, and he struggled to find it.

When he could breathe normally, he finally asked the question that had bugged him for the past couple of days. "How do you do it?" It was more of a wheeze than expected, but at least he got it out. "I know it's in the pack on your back, but I can't figure out what you're doing."

Kal helped pull Locke to his feet. His voice, dry and edged, answered, "Ah, the Kid is learning. Not as quick as Kenzie, but I'll give you points for the observation."

Locke's eyes flicked to the device strapped tight around Kal's lower back. He never saw Kal fight without it, and even then, he wore it most of the time, anyway. "That thing, it's how you can do all this?"

Kal patted the side of the pack. "Yeah. This thing." He walked over to some of the storage crates and took a seat.

Locke figured he should follow. Cookie had left out metal bottles of water for them, and Kal took a drink from one of them. Locke grabbed his own, grateful for the thoughtful gesture.

When Kal spoke again, his voice was quieter and had a somber tone. "You know how I was in the Armada? I was a lieutenant out of Citadel, the first to do so, ever. Everyone else graduated as a Junior Lieutenant. Toren tried to pretend that it didn't bother him, but it bothered him." Kal smiled.

Locke smiled too and understood precisely what he meant.

"I remember you at graduation. I don't think I'd seen you since that first summer we stayed with your folks, but I recognized you. Well, anyway, I was made a lieutenant of the *Deepwarden*. Served there for several years, saw some nightmares I don't want to admit. The Armada promoted me to lieutenant commander after a conflict near Somerset, but it didn't spare me from the next hell. I got pretty rattled, had trouble adjusting, and made some poor decisions. Got in trouble for insubordination.

"Then one day, I get a message. They want me to volunteer for a program that would take me off the front lines and let me clear my head. 'Okay,' I said. The next thing I know, I'm at the Conchordia. I thought the city was beautiful, with its all-glass and steel architecture. I never thought I'd go with my grades and all."

Locke just looked at him and nodded. He had never heard the story and did not want to jeopardize the rest by interrupting.

"So, I meet the program leader, and I have to sign this document stating I won't discuss the program and its personnel. I sign that, and I'm told they want me for this covert anti-Rosari and anti-Altier program. *CaRaAP,* they called it. Military nerds are the worst, all of them, and it's not even just the naming."

Locke snorted.

Kal smiled, but kept going. "So I'm in the program, and they're running tests, something about compatibility. They run the tests, but don't tell me what the results mean. A week later, a team of Altiers bursts into my room and ties me up. They put me under, and the next thing I know, the director of Conchordia is operating on me. I'm bound to the table. I scream, and they put me back down. The rest was hazy."

Kal shifted uncomfortably. "I wake up in confinement, arms and legs still bound. The nurse and a doctor are standing there, detailing what happened. I had a device placed directly on my spine. Inside it are two 'hollow' shards, one Azure and one Rose, which can now interact directly with my nervous system. I could use both powers while also draining the powers from any Altier or Rosari I fought. They told me the device was called the Hollowline."

Kal sighed. "I was speechless when I woke up. I'm not too proud to admit I cried. Some officer of the Armada, huh?"

Locke gave him a consolatory half-smile. Kal continued.

"I asked for the director but was told he was unavailable and that I was to rest until I was able to move sufficiently. That took forever. The Hollowline messed with my nervous system, so I had to relearn how to use my legs. Eight horrible months. After that, they trained me on the Hollowline. How I could be as fast as an Altier and as devastating as a Rosari. Best of all, I could absorb any powers from a shard or shard-powered individual I touched."

"Wow, I didn't know that," Locke said, not knowing how to continue.

"Yeah. The perfect weapon against the perfect weapons. Draining them is usually how I fight now. Most of the people we encounter are enhanced."

Locke nodded in agreement.

"Anyway, the abilities are convenient in a scrap, but I'm not a fan of how I got them and wouldn't have agreed if they had told me everything up front."

"Wait, why?" Locke asked.

"This isn't that story, Kid." Kal took a second to look off toward the cargo ramp. His gaze lingered on the railing, as if he had seen something there. He closed his eyes and shook his head before he returned to the conversation. "Maybe one day, before our next suicide mission, I'll tell you that one. So, I'm pissed in the bowels of the Conchordia. They're letting me test out the powers, but only in limited doses. I get enough juice to run some tests, then it's back into my room. Time goes by, and I'm still down there. I think I'm never getting out. Then one day, a freshly promoted lieutenant is assigned to my detail. And guess who that would be?"

Locke shrugged.

"Val. She had herself transferred in. Not sure how she accomplished that. She must have had someone scrub our records, probably Uncle. Well, she oversaw the security detail watching me. At the time, I was close to losing my mind, but she found me and said, 'Four weeks. We're getting you out.' And we did.

"We took two weeks for her to learn the facility and systems, and two weeks to put a plan in place. Then we broke out."

Locke thought of their current situation. "Four weeks to break out and two days to break in?"

"Please stop asking questions. Where was I? Oh, right. Val." Kal shifted his weight against the crate.

"The night of the escape. Val and I were breaking out of the facility when we ran into a problem. Our final side door was broken, so we had to find an alternative route. When we did, we ran into the director, who recognized me immediately outside my cell. We made a break for it. Val headed for the underground hangar, and I followed. That's when we saw the *Days.*"

Kal gestured with his arms out, as if taking in the sight of his ship for the first time. "She was the latest in skyship technology, faster than anything else in the Armada and able to bypass all detection. Val and I had both minored in aviation at the Citadel, her idea. So we engaged the dock hatch and made our escape into the sky. We have had this beautiful girl ever since."

Kal stomped his boot, as if to make sure the dream was real.

Locke looked out over the cargo hold. Messy, smelly, with an elderly engineer in the corner. He could also see it the way Kal must. It was beautiful.

"I'm telling you that story for two reasons. You said our fight was unfair. I don't want you ever to think I have something unearned or that I am using to cheat you. Some might say these powers are a miracle or that this ship is stolen, but they did not see the director rip out my nerve endings to stick into this thing. The months of isolation. I did not choose that. They took my freedom from me. How much would you sell your freedom for?"

Locke looked at him but did not respond.

"That wasn't rhetorical," Kal said, laughing to himself.

"Oh, um, I don't think I would ever sell that."

"Exactly. Priceless. The Hollowline and the *Days* are priceless. I have already paid that."

Locke looked down in thought.

"And two, I know you're angry, and that's fine. Your brother made his choice that night, and it got him killed. That isn't easy to hear, but it is the truth. I wish he had chosen differently. I wish we all had more time. The choice was his, and now we must live with what remains. You are going to feel a lot, Locke. The farther away you get from it, the deeper it will hit. Rage, guilt, grief, those emotions will either burn through you or crush you. You will need to find your feet while carrying them. When they have finally spent themselves, the one thing that should still stand in your heart is kindness. It's the core of who we are, always. Extend it to yourself first. I could tell you it will be a choice, but when the moment comes, you won't have to choose. Not really."

Kal approached the center of the hold. "To finish our little fairy tale, after Belfield, Val, and I became skypirates to make ends meet. Figured we could do a little good along the way. The Armada, Aurelian Fleets, and the Shipping Guild all chase us, but they can never catch what they can't find. After that, well, you know the rest."

Locke wiped a tear from his eye and followed him back to the center of the hold. "Who was Rook?" he asked.

"They were Lucan's chief strategist. They led him to the Colossus and created the plan to raise it."

"How'd they know where it was?" Locke asked.

"We think they stole a tome from Breezewaltz."

"They were tied to Breezewaltz?" Locke thought for a moment.

"Not sure, but they're off the board. They disappeared the night the Colossus rose. They're someone else's problem if they're still around. I told your brother as much when I saw him." Kal shrugged. "I wish I could tell you more, but that's the truth." He waved a hand for Locke to follow.

Locke took his position in the ring. "So you can take people's powers?"

"Yeah, with a touch, I can suck it right out of you." He made slurping sounds that the few crew members in the cargo hold apparently could have gone without. "Shard users are easy. Just a tap and I got it all. Shards themselves take more time, but give more energy. I have a limit to how much I can store. Both too much and too little are problems."

"Have you ever given it back to somebody?" Locke asked.

Kal thought about that for a moment.

"No, never had the need. If someone is attacking me, it usually means they don't deserve the power to begin with. That's what most of them are, just bullies who think they have a bigger stick." Kal smirked. "You can be my first test subject if you want."

"No, are you crazy? I just got these powers, and we'll need them for what comes next."

Kal's smirk flashed, but it didn't reach his eyes. "C'mon, gimme a hug. That was a big chat back there. I think we could both use one."

He strode toward Locke, but Locke ran. The two of them moved in circles until Locke dilated time and fled from the hold. His feet left minor dents in the metal outside the inertial dampener field.

Kal looked over at Jules and grinned as he motioned with his thumb. "I trained that one myself."

Jules grunted and continued working on the engine component at her workstation. She pointed at the dents. "I'm not fixing that."

CHAPTER 38: KALISTON

3 Days Until the Colossus Attacks Orleans

The hum of the *Days* was different at night, in the air where she was meant to be.

The crew had spent the day preparing for Belfield and beyond, but they hit the bunks under Val's orders. She was a stickler for curfew. She had inherited the self-discipline rule from her father. Kal always appreciated it because sleep was important. He just hated it when it meant he was alone on night watch.

He moved through the corridors barefoot, the cool deck plating grounded him to his beloved ship. Autopilot could manage the brief dereliction of duty.

Kal made sure he pulled a night watch like everyone else. Sure, he'd bribe or cajole a crewmember to swap shifts occasionally, but he tried to keep it somewhat fair.

Kal didn't just hate the night watch because of a lack of sleep. He hated it because that's when they came, when he was alone in the dark.

He reached for his pack, and his fingers brushed the hidden clasps. Just a flick, and it would be off. Instead, he froze. Without it, everything felt worse. All his confidence, clarity, and control lived in that polished shell. The Hollowline didn't just make him stronger. It made him sure, and Kal had worried it was the only thing that made him who he was nowadays.

It was in that moment of hesitation that he felt it before he saw it. A flicker, just at the corner of his vision. His fists clenched, and his eyes snapped left. Nothing. Just the empty corridor.

He exhaled through his nose, but his chest stayed tight. He told himself to keep walking.

The familiar path pulled him toward the galley, but he didn't enter. He passed it and brushed his fingers along the wall. The metal was warm from the pathing lights.

His route wasn't random. It was instinct, and it drew him somewhere he rarely allowed himself to go. He needed to be with someone, and there was only one good choice.

Val's quarters.

Kal knocked. No answer. He waited a moment before he pressed his hand to the plate. The door slid open with a soft hiss. No one inside.

There were three or four options for where she could be. Kal would have to ask tomorrow.

His hand hovered over the panel to close the door. He could rouse Haruto, or Avery, or even Locke for a drink. He could, but he wouldn't. He barely wanted Val to see him like this. The rest of the crew could never. He knew they had their thoughts, but it was best to keep those to rumors rather than confirm them outright.

The door stayed open, and Kal looked into the room from the doorway. The air inside was still and carried a trace of her, something faint and warm beneath the ship's recycled air. She kept the room neat and mostly impersonal. However, he knew what to look for.

His eyes flicked to the small details that told the truth.

The old flight jacket hung neatly over a chair. A worn datapad on the desk, its corner chipped from a time she threw it at Kal. The silver chain with service tags on the nightstand belonged to her father. She never wore them, but she always kept them close.

He stood in the doorway, the pit in his chest sinking deeper. He shouldn't be there.

"You kept silence, even to your love." The voices, soft and cold, brushed his ear.

Kal spun, his heart slamming against his ribs.

The hallway was empty, but he felt it. Two presences just behind his shoulder that brushed the edges of his mind. The voices were familiar, but they didn't belong to anyone he could name.

He squeezed his eyes shut. *They're not real.*

His fingers twitched at his side, and he pressed his hand to the plate. He turned sharply and left the room as the door sealed behind him.

The corridor felt longer than before. The hum of the ship, once a comfort, itched beneath his skin. His stride quickened without meaning to. He didn't think about where he headed, only that the chill in his chest wouldn't leave, no matter how much he rubbed his arms.

He hated this part, the shift from control to chaos. In daylight, with people around, he could act like nothing was wrong. He was the great Kaliston, and he made sure everyone knew it. It was when he was alone at night that the buzz behind his eyes crept in. He knew the price of using the Hollowline. He just never liked paying for it.

Eventually, he stepped into the cargo hold. The space had been Locke's training ground for the past three days. Kal had cast himself as the master. He felt like a stranger to that man tonight.

The movement sensors triggered the lights, bathing the cavernous space in a dim amber glow. He stepped into the center and his feet scuffed the worn deck. The makeshift sparring ring stood utterly empty except for two figures. He wasn't alone. Neither moved. Both figures were Val.

His breath caught. His heart hit his ribs once, hard. "Val?"

The figures did not react. One looked like the modern Val. She wore her flight jacket with her hair in a ponytail. The other was younger, a memory pulled from a dream. She wore her cadet uniform, hair loose. Both of their expressions were unreadable. They watched him, but their eyes were wrong.

The eyes of the older apparition were totally blue, and the eyes of the younger version were completely red.

A cold sweat broke out along his back. "Val." His voice was tight. His fists clenched. "No, stop."

The lights flickered. The figures dissolved and vanished like mist.

Kal's breath came hard and ragged. His pulse skittered beneath his skin. He tapped the Hollowline to slip into the dilated world. He hoped the limited awareness and fragmented reality would numb him to the real world.

It wasn't enough, not then, not ever. Even in a shattered world with limited perception, they were there and watched him with contempt. Using the Hollowline to escape them was pointless. It was their power. It had always been that way, and they only let him borrow it.

His knees buckled, and he hit the deck.

Kal's hands braced against the cold metal, fingers splayed. His head dropped, and for a long, brutal moment, he stayed there in a silent scream. Tears fell to the floor. The hum of the *Days* pressed in, deafening in the silence.

They had gotten worse, the apparitions. They twisted the world around him and turned the things he loved against him. He could beat them back in the daylight while surrounded by those he loved. It was at night, when he was alone, that they held all the power.

He squeezed his eyes shut, and his voice scraped out. "You're not real." His chest heaved with a truth he couldn't outrun. They didn't feel like lies. His voice broke the silence again, low and raw. "You're not her."

The apparitions didn't answer. They only spoke when it served them.

His head lifted, and tears held at the corner of his eyes. "You think I don't know what this is?" His voice echoed bitterly. "You're it, the price. My payment for this damn Hollowline and the *Days*." His hand curled into a fist against the floor. "I didn't ask for this! I never asked for this! Why can't you leave me alone?"

The whisper returned, just at the edge of his hearing. It was soft, intimate, but distorted. Val's voice. The apparitions moved around him, ghostly fingers trailed over his face and back.

"Love withers in shadow, and you wrapped her heart in lies," one said.

"She turns from you not by our hand, but by thine own," intoned the other.

His fist slammed the deck with a dull, echoed thud. "Because," he ground out, his voice hoarse, "I didn't know if I was losing my mind. I'm still not sure." His breath hitched. "If any of this is ever real..."

The air felt too still, and he could no longer feel the hum of the *Days* over the buzzing in his ear.

His voice dropped, raw and cracked. "I didn't tell her because I didn't trust what I was becoming... had become." He pushed out a breath and blinked back tears. "And I didn't want you around her."

That was the heart of the issue. The awful and beautiful truth. He loved Val, still, but he didn't trust the things living behind his eyes to leave her untouched. It wanted him dead, but for some reason, it wanted her dead first. It compelled him at all times to violence. Sometimes with visions, sometimes in other insidious ways. Kal had fought it constantly, but it was growing cleverer. Recently, Kal wasn't sure what was real or not.

The hold swallowed his confession. No reply came, just the deafening buzzing in his ears.

Kal's shoulders sagged. He couldn't get off his knees. His voice was barely above a whisper. "Take it off. You don't get to wear her face."

The apparitions laughed. With Val's beautiful face, they laughed.

Kal's resolve hardened, and in an instant, he reached back to remove the pack. Just like that, they were gone. Their echoing laughter cut off, and the *Days'* hum refilled the air.

The high disappeared just as fast. He was cold again and exposed. It felt like there was a hole in his heart, and all his confidence had drained out. The word fit. He hated to admit it, but the nerds had named it right.

He felt hollow.

CHAPTER 39: KENZIE

2 Days Until the Colossus Attacks Orleans

The *Days* dropped out of cloud cover just before midday and descended toward Belfield with steady precision. From the bridge, Kenzie watched the city rise beneath them. It sprawled, sharp-edged and glass-veined. It butted against the banks of the Cinnabar Sea. While it didn't have the grandeur of Orleans or the spectacle of Breezewaltz, it didn't try to. Belfield was its own kind of efficient machine.

An old city, but never ancient. There were no crumbling monuments. No history left exposed to the air. What didn't work anymore was torn down, and whatever replaced it was sharper, faster, and more efficient. Towers of glass and crystal gleamed in the sunlight. Their frames constantly evolved. Entire districts looked mirrored from above. They reflected the sky in steel skeletons that never stopped shifting.

Kenzie had never seen anything like it. Even the streets moved. The city featured extensive elevated tram lines that wove through the city. There were no alleys filled with rust, no corners that remembered how things used to be. Belfield didn't have time for nostalgia.

At the city's core sat Conchordia Institute, all sleek spires and interconnected skybridges, an academic citadel fused into the skyline like the city had sprouted around it. Mostly because it had. Kenzie didn't need to ask. She knew the place mattered to Kal. She could feel it in the way he'd gone quiet as they approached, how he leaned back in the captain's chair with his fingers steepled beneath his chin.

Kenzie had heard Belfield's skyline had changed every generation, but whatever ghosts that followed Kal from there were ever-present. She could see it in the dark rings around his eyes.

Kenzie glanced at him out of the corner of her eye. Something was off. Kal had swagger even when he was exhausted, but he was different today. He looked wired too tight. As if his body had moved ahead of his brain, and his thoughts tried to catch up. He didn't speak unless he gave orders. That alone was enough to put her on edge.

Below, the city pulsed with movement. Everything was built to be replaced, and nothing was meant to last. Even the older buildings had been swallowed by progress, repurposed and consumed, as if the city tried to erase the concept that buildings were supposed to last.

From the captain's chair, Kal's voice finally cut in. "Haruto, get a read on traffic and anyone with a shardshot pointed at us."

Kenzie didn't look at him, but she felt him pull himself back into the moment. Something about the way he said it sounded like he'd been farther away than anyone realized. She wasn't about to ask, but it was little things like that that told her he carried more than he admitted.

Haruto's fingers danced over the controls. "Port's busy, but nothing unusual. Military presence is light. The *Belepoch* has moved to Orleans. A couple of fighters on patrol, and the city's defensive cannons are live, but nothing out of the ordinary. We should be able to slip in without drawing too much attention."

"Good," Kal said, without looking up.

"Transmit codes?" Haruto asked.

"No. We pushed our luck with them in Somerset. Too many eyes here double-checking. Land in Baker's Clearing, if no other scoundrel is there already."

Avery gave a small nod, hands steady on the controls. "On it."

The *Days* banked gently and angled toward a wooded stretch just outside the city perimeter.

Kenzie sat next to Avery and tapped her fingers against the armrest. The movement was half impatience, half habit. "Why can't we land in the city?" she asked Avery.

"This city and the *Days* have a history, and it's not good," Val cut in.

Kenzie hadn't thought she had asked it loud enough for anyone else to hear, but there Val was. Her tone was neutral as always.

Val stood beside Kal, arms folded. "This might be a pain, but it's safer. We'll shuttle the crew in on the transport."

Locke leaned against the bulkhead near the door, arms crossed, his weight balanced with practiced indifference. "What if they stop us at the gate?"

Kal flashed a grin. "Then we'll have to be very, very charming."

Locke sighed. "That's what I was afraid of."

Kal mirrored the sound exaggeratedly. "Fine, I'll be very charming. You mope about somewhere else."

Kenzie didn't smile, but the exchange felt normal. Something had changed since Breezewaltz. The two almost acted like brothers. That was something.

The ship set down with barely a tremor. The landing gear felt like a whisper, just the quiet locking thunk beneath her boots and the pitch shift of the engines as they cycled down. Through the viewport, she spotted the domed roofs of Conchordia in the distance, clean and precise.

Then the scent of the sea reached her nose. It was sharp and briny. She loved that smell.

Locke smelled it, too. "A funny place to build an academy with so many things the salt air could corrode," Locke said.

Kal stood and stretched slightly as he pushed away from the captain's chair. "I'm sure they're working on that. Alright, everyone but Avery is with me. Command table, now."

Kenzie followed the others below deck to the war room. The central console had already powered up and cast a soft blue glow across the room. It displayed a detailed map of Conchordia. Security nodes, patrol routes, and a faint red pulse that marked their destination dotted the map.

Kal leaned over the table, his hands braced on the edge. "Alright, let's go over this before the big show. Our target is the office of Conchordia's director, located here." He pointed to a sector near the heart of the campus. "The records vault should be just off the office and, by policy, holds all research notes of all former directors and staff."

Haruto's eyes stayed fixed on the projection. "He was kicked out, Kal. They deemed his research unethical. You're sure he didn't take it with him?"

Liam jumped in. "Or what if they wiped the files when he left?"

Kal shook his head. "I hear he had to flee in the middle of the night. Doubt he took much with him. Makes sense that he ended up in Aurelia. The one place they would accept someone like that." He looked at Liam. "Conchordia doesn't delete data. It doesn't matter if it's unethical or dangerous. If it's information, they keep it."

Kenzie crossed her arms, and her eyes drifted between the glowing grid and Kal. He was calm, but too still. He was focused in a way that made her nervous.

She didn't know what Conchordia meant to him, but she had heard the crew imply something, and it felt like this wasn't just another job.

Kenzie frowned at the map. "Are these accurate?"

Val stepped up beside her. "We have my uncle to thank for these. They're three months old and will be as accurate as you get in this city. The street-level city changes every decade or so, but the underground tunnels remain untouched. They crisscross beneath the city, unseen and generally forgotten. Some have found second lives as utility tunnels."

Kenzie nodded slowly. If that were true, then the chances of sneaking in would have improved. The tunnels were tight, likely outdated, but manageable. She continued to scan the layout and mentally mark routes.

Haruto traced a path across the schematic. "There's an underground utility tunnel connecting this operations facility just off campus. We want a tunnel we know hasn't caved in."

Kal nodded. "I agree. That's our best bet. Haruto, you'll stay on the ship and monitor local security. If they flag anomalies on their comms, you let us know."

"Already patched into the city's peace officer grid, civilian signals, and Conchordia's comm net," Haruto said. "We'll have a leg up, but not perfect visibility. There'll be a delay, and I could use help to sort the data."

"Tia and Liam, you're on comms with him," Kal said.

Jules stepped forward and unfolded her arms as she tapped the screen. The operations facility lit up with red defensive markers. There were turrets, wall sensors, and dead man gates. "You still haven't answered how we're getting through this."

Kal didn't miss a beat. "Ah, have you met our master thief?" He gestured toward Kenzie.

Kenzie blinked. "Me?"

"You," Val confirmed, without a hint of humor.

There was a pause. Kenzie looked at Locke, who gave her the smallest smile, then back to the glowing map. She gave a quiet nod and stepped closer. "So, we're sneaking in through a sewer."

"Not quite," Kal said. "The tunnels are used for more than wastewater. That facility handles operations for all of Conchordia. Bottom level is sewage, but there are platforms above. We should stay dry." He pointed to a spot on the schematic.

"Once we're on campus, we move through the utility levels, then up through the sublevels. There's a side access point to a lift that reaches every floor. Assuming we can bypass the lockout."

Locke straightened as he leaned against the wall. "Where do I come in?"

Kal nodded to him. "You, my recently speedy friend, will escort Kenzie to the upper floors. Val and I will hold the lift. A smaller team means a lower risk of detection. Once we have what we need, we exfil through the same route. If we're lucky, no one will even know we were there."

Kenzie leaned back, crossing her arms. "And if we're not lucky?"

Kal gave her that usual half-grin. "We have a First Altier, a dashing pirate with mysterious powers, and the best damn crew this side of the Cinnabar Sea. I'd love to see someone press our luck."

A few chuckles rippled around the room, but they didn't last. The quiet that followed said everything. Conchordia wasn't a simple mark. It was the center of Iveria's military research. If something went wrong, it wouldn't just be dangerous, it would be catastrophic.

Kal's tone shifted, his posture sharper. "We take tonight to verify the intel. We strike tomorrow night. Everyone has an info packet on their datapads. Confirm your assigned locations. Be discreet and be smart."

Val took over, her voice cool and even. "Kal and I will stay aboard the *Days* until the operation. No point risking our faces getting recognized. Avery will shuttle the rest of you for recon. Teams of two. Your schedule and return times are in the packet. Assume you're known associates. Protect your faces and move accordingly."

Locke exhaled. "Hell of a way to spend an evening."

Kal smirked. "Could be worse."

Kenzie raised an eyebrow. "How?"

Kal headed out the door. "You two pulled the short straw. Have fun at the maintenance facility."

Kenzie said nothing back. She just shook her head and looked at Locke. She was surprised by how much she disagreed with Kal. A night spent with Locke didn't feel like a short straw.

CHAPTER 40: LOCKE

Belfield buzzed with quiet efficiency. The streets were clean, orderly, and lined with storefronts that sold everything from refined crystal technology to the latest military-related innovations. Unlike Breezewaltz, where every sector had a distinct personality, Belfield felt cold and calculated. Its people moved with purpose, and overheard conversations were clipped and businesslike.

Kal had tasked Locke and Kenzie to observe the operations facility about two miles west of Conchordia's campus. They took the levitating tram from the city's gate to a stop about three blocks away. They passed shops with their windows open to let in the sea breeze.

Kenzie had insisted on a cover story. Locke didn't think it was necessary, but went along with it. She had thought about it for a few seconds before she excitedly explained she would be an independent merchant, and Locke would be her tech-savvy partner who handled the package. She had insisted he was more than just a "courier boy" in the scenario.

They would look at the shops around the facility, or maybe they were there to pick up a shipment for a private contractor. There was a cute café across the street from the facility. Perhaps they stopped there between business meetings. Kenzie hadn't decided yet.

All of it made Locke feel silly, but he wasn't about to say no to Kenzie. Kenzie, however, had grown more agitated the farther they got from the *Days*.

She adjusted the collar of her jacket and scanned the street ahead. "I don't like it. No slums, no alley markets, no one looking over their shoulder. This place is too... clean."

Locke smirked. "It is clean. You say that like it's a bad thing."

She shot him a look. "It is a bad thing. All cities have rough edges. They do because people do. This place...not having any feels...off."

Locke rolled his shoulders to adjust the weight of the small courier bag slung across his chest. "So, what? You'd rather people be lying destitute in the streets or getting mugged out in the open?"

Kenzie ignored him and stopped near a small stall that sold refurbished crystal interface modules. She picked up a processor unit to inspect absently while she lowered her voice. "Conchordia security stations are every three blocks. They aren't patrolling, they're monitoring. We need to assume Big Boss isn't the only one in their system."

She had made Locke promise to call Kal "Big Boss" in public before they left. That had made him laugh at the time. Kenzie had not found the humor in it.

Locke plucked a tiny processing chip from the display and flipped it between his fingers. "Right, it's probably Peeping Pat and the Omnipotent Overlord."

She elbowed Locke in the ribs. "Take this seriously," she hissed.

The shot shocked Locke, but he did as she asked. "I thought Haruto scrubbed our records?"

"He did, but Belfield is different. The underworld avoids this place like the plague. It operates on its terms. If you're good enough to operate here…" She let the sentence hang and glanced over her shoulder before she set the processor down.

Locke nodded, slipped the chip into his pocket, and handed the vendor a few credits. A minor purchase to justify their stop. He turned and fell back into step beside her as they crossed onto one of the main thoroughfares that led further from the Academy District.

"How do we scout the entry point?" he asked.

Kenzie didn't respond right away. Instead, she tilted her head toward a cluster of buildings closer to the operations facility. One was the café across from the center. She made a beeline for it.

"Lightly guarded compared to the other parts of campus, but more heavily guarded than a typical operations facility," she murmured.

Locke looked around. "Is that good or bad?"

"It means we're in the right spot," she replied, looking over her shoulder.

"Well, that's good. Now we need to get in. Thoughts?" he asked.

"We wait and let the universe show us the way," Kenzie replied and took a sip.

They sat there for a while, neither speaking, simply observing.

The café was quiet, a place where people sipped their drinks without lingering too long. The chairs were bolted to the pavers, the tables were spotless, and the servers worked with mechanical efficiency. Even the soft hum of conversation felt measured and lacked the relaxed, chaotic energy Locke expected in public spaces.

They once again found themselves in the space between words. Kenzie was observing, and Locke wasn't sure what to say.

They had barely spoken about anything outside the mission since they arrived in Belfield, and part of him wondered if Kenzie kept her distance on purpose. The last ninety-six hours had stripped him of nearly everything before the *Days*. His brother, his home, and his family's legacy. Kenzie had been there for all of it and was still as she sat across from him. She sipped her drink in silence. Locke let his cool off in the evening's chill.

He wasn't sure where they stood anymore. He never really had, but he somehow felt less sure now. The only thing he was sure of was how he felt.

That realization came with a sharp and immediate sense of guilt. His world had collapsed, yet there he was, thinking about her. He knew it wasn't the time for it, but maybe there never would be either. Locke was afraid he would just add it to the growing list of regrets he carried since Breezewaltz.

He watched her stir her drink idly. He thought she was the most incredible person he had ever met. She had her secrets, but that was fine. Wonderful even. Something to discover down the line. He knew physical attraction wasn't the end-all be-all, but he still thought she was the most beautiful person he had ever seen.

He only wished he knew how to express that. Knowing how she felt would help, too. Regardless, it wasn't the time. Locke would settle for this quiet moment alone with her. A coffee in hand, on a crisp night in Belfield with more danger. That would have to be enough for the moment.

Kenzie took a sip and watched a group of workers exit the treatment center across the street. They wore neat, standard-issue jumpers, and all moved at the same pace, their chatter nonexistent as they filed toward the lev station.

She sighed, and Locke felt the urge to break the silence. "Still think there's something wrong with this place?"

"You don't?" she replied.

Locke smirked. "Because it smells nice and the streets are too clean?"

"Because this place is sterile. Have you ever been in a place where nobody stops to chat on the street? I haven't witnessed a single argument or a single person crossing the street when they shouldn't. Look at them." She gestured toward a couple who walked in perfect step with one another. "Even their casual strolls look like they've been programmed."

Locke leaned back in his chair and stretched out his legs. "The people here are the best minds of Iveria. It takes a special kind to be accepted here. An 'engineer brain,' as Toren used to call it. You're acting like they're secret automatons or something."

Kenzie huffed. "If they were, at least then they'd be interesting."

Locke chuckled and shook his head. "You know, for someone who insisted on this whole 'cover story' thing, you're not precisely blending in right now. You keep glaring at the city as if it personally offended you."

Kenzie let out an exaggerated sigh as she slouched in her seat. "Yeah, well, maybe it did. A city without a little grime feels like a city without a soul. Anything that comes out of here is equally soulless."

Locke studied her for a beat, then leaned in slightly. "Sounds like someone grew up with a lot of rules."

Kenzie went still. For a second, Locke thought she might brush off the observation.

Instead, she frowned and stared into her drink like it might hold the answer. "Sort of," she admitted. "Not exactly. Not like this, but close enough."

Locke tilted his head. "What does that mean?"

Kenzie's fingers traced the rim of her glass. "It means you ask too many questions for a lackey, courier boy."

Locke held up his hands. "Hey, that's not what we agreed to, and the least you could do is answer my very reasonable curiosity."

Kenzie smirked. "You agreed because you didn't want to argue."

"I agreed because you get scary when you're determined."

"Exactly." She tapped her cup against his. "So shut up and drink your whatever-this-is."

Locke took a sip and regretted it immediately. "This tastes like burnt dirt."

Kenzie shrugged. "Maybe that's where they put the grime I was looking for."

He set the cup down and pushed it far, far away. "If that's the case, I'll just have to be fine being thirsty."

Kenzie laughed, and for a moment, the tension of the mission eased.

Across the street, groups of workers started to file in.

Kenzie's gaze followed their movements. "And just like that, the universe gives us an opening."

Locke leaned forward. "Shift change? Think we can blend in?"

Kenzie grinned. "Think you can carry a crate without whining?"

"I'll have to ask Jazz for pointers."

She shook her head as if that was a bad idea and stood. "Pay for my drink, courier boy. I'm going to find us some uniforms."

Locke tossed a few credits on the table and watched as she crossed the street.

Kenzie didn't look back as she moved, but she didn't head straight for the entrance either. Instead, she angled toward a small group of women in the uniform jumpers who approached from the opposite end of the block. With a casual stride, she blended into their ranks, her movements effortless, as if she had always been part of their group. She struck up a conversation with one of the workers, and they talked as if they were old friends.

Locke tensed and watched the cluster of workers turn into the gated facility. They slipped past security without a second glance. Locke saw Kenzie through the gate as she moved with the workers and approached the central office.

A minute passed and another. Locke didn't realize he was holding his breath until he felt lightheaded. Then he focused too much on his breathing. It rattled in his ear.

A man in security gear with a shardshot approached her. Even from across the street, Locke could tell it wasn't just small talk. Their conversation was animated. The man gestured toward the central building while Kenzie nodded. She shifted her weight slightly and rocked from her heel to the balls of her feet. Kenzie tucked her hair behind an ear. She was working him, but would it be enough?

The man's face betrayed nothing from this distance. Without warning, he pointed and followed her inside.

Locke exhaled slowly. *She's busted.* He leaned forward in his seat, fingers flexed against his knee. *Damn it, Kenzie.*

Locke started looking at the facility. He might be able to use a parked speeder to vault the wall and blaze in using his Altier speed. He could grab her and get out before anyone noticed. It would be risky. He never had any practice carrying others. His father had done it a few times when Locke was little, but he wasn't sure if there was a trick to it.

Then she was back.

She strolled out of the facility like she had every right to be there and flashed an easy wave to the security guard and the other workers before she crossed back to Locke. She carried something.

Locke narrowed his eyes as she approached. "What was that?"

"Nice guys. They're almost done with their shift. Asked if I wanted to meet them for a drink afterward." She placed a stack of folded jumpers on the table, along with four ID badges.

"Uh, okay, no, wait. We'll come back to that. I can't believe you just walked in there like it was no big deal?"

"Yeah. I told them my uniforms never arrived, and I needed to pick some up for my shift next week. I pinched the ID badges on my way out. Haruto will have to reprogram and insert our pictures, but that should be easy enough for him."

"And that worked?"

"Sometimes the best place to hide is right in plain sight. Plus, it's amazing what a girl can get away with after just a little flirting. They thought my name not being in the system was a glitch."

Locke smiled. "What did you tell them your name was?" Locke asked.

"Not important," Kenzie replied.

"It is to me."

Kenzie rolled her eyes. "Lyla Luinondo. I'm bad with names, okay?"

"You're kidding." Locke's smile widened.

"Probably." Kenzie laughed and gestured to the uniforms. "You're carrying those."

"Fair." Locke scooped up the jumpers and badges. "But you're not meeting them for a drink, right?"

"Maybe. Lyla wasn't the type to stand someone up. How much time do we have?" Kenzie laughed.

It was Locke's turn to roll his eyes. "Just remember who bought you the last one."

He stood, and they made their way back toward the *Days*. "So, what's it like on the inside?"

Kenzie sighed. "I hope you're not squeamish. It really is a waste center."

"I'm not. Just questioning my life choices if we have to walk through the sewage."

"A bit late for that, don't you think?"

Locke huffed a quiet laugh. "More like I should have started long ago."

Kenzie took an unexpected left. He followed without hesitation, though the detour put them further from their planned route. She looked into a glass storefront, but it was like she was looking past the glass. Her voice came out low. "Don't look, but we've been clocked. Three of them. Not peace officers, too casual."

Locke exhaled slowly and stopped near a transit schedule posted on the station wall. He let his eyes scan the board without reading it. "Not as good as you think you are? From the center?"

"No, they were already on us before that," she said. "I just wasn't sure."

Locke grinned. "So, what's the plan? Lose them or play along?"

Kenzie hesitated for a fraction of a second, then slipped her arm through his. Locke blinked. "Uh…"

"Shut up and walk," she muttered through a tight smile. "If they're watching, let's give them something harmless to see."

Locke adjusted his stride to match hers. "You could have just said so."

Kenzie shot him a side-eye. "You would have made it weird."

"I'm not a good liar. You can't surprise me like this."

"Just act normal."

"Define normal."

"Not whatever this is," she muttered and steered them toward a bench as if they were just another couple waiting for the lev.

Locke draped an arm along the back of the bench and leaned in slightly. "You're committing to the bit."

Kenzie smirked. "Shut up and look cute."

Locke exhaled through his nose and fought a laugh as he studied their pursuers without looking directly at them.

They had separated to blend in naturally with the shifting crowd. One stopped near a food vendor, another flipped through a datapad, and the last leaned against a support column. None of them acknowledged each other, but their positions were too precise to be random. Their spots provided clear lines of sight to each other and the duo. Locke glimpsed concealed shardshots on two of them.

Locke kept his voice low. "Think they're professionals? Not just some street thugs looking for an out-of-town mark?"

Kenzie traced a finger along the stitching of his sleeve to keep up the act. "Yeah, and they're not reporting to local security."

"How do you know?" Locke asked.

"We'd have already been picked up. These men are watching. We're not their target."

"We can't lead them back to the ship," Locke murmured.

He glanced at the transit map but didn't look. The lev was a risk, but waiting was worse. At least if they moved, they controlled the pace. "Maybe get on and off at random stops?"

Kenzie nodded. "Sure, we keep moving until we shake them."

"Or until they make a move."

"Let's not let it get that far."

The overhead intercom buzzed to announce the arrival of the next lev.

Locke shifted slightly. "If we get on, we lose control of the environment."

"If we don't, we lose an easy getaway."

Locke met her gaze. "So what's the call?"

Kenzie held his eyes for a long second. There was something distant in her stare, something that didn't feel like it was about him at all. Locke had seen that look before, the kind she wore when her mind was somewhere else. She looked away and began scanning around them. He could almost see the calculation in her expression, the quiet tally of streets and exits, the way she mapped a city without moving. She had once told him she knew every alley in Seaforth by name. She looked like she was remembering what it felt like to disappear. Locke wasn't sure if that was a good thing.

Then she met his eyes again, and something shifted. Whatever instincts had been steering her toward flight or escape seemed to fall away. Locke didn't know what she had decided, not exactly, but her posture changed. She was looking at him as if he were part of the plan.

The chime dinged, indicating the doors were closing. She exhaled and stood quickly, pulling him up with her. "We get on."

Locke didn't argue. He followed her lead.

As the doors slid shut behind them, he glimpsed one of their watchers move to speak into a concealed comm.

Someone was interested in them, and he was sure they would find out who before they left town for good.

CHAPTER 41: KALISTON

1 Day Until the Colossus Attacks Orleans

The command room lights were soft. Kal liked to leave the dimmer low, and daylight couldn't reach them where they docked.

The central display cast its glow across a four-person team. Kal, Val, Locke, and Kenzie stood around the projection of the Conchordia campus. The map cycled between thermal, structural, and surveillance overlays. The rest of the crew stayed back. They were quiet as they watched the pieces move.

Kal tapped a corner node, and the screen snapped to the route Haruto had prepared. The route showed their entry through the operations facility, down into the underlayers, and up through a maintenance hatch. It was a ghost path, sketched in clean blue lines.

"This is it," Kal said. "Last details are locked in. Ready or not, we go tonight."

Kenzie crossed her arms, eyes locked on the screen. "You sure the tunnels won't have collapsed since Uncle got this map?"

Val answered before Kal could. "No, but we would know if the campus no longer had a maintenance shaft. The fact you confirmed the facility is operational tells us all we need to know."

Locke adjusted the cuffs of his fake uniform. "And if the guards clock us?"

Kal gave him an incredulous look. "What? No. Don't get clocked. Are you trying to jinx us?"

Val added, "Stay close. Move like you belong, and no unnecessary chatter."

"Aye, aye," Locke muttered.

Val looked at Kal. "That goes double for you."

"You take all the fun out of risky missions, you know that?"

Val's smile was thin, but it was there.

Behind them, Haruto stood by the secondary terminal to cross-check guard rotations and traffic spikes on city grid channels. "I've hacked the cameras with the info Uncle gave us. You will need to hack the doors manually, but I've prepped a terminal."

"I'll handle that," Kenzie said.

Tia leaned over his shoulder. "What if the doors don't have security ports?"

"Then we'll rely on our master thief to pick the locks," Haruto replied, nodding toward Kenzie.

Kenzie gave him a lukewarm thumbs-up.

Liam passed out modified comm units to the four, but he spoke directly to Locke and Kenzie. "These are short-range only. Encoded to speak to each other and the Days. We're not risking an open band. If you go dark, you stay dark until exfil. No heroics."

Jules, seated at the systems desk, didn't turn. "I'm not powering engines unless I hear an explosion."

Jazz grinned. "I give it twenty minutes before that happens."

"Jazz," Rina warned. "Don't tempt fate."

Kal looked around the room. His gaze landed on the crew, his crew, each one prepared in their own way. They took it seriously, but that did not stop the smiles and jokes.

It felt like a dress rehearsal for something bigger. They needed a win, but a clean win would be all the better for what came next.

Kal adjusted the pack on his back. "Once we're inside, Val and I will hold the lift. Kenzie and Locke push to the director's office. They'll copy what we need, and we all walk out of there together. If we're not out in ninety minutes, Haruto jams the whole comms network and makes a lot of noise elsewhere."

"Not subtle," Haruto said, "but doable."

Kal nodded. "Everyone else, hold the ship. Keep to your stations. Rina has the bridge." He looked at the doctor. "You have my permission to crack open Conchordia if this goes sideways."

The room stilled at that. Everyone knew more or less about his hatred for this place. The whole city felt like a scar he kept pretending wasn't there. He'd run from it for years. Now he was walking straight back into it, his spine humming with a power he never asked for, chasing answers to questions that weren't his to solve. None of that mattered now. They were here, doing this. What mattered was getting in, getting the intel, and getting his people out alive.

"What about the tails from yesterday?" Kenzie asked.

"What about them? Did you get names or who sent them?" Kal asked.

"Obviously not," Locke jumped in.

"Then it's just another day. Someone always wants a piece of me. Do I need to remind you about the Guild and Somerset? The trolls in Breezewaltz? I'm fine if this is a trap. It wouldn't be the first this week. Just stand behind me." Kal sounded as irritated by the concern as he felt.

It was Val's turn to jump in. "What he's saying is that if variables arise, compartmentalize and work the problem. Do that and we'll make it back."

Rina stood and handed Val a small medic pack. It had a gray circle on it, the symbol for Gaia. Kal knew that the pack hadn't always belonged to Rina.

"Know that if you don't, we're cutting the city open to find you," she said.

Val's eyes softened. "Noted."

Kenzie drew a breath and stepped forward. She bumped her shoulder lightly against Locke's. "Ready?"

He didn't answer right away. Just nodded. His eyes focused on the display.

Kal observed as the silence settled again. The kind that came before bad news broke hearts. "Alright," he said. "Let's get this done."

The infiltration team turned and filed out to get ready. They were eight footsteps against the idle hum of the ship. Behind them, the crew of the *Days* returned to their stations. No one said goodbye, not really. They all knew saying it aloud would pit fate against Kal's luck, and that was a battle no one wanted to invoke.

CHAPTER 42: LOCKE

The four of them stood at the edge of a narrow maintenance alley. The glow of Conchordia's campus cast long shadows across the damp pavement. Its operations facility loomed ahead, a squat, reinforced structure designed for function over aesthetics. Thick pipes ran along its exterior to feed into the city's underground system like artificial veins.

Locke adjusted the collar of his stolen jumper uncomfortably. "I don't know how Jazz does this all day," he muttered, rolling his shoulders. "Feels like I'm wearing a damn furnace."

"Quit fidgeting," Val said, dressed in her jumper. The worker's ID badge clipped to her chest gave her an air of authority and made her look like she belonged. "The real workers don't mess with their uniforms unless they're adjusting their gloves or goggles. You do anything else, and someone's going to notice."

Kal had taken a more relaxed approach. He had tied the top of his jumper around his waist. A stained white t-shirt hung on his torso. A smudge of grease marked his forearm and cheek. Val had mentioned it was unnecessary before they left the *Days*. Kal had insisted, and Kenzie had enthusiastically agreed. The girl loved making up a character.

Kal flicked a glance toward the facility's double gate. "You're all acting like we've never done this before," he said.

"Yes, exactly, I've never done this," Locke hissed. "I'm a terrible liar. I'm freaking out!"

Kal brushed him off. "Kenzie, how's our window?"

"We're good," Kenzie whispered. "Night shift swaps in five minutes. We pass through security with our ID badges and enter the tunnel."

"Everyone good?" Val asked.

"Yes," Kenzie said.

"Of course," Kal replied.

"No," Locke muttered and wiped sweat from his brow.

"Good, let's move out," Val said.

The four of them moved to the gate where the badges Haruto had created the previous day were scanned. All passed. Kal, Val, and Kenzie moved ahead naturally. Locke smiled and waved, but then realized he had made a bigger scene. He quickly put his head down and took large, unnatural steps.

Once they were around the corner and out of sight, Kenzie turned on him first. "What is wrong with you?" she seethed.

"What part of *bad liar* don't you understand? It's not my fault," Locke shot back.

"Get it together," Kal said.

Val made a *cut-it-out* motion. "We made it through. Now we move."

They approached a security door, but the maintenance badges wouldn't work.

"These must not have the right security clearance," Val said.

Kenzie worked fast and bypassed the electronic lock with the breach terminal Haruto had given her. The door hissed open to release a faintly acrid smell of processed wastewater.

Locke wrinkled his nose. "Great, now the fun part."

"Just pretend it's one of Cookie's stew nights," Kal quipped as he stepped inside.

Locke frowned. "I like Cookie's stew."

Kal grinned. "Then you'll be fine."

Val gave them both a sharp look, then gestured for them to move. "Save the quips for later. Let's go."

They filed inside, and Kenzie took point with her datapad. Haruto had set it to show her staff movements in real time based on information that filtered in from the cameras. Locke and Val flanked either side. Kal brought up the rear and shut the entrance behind them with a soft click.

The tunnels were narrow and humid, lined with thick pipes and reinforced grating that hummed faintly with the flow of liquid beneath their feet. The air carried a distinct chemical tang and masked any natural odors.

Kenzie glanced at her datapad, then whispered, "This way."

She led them through the winding maintenance tunnels. They stopped only when the datapad loaded information from the next camera.

"Hold," she murmured as she pressed herself against the wall. The others followed suit.

A mechanical whir approached, followed closely by a small floating drone with a camera mounted on it. The team pressed themselves against the piping that lined the tunnel. After a few tense seconds, the drone disappeared down another corridor.

Kenzie exhaled. "That was closer than I like."

Kal smirked. "What, you don't enjoy the challenge?"

She shot him a look. "*You* can enjoy the challenge. The rest of us will be too worried about our lives."

"Fair point," Kal conceded.

They moved deeper into the complex as Kenzie guided them through the complex maze of tunnels. Conchordia's waste system wasn't just for sanitation. It also handled the disposal of biohazards and other classified materials, making it one of the few places with restricted personnel access outside the campus itself.

Locke kept an eye on their surroundings and resisted the urge to check over his shoulder too often. "So far, so good," he murmured.

Val gave a slight nod. "We're past the first sublevel. Next stop, Conchordia."

They walked for another twenty minutes through the sublevel tunnels. Kenzie's datapad indicated their current location. Without it, the labyrinth would have been impossible to navigate. Time meant nothing in the tunnels, and to Locke, it felt like they had been down there for hours. Each tunnel looked like the one before it. He was glad Kenzie had a map, but Val seemed to move like she knew the place as well.

After a couple of right turns, they approached a steel door. Val moved past Kenzie and tested the handle. It was locked and had no interface panel. "Kenzie?"

"Give me thirty seconds," she said.

The other three stood watch as Kenzie wove a tool in and out of the keyhole. Eventually, the strike clicked, and the door slid open to reveal a maintenance shaft that led up to Conchordia.

Kenzie tucked her tool away. "Looks like we're climbing our way out of hell," she said.

"You mean hell's toilet," Kal joked and pinched his nose. No one laughed.

Val stepped forward first. "I'm on point from here. Follow me. Quiet and fast."

The four of them climbed out of the tunnels and entered a dark corridor. The only illumination came from the soft glow of maintenance lights that lined the floor. The air was cooler, sterile in a way that made Locke feel like they had stepped into an entirely different world. Gone was the damp heat of the tunnels, replaced with crisp, recycled air.

Val was all business as she led the way. Her focus remained forward, and she looked for any movement.

Locke tried to do the same. His gaze caught the recessed security cameras in the corners. "Should we be worried about those?"

Kal shook his head and kept his voice low. "Haruto looped the feeds before we left. We're ghosts unless someone has overridden them in real time."

Locke wasn't sure how much that reassured him.

Kal moved with practiced ease behind him. He tucked his hands casually into the pockets of his stolen jumper. Kenzie's steps were precise, almost too comfortable for someone sneaking into one of the most heavily guarded research facilities in Iveria.

Val stopped at the first junction. She didn't reference any notes or a datapad. She looked left, then right, before she moved left.

Kenzie asked, "How do you know where you're going?"

Val hesitated. "Not our first time here. I studied the maps of this place for weeks."

"What for?" Locke asked.

"So she could avoid idiots asking her questions," Kal said.

Val shot them both a sharp look. "Focus, both of you."

The two wordlessly pointed at each other before they followed Val. They slipped through the corridors and avoided open spaces where someone could spot them. Conchordia was eerily empty at that hour, though the hum of ventilation systems and the distant sound of machinery reminded them it was never truly silent. They reached a side door, which read: RESTRICTED ACCESS: AUTHORIZED PERSONNEL ONLY.

Kenzie crouched near the control panel to pull out the breach terminal. "Give me a second."

Locke shifted to keep an eye on the hallway behind them. "Any chance Haruto could have just unlocked this remotely?"

Kenzie scoffed. "Sure, if he had direct access to Conchordia's CrystalLine and about six weeks to work his way past whatever encryption they use for the doors. An outside security contractor, with way less security, operates the cameras. We get one tonight."

Kal leaned against the wall to watch her work. "So what you're saying is, we should have left Breezewaltz before the Colossus arrived?"

Kenzie smirked as the door let out a soft chime and the security panel flashed green. "I'm saying you should be grateful Haruto and I are good at our jobs."

She pushed the door open, and they slipped inside.

The room beyond was a bit cramped, with only one set of doors on the opposite wall. It was a maintenance lift that serviced the director's office above and the sub-basements below. Based on Kal's story, the basements were where Conchordia kept its worst secrets.

"Okay, this is where you leave us," Val said.

"Remember, we're looking for anything…" Kal started.

"Related to the previous director, we know," Locke cut in.

Locke and Kenzie entered the lift, and Kenzie overrode the controls. It ascended. The room beyond was larger than Locke expected when the doors opened. The director's office was opulent, with glass cases and large artwork that lined the walls. A desk sat under a wide window, a large clock inlaid in its surface. The room was dark, with some emergency lighting, but no one was around.

Kenzie pointed at an unmarked door behind the desk on the right-hand side. It was locked, but she bypassed it manually. Rows of storage consoles embedded into the walls lined the next room. The air smelled faintly of metal and old paper, a rare scent in a world where most records were digitized.

Locke stepped inside the dark. "Kenzie?"

She had already moved to one of the data terminals. Her hands flew over the interface, and the light from it illuminated her face. It was the only light in the room. "I'm looking for anything related to the previous director. These drives are old tech, but they're sturdy. They're just a pain to search."

Locke walked the perimeter, his eyes scanned the few shelves. "What exactly are we looking for?"

"Anything from the years between 972 and 996," Kenzie said. "I guess that's when he was here, according to Kal."

Locke ran a hand along one of the labeled storage cases and paused when he saw a familiar name etched into the side. He hesitated for a fraction of a second before he pulled the case free.

Kenzie caught the movement. "You got something?"

"Not sure, but I think it has Kal's name on it."

Kenzie barely looked up from the terminal. "His what?"

Locke didn't answer right away. The case was heavier than it looked, reinforced with a security lock that hadn't been opened in years. Locke exhaled and tried to open it, but to no avail. He decided to take it. They were already stealing from Conchordia tonight. What was one more parcel?

The comm crackled to life. "Kenzie, how much longer?" It was Val.

Kenzie frowned at the screen. "I found some logs, but this is all tame. Experiments on fruits, whether animals can see color, things like that. I need to search deeper, but it's going to take another minute."

"Get it done." Val's urgency was palpable over the comms.

Kal jumped in. "We're on borrowed time."

That's when Kenzie's hands stopped, and she looked at the door. Kenzie quickly shut down the terminal, and the illuminated screen went dark.

"What? What's happening?" Locke whispered.

Kenzie's expression darkened. "Someone is in the office."

Locke heard it too. There were voices coming from the office on the other side. He straightened as he listened. The voices beyond the archive door grew clearer. It was two distinct people, a man and a woman. Kenzie met Locke's eyes and placed a finger to her lips.

A chair creaked as someone sat, and the clacking sound of terminal keys being typed filled the air.

The first voice, a man's, was calm and measured. "The Council wants an update. I told them we don't have one."

The woman sighed. "That will not be good enough for them."

"They can want whatever they like," the man replied. "The truth is, we are no closer to understanding this Colossus now than when it first appeared. We can't get close enough to study it. Our only real data comes from the Rose Colossus in Aurelia, and those dusty records are obviously not enough."

HALCYON DAYS: THE COLOSSUS

There was a pause. The woman's tone was cautious in reply. "Do you think they're connected?"

The director scoffed. "Of course. The monsters and the Crystals." He paused, as if to consider what he said. "Humanity feels like pawns in this."

"Hopefully, we'll still be here when the board is cleared," she sighed. "What about Syd's research?"

"That lunatic?" The director exhaled sharply. "I wouldn't trust anything he left us after what happened. He fled with twenty staff members and one data drive. We had a backup of it, but his research was dark, tainted. Some things are better left in the past."

Another pause. "The military will want to intervene if this thing reaches Orleans," the woman murmured. "If we don't understand it, we risk making things worse. The princess is asking us for answers."

"What do we care about the princess?" the director asked. "The Armada are brutes who think all our problems can be solved with the right end of a shardshot…" He trailed off, and the typing began again.

The woman spoke again. "And Syd's notes?"

The director sighed. "They're in the archive. Feel free to dig them up if you must. I cataloged them under 'DNO.'"

"DNO?" she asked.

"Do not open," the man replied, but his voice sounded distracted.

A set of footsteps moved toward the door, and Kenzie's grip on Locke's arm tightened.

"Wait," the man's voice called out, and the footsteps stopped. "Actually, we have something more pressing," he continued. "Says here we have a man caught near the water treatment facility."

The woman made a thoughtful noise. "So what?"

"It says he's one of Syd's lackeys. They found him installing some gadget in a maintenance grate."

"Do we know what it does?" she asked.

"Some aerosol dispersion device, limited range. No clue what the application could be. He refuses to talk. No notes or instructions on his person, either."

"Was he one of the twenty that fled?" the woman asked.

"Correct."

"Maybe he knows something we don't?" she asked.

Another pause. Then a chair scraped softly against the floor. "Exactly. It might be a lead. We should visit him." The man's footsteps moved away from the door.

"Now?" she asked as she followed.

"It beats having to answer questions from the princess."

The voices faded as they stepped into the hallway.

Kenzie and Locke exhaled. They looked at each other and mouthed *DNO* at the same time. Kenzie restarted her search and loaded a data drive into the memory terminal.

Locke shook his head. "They didn't mention us."

Kenzie frowned. "Should they have?"

Locke adjusted his grip on the storage case. "I assumed the tails yesterday were from Conchordia."

"Sounds like there are more parties in play than just us and them. Syd's goons or whatever."

Locke had heard of Syd as a cadet at the Citadel. A brilliant man creating wonders. Kal and Val seemed to know him, but Locke wasn't sure how the scientist played into this story. He guessed the information they were about to pull out would shed some light on that particular narrative.

"Got it," Kenzie said as she grabbed the data drive from the terminal and stuffed it into her pouch. "We have what we need. Let's go."

They slipped back into the director's office. Thankfully, no one was there. They moved quickly and silently toward the lift. No alarms or alerts, but something wasn't right. The overhead conversation made something in his brain scream about imminent danger. As the doors slid shut behind them, Locke kept his hand near his suda. He had a feeling their real trouble hadn't started yet.

The lift led them down to the cramped room. The doors opened to reveal Kal and Val amid piles of unconscious bodies. Kal pulled one onto a pile in the corner.

"I told you time was running out!" Kal scream-whispered.

"We had to knock out like twelve people!" Val scream-whispered as well.

"Sorry, we had interference, but we're clean and we got the data," Kenzie said and held up the pouch with the drive.

They slipped back into the corridor, their path clear. Something about it still felt wrong. Locke could feel it in his bones. It was the way the man in the office mentioned Syd's man that gave Locke the feeling they weren't the only ones trying to operate unnoticed in Conchordia tonight.

Val led the way while Kenzie stayed close. Both moved fast, careful not to make unnecessary noise. Kal lingered at the rear and scanned the hallways with an ease that Locke didn't trust. An overhead camera tilted to point directly at them. All four of them noticed the tilt.

Locke exhaled slowly and kept his voice low. "Tell me we're not walking into something."

Kenzie glanced at her datapad. "It still shows as ours, but... someone accessed security manually just then. That's not an automated sweep."

"Then we're on borrowed time," Val said.

The four broke into a sprint and booked it back through Conchordia's sublevels. They retraced their steps toward the maintenance corridors that would lead them to the utility tunnel. Locke tried not to panic, but the camera meant something, and all four of them knew it.

They reached the final stretch of the hallway that led back into the operations facility. Kal reached for the door controls, and the system responded normally. No sign of interference. Locke's shoulders tensed as they moved. The dread hung between them like a fog, but no attack came.

They moved through the facility and slipped through the security gate without incident. The guard barely reacted as they scanned their badges, just four workers heading out.

The cool night air hit them as they stepped onto the street. Kal whistled ahead of the group. There was a giddy sense that they had just pulled it off. No one spoke, but the smiles and small chuckles exchanged said the most.

They rounded a corner, Kal first. He stepped onto some maintenance grating, and a rush of vapor exploded around him. Kal staggered, and Locke barely had time to react before Kal swayed on his feet. His breath hitched. It was some kind of noxious gas. Locke covered his face and pulled Kal back.

"Kal?" Kenzie grabbed his arm.

His voice came slowly and sluggishly. "That's... not good." He went limp.

Val swore and checked his pulse. "He's alive, but that wasn't an accident."

Then the other shoe dropped. A broad-shouldered man stepped into view, flanked by five others. Three were the same tails from the previous day. They pointed their shardshots at the team, fingers ready.

"Why don't we make this easy?" the broad-shouldered man said. "Give us Kal, and the rest of you don't need to die. You can even keep whatever you just stole from Conchordia."

Val crouched, her hand hovered over the semi-secret shardshot she kept in her boot. She looked at Locke, then at Kenzie.

Kenzie's voice was quiet, but firm. "What's the plan, courier boy?"

"No plan, miss, please," the broad-shouldered man said, apparently having overheard her request. "Dr. Syd just wants what is his. This doesn't have to get ugly."

Locke exhaled and responded to Kenzie's question. "We improvise."

The goons hadn't fired yet. That meant they didn't want to accidentally kill Kal. It also meant Locke had a window, and he wouldn't give them that chance. He moved while he tapped the energy. Something clicked inside him, like a gear slotted into place. His vision narrowed and his pulse slowed. The world stretched at the edges of his vision.

Before any of them could react, Locke closed the distance. He did not reach for his suda, but kept his hands open. He used the fighting style he had learned at the Citadel. Calm precision. From thought into action. That was his mantra on the training ground. It served him well in this moment.

Locke struck his palm into the first man's wrist to dislodge the gun. He then placed his other palm into the man's solar plexus. Locke pivoted, stepped into the second man, and struck his wrist as well. He might be breaking them when time returned, but the goal was to disarm, not maim.

Outside the dilation, he imagined what Kenzie would see. In a flash, she would see the first two goons crumple in pain. A third gun would clatter to the pavement. The fourth attacker would twist away, clutching his hand. The fifth would stumble back as their weapon twirled through the air.

Then the world snapped back into place for Locke as he stopped using his Altier abilities. He staggered at the exertion, and a pain filled his chest. He struggled to breathe. The five men reeled and clutched their arms, weapons lost. Their leading man looked around, terrified, and bolted. The others followed his example.

Locke's breath came sharply. He didn't know if he felt satisfied or sick, maybe both.

Val adjusted Kal's deadweight on her shoulder. Kenzie stood tense on the other side, her face contorted, trying to understand what she had just witnessed.

Val turned to Kenzie, her voice steady. "Safe house, now."

Kenzie nodded.

"I have a contact two blocks from here that owes me some favors. We lie low until Kal can move. Hopefully, a couple of hours. Locke, you're on point."

Locke scanned the street. He didn't know if they just had a window of safety or the rest of the night to move, but he wouldn't wait around to find out.

CHAPTER 43: KALISTON

The room was dim, lit only by the soft glow of a lantern on the table. The safe house was small, with the couch dominating most of the living room. Kal had been in it once before and recognized it as belonging to a connection of Val's. He wondered if she had asked to use it. She would wire credits when they were back aboard the *Days* for the trouble.

Kal lay on the couch, his breath steady but shallow. The aftereffects of the gas still weighed him down. He wasn't sure how long he had been out. He didn't need to look to know who was sitting beside him.

"About time," Val murmured.

Kal blinked as his vision adjusted to the dim light. Val sat in a chair near the couch, arms crossed. She watched him like a sentry with her shardshot on her lap.

She was always like this. Fiercely loyal and unwilling to leave his side, even when furious with him.

He tried to push himself up, but the ache in his chest told him he wasn't quite there yet. His lungs dragged with every breath, and they labored under something he couldn't shake.

He groaned, "This is why we never experimented with gas at school. Did you carry me?"

Val didn't smile. "Kenzie helped."

Kal let out a groggy chuckle, then winced and pressed his hands to his head. "Who gases someone like that?"

"Takes an idiot to bag an idiot," Val said. There was something in her tone, not quite amusement, not quite sadness. It was softer than she would admit to herself.

Kal shifted and noticed something was missing. His hand went to his lower back, but the familiar weight wasn't there. His pack was gone.

Kal's eyes snapped to Val. She didn't need to say anything. It sat on the floor behind her, straps folded neatly, placed deliberately out of his reach.

"Thought I'd lighten your load," she said.

Kal sighed and let his head rest back against the couch. "You're never subtle, are you?"

"Never saw the point."

The usual banter, but it didn't settle right.

Kal exhaled and closed his eyes for a moment. "How long was I out?"

"A couple of hours. You took a full dose of whatever that was." Val leaned forward, elbows on her knees. "The men mentioned Dr. Syd while you were out. Seems he still wants you back."

Kal's mouth tightened. That man's name always hit different when Val said it. She always dipped it in some kind of venom before spitting it out. Kal took it as a sign she still cared.

"He doesn't get to want anything more from me." Kal shifted on the couch. "Besides, he's smart enough to figure it out on his own."

She uncrossed and then recrossed her legs. A nervous habit he had seen a million times, but she'd never admit to. "Locke and Kenzie are keeping watch. No sign of pursuit."

Kal smirked. "And they trusted you alone with me? Brave."

Val didn't laugh.

"Did the goons say anything else? Like, where Dr. Syd is, or where they would take me?"

"Locke didn't give them the chance," she said.

"Sounds like he had a good teacher." His gaze drifted to the pack, almost unconsciously.

Her gaze flickered toward the pack again as the humor drained from her face. "How long are you going to keep wearing that thing, Kal?"

Here we go. He pushed himself up more slowly and leaned against the wall behind the couch. "You always ask questions you don't want the answer to."

Val scoffed. "No, I ask questions you don't want to answer."

Kal ran a hand over his face to shake off the last of the lingering haze. "It's not that simple, Val."

Her jaw tightened. "You say that every time. Every time I try to talk to you about this, and yet, here you are. Still wearing it. Still keeping me at arm's length. I see what it's doing to you, and I know you do, too."

Kal stared at her for a long moment. There it was, that old familiar edge between them, the thing neither of them wanted to name. He swallowed and forced a slight smirk. "I figured you'd be used to that by now, but nice to know you still care."

Something flickered in her expression. Hurt, maybe.

"You're still carrying what he did to you every time you strap that thing to your back like it's the only thing keeping you upright." Val shook her head, pushing herself out of the chair. "And you're pretending this is funny?"

Kal hesitated, then shrugged. "I don't get mad at the sun rising or the tide coming in and out. Some things are just the way they are. I didn't ask to have that pack strapped to me, but that's who I am now."

She turned away, hands braced against the edge of a side table. For a second, she just stood there, her fingers tapping against the wood, caught between silence and whatever followed.

Finally, she spoke. "I know what happened changed you. But this recklessness? It's not just about the power that thing gives you. It's like you don't care if you make it out at all."

Kal's smirk faltered. "No," he whispered. And for the first time, he wasn't sure if he was lying.

Val turned back to face him, and for just a second, her fire dimmed. "Then why do you keep rushing us into danger like this? You're asking us to take down a monster taller than Breezewaltz and tougher than hardened steel. This is a suicide mission with no upside at the end."

"The upside is we get to live in a free country, not under the boot of those bastards," Kal said, his voice tight. "I'd rather die than live under their rule. Aurelia's, the Director's, and any other tyrant."

Val met his eyes. It was a look that saw past Kal's charm and bluster. She had him cornered. There was only one question left, and she didn't hesitate to ask it. Not even when she knew she would hate the non-answer.

"Why do you keep pushing me away?" Her eyes softened as she asked it, not completely, but enough.

Kal didn't answer. His gaze drifted to the pack. Like Val, it would ask for more than he could give, but he wouldn't feel like he was letting it down when he did so.

Which answer did he want to give her? Because of what he had become? Because of what that thing had made him? Or because he didn't trust himself if he let her in?

Instead of saying any of that, he reached past her and grabbed the pack.

Val's lips pressed into a thin line. She didn't move, but something in her stance shifted. "Kal…"

He sat up and slung it around his back. He pushed, and it clicked into place. His muscles seized and spasmed for a moment before he forced them back under control. He secured the straps around his waist with practiced ease. The familiar weight settled against his spine.

Kal exhaled. The high rushed in, cold and clean. There it was, that feeling of invincibility. He had felt naked without it. It was as if his body knew how to breathe again, even if the breath felt borrowed.

Val didn't move. She just watched. For the briefest second, a shadow crossed her face, something tired and hurt. Like Kal had chosen the pack over her. Mainly, because he had.

Kal forced a smirk. It felt hollow, but he gave it to her, anyway. "You know me, Val. I always bet on us."

She exhaled and shook her head as she stepped back. "Yeah. That's the problem. The house always wins in the end. Everyone knows that."

She turned toward the door and picked up the case Locke had been carrying. "I'll let the kids know we're rolling out in five." She hesitated, only for a second. Then she was gone.

Kal sat there in the dim light, the Hollowline pressing against his spine like a second heartbeat. Syd's design and his legacy. Kal carried it even though he hated it more with each passing day because he didn't know who he was anymore without it.

No matter how much he wanted to, he wasn't taking it off. Not for her. Not for himself. Not until his work was done.

CHAPTER 44: KENZIE

The stars looked the same as always, but they felt different. It was just after midnight, and Kenzie leaned against the edge of the bridge as the *Days* banked east. They pulled away from the lights of Belfield and headed toward Orleans. The readouts across the console were calm and steady. No warnings or alarms. Just a clean flight path and an ETA that left enough time to link up with the Armada before the Colossus showed up later that day.

Haruto wasn't sure if it would be afternoon or evening, but they knew their time was running out.

From behind her came the quiet hum of the ship's engines. Everything was in motion, but it felt strange. Kenzie was still of the opinion that skypirates should always run away from danger, but something about flying into the storm felt right this time.

Val stepped onto the bridge, a blanket tucked under one arm. Her hair was half undone, and she had put her flight jacket back on. Her eyes moved over the bridge. She scanned the instruments and systems, then the faces, and finally, Kal.

The two of them hadn't talked since the safe house. Not really. The only chatter between them was updates, tactical notes, and need-to-know exchanges. Kenzie had picked up on the difference right away. She wasn't privy to what they had discussed in that room, but whatever was said made the air tense between them. Val didn't pretend, but she also didn't say what it was.

Avery sat in the pilot's chair, posture loose but alert. Haruto flipped through low-band surveillance without blinking. Half of Liam was inside a console, and he swore as buzzing and sparks intermittently erupted.

"Everyone's trying to get some rest before Orleans," Val said. "You should, too. I'll take the watch."

Avery glanced at the readouts. "Course is locked and autopilot's stable. Twelve hours to contact at this speed. Could make it in eleven if we push her."

"Twelve is fine." Val stayed near the XO's seat, arms crossed.

Kenzie didn't need to look to feel the awkward air between Val and Kal. She knew that kind of silence. It was her default, too, when something hadn't settled in a way she agreed with.

There was a zap, and Liam swore again as he shook his hand. "At least we know it's wired now," he muttered.

Kal adjusted the trim and made a slight heading correction.

"Kal, autopilot's on. Why adjust the route?" Val asked without turning.

"Winds are bad this time of year. If we cut southeast, we'll pick up better lift coming into Orleans," Kal replied.

No one said anything, but Haruto's eyes flicked to Val instead of Kal. A small, unconscious movement. Like he checked if she agreed. Kenzie had turned and caught it, too. Liam had stopped what he was doing and poked his head out of the panel to look at their XO.

Val gave the slightest nod. That was enough. Haruto turned back to his panel, and Liam repacked his kit.

Kal kept his eyes on the forward glass. "Like Val said. If you're tired, now's the time."

"We're good," Avery said. "We're with you."

Time passed. Haruto and Val went quiet as they ran through flagged intercepts. Liam sat back in his chair and clasped a mug with both hands. Avery didn't let go of the controls, even though there was no reason to stay on them.

No one left the bridge.

Kenzie stayed quiet. She understood what this was. Val had stayed up to make sure Kal didn't spiral. The others stayed up because they backed her and loved him. None of them would say it, but that didn't make it less true.

Kal probably knew. He hadn't looked at anyone since Val stepped in. Kenzie wasn't sure what went through his mind. He might have been grateful, or maybe he was angry. All she got from him was the same wry smile he showed the world.

CHAPTER 45: LUCAN

Lucan watched the beginning of the Iverian Armada's end. To him, it felt less like a battle and more like a ritual. A sacrifice to all he believed in. He took great pleasure in knowing how it would happen before it occurred. He observed the battle unfold below with calm detachment from the bridge of the *Inquisitor*. Through the reinforced viewport, Brittlebark Forest stretched below. It was an ancient and unyielding expanse of towering trees. The forest pressed against the Jotunn mountain range, a natural fortress for a last stand. The dense woodland would slow the Colossus and break up its advance, while the mountains forced a bottleneck.

Clever. Not that it mattered. The Colossus strode through the treetops. It shattered ancient trunks as if they were little more than bones beneath its feet. The forest gave way before it, each splintered tree a tithe to Lucan's pet god.

The Armada had drawn their defensive line at the forest's edge, where the trees met the mountains, to use the terrain to funnel the Colossus into a controlled kill zone.

Iverian Capital skyships of the line held position. Their shardshot cannons trained on the true monster in the field. Then, all at once, the Armada opened the heavens, and shardshot rained down below.

Lucan's lips curled as he turned his gaze to the Colossus.

It strode through the treetops and tore through the ancient woodland with indifference. Its towering form absorbed the hailstorm of fire from above.

Shardshot blasted against its crystaline frame, hammering its shoulders and limbs. The impacts careened against its surface, and a fine mist of shattered crystal flew into the air. The creature did not falter. The shardshot only fed its rage. It moved with the purpose of a god roused from slumber, indifferent to the mortals it crushed beneath its feet.

Lucan clasped his hands behind his back. "Push the western flank. Focus fire on the *Black Bastion*."

His order carried through the Fleet.

The Armada's twelfth ship of the line, the *Black Bastion*, had drifted forward and positioned itself dangerously close to the Colossus as it rained fire down on the beast. It was a calculated risk, but one that left its flank exposed.

An army is only as strong as its weakest link. Lucan's faithful Fleet adjusted. Their formation shifted to create a kill box around the *Bastion*. Each ship was a blade in his hand, each volley a verse in his hymn of conquest. He did not merely command a Fleet, no; he conducted a ritual of annihilation.

A century-old cruiser led the charge as it wove through enemy fire. Its broadside batteries lit up the sky in streaks of red-hot shardshot. The *Bastion's* cannons roared to meet the assault. It lit its engines to reposition, but it was already too late.

Lucan watched with calm satisfaction as his ships shattered the *Bastion's* armor. A concentrated blast from three heavy cruisers pierced straight through its hull. A chain reaction rippled across the *Bastion's* spine, its hull ruptured like dry wood split beneath an axe. The ship listed sharply to port, a final desperate maneuver, then it broke apart, its burning wreckage plunged toward the trees below.

One down, and the skies had opened. The *Berkshield*, another Armada Capital skyship, surged forward to fill the gap.

"Now!" Lucan's gaze flicked to the Colossus as the crew relayed the command to the units controlling the Hollow Crown.

The *Berkshield* either hadn't considered the monster's reach or thought it was mindless. Both were miscalculations. A ripple of energy surged through the Colossus's frame. Its limbs moved faster than anything that size should be capable of. A massive hand closed around the *Berkshield's* stern, the grip absolute. The ship's engines screamed, and thrusters fired wildly as it fought against the impossible hold. It unloaded all its shardshot battery straight into the creature's face. For a brief moment, it seemed as if it might break free, then the Colossus slammed it into the gaia.

Lucan exhaled sharply. To tame a god, one must first believe oneself worthy of divine power. Lucan had done more than tame the creature. He had become its will, its purpose, and the divine judgment that moved its limbs.

The fireball that rose was light blue and massive. The debris rained down on the hull of the *Inquisitor*.

Lucan's smile deepened at the destruction before him. He glanced back to see his crew in awe of the spectacle. Good, let the Emperor hear about what *his* weapon could do in the hands of a true commander.

Lucan's Fleet pressed the exposed edge of the Armada to carve through one ship at a time. His ships were old, cobbled together from whatever ships his father could spare. Still, when they moved as a single, massive unit while a god of war covered them, they were unstoppable.

Not for the first time, he felt the rush of his destiny manifest. The world bent to his will, and the unworthy crumbled beneath his shadow. He had become more than a man, a commander, or even a prince. He had become a living myth.

He wondered if his father would be pleased or if his mother had seen this future when he was a boy. He told himself he was finally beyond caring. The reaction of Iveria was all that mattered.

Let them tremble.

CHAPTER 46: KENZIE

0 Days Until the Colossus Attacks Orleans

The air inside the *Days* felt heavier than usual. Maybe it was exhaustion, or perhaps it was everything they'd stolen from Conchordia that sat on the table between them.

The ship was on approach to Orleans. In the solitude of the morning sky, they finally had time to look at what they'd taken.

Kenzie exhaled. "Alright. Let's see what was worth nearly getting killed for."

Liam picked up the drive and slotted it into his datapad. The screen flicked to life, lines of crystal code scrolled before it decrypted into folders of research notes, project logs, and sealed documents.

Locke leaned in. "Okay… That's a lot of classified info. Kal, I don't know if we should read this."

Kal winced, apparently from the effects of the gas. "Just read it. It's not like we can become public enemy number zero."

Liam's eyes scanned the directory to narrow his search. "Here. 'DNO Files.' That's what the director mentioned, right?"

Kenzie nodded. "Yeah."

Liam pulled up a document and uploaded it to the table. A series of schematics and logs flickered to life on the display.

NEURAL	LINK	INTERFACE
Status:		INACTIVE

Synchronization Method: Direct Connection to Nervous System

Director: <Redacted>

Liam read out, "Directly linking the subject's nervous system to the Crystal shard results in interesting phenomena. The synchronization enables knowledge outside the subject's purview to become available. The crystal also gives the subject direction."

Locke frowned. "Synchronization? He linked people to shards?"

Haruto leaned in. "Is that worse than forcing kids to swallow them?"

Val gave him a look, and Haruto turned back to the table.

"Probably not, but it's barbaric all the same," Kenzie muttered, still focused on the notes.

Liam stood next to her. "This is a case study, but if it's true, it looks like the Crystals broadcast signals to anyone directly interfacing with them."

Everyone turned to Kal, then Locke.

Locke held up his hands. "Don't look at me. I haven't heard anything."

They looked back at Kal. Kal rolled his eyes and stepped forward. "So, the Crystals are sending a signal to the Colossus?"

"Yeah, but not just a signal. It looks like the Crystal is guiding it," Liam said. "If this is true, the signal can be hijacked and altered. There are schematics for some device."

"Did he ever finish it?" Kal asked and leaned in closer.

"It says he never got it to work. Something about it desyncing." Liam looked from the datapad to Kal, then to Val.

"We can assume he found a workaround," Val said. "That bastard wouldn't let something like failure stop him."

Liam nodded. "That tracks. There's a linked log here." He tapped the screen, and a new entry flickered to life.

Syd's voice crackled from the table, and a picture of the scientist appeared.

"A masked man named Rook came to me today. He claims to represent an upstart prince of Aurelia named Lucan. This prince just assassinated another of his rivals for the Emperor's seat and has similar ambitions for Iveria."

"Bastard." Kenzie pounded a fist into the table. It came out too fast, too hard. Everyone looked at her. She blinked, as if surprised by her voice, then gave a slight shrug. "What... I thought we were all on the same page about that guy? Just me?"

Her tone was sharp but controlled. She hadn't expected to hear it out loud, but hearing Syd's voice say Lucan's name had triggered something in her. She knew enough to know Lucan hadn't just wanted power. He had wanted it at any cost, and she remembered who had paid the price. She breathed once, slow and steady, then focused back on the table.

The crew was in it for Iveria, Toren, or their fellow crew members. Whatever the twelve other reasons were, they were fine for them. She was in it to watch Lucan's face while his world crumbled to dust around him.

She leaned back slightly and uncoiled her fingers one at a time. No one asked, and the recording continued, but Kenzie remained quiet.

"I do not know how he learned of it, but Rook brought evidence of a dormant Colossus under White Hill, just waiting for the spark of life. This Rook had heard of my research on Crystal interfacing and wanted to know if I could make it walk again. I told him it was possible. My research suggested there might be a way to control the creature, much better than the Aurelian barbarians had done six hundred years ago. The ladies were practically giddy at the news, saying it was all part of the plan. I wish they had told me sooner. Creating a power interface should be simple enough. I can advance my research using human test subjects. I will need a heavy shard for the final version. Rook said he would handle that. The control device will be the actual challenge, but once complete, it will be my masterpiece. I will call it the Hollow Crown. Rook advised me to remain at Conchordia and work from here rather than attempting development in the field or substandard labs in Aurelia. I will begin work in earnest tomorrow. This project must remain top secret. Luckily, my team is absolutely loyal to me. If all goes well, I will have working prototypes for both by winter."

A thoughtful silence settled over the group.

Kal exhaled sharply. "So that's how it started. How did it finish?"

Liam scrolled. "Next project looks like it follows from there." He pulled up another file.

BIOLOGICAL APPLIED SHARD-POWERED INDIVIDUAL (BASPI)
Status: INACTIVE
Synchronization Method: Direct Connection to Heart and Brain
Director: <Redacted>

Kal frowned. "The worst names." He shook his head. "What is this now?"

Liam skimmed the text. "Looks like they experimented with using shards to power the subject directly instead of converting chemical energy into electrical signals."

Cookie spoke up, "You mean like instead of food?"

Liam nodded.

"The bastard," she said to herself.

A schematic flickered onto the display of a crystal-powered device affixed to a man's chest.

Kenzie paled. "Gaia's blood." The horror of it sank in.

Kal's voice was steady. "Was he successful?"

Liam hesitated. "Not exactly. Lifespans were limited, but one individual lived ninety-six days. All subjects eventually succumbed to some form of shard-induced poisoning." He paused, then added, "That is for humans, though."

Kenzie's lips pressed into a thin line. "So he wasn't just researching how to control people. He was trying to turn them into unstoppable monsters?" She glanced at Kal. "No offense."

Val shot her a look.

Kal shrugged it off like she had not said anything. "We have to assume he perfected both technologies and is using them on the Colossus," Kal said. "That would explain why it's moving after a millennium and is heading straight for Orleans."

"Okay, so we fly to Orleans and help the city's defenses," Val said. "Should be easier to sneak on with the Armada keeping the creature busy."

Locke leaned closer. "Do we land on the creature and destroy both the control and power source?"

"Or we just shoot both from the air," Tia interjected. "The *Days'* main cannon would make short work of whatever toys Syd created."

"It's not that simple," Liam muttered. "Give me a second." He pulled a finger to his pursed lips. "Destroying this... Hollow Crown... could cause more problems than it solves. Plus, we can't destroy the Crystal. That would defeat the point of this whole operation. No Crystal, no Iveria."

"I'm not even sure we can destroy the Crystal," Locke interjected.

Kal crossed his arms. "Noodle on it, Liam, and let's talk when we get to Orleans."

"I'm here when you want to walk through it," Val said.

Liam hesitated. "Yeah, give me some time."

He got quiet, gave Val the pad, and stepped back from the table. He paced for a second before walking out of the room. Hopefully, that meant he had an idea.

Meanwhile, Kenzie had fiddled with the lockbox. She had never met a lock she couldn't pick. At least, not since Seaforth. She had met a woman named Olivia on her first night there. She had taken Kenzie in and taught her all she knew. Kenzie looked up to her and even wanted to be her. That was until she learned Olivia was going to sell her to a street gang. That was the end of their friendship and the start of Kenzie's solo life on the streets of Seaforth. Still, Olivia had taught her to pick locks, and by Gaia's green garden, the lockbox would not be the first to beat her.

A click. The metal panels separated. She opened it to find a small data drive with Kal's name on it and held it up.

"I have no secrets," Kal said, and motioned to the console. "Or at least no good ones."

Kenzie plugged it in. Val frowned but pressed a symbol on the datapad. The table's display brought up a new file.

COVERT ANTI-ROSARI AND ANTI-ALTIER PROGRAM (CaRaAP)

Status:	INACTIVE

Synchronization Method: Direct Connection to Spinal Cord
Director: Dr. Baron El-Syd

"That is the worst program name I've ever read," Tia said deadpan.

"They didn't even do it ironically," Val replied.

A long silence followed. Kenzie was the first to speak. "At least they didn't redact Syd's name on this one."

Locke frowned, and Val quickly flipped through more documents as she scanned through them.

Kenzie read off the table interface. "There's a timeline here. Years of research on shard implantation, compatibility trials, subject viability…"

Val stopped, her eyes darted toward Kal before she shut off the table's display. Kal stepped forward. "Val."

She hesitated, then sighed and turned it back on before she handed the pad to him.

"Some things should stay buried, Kal." She said, but Kal clicked over.

SUBJECT	**FILE:**	**<REDACTED>**
Designation:	CaRaAP Test Subject	#001

Status: ESCAPED

The room went utterly still. Kal's gaze locked onto the screen. He took a slow breath and pulled up the file. He double-clicked, and the screen changed to display a personnel document. Kal's name, military record, and biometric data were all there. Kenzie's heart pounded, but her eyes caught something else, a photo attachment. Kal saw it, too. He clicked the icon, and the image loaded.

It was a picture of Kal, Val, and Toren. They wore their Armada uniforms, fresh from graduation. Toren and Val had their lieutenant junior grade insignia pins fastened, and Kal had his lieutenant pin front and center. They looked happy, like the world opened to them. Kal was in the middle, his arms wrapped around both.

Kenzie looked over to see Locke's reaction. His focus lingered on the picture. She looked back at it. Toren looked so young. His hair was longer, but still well-maintained. Locke and Toren had the same smile and eyes. They were the same eyes Locke had looked into when Toren fell.

Kenzie saw something stir inside Locke. He seemed to fight it, but he couldn't keep it at bay. She did not know what it was, but it resulted in Locke's face becoming pained as he looked away. Kenzie could only guess he thought about that night in Breezewaltz and their inability to make a difference in a no-win scenario. He couldn't save Toren or stop the rampaging Colossus. She knew he still blamed himself.

Kenzie put a hand on his shoulder. "You okay?"

"Yeah, I'll be fine… just didn't expect to see him." Locke looked back at the image, and Kenzie did, too.

Val had looked over. "He'd be proud of you and how far you've come in such a short time. He'd probably say you were farther along than you knew. It just took you until now to realize it." She spoke quietly but wasn't afraid if others heard her, either.

Locke snorted and fought back tears. Kenzie hadn't known the man long, but it seemed Val was right that Toren would say something saccharine like that. Kenzie wasn't sure if Locke knew the words to be true. They both looked at his brother again.

"She's right," Kenzie whispered to him.

He took a breath and then whispered to Kenzie. "We're about to attempt something that will more than likely get us killed. I want to meet him in the next life with my head held high. Not as the one who ran, or the one who failed, but as the one who stood when it counted. I'm done being the runt and letting someone else fix the world. I'm either going to protect Iveria or die trying."

"Well said," Val replied before looking back at the picture again.

Kenzie smiled at him and reached down for his hand. He wiped away the tears with the other one.

"I'm fine, really," he said, and Kenzie gave his hand a squeeze.

Kal swiped to the next image. It was a younger Kal, barely a first year at the Citadel, who stood stiffly beside Dr. Syd.

Syd looked more put together, but otherwise unchanged. The same calculating expression, same controlled posture. Kal had the same smile, but there was something more they shared.

Kenzie got it immediately. They weren't acquaintances. Their posture was different, but their faces were too similar.

"Dr. Syd is your father?" Kenzie asked.

The room felt too small.

"Yes, Dr. Syd is my father," Kal started. "A blessing and a curse. I don't have his scientific mind. He… never let me forget how much of a failure I was for not following in his footsteps and attending Conchordia. We had never gotten along, especially after my mom passed. Attending the Citadel instead of Conchordia had been the final straw."

Kal looked into the cold eyes of his father. "I often think about what must have happened to turn him into such a monster. He might have always been one, and it just took time to bring that part of him to the surface. It might have been my mother's death." He took a deep breath. "Now he's the man in the picture and something else entirely. We have to stop both, because no one else will if we don't. My father has already proven he will let cities burn just for some misguided ideal. We can't let him sacrifice the world, too."

He looked around the room at the crew. Kenzie felt like he had dropped the bravado for the first time since she met him. She wasn't sure how she felt about that.

"I spent the first half of my life trying to please this man, then the second running from him. Standing here with you all, I can see that both were wrong. I am lucky to be who I am, but my purpose has never been to follow or flee. My life was meant to stop him."

Val exhaled. "That son of a bitch…"

Kal tabbed back in the file. The image left the viewport, and he shut off the display. "Easy, Val. You're talking about my grandmother."

AC BISHKEY

CHAPTER 47: LOCKE

0 Days Until the Colossus Attacks Orleans

Locke had remembered Orleans as grand, but as he looked down at it from above, it appeared smaller.

The city sprawled along the banks of the Iverian River. Its alabaster towers rose against the sky like the teeth of a great beast that waited to bite down. The outer walls, reinforced with anti-air shardshot cannons, were lined with banners that bore the Imperial crest.

And yet, no airships patrolled overhead. No soldiers stood at attention along the fortified battlements. No checkpoints stopped travelers along the winding roads.

Locke adjusted his suda with a frown. "Everyone's seeing this?"

Val approached and nodded. "Where the hell is the Armada?"

That had been the question since that morning. They'd flown in from the west and expected to see a city that bristled with defenses as the Armada circled like a herd that protected its young. Instead, the skies were empty.

Earlier, Haruto had picked up a mass notification on all long-range comm channels. The CrystalLine was flooded with information about the Colossus. The King had revealed the nation's dark secret. Probably too late.

Skyship traffic had died off an hour before they reached the capital. The usual layers of royal security had vanished. Orleans stood unguarded, as if the war had never existed.

Tia scoffed. "Maybe they left."

Maybe, Locke thought. More likely, all the traffic earlier was the elite fleeing for their lives. The middle and lower classes were doomed to hitch their fate to the city's.

His boots scraped against the edge of the overlook as he stared at the city he had visited in his youth, twice with his father and Toren. The last time was with the whole family when the queen had died.

His eyes swept across the streets and traced old memories in the city below. The Royal Palace, the winding noble districts, the great markets that never truly closed. He had walked those roads long before he ever set foot on the *Days.*

Somewhere down there, he hoped his closest friend would be safe. He hoped she hadn't gone with the Armada, but knowing her, she was somewhere dangerous anyway.

His fingers twitched against his suda. How long had it been? Too long was the only answer that felt right. It was after Locke had left the Citadel, but before he had lost his memory. Life, his wild, unpredictable life, had just happened. He had thought about visiting, but Kal seemed to be allergic to Orleans. When he asked Locke why they should go, Locke was at a loss for words. So he left it unsaid, and they didn't go.

He wondered if she still had her father's old suda? She'd spun it in her bunk nightly. She was so talented, maybe the best Locke had ever seen. He smirked faintly.

A sharp whistle cut through his thoughts.

Locke turned to see Kenzie above on the observation deck. She leaned against the railing and gestured for him to join her.

Locke walked up the steps to see the trio at their stations.

"You're gonna want to hear this," Haruto said from the comm station as his fingers flew over the console.

Locke strode over, Val and Kal close behind.

Locke glanced back at Kal. He looked like himself, calm and composed as always. The bags under his eyes looked a little deeper, but that was to be expected when fighting a moving mountain capable of wiping whole cities off the map. It was good to know Locke wasn't the only one with sleepless nights.

Something still felt different. Not in Kal directly. He still commanded the room, even in silence. The difference was Val. It was the look she gave him. Her eyes lingered on Kal a second longer than usual. Her brow creased slightly before she turned away. Locke was a bad read, but things were starting to get obvious. Kal was overextending himself.

Haruto's frown deepened as he adjusted the signal. "I picked up something. A short-range military transmission. It's encrypted, but not heavily." He worked for a few more seconds, then the static broke, and a voice crackled over the speakers.

"Fleet engaged. South of the city... No confirmation on Colossus trajectory..."
The feed cut in and out before stabilizing.

"Armada redeployed to intercept... Brittlebark... Standby for further..."
Then, silence.

Haruto exhaled and sat back. "That explains where they went. Sounds like the King is with the Armada and the princess is handling evacuations."

Locke's jaw tightened. The Armada hadn't abandoned Orleans or Iveria. They had moved to fight the Colossus.

Kenzie crossed her arms, her expression unreadable. "They think they can stop it?"

Kal and Locke said nothing. Just watched the city below.

Val eventually spoke. "Probably not. They're just going out there to buy some time and delay the inevitable."

CHAPTER 48: KALISTON

0 Days Until the Colossus Attacks Orleans

Twilight had settled over Orleans, and the Days hung in the air over the city. The command table threw a pale light across the crew's faces. It sat beneath his captain's chair on the lower bridge and cast long shadows across the deck. The projection from it showed the Colossus in motion, with Lucan's Fleet spread around it. Haruto had pulled the scan from the *Fury*'s final transmission before it went silent. He kept the comms live. Background noise drifted from the overhead speakers. A quiet reminder that everything was already in motion.

Kal stood at the round command table. "I'm going over this one more time. We think there's a control device on the Colossus, the Hollow Crown. If we can take it, we steer the thing to the sea. If we can't, we destroy it so Lucan and Syd can't control it. After that," he looked to Val, "we go for the Azure Crystal at its heart."

Val tapped a finger against the map. "Most of the city on the Colossus is in ruins, but the shoulder section still has intact buildings. White Hill's City Hall is just below the neck. That's where the Crown is likely housed. According to Locke and Kenzie, the area's crawling with Rosari. We won't get two shots."

Haruto brought up the Fleet formation. "Lucan's skyships are flying cover. The *Days* can stay totally hidden if we move at night. Daylight will make it tricky. We get in quiet and fast. Once it reaches Orleans, we lose the window."

Jules stepped forward, tired but focused. "I can redirect power and keep her quiet. You'll get your run."

Kal nodded. "Avery's flying. Jules is in engineering. Rina has the bridge, and Cookie is second. Jazz and Lizz stay to keep things from falling apart."

"Security," Jazz added with a smile.

Lizz groaned. "That won't make anyone feel any better."

Kal let them laugh. It was better than silence.

"Tia, Liam, and Haruto. You're with Val and me. We hit the Crown. Disrupt their defense and gain access to the tech. Odds are they didn't stack extra security around it. They probably think Lucan's Fleet and the walking god are enough."

Tia leaned back and cracked her knuckles. "Get me in range. I'll clear the way."

Val raised an eyebrow. "You still have those pepper bombs from Warwick?"

Tia grinned. "No, but I resupplied in Breezewaltz. Cleaned the place out. Explosives and casings. We might have dipped into the Rose shards they confiscated from the guy Kal had locked up. I've got more than enough."

"I didn't lock him up," Kal muttered. "I just happened to be nearby when it happened."

Val shook her head. "Good. We need pepper charges and blueberries, too. Blueberry shardshot only, it's all that will dent the Rosari."

Cookie looked confused. "We're naming explosives after fruit, now?"

"They're the flavor of the explosives. Pepper means Rose. Blueberry is Azure," Tia explained, already too excited.

Val nodded. "Pepper bombs are for the Colossus. Make them bigger."

Tia's grin sharpened. "Is there another size?"

Val looked at the others. "Locke and Kenzie, you're taking the heart. The Crystal sits at the core. I don't expect guards. Anyone who gets close dies. Same rules as storage in Breezewaltz. Altiers should be immune, which means Locke's our guy. Kenzie gets him in, he plants the charge, and the Crystal should float up."

Avery chimed in. "I'll catch it. After I pick the rest of you up, of course."

Liam's voice stayed level. "It's been years since I've been in a fight. I'd prefer we avoid it."

Kal spoke quietly. "Leave any Rosari to me. You focus on the device."

Val picked up the thread. "Haruto and Tia will rig charges under the creature's shoulder blades. The *Days* can hover twenty seconds out. If anything goes wrong prior to the blast, call in and fall back. After that, we're locked in, no matter what."

A shift ran through the room. No one liked hearing the consequences should things go south.

Val kept going. "Ten-minute window. Get in, jam the Crown, steer the thing to the coast. The Colossus hits water about three hours after we start. Maybe less if the timing's tight."

Cookie looked up from her corner. "I'll pack rations."

Dr. Rina nodded. "Med kits are prepped. Try not to need them."

Jules spoke to the room. "Just don't let them shoot my girly."

Kal smiled and stepped back into the center. "Once the Colossus hits water, the *Days* will swing around and pick up both teams. Crown team exits through the front, back, or that panic tunnel."

"Panic tunnel?" Kenzie asked.

"Every city hall's supposed to have one," Haruto replied.

"The Crystal team sets their charges, dislodges the Crystal, and we grab it on the run." Kal glanced toward the cockpit. "The cloaking holds long enough to get us clear. Rendezvous at Somerset if we're separated. Better drinks there than at Port Royale. Hope you don't mind swimming."

Avery didn't look up. "Fast in, fast out. Even if we're spotted, they can't catch us."

The room shifted. The plan was solid enough. No time to make it better. That was when a chime cut across the table. The speakers flared with static.

"Armada…no more…Orleander…pulling back…"

Everyone froze. Haruto ran to the controls and cleaned up the signal.

"All ships evacuate Orleans airspace. The Armada is no more. The *Orleander* is pulling back. Evacuate immediately."

Liam's voice cracked. "Gaia, no. It wiped them out."

Kal felt the air sucked out in an instant, but Val didn't flinch. "This doesn't change anything. It just means we have no backup. We're it, but we always were anyway."

There she was, the level head he relied on. They all did.

Kal took a step forward. "I've never asked any of you to do something I wouldn't, and I'm not starting now. We can drop you off tonight if you don't feel comfortable with the plan. No judgment. You're welcome back if we make it out alive."

Jules stepped up first. "We're with you, Captain."

Cookie slammed her fist into the table. "If we're going down, we'll make them choke on us."

Haruto nodded. "They'll remember us, that's for sure."

The room went still. Kal gave it a beat, then smiled. "Seriously, thank you. Iveria never deserved a crew like this. We were always too good for her."

Around him, they exchanged knowing nods.

Kal's gaze landed on Kenzie. "It will come down to you two. You'll have to be our shadow. Slip through the cracks."

Kenzie smirked. "I'll be fine. Twinkletoes over here might be a problem."

Locke glanced at Kenzie, then at Jules. The two women exchanged a look and a smile. He would have to ask what that was about later. His eyes drifted across the room, taking in each of them.

Val stood at Kal's side. That was where she always was. It was the best place to lead from when the responsibility of keeping the crew alive grew too heavy for Kal, and she never flinched from it. Her expression was steady, and Kal appreciated what that resolve meant. She would not let him fall.

Dr. Rina stood nearby, calm and sure. She had always been more than just a medic. If Kal was the foundation, she was the one who kept the rest from collapsing. Her strength came quietly, but without it, the crew would have fractured long ago.

Cookie's arms were crossed, her face drawn with worry. She had already planned for everything that might go wrong, packed rations, and counted what they could carry and what they could leave behind.

Tia leaned against the far rail. She had a shardshot casing tucked behind an ear. The fire behind her smile said she was ready for whatever came next. Kal had seen that look before, usually right before a large blast.

Liam watched from a corner, quiet but alert. He hadn't signed up for the war, but he did his best, anyway. Sure, he would grumble the whole time, but he never stopped showing up. Kal loved that about him.

Haruto sat nearby and flipped a coin through his fingers. His expression gave nothing away, but Kal had known him long enough to guess the rest. He'd already run the numbers and probably had six ways this could have ended badly, yet he still chose to help.

Avery was a phenomenal pilot, but he had never really cared about anything but his own skin. Kal suspected the crew had changed that. Avery would get them in and out. That part never worried him.

Jazz stood by the door, brimming with restless energy, as if he might try to tackle the Colossus with his bare hands.

Lizz stood beside him, arms folded, jaw tight. She had something to prove, or maybe she just wanted someone to doubt her so she could prove them wrong.

Jules remained near the systems monitor, silent. Her hands rested on the rail, calloused and still. She never said much, but Kal knew she would keep the *Days* flying, even if it cost her everything.

It was his crew. His family, the one he found and founded.

"We're with you, Kal. You can count on us," Locke said.

Kal met his eyes and saw something shift. It wasn't guilt, and it wasn't just anger. It was steadier than that. It looked like the same thing that had carried Toren through the crucible of his upbringing for all those years. Kal was lucky enough to see firsthand the drive that had made Toren who he was. If Locke had found it, then he was ready.

Kal gave a small nod. "We've got six hours before the big dance. Get ready. Settle your affairs. Tonight, we bring down a god."

The groans were immediate. A few muttered "showoff," someone else said "cheesy."

Kal shrugged. "What? I stole that from Toren."

Cookie waved a hand as she walked off. "Yeah, but he could've pulled it off."

Kal smiled to himself. His father had built a monster to conquer the world. Kal had built a crew willing to save it. Soon, he'd see which endured. His bet was on the one fighting for the right reasons.

The crew dispersed, broke into quiet groups, and prepped for the impossible. Only Locke, Kenzie, Val, and Kal remained. Kal turned to go, but Locke stepped in front of him.

"You don't have to do this," Locke said. "You can drop me off on that thing, and I can still hit them where it hurts. No need to risk the crew. We're not an army. This isn't your fight."

Kal met his gaze. "I know you'd give them hell, but no chance, Locke. He was my brother, too."

That was the truth. The crew was fighting for Iveria, but for Locke and Kal, it was personal.

CHAPTER 49: LUCAN

The battlefield was a graveyard of fire and steel. In four hundred years, the Aurelian Fleets had toiled and harried the Armada for what amounted to a pitiful scratch. It had taken the Colossus a little under three hours to beat the Armada into Gaia's dirt. The *Deepwarden* and *Belepoch* were the most recent offerings.

Wreckage from Iverian Capital skyships littered Gaia below. Their broken frames jutted from the gaia like iron tombstones. It was not just a battlefield, but a testament to Lucan's might and a reminder of the price paid for his divine mission.

The sky smoldered with the ruins of vessels. The parts of the ship still attached to crystals drifted in slow, solemn orbits. Fragments of blue and gold banners fluttered through the ash-choked air, remnants of a nation on the brink of collapse.

The sound of Aurelian ships and massive footfalls ruled the space between the ruin.

The *Willowark*, *Daybreaker*, and *Golden Nexus* fled while they streamed shard-shot down on the Colossus. Lucan's Fleet swarmed from above to limit the altitude of the three massive skyships. Two were already ablaze, and the third operated on only a single engine. That one was the *Daybreaker*, and she listed lower and lower.

Once the Colossus grabbed her out of the air, it was over. The Colossus ripped off the single remaining engine and lined up the two airborne ships. It launched the husk of the *Daybreaker* at the *Willowark*, which then collided with the *Golden Nexus*. The *Golden Nexus* listed but still held altitude. Then it turned and powered its engines directly toward the Colossus. The explosion was exceptional, an exclamation point at the end of the Armada's final sentence.

The Colossus still stood among the fire and shrapnel. It was a perfect moment.

Lucan stood on the observation deck of the *Inquisitor*, hands clasped behind his back, a cold specter in the glass. He had insisted on being aboard for the battle. The view from the Colossus was limited, and he wanted to witness victory first-hand. His eyes, twin blades of calculation, carved every scrap of destruction into triumph.

"The Armada," he said, his voice smooth as polished steel, "is no more."

Dr. Syd lingered at his left, his teeth bared in a fractured wall of glee. "I barely believe it," he rasped, his voice thick with pleasure. "Those bastards are finally dead. The ones that threw me out, gone!" He laughed.

Lucan didn't respond immediately. Instead, he snapped his fingers, and a junior officer rushed forward with a goblet filled with dark, rich wine. Lucan accepted it without a glance. His gaze never left the carnage beyond the glass.

He raised the goblet to his lips. The firelight from the wreckage below danced on the goblet's gold surface. It was not a victory, but a coronation. Not the triumph of a prince or an Emperor. It was the ascension of something more.

They would not remember him as Lucan, Prince Lucan, or even Emperor Lucan. They would remember him as the right hand of the Rose Crystal. The chosen disciple of a divine mandate and the forger of a new Gaia wrapped in faith.

"You have given me a perfect weapon, Syd," Lucan said at last. He lifted the goblet slightly as if to toast. "And with perfection comes inevitability."

Syd chuckled, the sound coarse and indulgent. "I told you the heart was key, but the Hollow Crown… ah." He inhaled as if to savor the words. "That's my masterpiece. We can command the smallest detail. The Armada captains assumed they were safe, beyond the reach of a slow, mindless creature. An incorrect hypothesis."

Lucan's eyes narrowed slightly. The edges of his mouth curled into something that wasn't quite a smile. "Yes. Control. Perfect, efficient control." He took a measured sip, unhurried. "With it, Orleans is next."

From the ship's PA, the strings of a somber orchestral piece echoed through the command deck. Lucan had chosen it himself, a composition that made his pulse quicken. The crescendo was a prelude to annihilation.

Then, a voice cut through the music. It was small, urgent, and out of place in Lucan's perfect moment. "Sir…"

Lucan's eyes flicked toward the command terminals. His irritation flared. His voice struck like a hammer and slammed the room into silence. "Who said that?"

The bridge fell into a choked stillness. Officers stiffened at their stations, faces pale and tight. Someone dropped a datapad.

Lucan moved. His boots hit the floor in slow, deliberate steps, each one heavier than the last as he closed in. His tone dropped, soft but venomous. "Who. Said. That?"

A young woman stiffened at her terminal. Her throat bobbed as she swallowed; her fingers twitched over the keys. "I…I did, sir." Her voice trembled but held.

Lucan's eyes, cold as the void beyond the glass, pinned her in place. "Then it had better be worth hearing."

The technician's gaze flicked nervously to her screen. "Sir, it's the *Orleander*." She hesitated, then forced the rest out. "It's intact… and falling back to Orleans."

The world stilled. The strings from the PA, once a grand accompaniment to his triumph, mocked him. Lucan's expression darkened. He turned on his heel and strode across the deck, his goblet forgotten. The wine within sloshed with each step.

"I didn't get the King?" His voice simmered, coiled like a predator ready to strike. Then he snapped and shifted. "Dammit!" he roared.

He threw the goblet hard enough that it dented against the bulkhead in a splatter of crimson. A heartbeat later, he seized a chair and hurled it across the room. It crashed against the floor and skidded hard before it slammed into the far wall.

Syd, unmoved, watched with his usual passive detachment. His eyes, however, glinted with something that might have been amusement.

"I know, I know. I'll tell him," he said to the empty air. "Temper, temper," he said dryly. "Break Orleans, not the furniture."

They had cheated Lucan of his complete victory. The Colossus had crushed everything in its path, yet somehow the King had slipped away. It was an infuriating imperfection in his otherwise flawless conquest, and the heretic mocked his disappointment.

Lucan turned on him. His form flickered as he primed into his Rosari state. "Don't mock me, scientist! The King got away!"

Syd's smile remained fixed, a mask of indulgent superiority. "Maybe for a night, but that's all. The *Orleander* is of no consequence. Whether it burns above Orleans or falls into the field beneath us," he spread his hands with the grace of a conductor guiding a symphony, "the result will be the same. Twenty-four hours from now, Orleans will be no more, and our victory will be complete. We should stop the Colossus here to run diagnostics. I'm not sure if the *Nexus* damaged the Crown or the Azure Crystal itself."

The air echoed faintly around them. A tremor from the Colossus's distant footfall.

Lucan's breath slowed, but his eyes retained their edge while he reverted. "Fine, you have four hours," he said coldly. "Then we crush the *Orleander*, burn the city, and salt their bones. I will not leave a single stone unbroken."

Syd inclined his head as his grin sharpened. "With pleasure."

The strings in the PA surged toward their climax, and there was nothing anyone could do to stop it.

CHAPTER 50: LOCKE

The *Days* was a phantom that cut across the night sky. Her engines whispered against the wind. Inside, the crew prepped in near silence, save for the occasional quip to break the tension. It was 2:00 a.m. Usually, that would mean they were breaking curfew, but they had a reason to tonight.

Locke sat on a supply crate, rolled his shoulders, and adjusted his gear. Across from him, Kenzie checked her equipment for the third time. She seemed a little frazzled. Locke guessed that flying into a war zone would have that effect on everyone.

Val approached Kenzie. "Here, I got this for you while we were in Belfield. I guessed your size, but it should be a perfect fit."

"What is it?" Kenzie asked and unrolled the clothing.

"New field jacket. The white blend is cute on you, but it's going to be cold up there. It's form-fitting, you won't have to worry about it rustling."

Kenzie held it up. It was black. Not her color, but she also understood it was a night raid. "Thanks, Val."

"We look out for each other. You two aren't an exception. Be safe up there." Val moved over to her locker and examined her gear one more time.

Tia stood near the viewport and watched the Colossus in the distance. Locke looked out as well. Its massive silhouette glowed with the faint hue of crystal energy. Even miles out, Locke could see that every step obliterated the gaia below.

"Well," Tia said and stretched her arms over her head, "we've had worse ideas."

Haruto snorted. "Name one."

Tia shrugged. "That time we didn't get paid, so Kal had us..."

"I'm going to stop you there. I'd rather not have my last few thoughts be about that." Liam held up a hand.

A chuckle rippled through the crew. It wasn't much, but it was something. Tia smiled at Liam, but she visibly swallowed hard when she looked back out the viewport.

"Haruto, I wanted to confirm you got that transmission out to Orleans?" Val asked.

"Yeah. They know about our suicide mission. Someone will tell our families about tonight," Haruto said as he read something on a datapad.

"I'd prefer if you stopped calling it that," Val replied.

Haruto sighed. "Orleans knows about our happy, fun mission full of joy and wonder."

"Thank you." Val smiled and tossed a medical pack at him harder than she needed to.

Haruto dropped the sarcasm. "I also pinged Port Royale should things go sideways after we divert the Colossus."

Val stood there for a beat before nodding once. "Thank you," she said, this time without the smile.

The ship banked hard as Avery adjusted their course to match the Colossus's path. It felt like an easy sway to the crew with the dampeners active.

Liam panicked, like he'd just remembered something crucial. "Did someone pack the inertial dampeners?" he asked.

"They're in the duffel bag," Lizz called out as she moved from person to person to check their packs.

"Haruto, you're carrying those," Val said.

"Always with the short straw," Haruto muttered, hoisting the heavy bag.

"One day it'll be something good, I promise." Val headed toward the dock door. "Tia, did you hand out the detonators?"

"Yeah, I have one. Then there's you, Kal, and Kenzie. Detonators are immediate. I didn't have enough time to rig dead man's switches as well. Everything is color-coded. Just make sure you match the receiver to your detonator. Press the button and then boom."

"Final approach in sixty seconds," Kal called out. "Last chance to back out."

Val smirked and strapped in. "I'd like to see you stop any of us."

The crew chuckled again as they moved into position. Val checked her shard-shot was chambered and looked at Locke. "We're counting on you."

Locke exhaled at the comment. The Days had never felt so small.

Kal approached him and Kenzie. "You two scared the hell out of me at Breeze-waltz. I thought I'd lost both of you when you stole the transport. I was trying to keep you out of danger, but I know what drove you that night is the same thing that brought you here. That loyalty and passion will see you through this. Just…watch each other's backs out there."

He clapped Locke on the shoulder, then Kenzie. "Like Val said, we're counting on you. You're both crew. You were from the moment your boots touched the loading platform that first day. I trust you. Just… Val will yell at me for including you in this if things go south…" Kal's smile finished the sentence for him.

Kenzie responded with a lazy salute, and Locke just smiled at the recognition and gave a slight nod.

The ship swept low to circle the massive walking fortress. From their position, the Colossus was terrifying. A living mountain capable of annihilation. Lucan's Fleet had given it space and watched from a distance as the behemoth continued its march toward Orleans. Locke tightened his gear and rested a hand on his suda. They wouldn't get a second shot. Best not to leave anything behind, including his courage.

Avery's voice came over the comms. "Stations. We drop in ten."

Kenzie tugged at the sleeves of the jacket and looked at Val. "No matter how this goes, it was nice getting to know you."

Tia grinned. "Don't be dramatic, Kenz. We'll be fine. It's the boys you have to worry about."

Haruto sighed. "You said that before Breezewaltz."

Tia chuckled. "And all the big, strong men of the *Days* made it back alive."

Val smiled, but it did not reach her eyes. "Everyone does their job, and we'll be fine."

Kal's countdown started. "Three… two… one…"

The landing bay doors hissed open, and wind roared past them. Avery had brought them in just below the city hall, about five blocks away, if streets still held any meaning. The Crystal team would need to move fast and either climb or circle the ruins. The distraction team had a cleaner path. They could slip through the lower structures to set their charges. Kaliston, Valentine, Tia, Liam, Haruto, Locke, and Kenzie made the nighttime jump onto the beast's back to the side of a broken building. The *Days* peeled off and dropped low. None of Lucan's Fleet moved to intercept.

"All clear," Kal said into the comm.

They were on, and the suicide mission could begin.

CHAPTER 51: KALISTON

The Colossus was a city unto itself. A broken city, sure, but to call it anything else would be to downplay its size.

Kal had walked through ruins before, from coastal fortresses abandoned after wars to battlefields left to rust, but nothing like White Hill. The city on the Colossus's back might have been destroyed, but it was far from dead. It breathed and moved beneath them. Rosari patrolled the broken structures that clung to its spine. Every shifting plate groaned like old wood. Every pulse of Crystal energy beneath their feet sent vibrations through the steel.

He adjusted his pack and scanned the blue Crystal spires that grew beneath the ruined buildings of White Hill. That was new.

"It's repairing itself," Kal realized. The Azure Crystal embedded in its chest wasn't just a power source. It made the Colossus stronger.

Tia crouched behind a fallen girder and tapped the charge pack slung heavily across her chest. "So… we're setting these, or are we just taking a climbing tour?"

Kal exhaled with a nod. "What is with you and explosives?"

Tia grinned. "I just like knowing my problems will go away in a big, satisfying boom."

"Here," he said and reached out for the heavy pack. Tia begrudgingly handed it over.

Val's voice came over the comm. "Kal, we're set. Moving to rendezvous."

That meant Val's team had finished planting their charges beneath the Colossus's other shoulder blade. Kal heard her, but didn't respond. Instead, he held his breath and listened. At first, nothing, then the sound of footfalls came from a ruined building above.

It was faint but grew stronger. Rosari. He clenched his jaw as three appeared on the upper walkways above them. They were fully primed, and their fur glowed red. The heat caused the air to shimmer around them. It looked like their bodies slowly dissolved into ember and smoke, only to regenerate immediately.

Tia flattened against a column, hands on her weapons. Kal's fingers flexed. He debated how fast he could drop all three.

A faint chime echoed. "All guards and sentries, as we approach Orleans, return to designated battle stations."

The Rosari hesitated, and Kal didn't breathe.

One muttered something before they turned away and disappeared through the broken ruins. The others followed, their glowing forms vanished into the dark.

Tia exhaled first. "Close."

Kal shook his head. "Not really." He turned to place the charge. "We're done here. Move."

The teams met up at an abandoned transit platform near the Colossus's spine, about two blocks below City Hall. They used ropes with hooks to move between elevations and debris to form walkways between buildings. Luckily, most of the crew wasn't bothered by heights, the only exception being Dr. Rina, who awaited their safe return on the Days.

Kal and Val crouched next to each other.

"All charges set?" Kal asked.

"Confirmed," Val said. "Ready to go."

Tia tapped the ground beneath their feet. "We're at a safe distance here."

Kal held out the detonator. For just a second, the weight of everything his father built pressed against his back. He paused and gave a slow breath.

Then... *Click.*

A deep tremor rocked through the Colossus's back. Then another. Explosions erupted from under both shoulders. Fire and smoke billowed into the night.

Kal dropped low and pressed against a steel beam as Rosari soldiers surged forward from the east and west. Some held weapons, but most Rosari were weapons enough by themselves.

"Crown team, move," Val ordered once the squads had moved out of sight.

Haruto and Liam threw up their grappling hooks. Both tested the ropes once they were secured. They would be on level footing once they reached city hall, but they still had two city blocks to cover. They looked at the group, then engaged the climbing devices.

Kal climbed up the rope behind Liam by hand.

No signs of Rosari. The limited security staff must have all moved out. Kal guessed they probably operated with a skeleton crew after the Battle of Brittlebark. Good, something in their favor. They would need all of it.

As they scaled the ruins of White Hill toward the Colossus's head, the buildings flattened out. By the time they arrived at city hall, the ground was practically level, extending from above the shoulder blades to below the neck.

"Pull off those inertial dampeners. They have double what they need for the room. Keep the ones on the walls. We'll need those to reinforce the structure. Everything else goes to the barricade." Liam was pointing as he walked to the egg-shaped device on the dais.

"What barricade?" Tia asked.

"The one we're about to build," Val replied for him.

Liam moved to the Hollow Crown and immediately swore. The interface was dark and wouldn't respond to keystrokes. "It's locked."

Tia, Haruto, and Val began pulling off dampeners in the center of the room and moving them to the front entry. Kal was half observing Liam and half grabbing furniture to shove into the opening.

He yanked open a maintenance panel. Sparks flew. The Colossus lurched hard left, throwing Tia against a column.

"Whatever you're doing, do it faster," Val said, moving to help Tia up.

Liam's hands flew between exposed circuits and crystal lattice panelboards. "I'm trying to convince a brain-damaged giant to turn around using the designs of a madman." Liam connected something, and a loud jolt rang out through the room.

Kal saw Liam spasm for a second. That must not have felt good.

The tired engineer pulled himself out of the hatch and pressed a single key. He looked at the crew as the device booted, finally. He began to type into the interface.

The floor tilted as it started turning East, toward the shore. Tia and Haruto hugged. Val grabbed Kal's hand and squeezed.

"This thing moves about fifty-three miles per hour. We're a little over double that to the coast, so two hours." He pulled out a comm. "We should reach the coast in two hours." Kenzie, Locke, and the *Days* would now know they were moving into the next stage.

Kal looked at his team with pride. They had completed the first step. That's when the alarm started to sound. It was coming from both outside and inside the building.

"What's that noise?" Haruto asked.

Liam's face went pale. "They know we're here."

The first Rosari patrol rushed through the billowing smoke. Their eyes and fur glowed a deep red.

"Alright," Kal said to his team, "finish the barricade. I'll hold them off." He bared his teeth and charged.

CHAPTER 52: LOCKE

The wind howled over the Colossus's back. Every step kicked up dust and debris below Locke. He pulled himself up over the edge of a collapsed bridge and offered a hand to Kenzie. She ignored it and pulled herself up beside him in one smooth motion.

"I'm fine," she muttered.

"Sure," Locke replied and brushed off his coat.

The two of them crouched behind the remains of an old transmission tower to peer ahead. Rosari patrolled the ruins. Their bodies shimmered with residual heat and left trails of red mist in the cold night air. They leaped from ruin to ruin in this vertical city.

"We're not fighting," Kenzie whispered.

"No argument there."

Locke scanned the path forward. They needed to move toward the front of the Colossus, where the stolen Azure Crystal was embedded in its chest. That was easier said than done between the Rosari patrols and the ever-shifting landscape. Debris constantly fell off the creature's back, and routes that existed seconds earlier plummeted toward Gaia the next.

Then there was the creature's crystalline skin. It emitted a faint blue glow, each pulse a steady, living rhythm. Locke felt the crackle of energy as he approached. He flexed his fingers and caught the familiar tingle of power that danced beneath his skin. He would be fine, but Kenzie couldn't pass. Tall crystalline towers jutted out between city streets, their growth uneven and organic, more like the living veins of the Azure Crystal than the jagged shards he had known before. It felt less like armor and more like the creature allowed the Azure Crystal to grow through it. It was a reminder that he and the creature had that in common, for better or worse.

Kenzie exhaled through her nose. "So... that way?" She pointed at a pile of collapsed steel beams that led up toward its left shoulder.

Locke sighed. "Yeah, we'll have to be quick."

"Keep up then," she said and left their position in a crouch.

They moved together, ducked behind collapsed walls, and hopped over shattered steel beams. They came to realize the patrols avoided areas that were too unstable. That was great for evading the patrols, but it made their climb precarious.

At one point, Kenzie stepped onto a wall just as it crumbled under her foot.

Locke snagged her wrist at the last second. "Looks like the road is closed," he muttered.

Kenzie grinned as she pulled herself back. "Then we take a detour."

She scampered up a side wall, and they continued on their way.

"Ever wonder why we keep getting paired up?" Kenzie asked.

"Not sure. I assume it's because they see we have a good working relationship," Locke said.

"I think Val has ulterior motives," Kenzie mused and vaulted over some debris. She scaled up a collapsed wall and turned to help Locke. He took her hand.

"Remind you of anything?" Kenzie asked.

"Beggars Trail?" Locke responded.

"Yeah. Let's hope we don't run into any cliff cats," she said.

"I think the Rosari would be worse."

The natural motion of the Colossus wasn't random. There was a rhythm to it, and they found they could use the creature's momentum to help them navigate the ruins of White Hill more easily.

Kenzie watched one patrol move across a section of crumbling catwalk. They stepped just as the Colossus shifted to support them. A second later, the path they had crossed dropped into the abyss.

Kenzie nudged Locke. "I think I got it."

She pointed ahead at a section of ruins that jutted out over the Colossus's shoulder. The patrols avoided that area, which meant it wasn't stable, but that also meant no one would expect them to be there.

"The faster we move, the better our chances," Locke said.

Kenzie smirked. "So don't get caught enjoying the view."

She took off ahead. She moved low, and her steps were quick but measured. Locke followed, his boots crunched over loose rock and shattered glass. The wind was brutal. It howled past as the Colossus moved, and every gust carried flecks of crystal dust that shimmered in the air.

They climbed over a collapsed building and used its skeletal remains as a makeshift bridge toward the front of the Colossus. Locke reached for the next ledge, only for his fingers to brush against something warm. He pulled back.

The surface glowed a faint blue. "Crystal plating," he muttered. He held out his hand, and blue lightning arced from him to the creature.

Kenzie crouched beside him. "It's electrified," she whispered. "Think it would kill me?"

"Not sure, but we probably shouldn't put you in a position to find out. Use the buildings whenever possible and avoid anything made of Crystal. The skin between the plating looks fine."

Locke eyed the veins of energy that pulsed beneath the surface. His eyes followed and led him to what looked like a small home. There was scaffolding just beyond that, which would be an ideal path. He approached and opened the door.

The scene made him freeze when he stepped inside.

Three bodies lay on the floor, crushed under rubble. Locke hadn't thought about the human cost of the ruins until then. The poor people looked like they had sat down for a meal. Their corpses rode on the back of their killer.

Locke whispered a quiet prayer to Gaia. The words came without thought. It felt right, more fitting than any plea to the Crystal. The people were dead, and there was nothing the Crystal could do for the dead. Locke just hoped they would find their way back to Gaia. He hesitated at the door and cast one last glance at the crushed forms before he stepped back into the cold wind.

If Kenzie noticed, she didn't say anything. They took a moment on the other side of the door to observe. No patrols.

"Go," he said.

Kenzie didn't hesitate. She sprinted across the gap to the scaffolding, her boots barely making a sound. Locke followed. His gut tensed, and he anticipated an alarm to flare at any time.

Nothing.

They leaped onto the framework. Their fingers scrambled for holds as the metal groaned beneath their weight. The scaffolding swayed with every movement, and rusted bolts strained against the pull of gravity. Locke's foot slipped on a loose panel, and a few chunks of debris clattered to the depths below. Kenzie didn't stop. She moved ahead with practiced ease, her grip firm and breath steady.

The structure shuddered as the Colossus took another step. A deep vibration rolled through the steel.

"Not a fan of this," Locke muttered and forced himself to climb faster.

"No, I'm allowed to be bad with heights. There can't be two of us," Kenzie shot back.

"Heights and this are two separate things," Locke asked.

"Are they?" She pushed past some rubble.

"The Beggars Trail was heights. This is the living embodiment of vertigo."

"That explains why I'm doing better than you. It's well known I'm better on my feet."

Locke heard the smile in her voice.

"The dance wasn't my fault," he said

"Mm-hmm," she replied.

"Like you've never tripped," Locke said to himself, or so he thought.

"You should know by now that I never hold myself to my own standards," Kenzie called back.

Another metal beam cracked and shifted dangerously under them. For a moment, Locke thought the entire thing would collapse and send them both tumbling into the abyss. Instead, it settled with a harsh groan and left behind only the sound of their hurried breaths.

Hand over hand, they climbed and pushed through the ache in their muscles until finally, they reached the top.

Kenzie pulled herself up first. She rolled onto her back and exhaled sharply. Locke followed a second later, his hands pressed into the solid ground beneath them.

They had made it: the shoulder.

The movement around the shoulder and toward where the Crystal was embedded was more straightforward. No major structures had survived or existed on that side of the creature.

Good and bad. They wouldn't have to worry about navigating structures, but the crystalline plating was very exposed. There were seams of blue skin between the plating, but movement would be slowed. Some crystal growths pocked the skin. That would have to do, since the safety of the buildings ended.

Locke and Kenzie moved between cover. They avoided patches where the plating hummed with an electrified tone.

Locke was rounding a crystal the size of a boulder when Kenzie's hand found his arm and held him still.

A Rosari paused just on the other side and listened. Locke held his breath.

That's when the detonations went off on the back. The creature rocked, not enough to fall, but enough to make Kenzie shoot Locke a nervous grin. It reached back to where the explosions occurred, like a person who tried to swat a fly, and knocked off some ruins that had survived the blasts.

The Crown team would move into place shortly.

A chunk of debris tumbled into the abyss. The Rosari turned toward the blast and leaped off toward the distraction.

Kenzie grinned. "You could've taken him."

Locke exhaled slowly and looked at his hands. "Yeah, maybe," he said and turned his palms over. Like the Colossus, the power flowed just beneath his skin. He wondered if that was a good thing.

Crystals grew thicker and rose like spires. They forced them to weave between narrow gaps.

"We need to hurry," Locke said.

"Hurry where? We're already at the fun part." Kenzie pointed.

It was the front edge of the shoulder. The chest was beneath them. Now, they just had to get down to the cavity where the Crystal was housed. On a walking giant that rattled with every step.

Easy work, no trouble at all.

Liam's voice came over the comms. "We should reach the coast in two hours."

A brief communication was sent to inform the team that the next stage was about to start. Kal's team would have its hands full shortly. Locke and Kenzie had their own problems to solve.

"I guess we wait here until the coast is closer," Kenzie said.

"Yeah, let's head back to the structures and find some cover while we wait. We should modify the plan since we know the terrain."

She dusted off her hands. "Sure, sounds like a plan." She followed him toward some ruins by the creature's neck. "All things considered, that wasn't so bad."

Locke shot her a look as he worked to catch his breath. "You think?"

"Yeah," Kenzie replied, "you didn't have to push any animals off a cliffside. Definitely an improvement."

CHAPTER 53: LUCAN

2 Hours Until the Continental Shelf

The deck trembled as the detonations rocked the Colossus. Lucan watched from the command bridge of the *Inquisitor* as the columns of fire and smoke bloomed from the beast's back.

He clenched his jaw so tightly that the muscles in his neck strained with frustration at the incompetence, not from his enemies, but from his troops. To allow for such failure was unacceptable.

Lucan's fingers curled into fists at his sides. Even the slightest failure was intolerable. A minor flaw in execution could be the seed that blooms into disaster. He had worked too long to turn himself into the blade that would cut at the heart of Iveria. He willed the Colossus and his troops to make his dream a reality. Now, in the wake of his decisive victory at Brittlebark, they dared to grow complacent.

That wouldn't happen, not under his watch. This *would not* slip.

"Status," he said, his voice cold, each syllable sharpened to a point.

The crew snapped into action, each one afraid to be the first to disappoint him. "Sir, we're scrambling patrols to the sites. It looks like two localized demolitions. Nothing to suggest it was shardshot from an unidentified ship."

One of Syd's engineers hesitated before they spoke. "Surface-level damage expected. The blasts were not significant enough to get past the creature's skin."

Lucan exhaled slowly, measured and controlled. The crew had no idea how fortunate they were that the damage was minimal. "And the Azure Crystal?"

"Still in place," Syd responded.

"Should we scramble fighters?" an officer offered.

"Overkill, you don't kill flies with shardshot," Lucan replied. "They're on foot, lieutenant, we can manage." Although Lucan also considered himself overkill for the situation.

Lucan gave a single nod. "Then we stop whatever this is." His coat flared as he spun toward the exit with the impeccable, rigid discipline of a man who never second-guessed himself. "Prep a transport," he ordered. "We're going down there."

Syd tapped his datapad and skimmed the schematics. His fingers twitched, and his head tilted slightly to the side. His lips pressed together in thought before he exhaled, almost amused. He raised a hand to his heart to tap on something glass under his shirt and jacket.

"No, I suppose it was inevitable," he murmured, his voice barely above a whisper.

A nearby officer gave him a quick, uncertain glance, then refocused on his station. Syd didn't seem to notice. He adjusted his glasses, and his focus drifted past the screen.

"Yes. I see that now," he said. A pause and then a tiny chuckle. "Of course, he came. I told you he would."

Lucan moved toward the exit, his pace quick, controlled.

Syd finally spoke up, his voice stronger. "The intruders are at the Hollow Crown."

Lucan stopped mid-stride and turned his head slightly. The temperature dropped, and the crew all wilted around them. No one spoke or moved. Even the hum of the ship's systems seemed afraid to intrude.

"How do you know?"

Syd blinked and shook his head as if to clear a thought. His smile was sharp. "Because it's the only thing that makes sense. Their explosives targeted structural weak points, not the Colossus itself. That means they're not trying to destroy it. They're trying to draw our attention."

Lucan's gaze lingered for a moment before he nodded. "Clever."

Lucan was already halfway off the bridge. There was no use arguing. With a weary sigh, Syd adjusted the straps of his equipment bag and followed. He pointed at three of his technicians, and they fell in behind him without a word.

The Praetori had already formed up in the loading bay. They all had shifted into their Rosari forms. Around their necks were signaluca of pressed bronze. All other clothing and jewelry were hidden beneath the transformation. These bronze discs on chains would be worn after the transformation to mark the Praetori. They were ceremonial, elegantly designed to remind everyone who looked upon them that they belonged to something greater than themselves.

Lucan's soldiers didn't speak, didn't hesitate. They were more than loyal. They were conditioned. No wasted movement or thoughts. Every one of them would lay down their life for the good of Aurelia, and even better, at Lucan's command. Lucan didn't see a difference anyway.

Lucan's vision for Aurelia was one of absolute control. The Praetori were just the first disciples.

The dropship sat ready, its angular frame bristling with armor plating, a transport built not just for deployment, but for intimidation.

As the ramp lowered, Syd stepped inside alongside the Praetori and wedged himself between two broad, silent warriors. The soldiers didn't seem to scare him. He acted like he was above it all, but the charade was wearing on Lucan.

Lucan didn't sit. He stood at the front of the compartment. His fingers twitched at his sides as the ship trembled and lifted off from the *Inquisitor*'s loading dock. He wasn't there as a general to inspect damage or to punish failure. He was there to pass judgment. Holy, divine retribution.

He alone had been chosen. The Rose Crystal had answered his prayers through victory, and through the trembling of the gaia beneath the feet of the Colossus. The Azure Colossus marched to his will, and once he cast the interlopers aside, the whole world would, too.

This interruption was a stain on perfection, and he would cleanse it from the world. He hated the sight of it, but oh, how he loved the work. Behind him, Syd's team stared at their datapads and tried to focus on something, anything, other than how Lucan's presence seemed to drain the very air from the cabin.

It would be a long descent for such a short distance. The anticipation was like a collar, chafing Lucan's neck. When they landed, some would pay for the failure, while others would pay for their blasphemy. The Rose Colossus could sort out the two after Lucan was done with his bloody work.

CHAPTER 54: KALISTON

1.5 Hours Until the Continental Shelf

The air reeked of sweat, smoke, and the smell of burned Rosari. Kal thought he had smelled worse in his time in the Armada, or maybe he was just coping. Something to think about while his hands worked.

He drove his fist into a Rosari's chest. The crystalline fur cracked, and energy pulsed beneath his fingers. The Rosari stumbled, flickered, and struggled to reform. He didn't give it a chance. His fingers locked around its wrist. A surge of power ripped from the Rosari's core straight into Kal. It convulsed once, its body shuddered as its energy drained, then it dropped.

Another one down. He hated it when they required a double-tap.

He moved before the next could react. Kal ducked under a wild swing and drove his palm into its ribs. The impact threw it backward into the barricade. Its form flickered before it reverted to a human midair. It struck the stacked wood hard and crumpled.

Kal stepped forward and scanned the barricade. The piles of furniture and debris they had jammed across the entrance trembled under another impact. A wooden desk splintered. A chair leg snapped. The Rosari, on the other side, relentlessly pounded at the blockade to force their way through.

Liam had set up the inertial dampeners to make the barricades as compact and immovable as possible. The Rosari could punch through a mountain, but anything caught in the dampener's field would be hard pinned. He'd spliced in power from the dampeners that were already present. Liam had been surprised to find the room had its own field installed, but he was happy to adjust the position and crank it to the max setting. The room would hold, just like the barricades. They just had to be mindful of the side entrances and holes in the ceiling.

"Reinforce the left!" Val shouted. She and Liam slammed more debris into the pile to wedge more between them and the legion of furious Rosari.

A burst of shardshot rang out. Tia fired into the narrow gap between two overturned bookshelves. A glowing round slammed into a Rosari's face. The bolt was blue, but the mist was red. The target snarled, jerked back, and clawed at her face.

"Damn it," Tia hissed and cycled the weapon.

"Vitals only!" Liam called out. "Eyes, throat, joints. Make your shots count!"

"I know, Liam!" Tia yelled and lined up another shot.

Haruto lobbed another blueberry charge over the barricade. The explosion rocked the hall outside. Heat and smoke billowed into the room.

For a moment, the hammering on the barricade stopped. Then it started again. Harder.

Kal did all he could with the single units passing through the side openings. He used their unconscious bodies as makeshift barricades in the gaps and hoped the Aurelians would at least hesitate before they trampled their own.

"This isn't working," Val muttered, breath ragged. She wiped sweat from her forehead and flicked it onto the dust-covered floor. "They'll overrun us before we get close."

Kal didn't argue.

Another Rosari lunged through one of the smaller openings. Kal caught the thing midair, pivoted, and slammed it headfirst into the floor. It twitched once, then went still.

He threw the reverted man toward the opening from which he had come. The unconscious body collided with two incoming Rosari, who stumbled under the weight.

"How long have we been holding?" he asked.

Val checked the timer on her wrist. "Forty-seven minutes."

Kal exhaled. Seventy-three more to go.

Another crash. A bookshelf cracked in half, and a Rosari's head forced its way through the widened gap, snarling. Tia obliged with a shardshot to the mouth. That one was messy. She shoved a desk into the hole. The inertia dampeners made it impossibly heavy as she wedged it into place.

Kal watched the chaos unfold around him. His crew desperately tried to reinforce the position. He knew the barricade wouldn't last. The bigger question was, would he?

CHAPTER 55: LOCKE

1.5 Hours Until the Continental Shelf

The Colossus groaned beneath them, the sound deep and ancient, as if its crystalline plating rubbed against itself and resulted in a deep thrum.

Locke sat with his back against a half-collapsed support beam, boots planted firmly on the edge of the ruined structure. From there, he had a clear view of what lay before them. The moons were still up, and they had under two hours before sunrise. The sky was cloudless, and Locke could see the coast on the horizon, illuminated by the reflected light of the twin moons.

Kenzie sat a few feet away. Here arms were draped over her knees, and she fidgeted with her boots.

They sat in silence. An unmoving person lay before them. It had been Rosari ten minutes earlier. The patrols had been sparse since the detonations, but some still passed by, and Locke had to put that one down. He was surprised how easy it had been, and now, sitting with the corpse felt harder.

"How're you feeling...after... ?"

Locke looked at the corpse, and it reminded him of pushing the cat over the edge of Breezewaltz's mesa.

"It was either him or us," Locke replied.

"Yeah..." Kenzie let the words hang there as she stared at the corpse.

"Want to move?" Locke asked.

"Yeah...probably should," Kenzie replied.

The two moved silently into another structure. The ceiling no longer existed, but they found shelter under a staircase that was only half knocked down.

The wind carried the distant echo of explosions and shardshot. Kal, Val, Liam, Haruto, and Tia fought for their lives somewhere back there. Meanwhile, the two rookies sat, waiting.

Locke exhaled sharply and rubbed a hand over his face. "You ever just... stop and think, 'what the hell am I doing with my life?'"

Kenzie snorted. "Locke, I don't think I've stopped thinking that since, well, since Seaforth."

He smirked and let his head tip back against the beam. "You always mention Seaforth, but you never say anything about it."

"What's there to say? I was there, and now I'm not. Oh, and uh, George's Garage has excellent chowder," Kenzie said.

Locke smiled. "Thanks. You'll have to take me there if we survive this."

For a moment, neither of them spoke. The night stretched out in front of them, vast and indifferent.

"I don't think I'm supposed to be here," Kenzie finally said.

Locke glanced over. "What, on the Colossus?"

"No, in general." She gestured vaguely at everything. "Like, somewhere, there's a version of me who made different decisions, or had different decisions made around her. And she's... I don't know. Somewhere else in Iveria, running a bar, or across the sea, leading a very different life."

Locke huffed a laugh. "Instead, you're sitting on top of a moving mountain, waiting for the right moment to steal a Crystal that's worshipped as a god."

Kenzie clicked her tongue. "Yeah." She took a long breath. "I guess that's what happens when you make it up as you go, huh?"

Locke stretched his legs out and tapped his fingers against his knee. "Better Kenzie sounds nice. I wonder if she ever settles down?"

"Fat chance." She grinned. "You thought I was gonna say 'married to a nice guy with a respectable family' or some junk like that?"

"What's wrong with that?" Locke asked, wounded.

"Disgusting." She shuddered dramatically.

Locke chuckled and shook his head. The exhaustion settled deep. Not in a way that made him want to sleep. More like his brain had given up on rational thought and went with whatever came next.

"Alright." Kenzie shifted her weight against the rubble. "What about you?"

"What about me?"

She rolled a hand. "If you weren't here, if life had played out differently. Where's 'better Locke'?"

He opened his mouth, then hesitated. His first instinct was to say he didn't know, but that wasn't true. He did know, but didn't like thinking about it.

"Better Locke doesn't exist," he finally said with a forced smirk. "I've made all the right choices."

Kenzie snorted. "Yeah, okay, Mr. Mystery First Altier. You've got something. Spill it."

"Says the woman with a house full of skeletons." Locke ran a hand through his hair and exhaled through his teeth. He didn't want to answer, but he did anyway.

"Better Locke..." He rubbed his thumb against his palm and frowned. "I used to be angry. Like, really angry. At everyone and no one. Everyone always looked down on me, and the only time people saw me was when I pushed myself past my limits to compete with Toren. But I mostly failed, so I looked even more pathetic than I already was. I hated my family, Breezewaltz, Iveria, all of it. This stupid war we keep fighting, and for what? How many lives has this conflict claimed or ruined?

"Then I was old enough to enlist and entered the Citadel. It's what my father wanted, so I did as he demanded. I wasn't making any new friends, mostly just studying and sulking. My grades flourished, which was nice."

"Then my father invited us to Seaforth, the whole family, for a diplomatic mission. The funniest part was that we all got along on the trip. Father was so proud of what I was accomplishing at the Citadel. Toren was, too, even if he was a little jealous. He was an amazing person and older brother, but everything was a competition to him. My mother was overjoyed to have her boys back with her, even for a brief trip. It was a genuinely great moment, until it wasn't.

"I don't remember a lot of what happened next. Aurelia attacked Seaforth, one of those surprise indoctrination incursions. My last memory is the *Arcadia* unleashing a full broadside into the Aurelian Fleet overhead. Next thing I know, I'm on the *Days* with the crew. I was told I had a bad head injury and that part of my life might not come back to me."

He took a drink from his canteen. "I was told I found Kal and joined the *Days*. That's about as much as I know from that time. I do remember being angry. So angry that I could hurt people to get away from it. I still see that Locke inside me, but I'm not sure how much of him existed in the world. The crew never talks about what I was like in those days, thankfully.

"I think Gaia gave me another shot at this." Locke rapped his knuckles on his head and smiled. "It's just... I see that anger for what it was, and still is. It was fuel. It allowed me to see past the means and only the ends. It drove me like few things could. I'm doing my best now to focus on the good and see the positive, because I know anger can consume me if I don't. It feels like the anger is still there, will always be there, waiting for one bad moment. I don't know what I would become, where I would draw the line. Now that I'm an Altier... well, I think that anger would do great and terrible things, and that scares me."

Kenzie didn't say anything.

The silence stretched just a little too long.

Locke cleared his throat and shifted in place. "Or, you know, maybe he's running a bar in Breezewaltz, too. Just... real different clientele."

Kenzie arched a brow. "You'd be terrible at that job."

"Oh, for sure."

She smirked, then sighed and tilted her head back to stare at the sky. "If it makes you feel better, that doesn't sound like the Locke I know."

Somewhere below, a distant explosion rattled the framework beneath them. Neither of them reacted.

"Do you think we're making it out of this?" Kenzie asked.

Locke let his head fall against the beam again. "Ask me when we hit the shore."

"You're more like him than you like to admit." Locke looked at her quizzically. "Toren, that is," she continued. "Keep working at it. The person you described, the angry one, doesn't sound like the Locke I know. My Locke knows he has faults, seeks to overcome them, and still extends grace. That's the kind of person others follow. Just look at Kal."

"Dear Gaia, he can't be our role model," Locke begged as he looked up at the stars.

"He's not mine," Kenzie replied, and they laughed to themselves. She took a breath and continued. "You'll become an amazing First Altier one day. I know it."

"Thanks. You're kinder than you let other people know."

"You think?" she asked.

"Yeah, it's my favorite thing about you. You're one of the few people on the *Days* who doesn't call me 'Kid.'"

"Ever ask them to stop?" Kenzie inquired.

"Yeah. Val said I would have to pass Jules's test or..." Locke cut himself off.

"Or what?" Kenzie asked.

"Or get a kiss from you," he said, sheepishly.

Kenzie laughed, not cruelly, just at the absurdity of the situation. "Tell you what, First Altier. We make it off this thing alive, and I'll kiss you in front of Val so she can't call you a liar."

"Deal," Locke nodded. That was a promise to live for.

Kenzie stood up and looked toward the front of the creature. "What's the plan to get down there?" she asked.

"We don't have any rope. I might be able to scamper down, but you'd be exposed up here while I set off the charge."

Kenzie tapped a finger on her lips. "How many pepper charges do we have?" she asked.

"Five pepper, two blueberry. Tia made me swear to protect them as if they were my children."

"That woman and her explosives," Kenzie said.

"I hope they're alright." Locke looked back.

Dropships approached from the Fleet above. Kal would have more company soon.

"We have to trust them, right? Like they're trusting us to do our job."

"Right," Locke said. His face firmed up, and he looked back to the horizon. "So what's our plan?"

The wheels in Kenzie's head turned. "Did you see how the Colossus reacted when the charges went off? The detonations didn't hurt it, but it reached for the spots where they occurred. Tia must've used the pepper charges then. That's why it reacted like that. The Rose powder must be caustic to it…" The wheels continued. "Dammit, Val knew on the ship. How'd I miss that? Oh well, nothing to do about that now."

She stared at the arms, then at the shoulder. "What if we set one off here on the left shoulder?"

"Its right arm would cross its chest, and we'd be able to use that as a ramp to get to the Crystal," Locke said as he realized the genius of it.

"Exactly," Kenzie said. "And maybe it would take some heat off the Crown team."

"Maybe," Locke said. "But it's a solid plan for our objectives. I'll set the charge. We probably want it on the edge of the shoulder, right?"

"Yeah. We don't want it to be a place it can reach with its left hand."

Locke grabbed a pepper charge from his pack and raced off. He dilated and moved across the primarily barren shoulder. Locke slapped the explosive just off the plating and noticed for the first time that it had *Love, Tia* stenciled on the side.

He raced back to Kenzie.

They had a plan. His friends were in danger, and he knew what mattered. But in the quiet space between thoughts, he couldn't help but wonder what Kenzie's lips would feel like if he made it to that kiss. Just for a second, he let himself dream.

Then he pushed it down and focused forward. They had work to do.

CHAPTER 56: LUCAN

1 Hour Until the Continental Shelf

The dropship knifed through the night. Its engines howled as it plunged toward the Colossus. Wind shear slammed against its hull and rattled the reinforced plating. The turbulence was brutal. The ship's frame groaned under the pressure, but it didn't slow. It couldn't.

Below, the Colossus carved its path toward the sea, a moving fortress of steel and crystal. It's back crawled with Rosari. The twin fires still burned just below its shoulder blades from the detonations, and the Colossus reached as if to scratch an itch. The battlefield was a chaos of sporadic bursts of shardshot that cut the night air, the distant thud of explosions, and shadows that clashed in the ruins.

Their descent wasn't smooth. It was a free-fall, barely restrained. A straight shot to war.

Lucan stood at the front of the compartment. One hand gripped the overhead railing, the other rested on the pommel of his suda. He was still, except for his eyes. Lucan scanned the back of the Colossus and observed the hordes of Rosari that surrounded the city hall. He looked back at the troops he brought and met each gaze. A silent, suffocating reminder that failure would not be tolerated.

None of the soldiers flinched as Lucan peered into their very souls for weakness. They sat in perfect stillness, expressions locked behind their crimson faces.

Thirty soldiers sat along the walls, and all belonged to the Praetori, the elite among Aurelia's forces. The only ones considered better were those who guarded his father, and they did not have Lucan for a master. Lucan saw that the Emperor's standards had slipped for years. It showed Lucan that being considered and actually being it were two different things.

The other dropships would bring in the remaining Praetori.

Dr. Syd, however, adjusted the strap on his bag for the third time. His fingers twitched against the datapad in his lap. Lucan's gaze lingered on the madman. He was a better scientist than an actor.

"Nervous, Doctor?" Lucan's voice was calm, but the edge in it was unmistakable.

Syd exhaled through his nose. His lips quirked in something too amused to be nervous, but too anxious to be amused. "Anticipation. I have been waiting for this moment for years."

"It looks like they've barricaded themselves with the Hollow Crown. The Praetori will breach it, and it's up to you to secure my device," Lucan ordered.

"I'll make sure it's working, if that's what you mean," Syd said.

Lucan's grip on his suda tightened. He didn't trust Syd, but the man produced results. He was too clever for his own good. A trait that would get him killed one day. Lucan just hoped he would be there when it happened.

Across from them, a lieutenant held up a comm to his ear and frowned.

Lucan turned to the woman. "What is it?"

"It's chaos. We can't get a foothold in the structure. The team has some ability to negate Rosari. Additionally, there is a report of a missing patrol. Doesn't seem relevant."

Lucan's gaze held her. "Everyone else accounted for?"

"Yes, Prince. The troops that enter the city hall have not come out, but everyone else is reporting in."

"Where was the missing patrol?"

"The neck."

Lucan's expression remained stone, but a single muscle in his jaw ticked, a minute crack in his otherwise perfect control. He had anticipated resistance. The whole reason he headed down there was to confront it. But not scattered and unpredictable. How did multiple teams manage to operate without detection?

He wanted a clean execution. One decisive strike to crush them all beneath his heel. That was what he expected. Instead, they spread like vermin, slipped through the cracks, and forced him to divert attention. Efficiency had broken down, and that was unacceptable.

"Syd, do you know anything about this team that can negate our soldiers?"

Syd seemed to be debating what to reveal. Lucan's face hardened, and Syd relented. "Yes. It is my son, Kaliston. He has a device of my own making that allows him to fight shard users. Shame he's using it against us now."

Lucan let out a slow breath through his nose. The secrets Syd hid would be the doom of them all. Lucan wondered to himself if he had been too lenient. Results were one thing, but these layers of deception were beginning to mount. Regardless, it was not the time to interrogate him. Lucan would have to correct that after they contained the incident.

"How do we fight him?"

Syd adjusted his glasses. His fingers lingered on the frame a moment too long. His smile was small, distant. "I'm not sure *you* can," he said lightly, like the thought amused him. "My team isn't shard users, and I can hold my own against him. Punch us in, and we should be able to handle Kaliston while your unit finishes the rest."

Then, softer, almost under his breath, "She is there? Excellent. Yes... I know. It will be soon."

Lucan's eyes sharpened. "What?"

Syd blinked and refocused, like he had just remembered where he was. He waved a hand dismissively. "Nothing. Just... thinking aloud."

Lucan wasn't convinced, but he had little option but to accept it. He had long since decided the scientist wasn't entirely stable, but Syd's peculiarities were secondary to the mission. If he delivered results, Lucan would tolerate his eccentricities. It meant he could find the rats near the neck.

Lucan took a step forward. The air inside the dropship was suffocatingly still.

His men did not flinch. They did not adjust their weapons. Even their breathing was controlled, measured. They resembled statues, locked in perfect readiness.

They waited.

Lucan's voice cut through the silence. Smooth, controlled, razor-sharp. "Look at yourselves."

He let the words settle, his gaze passing over them slowly and deliberately. "And look at what they want to take away from you. Your moment. These fools think they can steal victory from you. You, the finest warriors Aurelia has ever forged."

He pointed out the glass front of the dropship, toward the resistance, which still clung to their fleeting moment of defiance. "They think they've earned this fight, that they've bought themselves time. That they can hold." Lucan exhaled and shook his head slightly. "They don't know what's coming."

He paced once, twice, his eyes flicked over his soldiers. "They believe they can hold, that they're already fighting the might of Aurelia. That they have endured the strength of our divine retribution."

His lip curled slightly. "They haven't. Not yet."

A pause. The tension coiled like a predator ready to strike. "They will break before you," Lucan continued. His voice lowered to become something quieter, something colder. "They will run, and when they realize there is nowhere left to run, they will surrender and beg." He tilted his head slightly. "Or, perhaps, they will not. Perhaps they will stand their ground. Perhaps they will fight until their last breath."

His eyes gleamed. "That would be preferable."

He stopped pacing and looked at them. "But leave one alive. One." His voice was soft, but it carried through the silence. "One to crawl back to whatever remains of Iveria and tell them what they saw here. One to remind them who they used to fear."

Lucan's voice sharpened for the final blow.

"I want the people of this forsaken nation to understand. In their final moments, resistance was never truly an option." He let the silence stretch, the moment before the slaughter. "You are not soldiers. You are not men and women." Lucan inhaled deeply to take in the collective faith of his troops. "You are my left and right hands. The sacred will of Aurelia. Go now and impose it."

The soldiers gave the customary salute and holler in uniform. Then, they stood as one.

The ship jolted as it neared its landing point, an open plaza near the edge of White Hill's city square, just behind the city hall structure. The massive plating of the Colossus's upper back revealed where the streets had fallen out. They had learned the hard way not to touch it. A ruined landscape of broken steel, jagged stone, and spiraling crystal formations.

The moment the ramp lowered, they surged out into formation. Silent, swift, and absolute. Lucan strode forward. His boots clanked against the steel as he stepped off the ramp and into the fray.

The air was thick with smoke and dust. The distant sounds of combat echoed from the city hall's direction. A blend of shardshot, the sharp cracks of explosions, and an echoed, rhythmic pound of something immense and unrelenting. The barricades and building still held. His troops would see to those shortly.

Lucan exhaled sharply. The whole thing was unacceptable. Why did it always fall to him to steer fate to the correct path? Why was his perfection the only thing he could rely upon?

He turned his head slightly. "Syd."

The scientist had stopped just outside the ship to adjust the collar of his coat. He looked entirely out of place among the soldiers, but at least he held it together. Three technicians stood behind him, clutching shardshots as if unsure which way to point them. None of the four belonged on a battlefield, but Lucan had no better option.

Lucan's tone left no room for debate. "You will re-secure my Hollow Crown. I expect to be basking in the destruction of Orleans by this time tomorrow."

Syd adjusted his glasses. He didn't look at Lucan. His gaze was elsewhere, fixed on the field lights lining the plaza, or perhaps on something beyond them. "Yes, he thinks the Hollow Crown is..." His voice trailed off, and he caught himself. Then he smiled. "Yes, Prince. We'll see to it."

Lucan's eyes narrowed slightly, but he didn't waste time deciphering the man's expression. He had more pressing matters.

He turned back to his soldiers. "Move."

There was no hesitation. No war cries.

The thirty warriors moved away from the dropship in perfect unison. They did not falter. They did not hesitate. Their formation adjusted mid-stride without a single spoken word, and they shifted into attack positions around the structure.

They were an executioner's blade, already mid-swing.

Lucan watched as the first of the Praetori reached the barricades, their movements precise and deliberate. Half of them tore it apart. They shattered wood and steel with heightened strength. Gaia, he would kill for an army of them. The others split off and moved around the flanks. They would pincer the team inside, led by this Kaliston.

Lucan knew, with absolute certainty, that their blood would stain the back of this creature before daybreak.

He did not run to his troops. He did not take a position alongside his soldiers or issue further orders. They did not need him. His fingers flexed at his sides. The battle unfolded exactly as it should have.

It was his turn.

Lucan shifted into a Rosari. He flexed his fingers again to test the difference. They felt better. Powerful and deadly.

Lucan leaped into the night sky. The speeches were over. Now, the real hunt could begin.

CHAPTER 57: KALISTON

1 Hour Until the Continental Shelf

Liam slammed another chair into the barricade. He braced his shoulder against the splintered beams to keep them upright. Around him, the Crown team hustled to form a makeshift defensive line. They had heard the dropships howl in and knew it was only a matter of time before Rosari flooded the room.

They had piled up the bodies of unconscious enemies near the side doors. The Rosari outside had enough respect not to barrel through their comrades.

"Liam!" Kal roared. "Get your fat ass over here!"

Liam pushed himself off the pile and ran toward the others, who defended the raised speaking lectern. He didn't have time to argue with Kal over the size of his ass.

Overhead, stars shimmered through cracks in the ruined ceiling. Kal remembered Liam had once said he told his daughter that each star was married to a planet, like Gaia and the sun. That was thirty years ago. She'd been gone twenty. Maybe he'd get to see her again this morning if things went too wrong.

"Hold that corner!" Val shouted and nodded to Tia and Haruto.

They pressed their backs to opposite pillars, shardshots raised, and picked off any troopers bold enough to push through the rubble. Tia had informed them she'd run out of explosives a while ago, but the thunderous footfalls of the Colossus made enough noise, anyway.

Kal stood at the center of the dais beside the Hollow Crown and fought with nothing but his hands. Rosari came at him with hammers, sudas, fists, and shardshots. Kal was either too fast or too invulnerable for anything Aurelia threw his way, but he was tired.

Liam slid into position and helped his friends hold the line. He shot one Rosari clean in the face. It dropped and didn't get up. He picked another target and fired. He turned to find a third, but there wasn't one. The flood of Rosari had inexplicably stopped.

Kal put the last one down and stood, breathing hard, dumbfounded by the reprieve. A few moments passed, and then Kal saw the realization forming on Liam's face.

That was when the barricade trembled. Something, or someone, new had arrived. They must have ordered the grunts to retreat.

A wave of Rosari wearing signaluca descended from the shattered ceiling. *Praetori.* The new squad moved toward the remains of the barricade and worked with precision and speed.

"Damn," Liam muttered. "They're disabling the inertial dampeners."

"Clear!" one of them roared.

The room exploded in a storm of debris. Wood and steel shattered into lethal fragments. The same material that had once formed their desperate defense became a legion of deadly missiles.

The lectern was all that saved Val, Haruto, Tia, and Liam.

Kal looked down to see that a jagged shard of wood had pierced his thigh. His exhaustion had caught up, and he had been too surprised to accrete fully. He clutched his leg, teeth clenched in pain.

Waves of red poured in through the broken entryway, taking positions around the room.

"Go!" Kal shouted. "Val, get out of here!"

She hesitated. That was never good. It meant she could see it, feel it. She was panicking at the thought of leaving him behind.

"The crew needs you!" Kal shouted again.

Val looked from Haruto to Tia and then at last to Liam. Her resolve hardened. "I'm going to find you in the afterlife and drag you back if you die," she said.

She kicked open the emergency escape hatch beneath the lectern. Every Iverian executive chamber had one, and White Hill's City Hall was no exception. One benefit of being at war all the time was that the architects designed for it.

"Go!" she yelled to the others behind the lectern.

They didn't need to be told twice. Haruto first, then Liam, then Tia.

Val took one last look at Kal, then vanished into the hatch's depths. A wall of Rosari surged into the space the crew had just vacated. The door gave little resistance, but the tunnel's narrow entrance was too tight for their massive forms. They tried to widen it, but progress was slow.

Then the tunnel exploded in a deafening blaze. Blue powder shot into the room. The immediate blast caught two Rosari. The rest staggered back, coughed, and shielded their eyes from the caustic cloud.

A final parting gift from Tia.

"Should've known she had one more," Kal muttered. He'd have to talk to her about holding out on him. He had assumed the one they planted under the Hollow Crown earlier was the last.

Kal looked up at the ring of Praetori surrounding him. Even wounded, he was a threat to all of them, and they seemed to know it.

Kal gritted his teeth and yanked the shard of wood from his thigh. He focused his Rosari abilities on the wound. It wouldn't heal any faster, but it would staunch the bleeding. The effort would also drain the Hollowline and wear him out faster, a necessary sacrifice.

"Who's first?" Kal shouted to the assembled killers. Better make it quick.

"That would be me." A figure stepped through the line of soldiers, someone Kal hadn't seen in a decade.

"Syd," Kal spat.

"Now, now. You know it's disrespectful not to address me as 'Father.' Or to purposefully forget my title. Ladies, wouldn't you agree?"

There they were, too. The blue and red apparitions that flanked his father. This time, they did not resemble Val. Kal refused to acknowledge the faces they were wearing. They nodded, smiling, and Syd reacted to the gesture. Apparently, Kal wasn't the only one who could see them.

A few of Syd's technicians moved through the spectral women and took up positions closer to Kal. They assumed that because they weren't shard-enhanced, they had some advantage over him. That was a bad call, but he wasn't about to stop them from making it. Just another reminder that education does not equal intelligence.

"Why don't you surrender? I can ensure your crew is returned safely to Iveria. Well, as safe as Iverian can be considered currently."

Syd turned his head toward one of the apparitions. It leaned in and whispered something in his ear.

"Oh, but not your wife. She dies here."

That was all Kaliston needed to hear.

He rocketed toward the techs. The pain in his leg was a dull ache. It slowed him, but not enough to matter against anyone who wasn't an Altier. He slammed his palm into the chest of the first tech, grabbed his discarded shardshot out of the air, and put two rounds into the other two.

In an instant, he accelerated toward his father and intended to end it with a single focused strike. He could worry about the Praetori after.

He didn't plan for Syd to catch his arm.

The world dilated around him, but Syd moved at the same speed. His father smiled, then drove a fist into Kal's chest with full force. Kal tumbled backward. He crashed toward the dais and the Hollow Crown.

The surprise was worse than the pain. He looked up at his father. "You did it to yourself?" Kal sputtered.

Syd ascended the short steps toward the floor where the dais stood. "Never ask anything of someone you aren't willing to do yourself. I taught you that."

Kal shifted and tried to think of an opening.

Syd continued, "I installed it after they ran me out of Belfield. A little bird chirped about my *unethical* experiments to the King and Council."

"Maybe a clue you shouldn't have been doing them," Kal muttered.

Syd ignored him. "Saddest day of my life. Nearly ruined everything I built. Was it you who spoke? I never thought you'd be so… ungrateful."

"Yeah, sorry, I didn't thank you for turning me into a lab experiment."

"Son, you'll never have to thank me. I did what any good father would do. I protected the offspring who couldn't protect themselves."

He paused and studied Kal as if he still expected recognition. Kal almost laughed.

"Protected?" he said, his voice quieter than intended.

Kal couldn't remember the last time he felt safe around Syd. It certainly wasn't in that lab, where the air reeked of ozone and decay. Even before that, Kal had recognized there was something broken in Syd. After Kal's mother had passed, it was only a matter of time before Kal cut himself on his father's edges.

"You didn't protect me." Kal was surprised that his voice was only a whisper, but he continued. "You broke me open and sifted through the pieces until only the parts you thought were useful were left."

Syd frowned. "Don't be dramatic, Kal. You're only here now because of what I did. Besides, you volunteered, remember?"

Kal shook his head but didn't have a retort.

"I knew it was you who reported me to the Council. They knew what I was doing at Conchordia, but they pretended not to. Still, you walking around was enough evidence to shut me down." Syd walked over and placed a hand on the Hollow Crown. He turned back to Kal. "I wasn't ready to leave. I wasn't ready to give up everything just because the Council got nervous. I mean, look at you, Kal. Look what you did tonight. Imagine an army of us."

"I don't need an army, I have the Days. We don't need monsters to win."

Kal surged to his feet and threw a punch, but he was a heartbeat too slow on his bad leg. Syd stepped in to rip two brutal right hooks into Kal's ribs. Kal absorbed them, just barely.

Impossible speed and unreasonable strength. Kal staggered and tripped over the steps of the dais.

Syd smiled and slammed a fist down on the gash in Kal's leg.

"You're resourceful, I'll give you that, but you always thought you were more clever than you are, Kaliston."

Kal howled in pain. Even with the leg accreted, the sensation blinded him under Syd's crushing hand. Syd didn't relent. He followed up with a brutal left cross to Kal's face.

Kal bounced off the marble floor and slid to a halt beside the Hollow Crown.

"I'm not going to kill you, Kaliston. I mean that when I say it. But I am taking the Hollowline back. I don't know if yours is more perfect than mine, or if it's the interface... Either way, you have secrets, and I'll need to extract them from you before I send you to your mother."

Kal spat on the floor, most of it blood. "You don't get to talk about her."

"Sure I do, Kaliston. She loved me before she loved you."

"Yeah? Well, they say it's not how you start, but how you finish." Kal spat on the floor and tried to get to his feet.

Syd laughed. "Then I'd say it went badly for you on both counts. I hope you had your fun in the middle."

Kal shrugged. "The whole thing was generally fine, except the time I was forced to spend with you." He inched back, slowly. "I know you don't care. You think you're above all this, but deep down, I know it kills you that she and I were the only two people who saw you for what you are. Not the great genius Baron El-Syd, but a small, scared monster of a man." Kal smiled. "I bet your parents saw that, too."

Syd's face twisted into a barely contained storm of rage. "That's the second time you haven't referred to me by my title. There won't be a third." He stepped forward and leaned back for a massive overhead strike.

"That's the funny thing about being your son," Kal said, and his thumb settled against the switch. "I know how to push your button."

Syd immediately recognized the detonator for what it was.

"Dead man's switch?" His eyes darted from Kal to the Hollow Crown and back to Kal. "Where?" Syd asked.

"You already know," Kal replied.

Kal had waited his whole life for that look of surprise on his father's face.

CHAPTER 58: LUCAN

1 Hour Until the Continental Shelf

Lucan stopped just short of the Colossus's crystalline plating. He was immune to most sharp or blunt trauma, but being electrocuted at that amperage would probably still kill him. Despite the distant boom of explosions, his senses felt honed as he charted the Colossus's back. He didn't need Syd to tell him they had overridden the Hollow Crown. He could smell the salt of the sea mingle with the tang of ozone in the night air. The creature strode inexorably toward a watery tomb, and Lucan wasn't sure how it would handle the crushing depths.

They were likely near Port Royale. A detour to destroy the famous shipping hub crossed his mind for a moment. *No*, he dismissed the idea. His focus remained: seize control and steer the beast toward his ultimate goal, Orleans.

With a burst of raw kinetic power, Lucan leaped to another crumbling structure along the Colossus's spine. Although Rosari were slower than Altiers, by adjusting his mass, he could launch himself an impressive distance. It was a shame that ordinary Rosari required decades of training to master such manipulation. For Lucan, a few years of ruthless discipline had sufficed.

He landed silently on a fractured platform and startled a pair of patrolling guards. "You there," he snapped at one of the bulky Rosari women with glowing red eyes. "Report."

They offered a quick bow. "Nothing special, my Grace, besides running into you."

A spark of satisfaction lit Lucan's thoughts. He relished being regarded as exceptional. "Very well," he ordered curtly. "Reinforce the troops outside the city hall. I don't want you to miss the excitement."

His gaze returned to the massive creature. The patrol that had vanished was near the neck, the region that marked his ultimate destination. For a fleeting moment, he considered summoning the guards to join his assault, but quickly dismissed the thought. His troops were loyal, efficient tools, but they were as blunt as hammers, only useful on nails. What he had in mind would fall to him and him alone.

Besides, if he was to suffer the fools who dared stand against him, he would at least get his fun from it.

Lucan advanced further. The dying embers of fires along the mid-back gave way to dark, ruined structures. His eyes adjusted to the faint silver glow of the moon, and he found himself on the creature's right shoulder, near its neck. In his mind, locating his hidden prey would be an effortless task. Unfortunately, he had underestimated the sheer size of the beast. Worse, the surrounding debris provided ample hiding spots for vermin-like saboteurs.

It was time to clear a path.

Lucan hardened his skin and began a brutal charge. He barely lowered a shoulder as he burst through the wall with such violent force that the shards embedded in the opposite wall. He continued into the next wall, then the next. Each breach was just as devastating, and Lucan burst through every barrier as if it were paper.

Lucan pulverized anything caught in his wake. He would charge from one side of the neck to the other until he eliminated every piece of cover. For him, it took no more effort than walking the same distance.

Walls crashed behind him with a satisfying crunch. White Hill had been mainly built from forged steel, oak harvested from the forests that surrounded the city, and white stone taken from the city's namesake. Those same timbers and stone proved to be as easy to crush as everything else on the continent. The steel bent and twisted around him.

Crack. Crack. Crack.

He barely registered the force he had become. The wood splintered at his touch. Even the stone was no match for his terrifying form and broke apart like brittle glass.

As Lucan advanced, the destruction grew with every step. Yet within the tumult, his focus remained razor sharp. His heart pounded with the thrill of conquest and a cold, calculated resolve. Each shattered barrier was a declaration: no saboteur or meddler would hide from him.

He understood the hunt, and soon, so would his prey.

The noise deafened, the destruction absolute. To stand in the rooms as he tore through would be like standing in the path of the Colossus itself. His quarry would cower. They would flee, and he, the hunter, would catch them.

Crash. Crash. Crash.

He burst through the wall and realized he had reached the opposite shoulder. He crouched low and strained to listen. All he heard was the distant sound of combat and the thuds of the creature's steps. With renewed determination, Lucan surged toward a piece of scaffolding for a better view.

"Come out," Lucan commanded, his voice a low, menacing growl that reverberated across the ruined expanse. "No use hiding."

For a long, suspended moment, only the howl of the wind and the distant thuds of the Colossus's stride filled the air. Then a faint rustle echoed from behind a fractured beam. Lucan's predatory eyes narrowed as he scanned the darkness. Somewhere amid the labyrinth of debris on this battered shoulder, his prey hid.

Lucan shifted his weight and crept along the jagged edge. The debris underfoot crunched softly as he advanced, each step measured and deadly silent despite the surrounding chaos. He expected that once he discovered his prey, they would scatter in panic. He relished the idea of hunting them down one by one, a solitary game against the fugitives who dared to oppose him.

A Rosari's form wasn't just for aesthetics. When shifted, his human eyes and ears were covered by his Rosari form, but the crystalline ears, eyes, and nose provided heightened senses. He could pivot his ears toward any sound. Scents that would be paper-thin to others were full books to him.

As he edged closer to a partially collapsed archway, Lucan's keen senses picked up subtle signs in the dust and chaos: the scent of fear, a stone nudged out of place, and the faint traces of someone who had recently spent time near an Iverian engine.

The sudden proximity made his heart race with the thrill of the hunt. Lucan quickly calculated the best way to flush them out. He had to force them into movement, to break their tenuous cover and make them engage. Lucan didn't just want them to run. He wanted them to know they had already lost.

Lucan took one step, then a second. He closed his eyes and sniffed. He paused. Then his fist shot through a nearby wall.

A woman screamed on the other side, but a man burst through the opening a heartbeat later.

For a second, Lucan thought it was Toren, back from the dead. He barely had time to densify his skin before the suda flew at his neck.

Lucan tried to trap the blade in a localized density, but he only caught an edge. He couldn't hold it and let go of the bit he had. The suda fell at his feet, but was picked up as soon as it clattered.

The cut on his neck was shallow and insignificant. Still, Lucan backed off to confirm it wasn't a specter he fought, but the attacker pressed the advantage.

Lucan leaped back with practiced grace, vaulted over a fallen beam, and landed hard on the open shoulder behind him, between the plates. The ground was still littered with debris from White Hill, but the amount of exposed plating was a concern. One step would be fatal for him. He doubted the same was true for his opponent.

For a moment, the man halted his assault, and Lucan saw his face.

He still thought it was Toren until the attacker shifted their posture in fading moonlight. It wasn't Toren. It was the runt.

His face, streaked with grime and dust, flickered with anger and fear. The woman, whoever she was, remained hidden. She did not matter. He would kill her once the runt was dead.

Lucan's quarry finally stood before him, and his eyes gleamed with predatory delight.

"I know you!" Lucan's voice was a shout laced with laughter. "You were rumored to be dead. Or worse, a coward."

The man was Toren's younger brother, Locke Luinondo. He had been in the dossier Rook had prepped before White Hill, with large red letters across his page: Location Unknown.

"Glad to see you came out of hiding. It's not every day I get to snuff out a family line twice."

Lucan watched the man grip his suda tighter. His body tensed, either to prepare to strike or brace to be struck, and Lucan figured either was acceptable. He noted the emotion in the man's eyes. It danced before him, clear and chaotic. The boy was an open book.

That's no fun, Lucan thought.

Between the stance and the wild emotions boiling off him, it was clear that Locke was a novice Altier. Lucan would have to toy with his food before he sank his fangs into it.

Locke shot forward at unbelievable speed.

Typical Altier, Lucan thought. His hand moved to where he assumed Locke would be, and he accreted his skin at the point he guessed the strike would land.

Both guesses were wrong.

Another shallow cut. So shallow ants would wonder if it had happened at all.

Locke kept up the assault. He slashed at non-vitals. Lucan wasn't sure if his targeting was clever or just naïve. Maybe the boy was sharper than he looked, or perhaps he was too green to know better.

Fine, Lucan thought. He raised his forearm to shield his eyes and endured. It felt like a million paper cuts. All of which were an insultingly easy task to withstand. Then, just as quickly as it started, it stopped. Locke reappeared as he panted.

In that instant, Lucan smiled and threw an impossibly strong punch. It missed, but only just. Lucan was confident the fight would be over before it ever truly began.

CHAPTER 59: LOCKE

1 Hour Until the Continental Shelf

Locke was scared right up until the moment the fist obliterated the wall behind him.

In that split second after the violence erupted, his heart hammered in his chest, and his mind screamed in terror. Then Kenzie's piercing scream cut through his panic and snapped him into action. There was no time for second thoughts. With no time to think, he did precisely what his instincts commanded: aim for the neck.

His blade was a double-sided dirk he chose for its speed. It found its mark and bit into Lucan's flesh.

For one agonizing, dilated moment, Locke believed Lucan had trapped the blade with his peculiar density control and frozen time itself.

Desperation clawed at him as he struggled to wrench it free from what felt like temporal imprisonment. The metallic tang of blood filled his senses as he barely had time to twist away from the sweeping arc of Lucan's massive hand. The suda fell at Lucan's feet, but Locke moved before Lucan could react. He regrouped, his free suda once again in hand, and he eyed the man who tried to kill him.

To Locke's dismay, his attack had produced no visible damage on Lucan's neck. In that heartbeat, his hope for a quick, decisive victory scattered like dust in the wind. For better or worse, there was no time to wallow in regret. Locke had to buy Kenzie time to get away.

Even so, a flicker of surprise stirred in his gut when Lucan fell back before he could continue the assault. With the grace of a seasoned fighter, Lucan had created space between them. He vaulted over broken debris and landed heavily in a swirling cloud of dust that rose from the shattered wall.

Locke allowed himself a brief nod of approval. At least Lucan moved away from Kenzie's position.

Then came the taunting shout. "I know you," Lucan bellowed, his voice a mix of mirth and menace. "You were rumored to be dead. Or worse, a coward."

The words, laced with a sneer, echoed every rumor and slight Locke had endured since his return.

Lucan's words continued to drip with arrogance. "Glad to see you came out of hiding. It's not every day I get to snuff out a family line twice." His smile, lit by the moon, was cold and predatory.

Locke's grip tightened around his suda. The sleek, liquid-metal weapon had first caught his eye in the watchsmith's shop. It had reminded him of the one his father had carried. He had loved and hated it. The imitation had turned to serve as an extension of his rage.

His fury unfurled like a banner in the dark. Every part of him screamed for retribution, even if Lucan were made of stone. Even if Locke was doomed, he would *not* let this monster go unscathed.

With a burst of desperate energy, he cut, not for the vital organs. Lucan would expect that. Locke aimed everywhere else. A flurry of shallow cuts fell on his enemy. Each one bled away a bit of hope from an already failed strategy. He struck again, and again, but the rhythm betrayed him. The attacks became predictable. Each successive cut landed with less force than the last.

The fight slipped away from him.

Lucan's eyes narrowed as he raised his arm to shield his eyes, a move that forced him to cover his vision for a moment.

Interesting, Locke thought bitterly as he watched how his enemy tried to protect himself while still engaged. As the fight dragged on, a sharp cramp bloomed in Locke's side. The power that had granted him bursts of speed and precision faded. He slipped out of the dilated world and gasped for air, his breath shallow and ragged.

Without warning, Lucan's lips curled into a predatory smile. He threw a vicious punch.

Locke barely had time to dilate again. He stepped aside just in time to avoid the crushing blow. Lucan's fist smashed into the broken street of White Hill. It shattered the ancient stone and exposed a crystalline stalagmite that had formed from the debris.

An act of violence that revealed something beautiful underneath. A reminder of the raw, unnatural forces at play.

Lucan took a step back, cautious. His eyes flicked toward the electrified crystal. He recognized the danger.

Then he scoffed. His voice dripped with derision. "I was told you weren't an Altier. Based on how you fight, I'd say you haven't been one for long."

Locke stood in the pale moonlight, unmoving. His heart pounded in his ears. He said nothing.

Lucan's tone turned almost celebratory. "Ah, that's it. You're the new First Altier of Breezewaltz." His gaze swept over Locke with a mix of scorn and amusement. "I'd say I expected more from Toren's brother, but this is about right."

At the mention of Toren's name, Locke's chest tightened. Grief and fury collided inside him, hot and cold at once. Images of his brother's last moments flashed through his mind: when Lucan stabbed him in the chest, Toren as he slipped from his grasp, and the final look in his eyes while he plummeted into the dark.

That hollow ache cracked open again, and the rage poured out. "Keep his name out of your mouth," Locke hissed, voice low and dangerous. "He stood for more than a monster like you will ever understand. He died protecting Breezewaltz from you."

Lucan laughed. A deep rumble that vibrated the very air around them. It echoed with cruelty, resonated with his overwhelming power. Then he moved. In a burst of blood-red fury, Lucan surged forward like wrath made of flesh. His suda sliced through the air with terrifying precision, aimed straight for Locke.

Locke reacted on instinct and primed his abilities. Blue crystals bloomed and evaporated across his skin as time dilated. For a moment, everything slowed around him. He dodged faster than seemed possible.

That's when his body began to fail. His limbs slowed. Every motion dragged like he fought through molasses.

Their blades collided with a violent crash. Sparks burst into the air and showered across the ruined shoulder of the Colossus. Liquid metal twisted and reformed in mid-strike as Locke flew backward and skidded hard across the stone.

Pain lit up his arms. The sheer force of the impact burned through his nerves, a raw reminder of what defiance would cost.

He gritted his teeth.

Locke pushed through the ache and hurled himself forward. He poured every ounce of strength into his legs. A final burst of Azure-primed speed surged through his body and propelled him toward Lucan.

Once again, he aimed for the neck. If only he could strike true.

Then came the backhand.

Lucan's strike crashed against Locke's face. The blow slammed him into a twisted support beam. His vision swam. His ears rang like a bell struck deep in a cavern.

For a long, disoriented moment, Locke's mind scrambled to reassemble itself. His head pounded relentlessly. The fact that he could still think at all felt like a small mercy.

Adrenaline surged through him, but it was futile. His limbs grew dull, and the power within him faded. There was no matching the monstrous power Lucan wielded with ease.

Then came the cry.

"Locke!" Kenzie's voice rang out, raw and desperate. It pierced the fog and dragged him back to the world. A lifeline.

Lucan turned at the sound. His attention shifted as if he'd nearly forgotten his second plaything. He tilted his head like he recognized her voice but couldn't quite place it.

Locke's eyes found hers. She was still there and hadn't retreated as they'd planned.

She stood her ground for some insane reason, one hand clenched around a detonator. Her gaze shifted from Locke and peeked at Lucan on the battlefield. She seemed scared, but her eyes looked determined. Ready to carry out the plan if Locke fell.

That thought galvanized him.

Fine, he thought. If she wasn't giving up, then neither would he.

He pushed to his feet. Pain and dizziness crashed over him like waves. There was no time for hesitation. He dilated again.

The world slowed as Locke surged forward, every muscle burned, every breath a jagged fire in his lungs. He didn't look at Lucan, didn't need to. The bastard would come to him soon enough.

Locke focused on Kenzie. On her eyes and her safety.

He barreled past, moved on instinct alone. A flicker of movement to his right told him Lucan watched.

Kenzie waited beneath a crumbled stairwell, tucked in just far enough to be hidden. She had a clear view of the battlefield, a sliver of quiet in the chaos.

A brief haven. Just long enough to draw breath. "I'm going to lead him to the shoulder," Locke panted, his voice resolute despite the pain. "Set off the charge when we're in position."

Kenzie's eyes met his. Despite the danger, a small smile played on her lips. "Will you be okay?" she asked, her voice a mix of worry and defiance.

Locke gave a grim smile. "Probably not, but I won't be okay if this fight drags on either." His words carried the understanding of someone ready to do what had to be done. "Oh, and Kenzie?"

She paused, eyes locking with his. Her expression shifted, with less fear and more focus.

"I appreciate your concern, but yelling from a hiding spot isn't staying out of danger. Promise me you'll run if something happens to me." Locke held her gaze. For maybe the first time, they truly saw one another's resolve.

"I promise no such thing, Locke Luinondo."

CHAPTER 60: KALISTON

1 Hour Until the Continental Shelf

Kal leaned against the shattered dais and gasped hard. Everything hurt. His ribs throbbed from where Syd had landed those hits, every breath a reminder. His leg bled, barely held together through sheer Rosari focus. In his shaking hand, the switch sat small and cold, the only thing that kept the whole mess from spiraling further.

He could feel it, deep in his bones. The Colossus moved, step by thunderous step, and made its way into the sea. If Liam's math was correct, and it usually was, it had maybe ten minutes before it reached the continental shelf. After that, no one could stop it.

Syd stood a few steps away and watched. The apparitions lingered near him, half-formed figures with ice-cold stares. Something about them felt wrong, or maybe it was something about Syd. The contrast between them screamed for Kal to recognize it.

Syd spoke before he could. "What's your plan, Kaliston?" Syd asked, voice smooth, easy. He clasped his hands behind his back, calm as ever. "You die no matter how this shakes out."

Kal huffed out a breath, more a bitter laugh than anything. "Yeah, I figured. At least I get a front-row seat to watching you lose everything, too." He tilted his head, and his voice dropped. "Pretty poetic, don't you think? The son you never wanted destroying the legacy you always did."

For a second, just a second, Syd's jaw twitched. Kal saw it and added it to the picture in his mind.

"You always confused tough love for no love, Kaliston. Just because I was hard on you doesn't mean I didn't want you. Quite the opposite. I thought you would carry the El-Syd name into the future. Shame it won't be the case."

"You always did talk too much," Kal muttered and shifted just enough to look like he could barely stand. He needed to sell the moment like a bluff at the final hand of the night.

Syd exhaled and shook his head. "And you always tried to make things mean more than they do." He gestured vaguely at the Hollow Crown. "But let's drop the theatrics. We both know time isn't on our side, after all."

Kal grunted. "Oh, good. Another lecture."

Syd crouched, his voice softened, and he tried to sound thoughtful. "Let's re-move the charge from the Crown," he said, like he offered some great kindness. "I'll spare your crew. They can go back to the *Days*, and maybe even you, too, in time. I want the Hollowline."

Kal raised an eyebrow. "Oh? Yours not working out?"

Syd didn't answer. That was answer enough.

Kal's voice dropped to a whisper. "I'm guessing you started working on a new design after mine. Knowing you, and what came next, you probably never finished it. You had to install one of your prototypes before you fled."

Syd stood. "Since when have you known me to make something flawed?"

"You made me, old man."

Syd chuckled at that, but Kal saw the sweat on his brow and the pallor that crept into his skin. Clear signs of withdrawal. Kal had seen that same look in the mirror after a hard day using the device or going without it too long.

"You can't keep it running. Burns too hot, crashes too fast. Must be painful, hitting overuse five minutes in."

Syd's jaw tightened. For the first time, the mask slipped. Just a fraction, but enough.

"You want mine because it works. You need me because I made it work. Too many variables."

"You never wanted it. I can take it away," Syd said. His face was hard, but Kal could tell he meant it. He knew Kal never wanted the Hollowline. It wasn't a trick. It was a genuine offer to remove it. To end the curse. "Let me help you... son."

Kal let the silence stretch. He needed the time. He let his fingers tremble slightly, just enough. Then he laughed to himself, low and humorless. "Pretending to be the loving father didn't work when I was twelve. What makes you think it'll work now?"

Something flickered across Syd's face, a shadow, quick and dark.

"If you were going to spare them," Kal continued, "you wouldn't have said it out loud. You would've just done it. But you wanted me to hear it first. Wanted me to doubt." He tilted his head, voice quieter, sharper. "And then, when you went back on your word... classic Syd."

Syd stood and brushed off his coat. "Classic Syd," he repeated mockingly. "You act like you know me."

Kal grinned. Blood still ran down his face. "I know exactly who you are." He leaned in slightly. "And I know what you're afraid of."

Syd's fingers twitched. Did his father always have those tics, or had they gotten worse? Was that what the Hollowline did to someone if they gave themselves over to it entirely?

"You're stalling," Syd said.

Syd's gaze flicked to the Hollow Crown and back. The Colossus lurched beneath them, another step forward. Water roared outside. It was close. Syd heard it too. They both were doing the math. The Colossus hadn't stopped its march into the sea.

Syd's face shifted, just slightly, and he knew the window to stop this was closing. He turned toward the Hollow Crown.

Kal lifted the detonator. "Don't."

Syd hesitated, then snapped, "Let me remove it. This is bigger than you. Bigger than both of us."

Kal studied him. He really looked at the man on the dais. Syd had been a father in some ways. Supported his education and motivated him to excel. Ultimately, however, Kal understood that Syd saw him as just a tool. An extension of Syd himself, to be used or discarded to further Syd's legacy.

Syd was someone who had burned every last bridge to further himself. He had stood on the shoulders of giants, seen farther than anyone before him, and knocked the ladder down so no one else could see.

"Nothing is bigger than me. You taught me that. That's one thing you gave me. The pride to stand on my terms."

"Cute sentiment, son, but that doesn't solve the present situation."

"No, it does. You see, my pride is exactly what allows me to see through your façade. You could've solved this a long time ago. All it would've taken was a shred of humanity," Kal murmured. "You sold yours the moment you strapped these things on us. Sold it to them, whatever in Gaia's name they are."

He pointed at the apparitions. Spittle flew with the words. "And for what? What did you get in return besides blood on your hands and misery? You used to be the smartest man on Gaia. Look at you. You're nothing but their dog who has come to fetch."

Syd stood there, speechless. Maybe for the first time. Kal knew it wouldn't last, but that didn't matter anymore. He looked at his father. The twitch in his jaw, the sunken eyes, and the desperation that clawed behind all that power.

That was what the Hollowline did when you gave it everything. Kal had seen that same look in the mirror, over and over. He knew he would see it in the morning, if he lived that long.

That was the difference between them. Syd saw the Hollowline as the achievement, the enlightened state that allowed humans to commune with gods. Kal finally saw it for what it was: a yoke his father had placed on them both.

He might as well use it to ruin a few well-laid plans first if it would kill him eventually. Cut the killer with their knife. He still had enough juice for one final push.

He tapped the Hollowline and moved. Time dilated, stretched every second. Kal hurled the detonator straight at Syd. Syd reacted just as fast and reached for it. His dilation warped the space around them. For a heartbeat, everything slowed to less than a crawl. The color drained away, and the world fractured into scattered frames. Syd's fingers closed around the detonator. He pressed the button, and it clicked. Kal hadn't lied about the explosives under the Crown, but he had lied about the dead man's switch. Syd's eyes went wide as he realized too late what pressing it had done. Kal waited to see his father's face, then fled. Only Syd, the Hollow Crown, and the detonation remained on the dais.

Kal didn't look back. He'd already moved and blasted past the Rosari on Altier powered legs. He didn't need to see what happened next.

The explosion roared to life behind him. Light swallowed everything. He knew the size of the charges Tia used. Whatever was inside the Hollow Crown had doubled the blast. Heat burst across his back, and he accreted. The Hollowline strained to keep up as he tapped into both powers.

Kal had wondered if Syd would fall for it, and of course, he had. Syd always assumed Kal would make the wrong choice. That was enough.

The shockwave struck a moment later and slammed into the remains of White Hill like a thunderclap. Kal didn't have to break stride. The pack on his back allowed him to tank it. Stone cracked above him. The floor rippled and fractured below. He jumped to the next structure and hit hard, rolled, and continued to move.

Kal knew his father would probably survive the explosion. Even without the Hollowline, Syd would have found a way to snake his way out. With a prototype, it was likely he'd walk away without a scratch.

Water surged through the broken structures below. It looked cold and relentless. The Colossus had reached the shelf, and there was nothing stopping it from going over.

Kal staggered to his feet and favored his healthy leg. He could feel the whole world tip. The creature groaned under its own impossible weight. Somewhere behind him, the Crown was gone, and the city hall had blown wide open. A small frigate flew by him overhead. It looked like Iverian in make. Likely one of Syd's. They'd likely find the bastard in the rubble or floating. Either way, Syd was in the past for today.

Kal didn't choose the Hollowline. Just like he didn't choose his last name, but from now on, he'd decide what they meant to him and the world. That would be his legacy.

Kal limped over the buildings toward the sound of shardshot. The growing flood would soon lap at his boots. He didn't know what Syd's fate would ultimately be when the sun finished rising, but it didn't matter. Let the old bastard drown with his broken dreams. Kal had to find his wife and friends.

CHAPTER 61: LOCKE

1 Hour Until the Continental Shelf

Locke pressed himself against the uneven rise of the Colossus's shoulder, every muscle coiled with tension. The wind whipped at his clothes, and the hum of the living titan beneath him vibrated through the soles of his boots. Far below, the western flank of the Brittlebark forest had turned to golden sand.

Locke didn't have time to enjoy the scenery. He kept his eyes on Lucan. The prince closed in, his gait slow, predatory.

Getting past Lucan wasn't the problem. The real challenge was feigning panic without actually feeling panicked.

Locke had figured out he could use the electrified plates to keep some distance. He used them to conserve what little stamina he had left and avoid getting a hole punched through his chest. *A few more steps. Just a little closer.*

Lucan's swing carved through the air with a crack, but Locke ducked and rolled clear just in time. He was exhausted, but not yet out of it.

His eyes flicked toward the crystal plate between them, where he'd planted the explosive earlier that night. Kenzie watched and waited for Lucan to be in the right spot.

Lucan stopped a dozen paces away, his monstrous face split into a grin.

"I know what you're trying, boy." The wind carried his voice. "You're trying to lead me away from your little friend back there. That's sweet of you. I can tell from your face that you care about her. A noble gesture. A shame it won't matter. I'll kill her after I'm done with you."

Locke let his face slip into concern to let Lucan believe he had him figured out.

Lucan sprang sideways before he charged. His footfalls rose against the living giant's exposed skin. Below, dry land had given way to the first hints of shallow water.

A flicker of movement to the right. It was Kenzie, crouched low behind a fragment of ruined architecture. One hand rested on the detonator.

Locke dilated just before the flash. A blinding burst of light right beneath Lucan. Locke doubted it would hurt the prince, but it would buy them a second.

He sprinted for Kenzie, muscles screaming and lungs burning. He reached her just before the blast wave hit.

A thunderous crack split the air. The edge of the Colossus's shoulder erupted in a spray of yellow and red. The Rose powder packed into the explosive made the blast resemble a firework. Chunks of stone from White Hill tumbled into the ocean below. The crystalline plating remained untouched.

Still, it worked. As predicted, the giant's right hand lurched toward its left shoulder and clumsily reached for the source of irritation. Kenzie was right. It couldn't stand contact with Rose shards.

"Move!" Kenzie yelled.

They bolted back toward the Colossus's neck and gave the massive hand a wide berth. Once they reached what passed for a safe distance, they turned.

"Where's Lucan?" Kenzie asked.

Locke scanned the debris. "I don't see him. Maybe the blast got him?"

"Not likely." Kenzie's voice was grim.

The hand slammed into the shoulder. The blast of air and sound deafened them. Locke wedged his fingers into some remaining debris and grabbed Kenzie's wrist as the sheer force threatened to sweep them off. They held on, breathlessly, until the shockwave relented.

"Maybe the hand got him?" Locke asked as he caught his breath.

"No, it didn't." Kenzie pointed.

Lucan stood beneath the colossal thumb and braced it with one hand. The massive pressure would have crushed any other person to paste. Not Prince Lucan. The weight of the Colossus's hand and the raw power behind it should have splintered his bones, flattened him into the stone-like skin. It would have done so to any other Rosari.

Lucan stood with his shoulders squared and his monstrous form braced against the impossible weight. His knees didn't bend. His arm didn't shake as if he dared the Colossus to try to break him.

He stepped forward, slow, deliberate, his smile widening.

Locke's stomach dropped. That shouldn't be possible. "How can he be that strong?"

"It's not strength," Kenzie said, her voice tight. "It's mass and density. I thought you'd have learned that by now. Nothing could crush him like that."

Locke swallowed hard and tried to keep his voice steady. "Right. So, uh… how do we beat something like that?"

"He's turning himself into a solid block." Kenzie's mind raced. "I don't care who he is. That's gotta be taking a toll. Aim for the eyes. You cut those, and he'll either have to fight blind or cycle the transformation. You can catch him when he's human."

Locke eyed the bloodthirsty prince, who still moved with that slow, inexorable gait. One step at a time under a thumb that must weigh five hundred tons. It seemed like he was more than a man.

"Okay, it's better than anything I've got," Locke muttered. "I don't have much juice left. It'll take most everything I've got to get in and out without being crushed by that thumb."

"You can do it," Kenzie said. Then added, "And if you can't, we're probably both dead."

Locke exhaled. "You have a way with words, Kenz."

He stepped away from her, toward the monster beneath the thumb. The wind lashed at him, and the salt air stung his eyes.

Lucan still advanced, slow and deliberate. Every muscle in his Rosari form appeared to burn the surrounding air. It seemed like the Colossus could feel it and redoubled the pressure to crush the Rose irritant.

Locke took a quick breath. Time to gamble it all on one final long shot. "Gaia's blood," he muttered. "I'm turning into Kal."

Locke moved straight at his opponent before he veered around him. His body screamed. Exhaustion clawed at his limbs, but he pushed harder. He had no idea how much longer the Colossus would keep its hand there. They just needed a few more seconds.

Lucan twisted to follow, but under all that mass, he was slow. *Good.* Locke picked up speed.

"Another trick?" Lucan bellowed. "And here I thought you were out of those."

Locke circled in tight arcs to gather speed. Then, as Lucan was turning, he dashed straight at the prince.

One shot. Locke lunged in a low arc and put everything into a single, desperate strike. In the dilated world, Locke's expression opened in anticipation of the hit. It would work. It had to. That's when he dropped out of the dilation.

His body had hit its limit.

Before he could plan his landing, the clawed hand of Prince Lucan van Ferro caught him in the chest. Lucan held him with one hand, the other still bracing the Colossus's thumb.

Lucan's grip tightened as he pulled Locke in close. The prince's Rosari teeth gleamed. Locke could see Lucan's mouth behind them. He wasn't sure which was more terrifying.

"Looks like your god abandons you," he gloated, his smile all predator. "As is the fate of all heretics."

Locke tried to wrench himself free, but it was useless. Lucan's fingers dug into his ribs and crushed the air from his lungs. He felt something pop. It didn't sound very good, and it felt even worse. A little more pressure and his bones would snap.

Above them, the Colossus's thumb loomed. Locke knew its presence was all that was keeping him alive. He also knew that Lucan's presence was all that was stopping it from crushing him to paste.

Locke gasped, his vision tunneled. He struggled, but Lucan's grip was absolute. The pain in his chest was unbearable.

That's when something hit Lucan like a cannon blast. A white blur.

The impact crashed into Lucan's side and drove him straight to the ground. Locke tumbled free and sucked in air just as his body slammed against the crystalline plating.

Lucan snarled, and Locke used the sound to reorient himself. He twisted onto his side to see another Rosari with stark white fur standing over Lucan.

Before he could move, the thumb dropped, and everything went dark.

CHAPTER 62: AVERY

30 Minutes Until the Continental Shelf

Avery's grip was iron on the *Days'* controls. His knuckles were strained, and his shoulders were stiff. He barely blinked, eyes locked on the battered skyline of White Hill. The ship was close, as close as the sinking Colossus would allow. The water was up to the creature's thighs. Something had happened on its shoulder, and the Colossus looked like it was trying to crush a bug there. Avery could see it all from his perch. Rina didn't call him Hawk for nothing.

He heard every hum, every vibration in the controls. He could feel the tension thrum through the ship. His palms were sweaty. They weren't supposed to do that anymore. He had seen too much and flown through it all unscathed.

Dr. Rina and Cookie stood nearby, quietly watching through the viewport. There was little they could do except wait. Deeper in the *Days'* belly, Lizz and Jazz operated the shardshot cannons, fingers hovered over the triggers, ready to light up the first thing that came too close.

The *Days* was built for that. Its stealth tech kept them just outside of harm's reach for the moment. The sun crept higher and painted the sky in shades of red, orange, and purple. The night wouldn't be their friend for much longer.

"Steady... steady..." Avery muttered. His eyes flicked between the instruments and the chaos outside. White Hill burned, fire and smoke curled through the shattered skyline. Kal's small team had turned it into a battlefield, but the Fleet above hadn't opened fire yet. Maybe too much collateral damage. Assuming the Aurelians even worried about things like that.

That silence, that waiting, worried him most. The Fleet hung still above them, and Lucan hadn't turned them loose yet. Which meant whatever was coming could always get worse.

The comm crackled to life. "Avery, we need you in position now. Kal's pinned." Val's voice was urgent. She left no room for argument.

Avery exhaled and toggled switches with quick, precise movements. "Are you together?"

"Negative," Val shot back. "Liam, Tia, Haruto, and I are a hundred meters from city hall. Same elevation."

Avery didn't waste time asking more. He flicked his shades down, then pushed the throttle forward. "On approach. Keep the ramp clear. You've got thirty seconds to get on or we're all swimming."

"Copy," Val answered, all business.

Avery's hands moved on instinct. Every flick of a switch, every adjustment, was part of a muscle memory built from a thousand hours at the helm. The ship purred in response, a low, steady growl.

Dr. Rina stepped up to the comms, voice calm. "Okay, everyone. This is it. May Gaia watch over us."

Avery didn't pray, but he understood the need for last words before they entered the crucible.

He slammed the accelerator. The *Days* surged forward. Thrusters roared to life and sent up clouds of ocean spray. "Jazz, Lizz," he barked into the ship's comm. "Get those turrets ready."

"Already spooling," Lizz fired back. "You just get us a clean shot."

Avery grinned. That was the spirit.

The *Days* cut between the ruins of White Hill like a blade as he dove. Engines howled while Avery wove through collapsed scaffolding and crumbling spires. The inertial dampeners struggled to keep up. The whole ship groaned under the strain.

Val's position came into view. Impromptu barricades barely held against the hailstorm of shardshot and feral Rosari who slammed against them.

Avery saw Tia hurl a broken rifle like a damn spear. Haruto and Liam crouched behind a fallen column, pinned down. And Val stood in the open, shardshot pistol smoking, teeth bared like a cornered wolf.

Too many Rosari. Too little time.

"Come on, come on…" Avery whispered as his fingers danced over the controls.

The *Days* banked hard.

"Twins, danger close. Fire!"

Jazz and Lizz unleashed hell. Blue arcs of energy ripped through the air, slamming into the Rosari below and scattering them. Smoke, screams, and chaos erupted across the ruined streets. Avery didn't stop moving. The ramp hissed open.

Val's voice crackled through the comms. "Hurry, people, the water's rising, and we're still missing a captain!"

Avery's stomach clenched. *That's right.* Kal wasn't there.

Too late to think. A section of the roof collapsed, torn free by the *Days'* thrusters, and sent a cascade of rubble into the street below. The ship lurched as debris smacked against the hull and rattled everything.

"Too close," Avery muttered and yanked the controls. "Val, now or never!"

"Not without Kal!" Her voice was a distorted scream.

Of course not.

Jules threw out six lines. Haruto moved first and grasped a line. He locked it in place, muscles strained as he pulled himself up with practiced ease. Liam and Tia followed.

Val didn't move. She'd hold the line until Kal or the afterlife came for her.

A shadow broke through the smoke. A Rosari, fast, too fast for Val to land a shot. It slammed into her. The pistol flew from her hand as her arm twisted awkwardly. She hit her head hard against some debris. Blood coated her forehead.

"Val!" Cookie snapped. The three of them felt powerless on the bridge. All the tension vanished in an instant, like air sucked from the room.

The Rosari loomed over their XO. Val threw rocks, but they bounced harmlessly off. It approached slowly, like a cat going for the throat of wounded prey.

Then, just before the killing blow, another figure crashed into the Rosari and tackled it into the rubble. A blur of movement. A familiar voice over Val's comms.

Kal.

Avery couldn't hear what he said, but whatever it was, the Rosari stilled. Its form flickered before it collapsed into something human.

Kal didn't waste time. He grabbed Val, hooked onto the nearest rope, and climbed.

"Avery, don't wait another second!"

Avery didn't. He hit the throttle.

The *Days* shot out across the waves. Avery had to keep it controlled, careful not to endanger the five crew members still tethered to the deck. One by one, they would scramble aboard.

Kal was last, and he pulled Val up with him. The second his boots hit the deck, he turned and yanked the line clear.

"We're all in!" His voice was raw, urgent. "Punch it, Avery. Let's get the kids!"

Avery didn't need to be told twice.

The *Days* banked, left White Hill behind, and tore through the sea spray like a ghost.

Dr. Rina had left the bridge to go check in on Val.

Kal came rushing into the bridge and took the co-pilot chair.

"The Crown?" Avery asked.

"Gone, I figured we were at the shelf, but even if we weren't, my choice was between this thing being free and Syd controlling it. I figured this thing was less of a monster."

Below, the Colossus moved, a titan sinking into the depths. Above, the Fleet waited. Ahead, Locke and Kenzie were still somewhere in the madness.

No time to think. No time to breathe. Just time to fly.

CHAPTER 63: KENZIE

30 Minutes Until the Continental Shelf

Locke walked to his death. Kenzie knew it. He probably knew it too, if he was honest with himself for once.

She peered out from the ruins, hands curled into fists. The sea roared below, and the wind ripped through the broken building around her, but her focus stayed on the two figures ahead. Lucan stalked forward like a wolf that had already won.

It wasn't a fight, and it probably never had been. Lucan was a legendary fighter, unbeaten. He was beyond what most reasonable people could imagine a Rosari to be. His ability to accrete had already shattered every rule she thought applied to Rosari. In theory, she considered herself something of an expert, even if she rarely said so out loud. She had known Rosari to be resilient, deadly, bloodthirsty, and incredibly powerful, even the novice ones. Lucan was something else, something worse.

Locke was either incredibly brave or incredibly naïve.

He followed her plan. Her impromptu idea had convinced him, and for some reason, he'd trusted it. She couldn't understand why. Why did she have to open her mouth? Why did he have to listen? A part of her had hoped he'd see it for what it was, call it stupid or desperate, and run. Then at least she wouldn't have to watch her friend die.

Kenzie swallowed hard. It wasn't supposed to be like that. The whole plan had been careless, maybe even reckless. No. Definitely reckless. But it had also always felt necessary. It had felt right.

The crew of the *Days* thought they could make a difference, and maybe they already had. At such a time, who was she to judge? Unfortunately, making a difference appeared to be about to cost the lives of her and Locke.

Someone should tell you about the costs of things upfront. Kenzie had always thought that. Otherwise, it was like they backdoor stole from you. How could a trade be fair if you didn't know the cost beforehand?

It just proved what she'd always believed: a person was only as safe as the people they choose to follow. You pick reckless leaders, and you get reckless plans. Kal was the poster boy for reckless. Her brother was, too. And now, apparently, she was counted among that growing, and dying, crowd.

Yet there Locke was. Someone she'd thought, until recently, was the sensible and boring type. He was on the verge of being crushed as he tried to fight someone he had no chance against. Maybe everyone was a little reckless. It only took one decision to be branded that way, and once you donned the moniker… well, what's done was done.

It shocked her that it wasn't just the recklessness that would get Locke killed. His fatal flaw was the hope he carried. A hope that things would work out and he would see a better tomorrow. She considered making a joke to herself about hope being his killer, but she bet on either the giant thumb or the maniacal monarch beneath it as the true culprit.

They could still run. The Colossus had already waded into the ocean. Maybe the waves would bury the thing, never to be seen again. Perhaps they didn't need to remove the Crystal at its heart. They should just run. That was what made sense.

Except Locke moved toward danger, and she couldn't bring herself to move away from her friend.

She should run. That was the rule, had always been the rule. When things got bad and death was a breath away, *just run*. It had kept her alive since before Seaforth.

Yet, her feet wouldn't budge. The only thing that moved was her heart as it slammed against her ribs.

Locke shot off. Not at full speed, but faster than any normal person. He made a beeline for Lucan before cutting around him to circle and time it just right.

He wouldn't be able to stop what came next if Lucan was as tired as she thought. He couldn't defend his eyes while he held up the thumb. Too many fronts, even for him. Maybe.

She saw it before it happened. Locke bled speed. Lucan's mass field was still up. Before she could scream, Locke broke from the circle and dashed straight at the bloodthirsty prince.

Then Lucan caught him by the chest with his free hand.

"Gaia's blood…" she said to herself.

In an instant, she knew. Locke would die unless she did something. Something she had sworn never to show to anyone.

Locke gasped, a sharp, desperate sound as Lucan's claws flexed and something cracked.

Kenzie's breath hitched. There was no time for hesitation, no more hiding. Before she even registered the motion, her hand was in the pack. She stood and charged, her body moving before her thought could catch up.

The power surged through her in an instant, hot and familiar. It welcomed her like an old friend, as if she had never left it behind. The shift was like she slipped on her favorite coat, one tailored for her, and waited right where she had left it.

She had never fought, never stood her ground. Even with the gift, she had only run. Not this time, though. She wasn't sure if it was her hate for Lucan, her care for Locke, or whatever alchemy of the two. Two things could be true, as Kal would say. It didn't matter. She would do something she told herself she would never do.

White crystalline fur extended from her chest to her arms and legs. Her stance and gait shifted mid-stride. She remembered what it felt like to be a Rosari, and she gained momentum. She closed the distance as fast as her new form would allow. She accreted as much as she could. Just before impact, she lowered her shoulder and hit Lucan like a shardshot cannon blast.

The collision cracked through the air. Lucan hit the ground with a crash, and the force rattled through the Colossus's shoulder. Kenzie stumbled, but caught herself before she landed on a crystal plate.

Locke was thrown, too, and he landed on the plate not too far away.

She'd done it. She'd knocked Lucan down. Before she could savor the moment, reality crashed back. Lucan was already rising.

His claws scraped against the Colossus's skin. His snarl was more annoyed than angry. He wasn't hurt, but he seemed surprised that anything on Gaia could move him.

Then his gaze fell upon her, and her white, crystalline form. Shock flickered across his face, followed by something closer to horror. "An Omen?"

Before he could process further, the Colossus's thumb descended once again on the irritants.

Lucan didn't hesitate. He threw both hands up and caught the wall of weight. He had to take a knee, but he stopped the immense mass with both elbows locked above his shoulders.

Kenzie ducked. Her breath hammered in her chest.

Lucan stood beneath the crushing force, muscles tensed. His Rosari form glowed with the strain. Even with one knee bent, he held firm. He didn't look at them as he held out. It was clear he was only saving himself.

Kenzie knew it was their shot. She ran up to their would-be killer and slapped a pepper charge onto his chest. Lucan flinched and reached for it, only for the thumb to slip an inch, forcing him to throw his hand back up.

She laughed, partially at the sight but mostly because of the adrenaline. "Keep being strong, big guy. We're counting on you." She turned to Locke, who had moved off the plate, and grabbed his hand. "Move!" Together, they ran.

"Kenzie?" Locke said as they shuffled out from under the thumb.

"Not now. I'll let you know if we make it out of this. Alive, preferably. Can you get the rest of the explosives?"

"Yeah, I think so. Where are they?" Locke asked.

"Stashed by where I was hiding. Meet me on top of the hand."

"Yeah, okay." Locke was about to run past Kenzie, but then paused. "Wait, what's the plan?"

"Back to the original plan. I'll explain more on the way to the Crystal. Just go!"

With that, Locke was off in a flash. When she got out from under the massive thumb, she turned, cleared it in one jump, and spun just in time to see Locke do the same with the pack of explosives slung over his shoulder.

"You could have at least shifted when we were trying to climb up the Colossus's back."

She laughed, partly at the comment, partly just because they were still alive. "One day you'll find out that timing is everything to a girl." She smiled. "Speaking of which, we don't have much of it."

They would have to run down the thumb and then to the wrist, but the arm would take them right where they needed to be. The Colossus just had to keep its hand there a little longer. Fortunately, it seemed Lucan's presence kept the Colossus occupied.

Two problems solved. A route to the Crystal and the murderous prince was firmly occupied with bigger concerns. Now they only had to remove the Azure Crystal. Maybe the reckless plan wouldn't get them killed if they reached it in time. Maybe not.

Too many maybes for a morning that was just getting started. Maybes always added up, and Kenzie wasn't sure how much longer they could keep riding that luck.

CHAPTER 64: LOCKE

15 Minutes Until the Continental Shelf

Locke watched Kenzie go first. She hit the Colossus's wrist hard and rolled with the impact before she pushed herself upright. The wind roared around them. Salt spray hit her face as the unstoppable titan waded deeper into the ocean. Each step sent tremors through its massive frame. They had little time.

Locke landed beside her and skidded a few feet before he righted himself. He still tried to catch his breath, still shook from what had just happened. He could feel it in his posture, in how his hands curled into fists before he forced them open.

"Well," she stretched out the word as she checked her shoulder, "that was incredibly stupid."

Locke let out a breathless laugh and ran a hand through his hair as he continued the descent. "Which part? The part where I tried to fight an unstoppable Rosari or the part where you tackled him off his feet to save me?"

She tilted her head and pretended to consider. "Tough call. I mean, I'd say yours, but only because mine worked."

Locke scoffed. "Right, but remember, it was all your plan."

"It worked, didn't it?"

He exhaled sharply and shook his head. "You're hopeless."

"Not true. Val seems to believe in me."

"She said this?" Locke asked.

"It's a vibe between us. You wouldn't understand," she said, sliding down to the next ledge.

"Uh-huh." Locke followed.

Kenzie kept her focus ahead and mapped their path forward. The plating was light but still present. They had to get to the chest cavity, plant the charges, and get out. All that before it collapsed, drowned, or shook them off.

Before he could get too lost in the plan, he glanced at Kenzie again. She was still tense, still working through what had just happened under the Colossus's thumb. She had revealed a secret to Locke. Sure, maybe that moment had forced her, but she still trusted Locke enough to keep it.

She bumped his arm lightly with hers. "So, you gonna tell me how you're doing?"

Locke blinked and glanced over. "What do you mean?"

"You. Lucan. The whole desperate last stand thing." She smirked. "It was brave, I'll give you that, but you must have been scared out of your mind when he grabbed you."

He let out a dry laugh, but it was short-lived. "Yes, that wasn't…pleasant, but I was trying to follow your plan."

"You could have said no," Kenzie said.

His gaze flickered downward. "Didn't feel like a choice at the time. It was either that or…" He felt her study him for a second before she turned back ahead.

"Yeah," she muttered. "It seemed that way to me, too."

The wind howled around them as they scooted down the forearm. They slipped and skidded toward the edge before Locke grabbed a protruding crystal and hauled them back up. Kenzie let out a slow breath and barely looked down before she nudged him forward.

Her white fur brushed against his arm.

"So, are you going to tell me about it?"

"About what?"

"Really? You're going to make me say it?"

"Oh, this?" She waved a hand over her Rosari form. "I got it from the store last week. I think it's going to be the biggest thing in fashion."

Locke groaned. "Gaia, save me. Can you answer one question about your past honestly?"

"As you said to me once, 'I have a complicated backstory.' "

"Har-har." Locke smiled despite himself. "I'm guessing you're not really from Seaforth?"

"I'll tell you when we're not in the middle of some idiot's poorly conceived plan." She grinned. "But for now, know I laid a few cards down to save your life. You're welcome. The rest are still firmly up to my chest."

Locke gave her a look, partly exasperated and partly reluctant amusement. "Kenzie."

She raised a brow. "Locke."

He exhaled sharply through his nose and shook his head. "You're right. This isn't the time."

"Right, everyone knows that scaling down a giant's arm is no time for complicated backstories. That's like the first thing they teach you at Adventuring Academy."

"Something about near-death experiences seems to lighten your mood."

"It's how my brain works. The more I joke, the closer we are to death."

"I'll keep that in mind for next time, but you've made your point."

A violent shudder ran through the Colossus and nearly knocked them off balance. They fell into each other to brace themselves. They exchanged a glance before they turned to the Colossus's shoulder they had just come from. The arm moved again. They were being pulled away from the chest. The hand was rising.

Kenzie sighed. "Fine. We'll table it, but we agree it was my point."

She removed her arms from around Locke and shifted back to her usual self. She reached into her pocket. Locke's hands were still on her shoulders as she took out the detonator and pressed the charge. Lucan shot out from beneath the hand, over the shoulder, and crashed into the waves below.

The explosion sent a shockwave through the Colossus's frame, and for a second, the massive creature hesitated. Then, like an animal that reacted to a bug bite, it returned its hand to the blast site and pressed down.

Kenzie smirked. "Told you he was tired." She pocketed the detonator before she shifted back to her Rosari form.

Locke let go of her arms and watched the figure of the man who had almost just killed them tumble into the ocean. The contradiction would have made him laugh if he weren't so tired. He smiled at Kenzie instead.

"That felt anti-climactic," Locke said, watching the sea swirl where Lucan splashed beneath the waves.

"All's fair," Kenzie said, shrugging. "His mistake was thinking it was a clean fight."

"Do you think we rely too much on explosives to solve our problems?" Locke asked.

"Tia would be very upset that you asked me that." Kenzie turned, and Locke followed.

"So you don't have pockets like that? Through your fur, I mean." Locke asked, sliding down the forearm.

"I'm still me under this. I wouldn't look like a fleshy wolf if you shaved off this fur. The fur is the transformation. I could break it and reach into a pocket, but it's easier to shift back and forth." She spoke as she moved down the forearm.

They moved faster as the chest cavity came into view. Crystalline formations had grown over the opening, as if the Colossus tried to seal itself shut. The glow of the Azure Crystal flickered through the structures and cast long, shifting shadows across the interior.

The water was getting close. Locke's breath hitched, and his steps slowed. Just like that, the banter died. They had reached the heart of the Colossus. Locke looked at Kenzie, re-secured the pack on his shoulder, and leaped across the chasm.

He landed hard on the other side and squeezed past the outcroppings to get inside the Colossus's chest cavity. His boots scraped against the slick crystalline plating as he steadied himself. The air was thick with static, and the sharp scent of ozone coated his tongue. The Azure Crystal loomed before him, an immense, pulsating shard embedded deep within the Colossus's core. It was alive, not like a human, animal, or plant, but in a way that made his skin prickle. It was like he stood in the presence of something too vast to comprehend.

Blue arcs of lightning coiled through the air, crackled along the chamber walls, and flickered against jagged crystalline growths that spread like veins through the Colossus's interior. Locke noted cable networks grafted onto the walls, probably a vestigial remnant from when Syd had powered the creature before Breezewaltz. The energy lashed out in chaotic bursts. One of the bolts struck him, and he jumped, even though he knew it couldn't hurt him.

It had been a considerable bolt.

At first, he felt nothing. Then he felt warm. It was as if the Crystal touched him, as if it saw him.

Then the voice came. "Thy fate lieth not within this path, Locke Luinondo." It was the same voice from the Rite. The one who had called him worthy. "Seek thou another course. Thou knowest the truth of it. Herein am I home."

The words sank into him, filled the space between his ribs, and pressed against something deep in his chest. He had wondered if the words he'd heard during the Rite came from the Crystal or if they were his mind's reaction to it. He had imagined that if the Crystal ever spoke to him again, it would be holy. Divine. Righteous. A moment of clarity or a guiding light.

It was different, certain. There was no anger or pleading, just a truth so absolute it left no room for doubt. Except the doubt was the same thing that had led him there.

His fingers hovered over the pack and the charges. His breath came shallow, uncertain. He had spent his whole life believing the Crystal was the one thing that would never fail him. The one thing that had always been right. So why did it tell him to stop, and why was he crying?

A memory surfaced, unbidden.

He was a boy again, and he kneeled in the temple beside Toren. The warm blue light of the sacred Azure Crystal filtered through stained glass. Their father stood before them, his voice steady, absolute.

"The Crystal is constant. It is beyond men, beyond nations. It does not falter, nor does it fail. It is our protection and our guide, always."

Toren was the faithful one, the better son. He kneeled with his eyes closed, hands clasped in prayer.

Locke looked from him to their father. The stern look wasn't an invitation for questions, but Locke knew he had to ask one, anyway. "Then why does it let bad things happen?"

Their father gave him the look, a mix of frustration, patience, and knowing. Locke was nine and had already become intimately familiar with it in his short time on Gaia.

"That is not for us to know. That is for our faith to provide. The Crystal works through us. All the good and bad we produce is inside us, but the Crystal makes us great."

Locke had believed that then, and still believed it. Even when his world fell apart at Seaforth and a bottomless, dark pit swallowed his memories, he had held onto that belief. If the Crystal was wrong and didn't watch over them, then what had it all been for?

But, standing next to the beating heart of his beliefs, he wasn't sure he could trust it.

The voice came again, resolute. "To wrest me from mine hallowed seat is folly most grave. Go hence, last scion of Luinondo. Peace attend thee, for thou hast fulfilled my will."

His chest clenched. The words struck something inside him. Something fragile. *Is this a mistake?*

Even if his faith wasn't rock solid, he had always trusted. Even in his darkest nights, he had believed in the life the Crystals had provided. The Azure Crystal was the hope and salvation of the Iverian people.

His hands trembled. He looked at the beautiful floating Crystal before him. "You're supposed to be our guide. You're supposed to protect us. So why did you let him fall?"

The thought formed before he could stop it. His father's words echoed in his mind. *It is our protection and our guide...*

Then a light flashed before his eyes, and he fell to his knees. Another voice cut through the uncertainty like a blade. Not his father's. Not the Crystal's.

Toren.

The memory that had threatened to rise during Landfall suddenly came to him. Locke was eleven, and High Priest Aldis had scolded Locke for breaking fast. Locke's parents had told him to confess his sins, but when he did, the priest just yelled at him. Aldis had called him unclean before he struck Locke in the face with a ringed palm.

Toren must have heard the strike. He had come into the room and pulled Locke out by the arm. They ran and ran and ran. Eventually, they headed to an old bridge, one of the many that spanned the outlets from the Grand Lake's mighty flow.

They hopped over the railing, onto the stone underpass, and sat together. "We'll stay here until they can't find us. Then, when we come home, Mother will be so relieved to see us she won't even care you broke the fast."

Locke looked at his brother. "But I sinned. Isn't that wrong?"

"Family first, Locke. That's what matters. We can figure out the rest together."

His breath hitched. He looked up, past the pulsing light and jagged crystalline formations that closed in around the chamber. Kenzie waited outside on the arm. Kal was out there and fought for his life. Val held the line with him. The whole damn crew of the best skyship to ever fly across Gaia's blue skies did everything in their power to keep Iveria from falling to this monster.

The Crystal had never fought for them. It had only ever made them fight for it. It had let Toren die.

Locke wasn't a priest. He wasn't a scholar. He no longer had the luxury of faith. All he was in the moment was the last hope for a family of skypirates. They needed him to put the monster down. He would do what he needed for his new family.

Locke firmly pressed the charges against the cavity walls and angled them to eject the Crystal upon detonation.

His hands were steady.

"I'm sorry." He wasn't sure whether he was apologizing to Crystal, his parents, or his faith.

Then the Crystal hit him with bolt after bolt and screamed.

The sensation tore through his skull and rattled his teeth, like the Crystal itself tried to crush his thoughts. He clutched his head and staggered.

The Crystal pulsed violently. The entire chamber shook. Arcs of blue light surged outward like flared nerve endings. The Colossus trembled beneath him, as if it fought to keep the heart in place.

"Locke!" Kenzie screamed. It was what brought him back. "The arm is moving. Hurry!"

She was right. The chasm widened, and the arm pulled away. The Colossus tried to position its hand into the cavity, attempting to prevent what was to come next.

Locke turned, sprinted to the edge, and leaped.

Kenzie caught him midair and yanked him up and onto his feet.

She looked down at him, eyes sharp with something between concern and understanding. "You good?"

He had to think. Was he? The arm continued to move while the ocean spray splashed their faces and the wind pulled their hair. Finally, he nodded.

"Yeah. Just a little crisis of faith."

"Good. Now let's bury this monster at sea." Kenzie smiled as she gripped the moving arm beneath her.

CHAPTER 65: KENZIE

5 Minutes Until the Continental Shelf

Kenzie sprinted along the Colossus's massive forearm, her boots slapped against its shifting surface. Each step sent a dull tremor through the titan's body, but it didn't collapse. It didn't thrash. It simply moved, slow and deliberate. The titan's other hand reached toward its chest, fingers outstretched, as if it felt for something it had lost.

Locke kept pace beside her. His breath came unevenly, but his steps were steady. The ocean stretched endlessly around them. The morning sun glinted off the surface. Its golden light caught the fine mist of sea spray kicked up by the titan's steady march. Wind whipped at Kenzie's clothes and tugged at her white fur. No time to look back.

Then, the roar of engines split the air and snapped Kenzie out of her focus. Without thought, she reverted to normal form.

The *Days* streaked overhead and banked hard as it cut across the sky. The boarding ramp was already down, and Jazz and Lizz were at the edge, one on either side, braced against the frame.

They watched and waited. Kenzie held the detonator in one hand and the comm in the other.

"Think they'll make it?" Jazz asked over the comm. Kenzie saw him squat on the ramp.

Lizz didn't look away, then spoke into the comm. "Now's not the time." She paused. "Fifty credits say they do."

Jazz considered it. "Two to one?"

Lizz nodded. "Deal."

"Guys, keep the line clean," Val yelled into it.

Kenzie smiled but didn't break stride. She and Locke ran flat out, the distance closing between them and the ramp with every second. That's when the Colossus moved as if it recognized its only real threat.

As the *Days* approached, the titan's massive hand pivoted and reached for the ship with slow precision. It was desperate and deliberate, its fingers stretched wide. Locke cursed under his breath, and Kenzie knew it, too. If the Colossus took down the ship, they'd be finished.

She held up the detonator, and her fingers brushed the trigger, but hesitation stopped her. *No, not yet.* They needed the arm above the waves. The Colossus still had a part to play.

The arm beneath them tilted and shifted beneath their feet. Kenzie stumbled but caught herself, her focus sharp as they pushed forward. She tightened her grip on the detonator. *Just a little farther.*

Locke glanced at her. His eyes were sharp. "Kenzie, blow it!"

She didn't, not yet. If she detonated it then, the lifeless arm would drag them down beneath the foaming sea. She pushed on, exhausted, and her mind raced. Kenzie almost told Locke to go without her, but she knew he wouldn't leave. What a hero.

The ocean rose up the arm. The *Days* banked hard and descended toward them as it avoided the creature's hand.

"Kenzie, now or the *Days* is done!" Locke snapped. His voice cut through the chaos.

She exhaled, pressed the trigger, and the violence behind them was unmistakable.

The chest cavity exploded. A column of blue fire shot outward, and the shockwave rippled through the Colossus's massive frame. The release of energy cracked the crystalline growths along its body. The Azure Crystal shot free. It burst out in a violent flash of light and tumbled end over end before it righted itself and hovered in place.

For the first time, the Colossus hesitated. Its outstretched hand paused midreach, fingers twitched as if unsure. Then it fell.

The *Days* was ahead, its ramp still down, engines roared to hold position just over the waves. The arm sank too fast, and if they didn't jump, they were going under with it.

Lizz's voice rang out in the comm and then echoed over the waves. "Jump!"

Without hesitation, Kenzie pushed off the surface. The air shifted, and gravity pulled her down faster than she expected. Then her chest slammed into the ramp. She scrambled for purchase. Her fingers caught the edge.

Locke was right behind her. He jumped, but the Colossus's arm submerged fully beneath him. The sinking force dragged water and debris in its wake. He hit the ramp hard. One hand gripped the frame, but his legs slipped.

Kenzie grabbed his wrist, Jazz grabbed hers, and Lizz grabbed his. With one final pull, they hauled them inside just as the ramp sealed shut. The ship tore away from the sinking titan. Locke and Kenzie collapsed onto the deck and gasped for breath. Lizz and Jazz lay nearby, still panting. For a moment, none of them spoke. Then Kenzie let out a weak, wheezing laugh.

Locke groaned and rolled onto his back. "That was the worst plan in a series of worsening plans."

Kenzie grinned, still breathless. "A plan can't be bad if it works."

Lizz laughed. "I can't believe it worked."

Jazz laughed too. So did Kenzie, and then so did Locke. The adrenaline still coursed through Kenzie, but exhaustion set in.

Kal's voice crackled over the comms, tentative. "Can we verify our favorite First Altier and second pilot are aboard?"

"Verified," Lizz said into the comm.

Kenzie picked up her head to see Val in the corner, being examined by Dr. Rina. "You two alright?" Val asked.

"More or less," Locke replied.

"You did well today. We might even get paid for this job," Val said with a smile.

Kenzie grinned, still flat on her back. "I expect a sizeable bonus." She stood and approached a porthole. She looked out the window as the *Days* climbed higher and the sinking titan's arm continued its slow descent. Its massive form tipped backward. It had passed the edge of the continental shelf. Its hand, reaching upward, was the last thing to disappear.

For a long moment, the ocean bubbled, as if it tried to boil the creature. Then, finally, a single bubble broke the surface. The immense ocean had swallowed the Colossus whole.

Kenzie saw Avery circle to pick up the Azure Crystal. That's when she looked up to see the Aurelian Fleet descend upon them.

CHAPTER 66: KALISTON

After the Colossus

The *Days* hummed with the aftershock of their narrow escape, the ship's engines steady as the crew struggled to catch their breath. Kal tried to imagine the mess in the cargo hold. Kenzie and Locke had just made it on, Jazz and Lizz laughed like maniacs into the comms. Their laughter had faded into quiet wheezes and groans of exhaustion, but there was no time to linger.

Val was somewhere in the hold with Rina. Kal guessed her arm was probably already in a sling. Rina was the best, and Kal was glad he didn't have to worry about them.

As if invoked, that's when Val's voice came over the comm. "We need to get moving." Val sounded like she was in some discomfort. "The sky is full of angry fascists, and we've got a job to finish."

Her words snapped everyone to attention, and the atmosphere shifted. The danger of the situation hung in the air.

Kal's voice crackled over the comms and cut through the tension. "Everyone, get to your stations. We've got a Crystal to retrieve, and I need you all sharpish. Comm channel open for all stations."

"On it," Jazz called into the comm.

Tia's voice came over the comms next. "We've got incoming, Val. The Aurelian Fleet's closing in."

"Stations, people, now!" Kal barked again, his voice colder, more controlled. "This isn't over yet."

Jules chimed in. "Ready to deploy the tow cable when you're set, Cap."

Kal took a breath and nodded to Avery in the pilot's seat. "Haruto, keep the data coming. I need to know what we're looking at. Liam, we'll need to divert power between camo and engines depending on how hot it gets. Jules is going to be busy with the cable." He scanned the sensor readouts Haruto had just sent to the monitor. "Probably more engines when the guns get hot," Kal added.

"All hands, brace for a bumpy ride," Val said and stepped onto the bridge. Her arm was in a sling, and she had a head wrap. Kal winked at her.

The *Days* roared through the skies, its engines burned hot beneath Kal's steady hands. The Aurelian Fleet loomed ahead, a vast swarm of enemy ships that closed in fast. Kal gripped the controls tightly. His eyes flicked to the sensor readouts. The Fleet was massive. Their formations tightened as they moved in on the Crystal. The *Days* would be vulnerable while retrieving the Gaia-forsaken thing, but there was nothing they could do about that.

"Steady," Kal muttered to himself and scanned the horizon. The *Days* wasn't the biggest ship in the skies, but it was by far the fastest. They had the advantage of speed and the element of surprise. The ship's advanced optical camo would help keep them hidden from the Aurelian Fleet, at least as long as no ships got too close to her.

"Liam, camo now," Kal said and put the *Days* into a hover beside the floating Azure Crystal.

"Ready to deploy the tow cable," came Jules's voice over the comms as it cut through the tense silence. It would be too large for the hold, but Jazz and Lizz were standing by to secure it to the aft.

"Deploy," Kal ordered, his voice calm but sharp.

Behind them, the tow cable system activated above the cargo hold. Its tendrils snaked outward and reached for the Azure Crystal suspended in the morning sky. Jules, operating the controls with precision, guided it carefully.

"Twins, are you in place?" Val asked over the comm.

"Yes, Mom," Jazz said back, half-sarcastic.

The twins would be suited up in protective gear to help Jules reel it in.

The crystal shimmered in the distance, bathed in the light of the morning sun. It was almost serene, taken out of context. In context, an entire sky of madness surrounded it. As the cable inched forward, Jazz and Lizz held position on the cargo ramp, braced against the shifting turbulence.

They had to turn off the ship's inertial dampeners in the cargo hold while the ramp was open. Every movement would cause the ship to buck slightly underfoot, and the cable needed to be steady to hold.

"Can't this reel work any faster?" Jazz spoke into his comm as the cable slowly drew the Crystal in.

"The camo should buy us some time," Lizz replied, focused as she guided the cable into position.

Meanwhile, Tia operated the main cannon, eyes locked on the Aurelian ships. Her fingers tapped over the controls, and she scanned the horizon for incoming threats. The Fleet set up a position over the Crystal, but one ship headed straight for it, closing fast.

"Captain, one incoming for the Crystal. Permission to fire?" Tia asked.

"And break our cover? We'd be completely exposed!" Liam said.

"Captain?" Tia prompted again.

"Kal, what good is staying hidden if we let them take the Crystal?" Val was the voice of reason, as always.

For a beat, Kal considered it. Let the Aurelians take the Crystal. It would be easy. Hadn't his crew done enough? It wasn't even their fight, not really. What did he owe Iveria? They were skypirates, forced to live outside the law. Iveria would just as soon wipe them off its boot as embrace them as heroes.

The thoughts were petty and small. He could admit that, and he already knew the answers.

Freedom was a wonderful thing. The ability to fly wherever his heart desired at any time. Answering only to himself. It was what he built his life around after Conchordia, after his father, but Kal knew that total freedom was a poison chalice. Drink too much and it's all you seek until it kills you. Untethered freedom made it easy to overlook the freedoms of others. Kal understood that people weren't meant to be completely free.

That thought made him look around at the bridge. These were his people, but he belonged to them just as much. He didn't care what road had brought them to the *Days*. He loved them and loved that they were standing with him now.

Saving Iveria was worth more than just whatever rewards would come next. It was about saving the only place most of these scoundrels had ever called home. Kal was right there with them. He loved the life they had built in the skies over Iveria.

That love was what forced him to speak next. "Fire, fire, fire. Weapons free."

Tia didn't need a second command. Her hand was steady on the trigger as she fired the main cannon.

The blast tore through the air with a deafening roar and slammed into the Aurelian ship that charged the Crystal. The shot punched a clean hole through its hull. Engines sputtered. The ship spiraled off course. The *Days'* first strike was true, but the danger hadn't passed.

Her optical camo flickered and vanished. It exposed their position to the entire Aurelian Fleet.

"Camo's off!" Liam shouted, his voice tinged with urgency.

"We've been spotted!" Haruto called from the bridge. Panic rose in his tone. "Aurelian ships adjusting course!"

Kenzie and Locke opened the turrets and sprayed shardshot into the morning sky toward the advancing Fleet. Kal's grip tightened on the controls.

"Cargo, brace for evasive maneuvers!" Val ordered.

Kal's eyes narrowed. They didn't have much time. "Jazz, Lizz, how's the retrieval?" Kal barked.

"Almost there," Jazz answered via the comms. "Maybe twenty seconds, Captain."

Kal's heart pounded. The pressure mounted as enemy ships closed in from all sides. Avery, stationed at the secondary controls, tightened his grip on the yoke and kept the skyship steady. That was when the sky turned red from the incoming shardshot. Kal adjusted the throttle and pushed the *Days* into a rapid ascent to avoid the enemy's fire.

"We lost it, Kal!" Lizz's voice was tense, almost breathless, as the cable jerked loose from the forced maneuver.

"We'll come back around. We need to clear some space!" Kal narrowly dodged a volley of shardshot that screamed past the hull. His knuckles whitened on the controls as he threw the *Days* into an evasive roll that crested sharply above another barrage.

The Aurelian Fleet's fire grew heavier. Their formation tightened as they clearly tried to encircle them.

"Copy that," Jules said. With a sharp tug, the tow cable retracted. The Azure Crystal drifted upward. Jazz and Lizz readied to secure the cable housing for the next shot. Jules would reseal the bay door and re-engage the dampeners.

The ship shuddered as another shardshot slammed into its outer hull. The impact rattled the bridge, and Kal assumed every other compartment. Even a brave crew would start to have doubts.

Liam's voice cut through the chaos. "We can't take much more of this, Kal. The hull's holding, but we're taking real damage."

"We need to get out of here," Kal said through clenched teeth. His mind raced. The *Days* had the speed to evade, but the Aurelian Fleet was everywhere and relentless. "Avery, close the distance. Tia, make a gap. We'll punch through, then come into their formation from starboard to port."

"Kal, what about the Crystal?" Val asked.

"We can't bring it back if we're dead! Now!" Kal snapped.

With a roar of engines, Avery pushed the throttle forward, and the *Days* surged ahead. She raced across the sky and narrowly dodged another volley of shardshot.

On the bridge, Tia fired the main gun at the oncoming Aurelian ships. She cleared just enough of a path for Kal to break through.

"Cut guns. Divert power to camo," Kal ordered.

The ship wove through the enemy formation and nearly vanished into the clouds as its camo cloaked the hull.

"Try to follow us up here," Kal muttered to himself as the ship banked hard to the right. He knew he tended to talk to himself when he flew. His heart pounded as his mind raced through the openings in the sky, wondering what gaps would exist when the ship finally came around. He had a route as soon as the *Days* lined up. "And just like that," he muttered, "the predators become the prey."

"All power to guns and engines. We're going in!" Val shouted.

The *Days* roared in on the Aurelian's flanks, their Fleet skyships still trying to reorient after chasing the *Days*' first evasive run through the Fleet.

Tia's cannon unleashed shot after shot, with each blue shardshot bolt erupting into red fireballs in the sky. The two turrets manned by Locke and Kenzie swept across the Fleet. Both sprayed shardshot into the crowd as they passed. The turrets wounded whatever the main gun didn't hit. The damage was one-sided but not decisive. It was still one skyship against hundreds, maybe thousands. Every enemy they knocked out of the sky seemed to be replaced by another.

The *Days* threaded and fired its way through the Aurelian Fleet, picking off targets as it passed. Very few of the skyships fired back at them. They were either too surprised, out of position, or both.

Kal knew the surprise wouldn't last. He had to peel away before the ships deeper in the Fleet had time to react and bring their guns around. He turned the *Days* back hard to port and punched back into the Fleet from another awkward angle. Same result. A merciless barrage of fire from the *Days*, but barely a dent to the overall Fleet.

"Kal, this is hopeless. We can't beat this, man," Avery said.

"I'm just clearing room. Haruto, let me know when we've got at least sixty seconds of distance between the Fleet's shardshot range and the Crystal so we can tow it in."

"Roger," Haruto said.

"They're going to close in on us, eventually. There are too many of them!" Liam cried out.

"We're not in trouble yet!" Kal shouted and pulled the sticks hard for another pass.

"Not by a long shot," Val said to the bridge before she spoke into the comm. "We need to get the Crystal on the next attempt before they realize what we're doing."

Kal's gaze hardened. They had one chance left to secure the Azure Crystal before they either scrambled out of there or died trying. "Is the Crystal clear?" Kal asked.

"Sensors say the Crystal has three bogies on it. Besides that, the rest of the Fleet is scrambling around us. I think we have our sixty seconds."

Kal steered up into the clouds, then looped back down. "Cut guns. Camo, now. Punch it!" he said, as he and Avery worked in tandem to rocket the ship toward the Azure Crystal.

Kal's hands tightened around the controls as the *Days* gained speed on a steep descent. The pressure mounted. They had only one shot left to secure the Azure Crystal before the Fleet overwhelmed them for a final time.

As they closed in, Kal spotted the Aurelian detachment trying to secure the Crystal. He brought the *Days* in low and floated practically between the enemy ships. "On my command... fire!"

Tia, Kenzie, and Locke engaged their guns in perfect sync. They shredded the enemy ships and dropped them toward the water before the optical camo even wore off.

Kal eased the *Days* back into position.

Jules aimed and launched the tow cable. "Good contact," she croaked through the comms.

The winch above the cargo bay reeled the Crystal in again.

"Jazz, Lizz, how's the Crystal?" Kal barked, his voice sharp as he stood to inspect the damage from the incoming shardshot visually.

"In one piece and almost here," Jazz replied, his voice tight with concentration.

"Faster, Jules, faster," Kal ordered. "Before they can regroup."

"It has one speed!" Jules shouted back over the comms.

The crew sat in near silence and waited for the all-clear. It was an eerie moment, like being in the eye of a storm. The reprieve was always only temporary. The entire ship lurched as another volley of shardshot ripped through the air.

"Brace!" Kal shouted. His heart pounded as the ship rocked from the impact. Tia, Locke, and Kenzie returned the volley.

Liam's voice came high and sharp. "We've got hull breaches, Kal! We're taking more damage!"

"Keep it together! This is just interceptor fire. The *Days* can handle this!" Kal snapped and fought the urge to launch into an evasive maneuver.

"Just a few more seconds!" Jazz called, tension crept into his voice. The *Days* shuddered again as enemy fire intensified. Shardshot from Aurelian heavy cruisers and frigates closed in and had nearly reached the Crystal.

"Kal, the Fleet's tightening around us. They're moving to encircle!" Haruto's voice was urgent. "We need to cut lines and run!"

Kal's gaze hardened. They were out of time. He shot a look at Avery beside him.

"Avery, get ready for a hard pull. We shoot straight up the moment we have the Crystal."

Avery nodded, and his fingers danced across the controls. "On your mark."

"Secure!" came Jules's voice over the comm.

"Now!" Kal shouted.

The ship rocketed skyward and climbed into the sparse clouds above. It was a desperate gamble. If it caught the Fleet off guard, it would buy the *Days* a few precious seconds to escape the range of the Aurelian shardshot cannons.

"We're not out of the woods yet!" Val shouted from the back of the bridge, her voice steady despite the chaos.

"Prepare for evasive maneuvers!" Kal's voice cut through the madness. He wasn't sure what he could do in their position, but he had to do something. They were seconds away from eating a whole volley of shardshot.

Then, an explosion shook the air below them. The sky turned dark as massive blasts lit up the horizon and cast an eerie blue and red glow across the battlefield.

"The *Orleander!*" Tia exclaimed, awe in her voice as the massive Iverian Capital skyship unleashed its firepower.

"They got your message, Haruto!" Val said.

The Orleander was a force of nature, its cannons powerful enough to shake the air with every blast. A series of shockwaves exploded from its main guns and rocked the Aurelian Fleet to its core. Their first volley struck an Aurelian warship dead-on. The massive ship crumpled under the impact, and debris scattered into the watery void.

The Aurelian Fleet, momentarily stunned, broke formation. Their ships scattered. Some fled in panic. Others tried to regroup and return fire, but the damage had been done.

"The *Orleander* is clearing a path," Kal said, a relieved breath escaped his lips as the pressure on the *Days* lessened. "Now's our chance to move."

With the Aurelian Fleet in disarray, Kal retreated. The *Days* pulled away and darted through the chaos as the *Orleander* continued to bombard the remaining enemy ships.

"The *Orleander* just wiped out a quarter of their Fleet," Haruto murmured, eyes glued to the viewscreen.

Kal didn't waste time looking back. He focused ahead and pulled out of the steep escape ascent.

"We're not done yet," he said, his voice hard. "Avery, move us toward the *Orleander*. Tia, we'll support their offensive with our firepower."

Tia kept firing the main gun as the *Days* arced away from the panicking Aurelian Fleet. The *Orleander's* overwhelming presence had cleared a path, but the

Days had to move fast before the remaining enemy ships regrouped and chased them down.

As the *Days* maneuvered to join the *Orleander*, the Aurelian Fleet splintered. Four separate formations pulled away to retreat toward Aurelia, back to the heart of their Domain.

"They're making us pick one group to attack," Val warned, and scanned the Fleet's movements.

"We'll leave it to the *Orleander* to chase stragglers."

The *Orleander* took off after one of the groupings, its shardshot cannon offering no quarter. Aurelian ships fell from the sky under its fury.

"Message from the *Orleander*, patching it through," Haruto announced.

"Privateer Captain, well done. We will meet you at Port Royale." It was a man's voice. Probably the King.

Kal looked at Val. She shrugged and rubbed her thumbs against her pointer and middle fingers to signal credits.

Good, the repairs on the ship were going to cost a small fortune.

Kal nodded and turned the *Days* toward Port Royale.

The greatest skyship Gaia had ever known streaked across the morning sky and over the waves. The battle behind them slowly died as the remaining Aurelian ships retreated.

The rising sun reminded them they lived to see a new day. Kal didn't realize he was smiling until he caught his reflection in the glass.

For the first time in his life, he didn't see his father in it.

CHAPTER 67: LUCAN

After the Colossus

Lucan barely registered the explosion before the sea swallowed him whole. He was already spent, his body wrecked from the fight. He barely had the strength to react.

The water dragged him down. Pressure crushed his ribs. His ears rang, muffled and distant, like the battle above had happened in another world.

Something worse cut through the noise, voices.

"You crossed the line, and you don't even see it…"

"To get you your fourth miracle…"

"I can march the Colossus straight to the King's doorstep…"

"I just like the sound they make when they break…"

"Temper, temper. Break Orleans, not the furniture…"

"They will break before you…"

"Keep being strong, big guy. We're counting on you…"

Lucan clenched his teeth, but his body sank. Bubbles rushed past and raced for the surface, while he dropped like a stone. *Move.*

Rosari weren't built to float. Accreting always meant adding mass and density, increasing weight. That was what they were. He had trained to accrete, to turn himself into an unshakable force. To lighten himself? That was something else entirely.

Lucan decided it didn't matter what he had trained to do. He wasn't dying in the ocean. He forced his body to shift, to let go of the mass and density that dragged him down.

The weight peeled away. His muscles unlocked, and his body shot upward.

Fish scattered and vanished into the dark. Wreckage drifted past. It was twisted metal, torn plating, the corpse of a ship that had seen its last battle. A piece still crackled with dying electricity.

He broke the surface and gasped. His lungs burned. Salt filled his throat. The sky was a mess of smoke and fire, metal grinding, and shardshot that ripped through the air.

A ship he'd never seen before knifed through the smoke overhead. It lanced Azure shardshot and screamed Iverian engines. It tore through his Fleet like it owned the sky.

The battle wasn't over, but the Colossus was gone. The Fleet would have to carry the day.

Lucan trod water and scanned the horizon.

A research frigate loomed a short distance away as it pulled another survivor from the water. His jaw tightened. He hated begging, and this felt dangerously close to that. He raised a hand and shouted.

The ship didn't stop immediately. He did his best to stay above the waves, waited, and screamed as loud as his lungs would allow.

Then, finally, it slowed and turned toward him.

The Iverian ship lowered the retrieval rig into the water. Lucan pulled himself onto it and waited as it reeled in. He shifted back to his human form as his boots hit the deck.

Medics moved in fast, but he shoved past them. "Where is Syd?"

No one answered.

"I know he's here. I saw you pick him up. Where is he?"

"In here," came a voice from the med bay.

The air inside smelled like antiseptic. Machines beeped in slow, steady intervals. Syd was in the far corner, bruised, wrapped in blankets. He looked up as Lucan entered. His expression was unreadable.

Lucan stopped in the doorway, his fists tight. "Did we lose?"

"Yes, or close enough to it to be indistinguishable."

His voice lacked its usual smugness. Lucan couldn't tell if it was pain or something worse.

"How?" Lucan asked.

A medic went to hand him a blanket, and Lucan threw the medic against the wall. He didn't need Rosari strength for that. He breathed heavy and stood over Syd.

Syd exhaled. "Overconfidence, probably."

Lucan scowled. He knew the game, knew what Syd was doing, and knew precisely what Syd thought of him. Worst of all, he knew Syd tried to make him suffer in it. It worked, and he hated that.

Lucan shook his head. "What ship was that, overhead? Never seen anything like it. One ship did all of this."

Syd tilted his head. "Ah, a skyship of my design. I named it after my late wife, *Enora*. But my son renamed it the *Halcyon Days*."

Lucan ground his teeth. More secrets the man had kept. Lucan thought about holding him up by his boots until all the secrets finally came pouring out.

For the moment, Lucan stayed silent and glared at the mad scientist. Syd could formulate his own opinions based on Lucan's scowl.

Syd leaned back. "The Colossus is sinking, but it isn't beyond reach. Not with the right tools."

Lucan's eyes narrowed. "What are you saying?"

Syd steepled his fingers. "Most of the connections we installed to power the creature initially should still be intact. It would just be a matter of getting power down there, something one of my designs might be able to achieve…"

Lucan exhaled and rolled his shoulders. The frustration cooled into something else: purpose.

"How long?"

"Nine months at worst. In the meantime, we'll have to make some modifications to that rust bucket you call an Imperial Capital skyship. I assume most of your troops are drowning beneath us, so it'll have to be a small strike team…"

Lucan spat on the floor. He would kill Syd eventually for disrespecting the *Inquisitor*, but not before he milked every drop of usefulness out of him.

He stepped back into the hold and ordered the ramp down.

The wind cut against his damp hair. The battle shrank in the distance, but it wasn't over. Not for him, not ever. The research frigate had turned and headed for Aurelia.

Lucan stared out at the seemingly endless sea. They might have lost for the time being, but the lessons learned would forge a brighter tomorrow.

His grip tightened. "They think they've beaten me," his voice low and steady, "but they've only ensured my victory."

Behind him, Syd left the medical bay to attend to something in his workshop. He instructed his surviving techs to gather around. They had plans to review for the long flight to Aurelia.

The frigate picked up speed and cut through the sky above the waves. Behind it, a prince watched the sea and planned his revenge. Not even the depths of this failure could drown his ambition. After all, the divine could only ever be delayed, never denied.

CHAPTER 68: KALISTON

After the Colossus

The *Orleander* followed the *Days*. Both ships pushed through the final stretch of open water toward the docks at Port Royale. The city had watched the battle above the waves, and it waited.

The streets were packed. Banners hung from balconies. People leaned over railings to shout, wave, and reach. It didn't feel real.

Kal squinted at the crowd. "Think they know we were just trying to get paid?"

Locke scanned the sea of faces and caught sight of a woman tossing a handful of flower petals into the wind. "You say that like you're not enjoying this."

Kal grinned. "Oh, I am, but you can't buy drinks with applause."

Then they hit the dock, and a wall of noise crashed over them. Cheers, music, and a damn parade formed on the spot. Someone blew a horn. A group of kids sprinted along the pier and waved blue and gold banners.

Before Tia even stepped off the ramp, someone had thrown a wreath over her shoulders.

Kal strode down like he was born for it. He tossed waves like a returning King. Locke followed, amusement playing on his face.

An Iverian commander, clad in full military gear, stepped forward. "Privateer, First Altier Luinondo, First Altier Robertson requests your presence in the city square."

"First Altier Robertson?" Kal asked.

"We lost First Altier Serge in the Battle of Brittlebark."

Kal nodded, solemn for half a second, before he slipped into a respectful smile.

The commander continued. "We've prepared speeders for you and your crew. This way."

Val ate it up, waving with the arm that wasn't in a sling.

Kenzie looked like she wanted to vanish.

Val nudged her with a hip. "Come on, wave, or they'll think something is up."

Kenzie sighed, but flicked her hand up. The crowd went wild.

Jazz and Lizz milked it and tossed high-fives like they were local legends. Jules kept her head down, tight-lipped. Avery flashed his megawatt smile but remained calm, as if it happened every day. And Cookie? She had already passed out an entire tray of pastries.

No one asked where they came from.

The commander approached three speeders and climbed into the driver's seat of the first. Kal slid in like he owned the thing. He stretched out with one arm slung over the side and grinned, just a little. It was like the whole parade was for him.

Val, Locke, and Kenzie climbed in after him. The rest of the crew followed in the supplied speeders. The engines kicked in, and the convoy hovered forward. Banners trailed overhead. People packed the streets shoulder to shoulder, and the noise rolled through the city like a squall.

Confetti rained down and stuck to hair, to boots, and even the damn seats of the speeder. Somewhere in the chaos, a marching band burst out onto a corner. An entire brass section blasted something loud and triumphant.

Locke grinned and waved like he was seen for the first time. Kenzie, despite herself, had fun too. The atmosphere was infectious.

Val leaned over. "So, Mr. Applause-Can't-Buy-Drinks. What'll be better, the crowd or the payout?"

Kal stretched again and settled back. "Oh, you think I'm just in this for the credits? You think I'm that petty? Please! I'm in it for the love of the people."

Val laughed and gave the back of his head a shove with her good arm.

Kal smirked. "Fine. The credits will be nice too. Especially with some of the damage we took from Avery's flying."

The three of them in the back seat looked at each other and knew full well who was behind the sticks.

The speeder turned into the city square, where the city had hastily set up a stage. A young woman stood near the podium, flanked by city officials. She couldn't have been much older than Locke and had to be the new First Altier.

Locke, who sat in the middle of the backseat, muttered, "She looks even greener than me."

"That's saying something," Kenzie said with a giggle.

"Ten credits says they make us get up there," Val said.

Kal adjusted his collar. "Obviously, they're going to make me get up there."

And sure enough, moments later, they were ushered forward. Kal, Val, Locke, Kenzie, and the rest of the *Days* crew.

The First Altier stepped up to the podium. Her voice was shaky, but it carried over the crowd. "Today, we honor those who stood against impossible odds. Those who faced the might of Aurelia and did not falter." She gestured toward the *Days*' crew, who stood to the side of the stage. "Port Royale, and all of Iveria, owes them a debt we can never fully repay."

Kal shifted his weight. He wasn't built for standing still, even when people talked about him. "Could've used a drink before this."

"It's like ten in the morning," Locke said.

"What part of skypirate do you not understand?" Kal asked.

The First Altier continued. She spoke about sacrifice, unity, and the strength of the people. Kal tuned most of it out. Speeches weren't his thing.

Locke, though, stood with his arms crossed. A grin tugged at the edge of his mouth, and he soaked it all in. He was exactly where he was supposed to be.

Then something shifted.

A ripple moved through the crowd as heads turned. A murmur rolled across the square. The First Altier hesitated and glanced past the stage.

Trumpets rang out, and the square fell silent. The King had arrived.

A massive royal caravan rolled in, banners snapped in the wind. Guards in polished armor took formation, each movement regal and precise. The air of it settled over the square, enough to hush even the loudest voices.

Kal had figured the voice over the comms during the skirmish belonged to the King. To see him in person made it real. He had never expected to meet the man. He wasn't eager to, either. Monarchs felt outdated.

To stand there, in the middle of it all? It was hard to argue with the gravity the crown still carried.

The procession moved with ordered precision. The King, draped in deep blue and gold, climbed the steps. He nodded once at First Altier Robertson. She stepped aside. Then he turned to face the square and let the moment breathe.

Everything stilled. The crowd. The city. Even the memory of the battle seemed to quiet.

His gaze found Kal. Then Val. Then the rest of the crew. His eyes lingered on Kenzie before finally settling on Locke. Locke was looking around, as if searching for someone who wasn't there.

"Today, we stand free. Not because of orders. Not because of laws. But because, when the moment came, free people stood." His voice carried. Calm. Measured. No need to shout. "They weren't soldiers, not bound by duty. No one ordered them to fight. They fought because someone had to."

The square was silent with every eye on him.

"At Brittlebark, we fell. I failed you. Iveria failed you." He let that hang. "War is never won in a single battle. Even when our Armada burned and our walls shook. When the world told us the dream of the Iverian League was over, a few brave souls said no."

He turned to them again. To Kal and Val. To Kenzie and Locke. And to the whole crew. "Trust. That's what it comes down to. A trust not just in government or flags, but in the people beside you. Trust is the difference between standing and falling. Between holding the line and breaking apart. Iveria still stands today because the trust you shared refused to let you break."

Another pause. Just long enough. "The greatest battles aren't always fought with shardshots or Altiers. Sometimes, they're fought with nothing but will. The kind that says, 'not today.' The kind that holds, no matter the odds." His gaze swept over the crew. "You held."

A breath. Then the roar came.

The city erupted. It crashed over them. It rang off stone and glass and nearly lifted the square into the sky. The King let it ride, let them have their moment, then lifted a hand.

The crowd quieted, but the charge in the air didn't.

"Four hundred years ago, we broke free from Aurelia. We fought, bled, and rebuilt. When they came to take it all away again and again, we stood firm. When they tried to wake a god to end us all, you stood in their way." His voice dropped, quiet, meant just for them. "Today was different. The stakes have changed. This was a fight like no other, and today, you gave this nation a second chance."

The applause started again. It rolled through the square, relentless. He let it crest, waited for it to fade. Then he smiled.

"I suspect the wind will take you elsewhere soon. But wherever you go, wherever that path leads, you will always have a home in Iveria."

A final beat.

"To the crew of the *Halcyon Days*, I speak for all of Iveria when I say thank you."

Locke barely kept his expression in check. Kenzie straightened her back, but was unreadable. Kal just waited.

The King gestured, and a soldier stepped forward with a small case. Inside, blue-tinted medals gleamed under the midday sun. Intricately crafted. The symbol of Iveria's highest honor.

One by one, they were called forward. Cookie first, then Jules, Jazz, Lizz, Haruto, and the rest of the crew. They had to drape one on Val gingerly because of her arm. The King smiled at Locke as it went over his neck. Locke asked a question that Kal couldn't hear, and the King shook his head. Kenzie looked uncomfortable with the medal hanging on her chest.

Kal was last. He debated whether he should let the King put it on him, but in the end, the smile welded to his face wouldn't come off. He decided to follow that feeling and lowered his head.

The crowd started chanting.

"Kal, Kal, Kal..." Kaliston blinked. He couldn't hide the shock on his face. They were saying his name. He wasn't just a skypirate or a disgraced former officer of the Armada. He wasn't Baron El-Syd's son. He was Kal, the captain of the *Halcyon Days*. The hero.

They saw what he had done and what he was worth. Recognition. It was all Kal had ever wanted, and it was finally his.

As the King stepped back, he addressed Kal directly. "Captain Kaliston, you and your crew have done more for this nation than most will ever know." Then, quieter, just for Kal, "I suspect you'll want your weight in credits for this?"

Kal smirked and closed his fingers around the medal. "And a royal pardon for any past... and future actions."

The King laughed and clapped him on the shoulder. "I'll talk with Thorne."

For the first time in a long time, they weren't running. For the first time, they could breathe.

CHAPTER 69: LOCKE

After the Colossus

The manor was too nice for them, too polished and still. Kal had said as much when they walked in.

"We're gonna break something before morning."

No one argued.

They'd spent the whole day drenched in victory. Food and drinks poured in while laughter spilled out. They were too exhausted to hold it in. No one cared about the speeches, the honors, or whatever half-scripted nonsense the officials had thrown together.

The King spent time with each of them throughout the day. Kenzie was the only one who kept her distance and had slipped away whenever he was near.

He didn't linger with Locke either, though he promised to bring him to court soon, since Locke was the First Altier of Breezewaltz. He mentioned his daughter had been leading the evacuation lines from Orleans, and she was looking forward to seeing Locke again.

The attention and glory were fine, but the exhaustion of the past twenty-four hours had caught up. All they cared about was the quiet of their quarters in the manor on the hill.

It was clear from the groans and dazed faces sprawled across the First Altier's oversized furniture that this moment, the shared breath, was everything. They were full, tired, and alive.

Val had taken over a couch, boots on the armrest, and a glass half-full yet went untouched. Kenzie sat sideways in an armchair, one leg draped over the side like she owned the place.

Kal had dragged a chair out to the balcony and soaked in the night air. The fireworks would start soon, and Kal had made a point that he wanted to watch them. The manor sat high above Port Royale, and the streets below were still lit with celebration. He watched the people dance beneath the city lights, as if he hadn't entirely accepted that it was all still real.

Jules, Avery, Liam, Tia, and Haruto had set up around a table to play cards. Their pockets overflowed with credits from well-wishers eager to express their thanks.

Jazz and Lizz had followed them back to the manor but left almost immediately when they realized the real party was somewhere else in the city.

Dr. Rina wasn't drinking. "I'm off to bed. Try not to have too much fun tonight. See me in the morning if you need anything." She waved and disappeared down the hall toward the guest rooms.

Cookie was half-asleep and mumbled something about "good stock" between sips of whatever someone had handed her earlier.

Locke had never seen the crew like that. Like a diver who had just come up for air. He exhaled, stretched out his legs, and let himself sink into the quiet.

"When did the King say he would transfer the funds?" Val asked Kal from the couch.

"He didn't," Kal said. "But we know where he lives if we need to collect."

"I don't like unpaid debts. Especially when they're owed to us."

"Unpaid debts," Kenzie said, and something sparked behind her green eyes. She stood and dusted off her hands.

Then her eyes met Locke's. That familiar smirk flashed across her face, and he barely had time to register it before she was on him. She grabbed his collar, yanked him up, and kissed him right there in front of everyone.

The room stilled for a moment, just as fireworks exploded in the night sky above Port Royale.

"Perfect timing," Kenzie said as she broke off the kiss. She smiled at Locke as green, blue, and gold lights spilled across her face.

Laughter broke out around the room. Val let out a low, amused whistle. Kal turned fully and blinked, as if he wasn't sure if it was a fever dream.

"There," she said. "Promise kept."

Locke blinked.

Val propped her chin on her fist. "Gotta say I expected that to take longer. Fine, I won't call you Kid anymore. You're promoted to…Golden Boy."

"That's a terrible name," Locke said.

Kenzie looked at Locke and shrugged. "Be happy with the promotion. I did all the same stuff as you, and all I got was a kiss."

Val laughed at that. Kenzie smiled at the XO, and the room returned to normal service.

"Did you know about the fireworks?" he asked her in a low voice.

Kenzie shrugged, stepped away, and moved on. "Timing's everything."

Locke touched his jaw. His lips still tingled, and he tried not to look like an idiot.

Kal just shook his head. "About time."

Someone passed Locke a drink. He took it, mainly to have something to do with his hands.

Kal left them on the balcony and joined Val on the couch.

"Is that why you kept pairing them together?" he asked and smiled at Locke.

"Me? I thought you were making the away teams." Val replied, smiling at Kal.

They both laughed and let it fade. "I couldn't have done this without you. We couldn't have done this without you," Kal said.

"By we, you mean…" Val asked, her eyes flicked to the pack.

"The crew, Val. I'm being honest with you. Can you give me a moment?"

"Okay, okay. Sorry. Go ahead."

Locke didn't move. He felt like he was overhearing something private, but maybe Kal figured the fireworks would drown out his words.

"I wanted to apologize for Belfield. You were worried about me, and I brushed it off. That wasn't fair to you," Kal said.

"Good start. Go on," Val said, tilting her head onto her hand.

"There's no easy way to say this, so I'm just going to say it. When I fought Syd and saw what that thing had done to him, I knew it would kill me too. Not just the physical toll, but the hunger for power. The chase for greatness and the isolation that comes with both." Kal took a sip. "That belief that nothing matters except being right." He stared off for a second before collecting himself. "He looked like a husk, like his soul had been traded away piece by piece."

Val dropped the cutesy look. "Kal?"

"Val, please, just listen. I can't pretend I don't feel the same pull. The Hollowline gives you this high, this clarity. It makes you feel untouchable, but it also makes you alone. It's not just power. It's loneliness distilled, and I'm done letting it turn me into him."

He let that hang for a beat, steady now.

"I've decided I'm not going to be defined by Syd or by the parasite he carved into my spine. This thing is trying to take everything from me, but I won't let it. Not yet, and not all of it. When the time comes and our work is done, it can take a part of me that I've given it. That's a fair trade, but it's never going to get you or the crew. From now on, I'm only going to use this to protect the people I love. I promise I won't wear it unless I need to."

With that, he unlatched the pack and set it aside.

Val smiled as tears formed in her eyes. She leaned over and gave Kal a big hug. He hugged her back.

She pulled away, then leaned in again for a kiss. One that said *I love you* better than words ever could. Then they sat together on the couch for a while. Val kicked her feet in Kal's lap. Smiles beaming on their faces as they watched the crew they built enjoy the evening.

The night stretched on, easy and warm, full of voices a little too loud and old stories a little too far-fetched.

At some point, the exhaustion crept in, and one by one, people peeled off.

Tia and Liam stood, ready to continue to cash in on the lifetime of free drinks they'd been promised. Haruto said he was too tired, but they dragged him back into the city, anyway.

Avery collected his winnings and made his way toward the guest rooms. He nodded at Val and Kal on the way. A mutual respect passed between them that was quiet, wordless, and unshakable. The unspoken knowledge that they owed their lives to Avery and the way he had flown.

The night grew, and Val went off to claim the most oversized bed. Said she was going to sleep in past sunrise for once, and no one should bother her. Kal walked to the balcony, slipped back out, and pretended not to follow in the same direction.

Kenzie stood, stretched, and then wandered back to the balcony. Locke wasn't sure how long he had sat there, stared into his glass, and smiled. It was then that Jules walked up, hands stuffed in her pockets.

She leaned on the back of the chair beside him and looked down at him like he was an unfinished project. "You still plan to give it to her?" she asked.

Locke frowned. "Give what?"

Jules lifted a brow. "The boot charm."

It took him a second. The watchsmith from Breezewaltz's market. The day he got the suda. He had almost totally forgotten about it with all that had happened since then.

Jules patted her pocket, then pulled something small and worn between her fingers: the rose-gold boot charm.

Locke blinked. He had barely remembered how the light played off it in the shop. The moment he saw it, the memory returned. Breezewaltz. The watchsmith. The charm on the chain. Training with Kal on the *Days* earlier that week. The last time he thought about it was when Jules had given him the repaired suda. With it in front of him, he couldn't believe he had almost forgotten the most important piece of metal on Iveria.

"Figured you could use it sooner than later," Jules said, twirling it once before handing it over. "Okay, my role in this story is done for the night. Remember, love is like an engine. You might not know how to name everything, but deep down, you already know how it works."

Locke smiled. "Thanks, Jules." Locke held out the charm. "Oh, Jules, what's your last name?"

She gave him a look. It was part 'why are you asking' and part 'I don't want to say.' She thought about it before saying, "Cole. Julie Cole was what my mother called me."

"Thank you, Ms. Cole."

Jules smiled. "Just remember," she said, softer than he expected, "be careful. She's a good one. She just doesn't know it yet." With that, she walked out of the room and left Locke and Kenzie alone.

Locke exhaled slowly. He stood up, walked to the balcony, and played with the charm in his pocket. He wasn't sure if he'd been more nervous fighting Lucan or giving her the charm.

Kenzie stood in the moonlight and basked in the energy of the city below. Her red hair caught the glow, vibrant even in the dark. She had a few bandages from cuts and bruises during the mission, but was otherwise her radiant self. She leaned over the edge of the railing, and in that moment, her frame seemed to glow with the moon.

Locke wished he hadn't noticed any of that. "So, uh, good day, huh?" he asked.

"It turned out pretty nice." She didn't turn to face him, but gave him a side glance and shifted enough to make space for him beside her. "Amazing what twenty-four hours can do."

"Been a weird week, hasn't it?" Locke said. He put his elbows on the railing and matched her pose.

"A lot has happened," she said. "I think it would take me another year to chart how we got here from there."

"I wish Toren could've been here to celebrate with us," Locke said, looking down.

"He is, Locke. You carry him with you, and everything you did today is part of the legacy you share with him. He's proud of you, wherever he is." She placed her hand gently on his.

"Thanks. I don't think I've had the time to think about it, with everything going on."

"Maybe that's not a bad thing, for now, but you should probably process it when you have a chance over the next few weeks."

"Yeah. Now's not the time." He wiped a tear from his eye. "Speaking of processing, can we talk about you being an…"

Kenzie reached over and placed her hand on his mouth. Her face was deathly serious. "Not another word, Golden Boy," she hissed. She removed her hand. "We can talk about it when we're not in a city surrounded by the King's delegates."

"Fair enough," Locke said. "A girl needs to have her secrets, right?"

"Now you're learning," she said, back to her typical self.

"Do you ever think about telling the crew your whole story? Seaforth, everything."

"Do you ever think about remembering yours?"

"You're deflecting again, but to answer your question, yes. I think about the memory gap every day. I wish I could lift the veil and see what is behind it, but it also scares me. Like the gap is a small mercy, and it's saving me from myself."

"That might be true, but I think it'll be important one day, whatever your story might have been."

"I just hope that I'm ready for it, if it does come back."

"Exactly, keep working on that, Locke, and the one from your past won't matter." She pushed her hair back over one ear and looked out over the sea. "I'll let the crew know about me when I'm ready. I'm not there yet, but I'm closer."

They stood there for a minute and let the warm sea breeze billow past them.

"I never did apologize… for keeping my family thing from you, back in Breezewaltz," Locke said.

"No, you didn't." Kenzie sighed wistfully.

"I wasn't trying to manipulate anyone. I just… didn't want to be that person. And I thought if I ignored it, I could become someone else."

"Someone without baggage?" she asked.

"Someone who didn't have to live up to my family name. I just wanted to be me."

"I get that, but our past has a way of catching up to us. It wasn't the lie that hurt. It was that you didn't trust me enough to tell the truth."

"I know," he said and picked at the railing.

"I can also see that I'm no better. The good news is we're not those people anymore. Our cards are on the table, and we can finally see each other for who we are. Mostly."

"Mostly?" Locke raised an eyebrow.

"Girls and secrets." She smiled and nudged her shoulder into his. "You ever lie to me again, though, I'm kicking you off the ship myself. I don't care if we're on the gaia or mid-air."

"Are we holding each other to that standard?"

She smiled at him, a knowing one that conveyed more than words ever could. The sight of her smiling made Locke twirl the boot charm in his pocket, thinking of what to say next.

"Which room do you think you'll take tonight?" he asked.

"Excuse me?" she asked and raised an eyebrow. "It was a kiss, Locke. Don't think…"

"No, not like that," he said, flustered. "When we sleep on the *Days*, your room is above mine, and your boots…"

"My boots?" she interrupted, clearly enjoying the effect on him. He felt like he was dancing with her again in Breezewaltz.

He tried to recover. "Yes. Your boots. They make a sound…"

"What about my boots?" she pressed and turned to face him.

Locke paused, then smirked, realizing she wanted to play with him. Fine, he could play too. "Your feet are louder than the Colossus. You could get notes from it on how to be quiet in the morning."

Kenzie gasped, scandalized. "You did not."

Locke continued. "It's like a drum ringing in my ears every morning. At first, I hated it because I didn't know what it was. I asked Jules if there was a system on the ship that was broken and making noise. She told me no system above my quarters could explain that thunderous sound. Then I realized one day that it was your boots."

Kenzie gasped playfully, but before she could reply, he reached into his pocket and pulled out the charm.

"And I wanted you to have this, because it reminded me of you when I saw it. You can throw it away or forget about it, but… I just wanted you to have it."

Kenzie looked at it for a long beat. Locke couldn't read her face, which wasn't anything new, but it felt different.

Finally, she smiled, tears in her eyes. "It's perfect, Locke. Thank you for sharing this with me."

She let the charm fall into her palm and held it up again. Then she stepped into his chest and hugged him before she reached up to kiss him on the cheek.

"I know that's anticlimactic compared to earlier, but let's just see where things go, okay?" She took a step back.

Things were going about as well as Locke could hope. "Yeah, that was nice."

"Just nice?" She twisted the charm in her hands once more, looked out at the city below them, then turned to leave.

"No, it was perfect, but I'm trying to play it cool."

Kenzie turned back. "Never pretend to be something you're not, Locke Luinondo." She smiled at him and pointed toward the guest corridor. "I think the third rooms on the first and second floors are unoccupied. I'll take the second floor."

Locke took the hint and smiled. "Goodnight, Boots."

"Goodnight, Locke. I'll see you in the morning."

It wasn't much, but it was a little promise she would still be with them when the sun rose. That was enough.

She walked away. Locke watched her until she finally turned the corner and disappeared. He turned back to the balcony and let out a long sigh.

The past three years were gone, lost in the dark. But the past week? He'd remember every second. The good and the bad were both a part of him.

He didn't know what came next. Didn't know if he'd stay with the *Days*, if Kenzie would ever leave, or if being First Altier meant he had to let all of this go.

That was tomorrow's problem.

Tonight, between the weight of the past and the pull of the future, Locke Luinondo felt ten thousand feet tall.

Practically a colossus.

A NOTE FROM THE AUTHOR

Thank you so much for reading my story! Ah, this is wild. I've been writing my whole life. I got my start on the mean streets of AIM chats, and now it's all Outlook emails, so putting together a novel feels surreal. I don't even know where to start, except to say this book wouldn't exist without the people in my life.

My wife, my son, our dog, my parents, my brothers, their families, and all the friends who feel like family. Special shout out to my wife's family. They support me by supporting my wife every day. What I'm saying is this book has a legion of authors, even though I'm the one (unfortunately) holding the pen.

I've been thinking about this story for twenty years. It changed, evolved, and refused to let me go. I've taken many cracks at putting it on paper over that time, just for my sanity, but none of them made it past Act 1.

Last Christmas, I took a long drive halfway across the US and back again. I had a lot of time to talk to the dog, my co-pilot, and he helped me rearrange the beats that cracked the story wide open. What I'm saying is that dogs are the best. My wife and son are the best-best, but our dog is, like, right there.

Last, but not least, thank you, dear reader, for your support of my work. I wrote this so that it could be read. I know it's not perfect, but I hope you find something to love about it, just as I did.

Love
A.C. Bishkey

PREVIEW FOR HALCYON DAYS: THE CITY IN THE SANDS

A glimpse of what's coming next...

PROLOGUE - LYLA

Lyla sat cross-legged on the velvet stool. She tried not to fidget while Mira, her attendant, wove copper threads through her braids. Each strand caught the lamp-light like tiny flames. The new girl polished Lyla's boots with a reverence usually reserved for holy relics. Lyla, for the life of her, couldn't remember the girl's name. It had started with a *K*. Her half-brother had sent her so she'd have to ask him later, after the parade.

Her mother's perfume drifted through the room: vanilla and something else, something that smelled like the desert wind just before dawn. Lyla breathed it in deep. In five years, when everything else had faded, she could still close her eyes and summon that exact scent.

Her mother was nearby, arms outstretched as attendants fastened the final clasps on her dress. She laughed. Not a laugh meant for court, but a real laugh, full and unguarded. Lyla hadn't heard the punchline. She only knew the way it made the room feel safe.

Her brother Noel leaned against the window, his hair caught the fading sun-light. He wasn't in his formal Rosari armor yet. Just a quarter-button shirt with loose, embroidered sleeves rolled to the elbow, a ribbon half-tied at the collar. He'd always been lazy with buttons.

"You're going to sweat through those boots before we even get to the square," he said with a smirk.

Lyla made a face. "They're new."

"They're impractical," he replied, not looking at her.

"They're beautiful." She scowled.

"They're going to give you blisters. Don't come begging me to carry you when you can't walk."

Their mother made a noise of mock exasperation. "Leave your sister's shoes alone. You'll both be late at this rate."

"I'm already ready," he said, arms wide.

"Yes, and unacceptably underdressed," their mother replied. "You're not escorting a patrol. You're escorting us."

He sighed dramatically and turned to get changed. As he passed Lyla, he leaned in and whispered, "Psst, take the knife Mother had forged for you. The craftsmanship will impress father."

"Where would I hide it?" Lyla asked.

"Isn't the answer obvious?" He pointed to the boots.

"I'm not hiding a knife in these boots," she whispered back. It came out as a hiss.

"Then get more practical boots, Lyla," Noel hissed back.

She thought about it, but didn't want to bring the knife to show her father. She wouldn't need it, not together during the festival. Especially not with her brother there. He had always been her shield. Someone she could stand behind and know she'd be okay. All her brothers had been. She had been lucky in that way.

The trio and their attendants left the manor just as the sun dipped behind the red sands. She looked to the skyline and saw the Scarlet Keep. She had gotten lost in there many times, but rarely unintentionally. Her favorite part was the holding cells beneath it. They were rarely used, but she had made one or two friends down there.

Getting lost in Rosewood was one of Lyla's favorite pastimes. She would sneak out and explore the city. Her third favorite thing in the whole world, after her family and the holding cells, was finding shortcuts. Between buildings, over hedges, and through holes in walls. The smaller and more secret, the better. She knew the back alleys of Rosewood better than her own room.

Lanterns floated above the street like low-hanging stars. They were paper globes strung between rooftops. They swayed in the breeze, each one painted in reds, golds, and indigoes that shimmered in the lamplight. Lyla danced beneath them, one hand clutched in her brother's, the other lifted a skewer of sunmelon to her mouth. Juice ran down her fingers with every bite. It was sweet, but with a sharp, tart edge.

Sunmelons always bloomed with a single brilliant red flower called the Desert Rose. Her father had nicknamed her that when she was little, said the fruit reminded him of her. Sweet, but with a bite. She never understood why he didn't just call her sunmelon, but Desert Rose sounded better, anyway.

The Festival of Sands was in full swing. Fireworks exploded overhead, each burst reflected off mirrored tiles in the street like shattered constellations. The dunes beyond the city were lit with streamers and banners that rippled like fire. Glass-flute melodies twisted through the air, high and sweet, while fire eaters juggled flame as casually as coins.

That was Rosewood. Lyla heard it said that it was the center of the world. Festivals made her believe it.

Lyla was in awe of the street performers, specifically. She always was. She had asked her mother if she could be one when she grew up. Her mother had just laughed. Becoming a street performer was romantic, but not realistic.

Admire the spectacle. Don't become part of it. That was her advice.

Her brother always had fast hands. He had taught her all he knew. She could already tell she was better, but he was the only one bold enough to actually use his skills in public. One second, the fire breather's kit of oils and sticks was on his belt. The next, it was in Lyla's hand.

She smiled, and once again, she felt lucky for him.

He winked. "For fun later."

It was a perfect night.

Her mother walked just ahead, resplendent in a dress of shimmering silk, and nodded politely to passersby. Lyla's brother was older, taller, and already a Rosari. He kept close to her side, answered her teenage questions, and always grinned when she giggled. She felt safe in his shadow.

"Stay close," he whispered. "Crowds like this can swallow you." He gave her an exaggerated chomp.

She nodded, still too young to understand what kind of warning he meant.

The attack came quickly, like a summer storm. A single scream. Then a suka in the crowd. It soon became dozens. Blades flashed through the festivalgoers. Noel transformed into a Rosari. Blood sprayed. Someone pulled a flute too tight, and it cracked in half as the player fell.

Her brother shoved her down just as a suka's blade missed her throat.

"Run," he said and drew his weapon. His face was all fire, his Rosari form all she could see. Red crystalline fur erupted from his face as a blade bit into his forearm.

She didn't run. How could she? She crawled back on her hands and feet under a table of fruit. She sat there and watched. Noel held the street like a fortress. He blocked every strike, even as they swarmed. Ten, twenty men, then more. He held.

Suddenly, she felt a tug and fought. She looked up to see her mother's face, her clothes torn. Her mom pulled her up, but Lyla had to watch Noel.

The last thing she saw before her mother pulled her into an alley was a splash of red across his face, and the glint of a dagger under his ribs. Still, he stood.

Lyla screamed as they rounded a corner and he was out of sight.

Her mother didn't flinch. She carried Lyla through the chaos like a wraith, eyes forward, skirts torn. They ducked into a side gate, a forgotten passage to the docks.

Her mother stopped and looked Lyla in the eye. "Take this." She pressed something into Lyla's belt. "If anything happens to me, get someplace safe. Don't trust anyone. Use your eyes and head. You're clever, Lyla, use it."

"What do you mean, if anything happens to you?"

"Don't argue with me, Lyla. Just say you understand."

Lyla's eyes welled with tears. "I understand, Mother."

Her mother grabbed her hand and moved further into the passage. They descended an ancient stone staircase to the docks. Lyla had to take the steps two at a time to keep up.

Her mother stopped at a railing and surveyed the docked skyships. "There," she pointed to a vessel at the far end. "That'll do."

Her mother grabbed Lyla by the wrist once again. The movement hurt, but Lyla wasn't about to say anything. Besides, she was already crying. What was a little more pain? She glanced back, but saw no one following them. Her legs hurt, and her feet stumbled.

They passed a shipment of fish from Saltimere. She would normally tell her mother how she hated the smell, but she did not hate it at that moment. She didn't know if she hated anything. The men at the table worked without noticing her. Knives flashed through the slick bodies of fish. It was disgusting work, but it meant nothing to Lyla then.

She turned back just in time to see one of the workers drive a knife into her mother, just below the ribs. Her mother staggered, kneeled, then rose again.

"Don't look back," she wheezed and lunged at the attacker. "Go, Lyla! Run!"

The last image Lyla would ever have of her mother was her fighting beside that fish stall. Her face was full of determination even while the blood ran down her side.

Lyla did as she was told; she ran.

She didn't know where to go. The docks felt unsafe. Too many eyes and uncertain motives. So she ran to her other brother. They had different mothers, but he was still blood. Up a staircase, under the balcony with the gargoyle, and past her three friends made of stone. She burst into the hall like a wild thing. Her shoes were gone, her dress was shredded, and her belt still held the tiny flask her brother had snuck from the fire-eaters.

For fun, he'd said.

Lyla's half-brother turned. Surprise flickered across his face for a half-second before in vanished behind a calm mask. "Lyla?"

She ran to him and threw herself into his arms with a sob. "They're dead. They're all dead."

He held her briefly, his hand in her hair. Then he stepped back. "Easy, Desert Rose. What's this?"

"Mother and Noel. We were attacked and they're, they're…" She couldn't finish.

"Attacked? Are they alright?" His gaze flicked to the guards, always at his side.

"Mother was stabbed in the chest. Noel was surrounded by Rosari along the parade route."

"I'll send my guards." He looked at one pair. "Go check the parade route. You two, go check the fish market."

Lyla froze. She had never mentioned the fish market. She let the tears continue to flow while the wheels in her head spun. The man in front of her had planned it. All of it. Luckily, he somehow thought she was still too young, naïve, or stupid to piece it together.

"Is there someplace safe I can go?" she asked through sobs.

"You can stay here. I'll keep you safe."

"No. They'll know you're my brother. They'll come looking here."

"True. Very clever, Lyla." He motioned to the remaining guard. "See to it that my sister is taken care of. No more pain."

Her brother had done it subtly. He probably thought she didn't see it, but she saw the shadow creep across his face. His words were not what he meant. He wanted her gone. His decision to have Noel killed was a step along the path. To have someone kill Lyla meant something different. There was a glimmer of enjoyment there, but then the mask returned.

He bent down to give her a hug. She shuddered, but played that off as part of the performance.

The guard took her by the arm and led her out of the well-appointed house. The crowds continued to swarm around them, but the guard's unrelenting grip held her. They pushed through the shifting tide toward a back alley. Lyla knew it wasn't far from the docks she had just fled.

The guard's grip tightened further, and it reminded her that the danger was there. She just didn't know when it would strike, but she knew it would come soon. The alley was too perfect a spot. Rosewood was huge and old, but the alleys had always existed, for better or worse.

She needed to escape or die. Those were her options, and Lyla knew her choice almost immediately. She thought of the knife she had left in her room, the one her brother had told her to smuggle in her boots. He had been right, as usual, but he had taught her other things. Like the streets and how to navigate them. She knew the alley from her time exploring Rosewood, and she knew there was a hole in the wall she could squeeze through in twenty-odd paces. She would need to break the guard's grip. Her hand brushed the kit her brother had given her.

She reached in and felt the soft flask of oil. The sparker that used a Rose Shard. It would be enough.

A flick of her free hand and oil sprayed across the alley, into the man's face. She pulled out the sparker and flicked it to life in the spraying oil. The flames roared. The man let go of her arm, staggered, and swatted at the blaze.

He shifted into his Rosari form to tank the fire. The flames did not stop, but they no longer bothered him.

Lyla ran. Her brother's voice echoed in her head. "Use your size to your advantage. You're smaller, find small openings. They won't be able to chase you if they can't fit."

She sprinted to the wall and slid through the opening. The Rosari was too large to follow and still on fire. He couldn't revert or risk the burns. He would have to go around, which would buy Lyla precious seconds.

She booked it toward the docks and grabbed a loose cloth to cover her red hair. Lyla avoided the fish market and passed the dock merchants who hawked their wares. She made her way to the skyship her mother had pointed to.

The crew finished their loadout. The ship would be mostly empty and it delivered its wares for imperial coin.

Lyla slipped past two crewmen who chatted about the parade while they lazily stacked crates. She moved between the stacks and leaped aboard. Lyla hid in a corner behind one of them. She kneeled and remained quiet.

The stacks rose around her as the dock hands set the crates down. They never noticed the red-headed girl who hid in a pocket. Eventually, the bay doors sealed, and the skyship pushed off.

She held the sparker with trembling fingers. *Never open these, Lyla. Never.* Her mother's voice had been sharp with worry the day she'd caught ten-year-old Lyla trying to peek inside one. *The shard isn't meant for children. Be patient, it waits for you.*

The ceremony should have been the next year in the Scarlet Keep. White robes, incense, the whole city celebrating as she joined the ranks of the Rosari with the initiates. Noel would have been there, grinning as she took her first transformation. He promised to train her afterwards. Instead, she was alone in a cargo hold, covered in blood, about to violate every sacred tradition she'd been raised to honor.

Her mind lingered on the word: patience. Lyla almost laughed, but it came out as a sob. Her mother was dead. Noel was dead. Her half-brother had looked her in the eye and ordered her execution with the same tone he'd used to request tea.

Her fingers found the threads and unscrewed carefully. The shard rolled into her palm. It was sharp, warm, and felt alive. She thought of shard sickness or of initiates who burst into flames. She had never witnessed either, but she thought of those consequences. It was her blessing and curse, a mind that would never allow her to think past the consequences. She thought of dying there, forgotten and alone.

She remembered Noel teaching her about shards after his ceremony. He had told her about the danger, the pain, and the power. She remembered her mother's smile and her warmth as she told her there would be nothing to fear when the time came. Then her half- brother's cold eyes and colder smile. *No more pain.* She closed her eyes, breathed deep, and swallowed before the fear could stop her.

The pain was immediate. It seared down her throat, bloomed in her chest. For a moment, she thought she heard a whisper, but maybe that was just the shock of the night. When her breath released, she was a Rosari.

She didn't know if she felt stronger, but she felt steadier. Her body had stopped trembling. That might have been the Crystal, or just the shock fading. She still remembered the horror. Lyla could still see the knife in her mother's side as she lunged beside the fish stall. She remembered what the fear felt like then, but it no longer seized her. She would learn from it. It wasn't a friend, but with whatever she had just become, it was no longer her enemy.

She would leave that girl behind. The one who froze. The one who screamed. And the one who felt the fear that taught you nothing except how to die. That girl was Lyla. She was someone else now. She thought of the pretty girl who had polished her boots that morning. The one who was quiet, capable, and invisible. Lyla finally remembered her name.

Kenzie.

That was the name of someone who forged her own path. That was who she would be from then on. She would be Kenzie, and Lyla would be an imagined dream of another girl.

There was blood in her hair. Her dress was singed. She didn't think about the life-altering decision she had just made. She thought about her half-brother's smile when he said it. *No more pain.* She spent the rest of time on board hiding and wondering why he had chosen the festival. Why then, when the whole city watched? Had her death mattered, or was it something more sinister?

No more pain. The last thing he had said. She realized what it meant the moment he said it. Now, she'd never forget, not for as long as she lived.

www.ingramcontent.com/pod-product-compliance
Lightning Source LLC
Chambersburg PA
CBHW061936130726
47909CB00013B/1895